When Spring Comes to the Heart

By Christine M. Conroy

Contents

Chapter One

On December 25, 2017, Mother Nature delivered a Christmas gift to the residents of Boston—a white Christmas! Like many of my fellow Bostonians, I did not accept the gift graciously. The snow and ice that the Christmas Day storm brought to the area made travel difficult and foiled the holiday plans of many people, including mine. Instead of spending Christmas with my close friends, as I had intended, I ended up spending the day in front of my television set, watching one yuletide movie after another. The bag of popcorn I slowly but surely ate was no substitute for the turkey dinner that I would have helped my friends devour.

A couple of days after Christmas, Mother Nature bestowed yet another gift upon the good citizens of Boston—a brutal cold snap. According to the weather reports, the cold snap was going to linger. On the 27th and the 28th of December, I did not venture outside for fear that if I did, the arctic blast of air would transform me into a block of ice.

When I woke up on Friday morning, December 29, I did so with a bit of wishful thinking. It was my hope that after giving us poor Bostonians the cold shoulder for a couple of days, Mother Nature would have a heart and send us some warmth. To see if the great lady saw things my way, I got out of bed, put on my slippers and bathrobe, and, in a half-asleep state, staggered into the kitchen. After opening my eyes as wide as was humanly possible at 6:30 a.m., I leaned over the sink and took a peek at the thermometer that was attached to the exterior frame of the kitchen window. An inhumane reading of four degrees stared right back at me. My wishful thinking was no match for Mother Nature's obstinance. I was tempted to do an about-face and return to the comfort of my warm bed, but I did not succumb to that temptation. I had an appointment that morning.

It was not essential that I keep my appointment, but I felt I should. December 29 was the first day I was scheduled to perform volunteer work at Elsbury Place, a residential facility for the elderly. As a volunteer, I was to serve as a companion to Constance Cranshaw, one of the residents who occupied an apartment in the independent living section of the community. I pictured Mrs. Cranshaw to be a lonely soul who would be disappointed if I did not show up that day. My meeting with her was scheduled for 10:00 a.m., and I fully intended to be there on time.

As frigid as the weather was, I was not going to allow it to chill the enthusiasm I felt about meeting the woman I intended to befriend. Elsie Wyman, the woman who ran the volunteer program at Elsbury Place, had told me a bit about Constance Cranshaw's background. I was eager to meet Mrs. Cranshaw, for I had learned that she had authored many a romance story and had been quite successful in that endeavor. On that day in December, I considered myself to be a romance writer but, unlike Mrs. Cranshaw, had not tasted sweet success. The three books I had self-published were not exactly taking off. I knew what a rough road an author travels to try to gain acknowledgement. Many fall by the wayside while traveling that road. The fact that Mrs. Cranshaw had stayed the course and had attained recognition for her literary efforts gave rise to my admiration for her and sparked my desire to meet her.

Wanting to make a good first impression, I reserved ample time that morning to make myself look presentable. After a rather meticulous grooming session that involved the use of several mirrors, I put on a tasteful slack suit. That suit was only my first line of defense against the freezing weather I would soon face. The fact that I did not own a car and would have to walk to the bus stop, two blocks away, made it all the more imperative that I bundle up. So, on went my red wool coat, earmuffs, knitted hat, cashmere scarf, ski gloves, and boots with cleats.

Feeling as "graceful" as a knight in armor, I grabbed my briefcase and then exited my apartment. Very slowly, I began to descend the staircase that led to the front door of the two-family home that housed my apartment. That door was meant to be shared by me, the sole tenant of the second-floor apartment, and by whoever occupied the apartment on the first floor. When my foot made contact with the bottom step of the staircase, the step let out a screech. The weight of my body clad in all that winter wear was almost too much for the tired, old step to bear. The oak floor in the square-shaped hallway did not fare any better when I traversed it to get to the door. Every single floorboard sounded its share of pain upon being subjected to my footsteps.

The white wooden house in which I lived was built just prior to World War II. It was certainly showing its age. To say that it was in dire need of renovations would be quite an understatement. I, however, had to convince myself that I was living in the lap of luxury. The rents elsewhere were beyond my means.

As I reached for the handle of the front door, I cringed at the thought that in a matter of seconds, I would be exposing myself to a wind chill factor below zero. After timidly opening the front door and then the storm door, I stepped onto the exterior wooden platform. The air was so bitterly cold that my common sense told me to retreat inside. In the end, however, my common sense did not reign. It was overridden by my desire to meet Mrs. Cranshaw and by my urge to escape the monotony of my apartment. So, with a slight slam of the front door, I set out on my journey to Elsbury Place.

In spite of the sand that my landlord had sprinkled on

the icy steps leading to the walkway, I looked upon those steps as potential tickets to the emergency room. The ice on them was so thick that I grabbed the railing with all the might my left hand could muster while I held onto my briefcase with my right hand. Quite miraculously, I managed to make it down all seven steps without falling on my posterior.

The cement walkway had also been sanded, but it felt slick under my feet. The downward slope of the walkway demanded that I place one foot in front of the other with the speed of a tortoise. Once I reached the city sidewalk, I figured the worst part of my trek was over. The remainder of my short walk would be on flat terrain, so I convinced myself that it made perfect sense to continue on.

It did not take me long to realize that I never should have listened to myself. The Christmas Day storm together with the current cold snap had created miniature ice skating rinks on the sidewalks. Whenever I encountered one of those rinks, I found myself walking in a zigzag fashion and, at times, through mounds of snow. Each second that I was exposed to the ice-cold air felt like an eternity. So much for my expectation of a short walk on flat terrain! My walk to the bus stop felt like a long and challenging trek through the Rocky Mountains in the dead of winter.

Amazingly, I arrived at the bus stop before pick-up time. The bus was due to arrive in six minutes. If it were delayed, I would have to head back home. The biting air had penetrated my gloves and even my boots, causing a feeling of numbness to invade my fingers and toes. My hands and feet simply could not endure much more, and I knew as I stood there shivering that the rest of my body would soon be in jeopardy. If there had been a shop nearby, I would have sought refuge in it, but my surroundings consisted of nothing but homes.

Thank goodness, the bus did arrive on time. As I boarded, I was not shocked that it was practically empty. With legs so cold that they would not cooperate, I waddled to one of the many available front seats and practically collapsed into it. Although I was shaking like a feather in front of a fan, there was one part of me that seemed incapable of movement —my jaw. It was so frozen that I doubted my mouth could emit any intelligible sounds. I could only hope that by the time of my meeting with Mrs. Cranshaw, my mouth would be in good working order.

The bus ride to Elsbury Place took about ten minutes. Luckily for me, the bus stopped right in front of the facility. I tightly grasped a bus pole, rose from my seat, and, with baby steps, made my way to the exit door. My *thank you* to the driver sounded more like *ta oooh*. A kind man he was, for he gave me a nod to indicate he had understood the gibberish that had come out of my mouth.

As I headed for the large brown double doors of the main building of Elsbury Place, I kept my eyes fixed on the walkway for fear that a patch of ice might send me flying. Although I did not dare look up at the building, it was tempting to do so. During my prior and only visit to Elsbury Place, I was fascinated by the looks of the main building. Its stone exterior, circular towers, and spires all contributed to its medieval look. In sharp contrast to the main building were two modern-looking buildings located behind it. One could gain entry to the newer buildings via passageways that connected them to the main structure.

I ascended the three steps that led to the front doors. In a lobster-claw-type action, my stiff right hand clutched one of the doorknobs and slowly turned it. I pushed the door open and entered the foyer, where I respectfully wiped my feet on the mat. About ten feet beyond the mat was a wooden bench that was positioned in front of a wall, the top half of which boasted an impressive stained glass window. I seized the opportunity to sit on the bench awhile in order to rest and to gather my wits. As I sat there, I tested my ability to speak clearly. Once I felt convinced that another human being could understand me, I rose from the bench and removed my hat, earmuffs, and gloves. Then I passed through the archway that led to the reception room.

My first impulse was to immediately approach the reception counter that was straight ahead of me. Signing in at the counter was a requirement for all visitors. The reception room was so cheerful looking, however, that I decided to linger near the archway for a few moments in order to take notice of the room's contents. On the light-yellow walls of the room hung impressive oil paintings of New England scenes that depicted all four seasons. The section of the room to the right of the reception counter was a sitting area. Recessed into the far wall of that area was a gas fireplace that emitted a warm glow. That glow made it all the more inviting for people to sit in the pale-green leather furniture that was cozily arranged in front of the fireplace. Mahogany bookcases, placed here and there against the other two walls of the sitting area, offered a large choice of reading matter. Adding to the cheery atmosphere of the room was a white artificial Christmas tree that was located to the left of the reception counter. It was so tall that it nearly touched the ceiling. Its twinkling red and green lights and gold-colored ornaments reflected the joy of the holiday season. Hanging above the counter, about two feet below the ceiling, were the words *Happy New Year* in big silver-colored letters. Although I was still physically frozen, my visual tour of the room gave me a warm emotional feeling.

I approached the counter. On the other side of it was a woman who was rustling through a stack of papers. Her gray hair was pulled back in a bun, and her large black eyeglasses were sitting halfway down her nose. In view of the fact that she neither looked up at me nor spoke to me when I placed my briefcase on the counter, I assumed that her role at the facility had nothing to do with the reception room.

After standing there for a minute or so, I finally said, "Excuse me. Is there someone here who can help me?"

In a tone of voice that sounded more efficient than friendly, she glanced at me and asked, "What is it you need?"

"My name is Linzie Cole," I said. "Today is my first day here as a volunteer companion. I'm supposed to call on Mrs. Cranshaw at ten o'clock. I understand that she resides in the independent living section of the community and that I have to sign in at the reception counter."

The woman furrowed her brow and remained silent for a moment, all the while scrutinizing me. She made me feel as though I were some sort of vagrant who had entered the building for the sole purpose of warming up. When she resumed speaking, her voice clearly conveyed some irritation.

"Have you been cleared by Elsie Wyman, the lady in charge of our volunteer program?"

"Yes. I filled out all the necessary paperwork in Elsie's office two weeks ago. Once Elsie approved my application, she arranged for this meeting today between Mrs. Cranshaw and me."

"And just how do you intend to spend your time with Mrs. Cranshaw?" she asked, her eyes widening with each passing second.

I nervously ran my fingers through my blond hair as I searched for the right words to answer her question. The woman's haughty behavior made me feel ill at ease.

"I learned from Elsie that Mrs. Cranshaw used to be an author," I explained. "I am an author. Elsie thought it would be a great idea if I read to Mrs. Cranshaw from the manuscript I have been working on for the past several months."

"Oh, Elsie thought that would be a great idea, did she?" the woman muttered while rolling her eyes. "Ms. Cole, does Constance Cranshaw know about your intention to read from your manuscript?"

Not knowing if Elsie had mentioned my manuscript to Mrs. Cranshaw, I shrugged my shoulders. The woman, in turn, slapped the top of the counter with her right hand to convey her disgust. That slap filled me with an anger characteristic of a bull that in being taunted by a matador. My pride would not allow me to be the victim of the woman's harassment. I would have to fight her rudeness with some of my own.

"I want to speak to the administrator of this facility!" I exclaimed. "If my volunteer work here is going to cause a problem, then I'll resign before I even start. Believe me when I say that if I quit, I will let the person in charge know why. Who is the administrator?"

It was against the grain of my nature to speak in such a fashion, but that rude woman had unleashed an anger inside of me that was about to reach boiling point. Apparently, it was a bit of a shock to her that I had lashed out. Her face reddened a bit, and she took a step or two back.

In a much more civil tone, she replied, "The administrator's name is Bonnie Tulley." Then, pointing to the name tag on her tweed jacket, she said, "Bonnie Tulley at your service."

Her introduction caught me off guard, so much so that I became mute.

"Ms. Cole, please take a seat. I'll phone Mrs. Cranshaw to see if she is willing—oh, I mean ready—to see you."

Bonnie Tulley disappeared into a back room. I wasted no time in heading for a seat on the leather sofa that faced the fireplace. My anger may have heated up, but my body had not. I desperately needed to feel the warmth that the fireplace was generating.

Once seated, I started to rub my hands in an attempt to restore circulation to them. It was tempting to take my boots off and let my toes sink into the fibers of the thick tan carpet that covered the floor of the entire reception room. However, I feared that if I took my boots off, I would be booted out of Elsbury Place by the "gracious" Bonnie Tulley.

As I gazed at the flames in the fireplace, I started to think of topics of conversation that might interest Mrs. Cranshaw. Deep in thought, I did not notice that an elderly gentleman had claimed a seat on the opposite end of the sofa.

"Good morning, young lady," he said in an upbeat tone of voice.

The sound of his voice was pleasant but unexpected.

After jumping a bit, I turned towards him and made an earnest attempt to smile. However, the cold weather together with the cold reception I had received from Ms. Tulley made it physically and emotionally impossible for me to form a full-blown smile.

"No one has called me 'young lady' for quite some time. Thanks for the compliment."

"Surely now," he remarked, "you can't be terribly old. I'm a pretty good judge of age. You, no doubt, are on the sunny side of thirty."

"Not quite," I said with a girlish giggle. "I turned forty-two a couple of months ago."

"You're just a kid," he commented with a twinkle in his hazel eyes. "I would love to be forty-two again. I'm in my seventies."

"You don't look it," I said as I continued to rub my pitifully cold hands.

He smiled, braced his chin on his right hand, which was atop the handle of his cane, and watched the fire for a moment in silence. Then he got up to grab a magazine on a nearby table. A rather dapper-looking man, he was slim and of average height. He was sporting an Irish knit pullover sweater and black denim slacks. His neatly trimmed goatee matched his white hair, which was considerably full for a man his age.

"Your hands must have taken a beating from the cold," he remarked as he reclaimed his seat on the sofa. "How far from the front door did you park?"

"Oh, I took the bus here. I don't own a car."

"Perhaps that's a good thing," he said. "Cars are expensive to maintain."

In my case, the very purchase of a car was out of the question. It was not my desire to bore the gentleman with details of my quickly deteriorating financial situation, but his next question would cause me to open up a bit about my poor-as-a church-mouse status.

"Are you applying for a job here?" he asked.

"No. I probably should be applying for one, though. Right now, I'm self-employed. I love my little business, but it hasn't been successful. Someday, I may have to call it quits and go to work for someone else. For now, anyway, I'm devoting a lot of time to my so-called business. If it doesn't take off, at least I'll know that I did my best to try to get it off the ground."

"I admire your gumption," he said. "So, you are visiting a friend or a relative here?"

"No. I have volunteered to be a companion to one of the residents. As a matter of fact, today is my first day."

"Truly remarkable and unselfish! By the way, my name is Norbert Rockfeld. You are someone I would certainly like to know."

He put the magazine aside and extended his right hand to shake mine. As I put my hand in his, the warmth of his skin felt comforting. My hands still felt like icicles, but he had rekindled my spirits a bit.

"I'm Linzie Cole. It's nice to meet you."

"Young lady, the pleasure is all mine. Will you be volunteering on a regular basis?"

"It was my intention to come here once a week, Mr. Rockfeld, but sometimes the best of intentions never get realized."

"Yes, Ms. Cole, I know all about good intentions and how they sometimes get dashed."

As kind as he appeared to be and as much as I could have used a sympathetic ear, it was not my place to discuss with him how Bonnie Tulley had almost dashed my good intentions. He appeared eager to continue our conversation, but Ms. Tulley approached the sofa and began to speak.

"Mrs. Cranshaw will be ready to see you at ten o'clock, Ms. Cole. Do you know how to get to her apartment?"

"No."

"Go to the elevator that is located in the hallway that runs behind the reception room. Take the elevator to the second floor," she continued. "When you get off the elevator, turn left and then—"

"It's all right, Bonnie," Mr. Rockfeld interrupted. "I can show Ms. Cole the way. I was about to head for the elevator to return to my own apartment."

"If you wish," Ms. Tulley said in a voice that betrayed some anger.

"I certainly do wish," he retorted. "After all, Ms. Cole is devoting time here as a volunteer and deserves a great deal of appreciation."

Bonnie Tulley glared at Norbert Rockfeld and, with no further comment, turned on her heel to head back to the counter.

No sooner had Ms. Tulley left us than Mr. Rockfeld said, "Ms. Cole, I did not realize you are here to see Constance Cranshaw. Is she going to be the recipient of your volunteer services?"

"Yes."

With a rather astonished look on his face, he asked, "Are you sure it is Constance you are meant to see?"

"Positive," I replied.

He shook his head in disbelief. Although I was perplexed by both his and Ms. Tulley's peculiar reactions to my appointment with Mrs. Cranshaw, I did not have the nerve or the time to delve into that matter with Mr. Rockfeld.

"I'd like to talk to you some more, Mr. Rockfeld, but I'm due at Mrs. Cranshaw's apartment in a few minutes. Are you sure you don't mind heading me in the right direction?"

"I don't mind at all. In fact, I'll take you right to her door."

"Thanks."

Mr. Rockfeld and I rose from the sofa. We passed the reception counter, where Ms. Tulley had resumed rummaging through the seemingly endless pile of papers. The previously talkative Mr. Rockfeld was quiet as we started down the hallway that led to the elevator. His silence caused me to suspect that Bonnie Tulley's rude behavior had disturbed him. Feeling that I had somehow ignited the fuse to her temper, I tried to think of some lighthearted topic that would return him to his chatty self. Finally, I decided to try to spark a conversation based on what was before my very eyes.

"I've noticed, Mr. Rockfeld, that the exterior and the interior of this building don't seem to click. The exterior looks like a medieval castle, and the interior looks like the inside of a modern apartment building."

"You are quite right about that, Ms. Cole. This main building dates back to the early nineteen hundreds. It used to be a parochial school for boys. The interior was completely renovated when Elsbury Place came into being about thirty-five years ago. Due to the growing number of people who wanted to live here, the two newer buildings in back were built fifteen years ago."

It seemed I had picked the perfect topic to get Mr. Rockfeld chatting again, for he seemed more than eager to tell me about some of the nice touches that had recently been made to the interior of the main building. According to Mr. Rockfeld, an interior designer had been hired by the trustees that past fall to give the inside of the building a facelift that would create a more cheerful ambiance. In all of the common rooms, the walls had been painted in pastel colors, the bare floors had been covered with wool wall-to-wall carpets, fine oil paintings had been hung on the walls, and new furniture had replaced the old.

Once we reached the elevator, Mr. Rockfeld pushed the button to summon it. He became quiet once again. As we stood there waiting, my curiosity prompted me to ask him a question.

"Do you know Constance Cranshaw?"

He nodded his head and replied, "Yes, I do."

I was expecting him to expand on his answer, but he added nothing. The thought of meeting Mrs. Cranshaw was beginning to make me jittery. The thought of being alone with her during my first visit was even more unnerving. Before I knew it, I blurted out something that reflected the anxiety I was experiencing.

"Here's a thought, Mr. Rockfeld. If you stay with me when I knock on Mrs. Cranshaw's door, she may invite you to join us."

Stroking his goatee, he said, "I'm afraid you are far too optimistic about that, my dear. In the four years that Constance has lived here, none of her fellow residents has ever received an invitation to come visit her in her apartment. Constance is practically a recluse. She refuses to attend any of the functions here. In spite of the fact that we have a great dining hall, she insists that all her meals be delivered to her room. Her rather demanding and belligerent personality has not endeared her to the staff. To tell you the truth, Ms. Cole, the fact that Constance is engaging your services as a companion baffles my mind. I've been of the opinion for some time that the only companion Constance Cranshaw can tolerate is Constance Cranshaw."

Now that Mr. Rockfeld had shared some information about Mrs. Cranshaw, my mind was just as baffled as his. I wondered what was going through Elsie Wyman's head when she assigned Mrs. Cranshaw to me. There must have been scores of ladies in the complex who were sweet and in need of a companion. It did not sound as though Mrs. Cranshaw was of that type.

The elevator arrived, and we entered it. As the door closed, I felt as though I were being caged with no hope of escape.

"May I give you a piece of advice, Ms. Cole?" Mr. Rockfeld asked as the elevator began its ascent.

"Please do."

"If the conversation between you and Constance does not flow well, do not try to fill in the lulls with idle chatter. Constance has little patience for chatter. Actually, Constance has little patience period. Let her come up with topics to discuss. She is definitely a take-charge person. Quite frankly, my dear, she can be very blunt and, at times, downright rude. So, do not blame yourself if things do not go well. My guess is that your visit will be a short one. Constance is Constance, and that's all there is to it."

The bell rang, the door opened, and we got off the elevator to begin our walk to Mrs. Cranshaw's door. The more we walked, the more my nerves became frazzled. Perhaps to calm them, I began to tell Mr. Rockfeld how I planned to spend my time with Mrs. Cranshaw.

"At the insistence of Elsie Wyman, the head of the volunteer program, I brought along a copy of a partial manuscript of mine. I've been working on a novel for the last several months, and even though the novel is far from complete, Elsie wants me to read what I have written so far to Mrs. Cranshaw. To be honest, reading a story that isn't nearly finished makes no sense to me, but Elsie was adamant that I bring it."

Mr. Rockfeld stopped dead in his tracks. He stared into my brown eyes and ever so gently placed his hand on my shoulder.

"Ms. Cole, are you a writer?"

I smiled and said, "I'd certainly like to think so, but my sales records may dispute that."

"So, that's the little business you were telling me about in the reception room?"

"Yes. I self-publish. I've put a few stories out there."

"Does Constance know you're a writer?"

"I'm not sure. I don't know if Elsie mentioned that fact to her."

"I bet that's it, my dear. I bet she knows you're a writer and wants to meet you. She was a writer once upon a time. You two have something in common."

As he said those words, his eyes lit up like bulbs on a Christmas tree. He obviously believed he had discovered the link that was joining Mrs. Cranshaw and me and seemed overjoyed by his finding. His joy mystified me, but his joy was not the first thing that had mystified me that morning. It was just one more piece in a puzzle that seemed to be expanding each minute.

I did not want to pick Mr. Rockfeld's brain, but I was extremely curious about something Elsie had told me about Mrs. Cranshaw. Rather than ask Mr. Rockfeld a question he might not want to answer or possibly could not answer, I decided to convey my curiosity in a passing comment.

"Elsie," I said, "told me that Mrs. Cranshaw was an accomplished writer, but for some reason, at the height of her career, put her writing pad away one day and never picked it up again."

"Yes, Ms. Cole, Constance made a name for herself and was well known in various literary circles. Many years ago, she abandoned her writing career, much to the disappointment of her readers."

He shed no light on the source of my curiosity—the reason why Constance Cranshaw had suddenly stopped writing while she was riding a wave of success.

When we resumed walking, there was a newfound bounce in his step, and the cane he had been relying on for support was barely needed. We reached about the halfway point in the rather long hallway. Mr. Rockfeld stopped in front of a door with the number 243 on it. Unlike the other doors we had passed along the way, door number 243 did not display any kind of decoration.

In a voice that was reduced to a near whisper, he said, "Well, my dear, this is it. Try to be patient with Constance even if she doesn't treat you the way she should. She may invite you back a second time, but don't get upset if she doesn't. You've done a good deed by coming here today. In fact, whether Constance is going to be in your future or not, I would love to meet with you again. Would you consider coming to Elsbury Place some other day to have lunch with me? You, of course, would be my guest."

"I would be happy to come back and join you for lunch."

"Wonderful. You can tell me all about your writing career. I'm an avid reader. May I borrow a pen for a moment? I would like to write down my phone number for you."

"Oh, of course."

I walked a few feet beyond Mrs. Cranshaw's door in order to place my briefcase on a small oak table that was situated against the hallway wall. I released the latches of the briefcase and opened it. My hands were still sore and shaky from the cold, so it was with a clumsy right hand that I searched for a pen inside the case. During the search, I managed to knock the case off the table. All of the contents, including a pen, found a new home on the floor.

"I'll put everything back in your briefcase, Ms. Cole. I'm afraid you have not thawed out yet. The good news is that we found your pen."

After Mr. Rockfeld neatly put my briefcase back in order, he reached into the right pocket of his slacks and took out a tiny notepad. He wrote his name and phone number on the top sheet, tore the sheet off the pad, and then handed me the sheet and the pen.

"Till we meet again, young lady, and I do mean *young* even though you're not on the sunny side of thirty."

I smiled and said, "I can't say I object to your flattery. I hope to come back for more of it soon."

"Please do," he said with a gracious bow of his head.

He then headed for the elevator that was located on the end of the hallway that was opposite the end from which we had just traveled together. I watched him until he pushed the button to summon the elevator. When he pushed that button, I pushed a button of my own—a panic button! As I knocked on Mrs. Cranshaw's door, my heart was beating fast. A neophyte was about to read an unfinished manuscript to an accomplished writer, who might prove to be a rather rude hostess. I suddenly had great sympathy for the gladiators of ancient Rome, who had no idea if they would survive what awaited them in the Colosseum.

When Mrs. Cranshaw opened her door, I was surprised to

see that she was not the hunched, haggard, and poorly dressed recluse that my mind had envisioned. In fact, she was quite the opposite—of good posture, fresh as a daisy, and impeccably dressed. Just an inch shy of my own height of five feet four inches, she was a slim woman but not fragile looking by any means. Her rosy cheeks conveyed the impression that she was a person who took good care of herself. Her gray hair did not dispute that impression, for it was neat and curly, leading me to believe that she had recently paid a visit to a beauty salon. She was wearing a navy wool jacket with a matching skirt and a fancy white blouse with ruffles around the collar and the sleeves. Her black shoes appeared to be made of fine leather.

As we stood on opposite sides of the threshold, Mrs. Cranshaw did not speak. She was engrossed in looking me over, with even more scrutiny than Bonnie Tulley had. As her inspection of me continued, I increasingly felt as though I were some sort of specimen under a microscope. I could not bear one more second of such treatment, so I took the initiative to try to put a stop to her visual analysis of me. It was my hope that if I began a conversation, she would stop her examination.

"Hello, Mrs. Cranshaw. I'm Linzie Cole. It's a pleasure to meet you."

"Come in, Ms. Cole. Remove your boots so that they do not dampen my rugs. After you remove them, put them there," she said as she pointed to a mat that was to the right of the doorway.

So far, Mr. Rockfeld's description of Mrs. Cranshaw was right on target. She did indeed come across as a take-charge person who had little use for idle chatter. After I placed my boots on the mat, I fully expected her to offer to take my coat, but she did not. That led me to believe that my visit would be a short one, just as Mr. Rockfeld had predicted.

"Follow me, Ms. Cole."

In my stocking feet, with my coat on my back, and with my briefcase, hat, earmuffs, scarf, and gloves in my hands, I began to follow Mrs. Cranshaw down a hallway. A yak transporting goods through the Himalayas would have moved more gracefully than I. My feet were still frozen from my walk to the bus stop and seemed incapable of flexing themselves. My shaky hands caused me to drop my gloves and then my earmuffs on the hallway carpet. Fortunately, Mrs. Cranshaw did not notice the trials and tribulations I was experiencing. In spite of her age, which according to Elsie was seventy-eight, she was quite spry and managed to maintain a five-foot lead in front of me.

Eventually, the hallway brought us to our destination—the living room. It was a spacious, rectangular room that was impressively decorated. Centrally situated in the far wall of the room was a large picture window. Through the pane of glass, one could look out at a magnificent view—rolling hills that seemed to stretch endlessly behind the facility. The many snow-capped trees that populated the hills were a stark reminder that summer was long gone, but they were also an attestation to the beauty of winter. To the right of the picture window, in the corner of the far wall and the wall to the right, was a black grand piano that faced towards the center of the room. It was tempting to ask Mrs. Cranshaw if she played it, but she was a woman of such few words that I did not dare ask. Against the middle of the right wall was a white curio with gold-colored decorative touches. The curio displayed a large collection of figurines. Towards the other end of that wall was a large mahogany bookcase, the shelves of which were filled to capacity. I wondered whether some of the books on those shelves were products of Mrs. Cranshaw's writing, but I refrained from inquiring. There was no telling how she might react to any question regarding her writing career, particularly since she had abandoned it so suddenly. Against the wall on the left side of the room was a French provincial sofa. In front of the sofa was an oval walnut coffee table with bowed legs and a glass top. On the other side of the coffee table, facing the sofa, were two matching French provincial armchairs. All three of the provincial pieces of furniture were upholstered in an attractive and, no doubt, high-quality material of pink and white stripes.

Mrs. Cranshaw took a seat midway on the sofa. I sat in one of the armchairs, the one closer to the hallway that had led us to the living room.

"Ms. Cole, do not sit in that armchair. Sit in the one to your right."

Her command seemed a bit odd, but I did what she wanted. I walked over to the armchair that was closer to the picture window and sat down. Other than telling me where to sit, she had not said one word since we entered the living room. I found her lack of communication to be not only rude but also unsettling to my psyche. To make her acknowledge that I was a human being, not an object, I made yet another attempt to initiate some conversation.

"Your figurines are beautiful," I said. "They remind me of my mother's. She was quite a collector of them."

My comment about the figurines was ignored by Mrs. Cranshaw. Mr. Rockfeld had warned me that she had little use for idle chatter, but I had not heeded that warning. From that point on, however, I was determined to take his advice and let her initiate the topics of conversation. The ball was now in her court.

"Now, Ms. Cole, I would like to ask you a few questions," she said as she reached for the notepad, pen, and gold-rimmed spectacles that were on top of the coffee table.

"Fine," I said as I began to fiddle with the handle of my briefcase, which was in an upright position alongside my assigned chair.

Mrs. Cranshaw placed the spectacles on the bridge of her nose with the same preciseness that a jockey exercises when putting on goggles before a race. She took a moment to glance at the notepad, which now lay on her lap. With the click of her ballpoint pen, she was off and running with her first question.

"What is your purpose in coming here today, Ms. Cole?"

Her interrogation had certainly started with a bombshell of a question. Perhaps Elsie had not told her I was a writer, but surely she had told Mrs. Cranshaw that I was a volunteer companion. Confused by her question, I cleared my throat in order to give myself a few more seconds to think of an appropriate answer.

"Well, I have always wanted to volunteer in a home for the elderly and—"

"So, Ms. Cole, are you trying to tell me that I am old?"

My cheeks reddened. The ball was suddenly back in my court, and I was not sure how to handle it. I had already insulted the woman.

Trying to smooth the waters I had just agitated, I replied, "No, of course I am not calling you old, Mrs. Cranshaw. It is my understanding, though, that no one under the age of sixty-five can live here. In other words, this is not a home for the young."

"Go ahead," she ordered. "Continue with your reason for being here today."

"Elsie Wyman matched me with you when I put in a request to be a volunteer companion here at Elsbury Place. She said you used to be a writer. I am a writer. I suppose she felt we had something in common. She even insisted that I bring the manuscript I have been working on and read it to you. However, I must warn you that the manuscript is not finished and —"

"I know about your manuscript, Ms. Cole. It is your motive that I am questioning. Are you trying to feather your own bed by coming here today? Are you looking for favors from me because I still have contacts with some influential people in the literary world? If that is the case, you better rethink your coming here."

Her comments caused me to become tongue-tied, but I knew I could not be silent too long. I feared that if I did not show some backbone, I would end up like one of the unfortunate gladiators in the Colosseum—unable to free myself from the jaws of an angry lion.

"Mrs. Cranshaw, I am not looking for any favors from you. Your contacts in the literary world are of no concern to me. My sole purpose in coming here today is to offer my services as a companion. Let me repeat the fact that it was Elsie who matched me with you. Let me also repeat that it was Elsie who instructed me to bring my manuscript."

She tilted her head up towards the ceiling and gazed at it with her greenish-blue eyes. Apparently, she needed to pause a moment—no doubt to reload her mouth with more caustic words to shoot at me. When she turned her head in my direction, I tried to brace myself against any verbal bullets that might be heading my way.

"Ms. Cole, do I look like a child to you?"

"Of course not."

"Then, why should you read to me as though I were a four-year-old?"

"I guess Elsie thought you would enjoy sitting back and listening to what I have written so far because you used to be a writer."

My response evoked a grunt from Mrs. Cranshaw that was loud and clear. Mr. Rockfeld's advice to let her take charge of the conversation could no longer be heeded by me. I believed it was time for me to ask a few questions and put her on the defensive. By doing so, I hoped that our conversation would become more rational and that she would come to realize that it was my intention to offer her some companionship, not to feather my own bed. So, I took a deep breath and began my own inquisition.

"Mrs. Cranshaw, did you request Elsie to send a volunteer to you?"

"No, I did not," she replied in a tone of voice that sounded a bit less hostile than her prior tone. "Elsie phoned me and told me about you. When I learned that you are a writer, I agreed to meet with you."

"Now you are telling me that it is because I am a writer

that you agreed to our getting together today. Based on what you said before, you have no intention of helping me with my literary career. You certainly do not want me to read to you. So, what exactly do you want from me?"

The previously articulate Mrs. Cranshaw responded to my question with a string of *ums*. Now at a loss for words, she turned her head to the left and gazed out the picture window. While she remained silent, so did I. It appeared that we had hit a roadblock in our conversation. A couple of minutes went by before I heard the sound of her voice again.

"Ms. Cole," she said as she continued to gaze at the hills, "I have a purpose in mind, but I will not share that purpose with you today. There are more questions I want to ask you. If you do not want to answer them, then leave."

My curiosity would not allow me to head for the door. Although, on that Friday, she had no intention of unveiling her purpose for meeting me, I was hoping that the questions she wanted to ask would give me an inkling as to what her purpose was.

"As long as your questions are not too invasive," I said, "I'll answer them."

She looked at her notepad and then continued with her interrogation.

"Are you married?"

The question seemed so ridiculous, I wondered whether I had heard it correctly.

"Pardon me?" I said.

"Are you married?"

Bewildered, I replied, "No."

"Have you ever been married?"

"No."

"How old are you?"

I started to say, "Would you believe on the sunny side of thirty?" but quickly bit my tongue. Mr. Rockfeld would have appreciated such humor, but it was obvious that Mrs. Cranshaw had not one ounce of joviality in her whole body.

"I'm forty-two."

"Do you have a boyfriend?"

"Now, I don't understand why that matters."

"Please answer, Ms. Cole."

"Okay, there is a man I've been seeing for the last two years."

"Has he proposed to you?"

I burst out laughing. Her poker face cut my laughter short.

"No, he has not proposed."

"Are you engaged in any work other than your writing?"

"No. At least not for the time being."

"Do you live alone?"

"Yes."

"Do you have any immediate family?"

"No," I sadly replied.

"Finally, will you leave your manuscript here with me? I'll make sure you get it back. I want to read it."

Of all the questions she had asked, that was the one that disturbed me the most. Many painstaking hours had gone into that manuscript. I did not feel comfortable leaving it with a perfect stranger, but I knew if I expressed any hesitation about surrendering it to her, she would take offense. I had to be as diplomatic as possible.

"My manuscript is still in progress. Leaving it here with you would serve no purpose to my way of thinking."

"Ms. Cole, I am well aware of the fact that your manuscript is incomplete, but I still want to read it."

She was obviously not going to budge an inch on the issue of my leaving the manuscript. Other than simply refusing to leave it, the only thing I could do was ask her a point-blank question.

"Why do you want to read my manuscript, Mrs. Cranshaw?"

With the look like that of an angry dog, she growled, "I already told you that there was a purpose for our meeting today and that I would not share that purpose with you right now."

"But my manuscript seems to be at the heart of your purpose. Is that correct?"

I feared that my question would add fuel to the fire and that she would dismiss me immediately. I was pleasantly surprised when she did respond without rallying any extra anger.

"What I will tell you is that if I find your writing satisfactory, we'll meet again. Otherwise, I'll leave your manuscript with Bonnie Tulley. It will be there at the reception counter for you to pick up at your convenience. Do not worry. If I hold onto the manuscript, it will be in safe hands, and if it ends up in the hands of Miss Tulley, it will also be in safekeeping. The only good thing that I can say about that goofy woman is that she is reliable."

With reluctance, I opened my briefcase, took out a box that contained my manuscript, and handed it to her. Had it not been for the fact that I had a copy of the manuscript in my desk drawer, I would not have parted with it. Not saying any kind of thank you, she rose to her feet and started walking towards the hallway. That was my not-too-subtle cue that it was time for me to leave, so I got out of the chair and followed her to the spot where my boots awaited me.

My boots were a lot easier to take off than to put back on. Mrs. Cranshaw did not offer me a chair to make the latter task easier, so I simply held the boots in my right hand with the intention of struggling with them once I left her apartment. I had no desire to perform a balancing act in front of the heartless woman. Apparently, she had no desire to watch a balancing act, for she opened the front door without making any comment about my exiting her place in my stocking feet.

"Goodbye, Mrs. Cranshaw," I said as I headed for the doorway.

Constance Cranshaw did not say goodbye. She merely nodded her head to acknowledge the fact I was leaving. Once I was beyond the view of her peephole, I leaned against the hallway wall and put my boots on.

As I retraced my steps to the elevator, all I could think about was Mr. Rockfeld's comment that my visit with Mrs. Cranshaw would probably be brief. Brief it was indeed, but *bizarre* was a much more appropriate word to describe it. I entered the elevator and watched the door close. The elevator's descent felt more like an escape than a simple means of transport. After the door opened, I quickly exited the elevator and then scurried down the hallway. When I entered the reception room, I noticed that Bonnie Tulley was still at the counter, huddled over that darn pile of papers. The thought that I should sign out at the counter did occur to me, but my desire to leave was too great to cater to that formality.

It was with a sense of relief that I turned the handle of the front door of the facility and re-entered the world outside. The frigid air had not mellowed one bit, but it was far warmer than the ice-cold treatment I had just received within the walls of Elsbury Place.

Chapter Two

Upon my return to my apartment, I flopped into my favorite armchair, which enjoyed a place of prominence near the fireplace in my living room. Clunky, worn, and plain, my chair was a far cry from the fancy French provincial one that I had occupied less than an hour earlier. Although many would have considered it worthy of the trash, I considered my chair to be a tried-and-true friend that offered me comfort when I entertained my deepest thoughts. My visit to Elsbury Place had certainly caused the wheels in my head to turn. As I sat, I tried to rationalize all that had happened at the facility that morning but could not. The haze of mystery surrounding my visit was simply too thick. Bonnie Tulley, Norbert Rockfeld, and Constance Cranshaw had all planted question marks in my brain, which was just as worn out as the chair in which I sat.

One particular thought was gnawing at my very soul. That thought revolved around the fact that my manuscript was now in the hands of a successful writer. Mrs. Cranshaw's social skills were far from polished, but her skills as a writer had obviously been polished to perfection. How would I react if my writing failed to meet her approval? Would a thumbs-down from her cause me to give up my writing career? As I agonized over the possibility that "Constance the Great" might turn her nose up at my manuscript, the need to talk to someone grew stronger. I picked up the phone and dialed the number of my boyfriend, Kevin, who worked at home as a self-employed financial advisor. To my relief, I got his voice, not his voicemail.

"Hello. Kevin Conway speaking."

"Hi, Kevin. This is Linzie."

Laughing, he said, "Is this Linzie, as in Linzie Cole, the famous author?"

I was so uptight that I disregarded Kevin's sense of humor.

"I haven't had the best of days, Kevin. Do you have time to chat?"

"I always have time for you, Linzie. You know that. Did you go to Elsbury Place this morning?"

"I did."

"So, did something go wrong while you were there?"

"Yes, that's for sure."

Kevin coughed to clear his throat. There was definite concern in his voice when he continued.

"Linzie, did you get hurt in any way?"

"Not physically, Kevin. The hurt I feel is emotional."

"I don't understand. How badly can volunteer service go, even on the first day?"

"Plenty wrong. I have never felt so insulted. I was not received well by the administrator of Elsbury Place. As for Constance Cranshaw, she was as rude as rude can be. She did not give a hoot that I wanted to offer her my services as a companion. All she focused on is the fact that I am a writer. Do you remember I told you that I was going to read my unfinished manuscript to her?"

"Yes."

"Mrs. Cranshaw insisted that I leave it with her so she could read it herself. I do not understand why Elsie Wyman was so adamant that I bring that manuscript with me today. Elsie knows darn well that the manuscript has a long way to go before I complete it. I also told Mrs. Cranshaw that it is a work in progress, but that did not put one dent in her desire to read it."

Kevin did not respond right away. When he did, his voice sounded more than just concerned; it sounded strained.

"Linzie, I know how hard you have been working on that manuscript. Do you have another copy?"

"Yes."

After heaving a sigh of relief, he said, "You told me that Mrs. Cranshaw was a great author but no longer writes. Why does she want to read your manuscript?"

"That's the thing, Kevin. She refused to give me a reason today. She said if she found my writing to be satisfactory, I would hear from her again. If not, she'll make sure I get my manuscript back."

A lull in our conversation ensued. During that lull, I could hear Kevin tapping his fingers on his desk. His tapping was usually a sign that he was perplexed and needed time to think.

"Hmm, it does seem strange," he finally said, "that she refused to give you a reason today for wanting to read your manuscript and even stranger that she will be judging your writing based on work that has not been completed."

"Kevin, what if she doesn't like it?"

Kevin did not need any time to respond to that question.

"Why should you care, Linzie, whether she likes it or not? Her writing days are over, right?"

"Right."

"And she'll be looking at a manuscript that you haven't had time to finish or perfect, right?"

"Right."

"Then, babe, I would not fret about Mrs. Cranshaw's opinion of your manuscript. It is the final product that will count, and it is your future readers that will matter. As for Mrs. Cranshaw, who knows what makes her tick? Don't strain your brain trying to interpret her intentions."

Kevin's comments put me at ease. In many ways, he was like a big brother to me, always protective of my welfare and feelings. I now realized how foolish I had been to magnify the importance of Mrs. Cranshaw's opinion of my work.

"You have a way of cheering me up," I said with a hint of a laugh. "I guess I'm overtired. This writing business of mine has been an uphill battle."

"Linzie, your writing is your passion. Most people are probably bored to death with their jobs. Don't you think you should feel good about devoting your time to what you love doing most?"

I paused before answering in order to gather and properly convey all the feelings I was experiencing at that moment.

"I feel good about my decision to write," I remarked, "but today upset me because my trip to Elsbury Place had nothing to do with my writing career. I simply wanted to perform some charitable work. When my mother was living in the nursing home in Cambridge, a lot of the residents there had no visitors, so I used to call on them. After Mom passed away, I began to seriously think about volunteering as a companion to the elderly. My good intention to bring a little joy into the life of someone who might be lonely sure backfired on me today. Mrs. Cranshaw does not want a companion. I am so confused as to what her intentions are. Although she insisted on reading my manuscript, she practically accused me of trying to use her as a stepping-stone into the literary world. Nothing could be further from the truth."

Kevin was silent once again, but this time his silence was accompanied by more than a mere tapping of his fingers on the desk. Rather, the noise that came over the phone sounded more like a banging of his fist. When he began to speak, his voice sounded agitated.

"Linzie, how dare she accuse you of such a thing! Listen to my advice. Get your manuscript back and stay the hell away from her. She sounds like a crackpot."

Kevin rarely got angry, but he was certainly angry at that moment. The harshness in his voice actually startled me.

I tried to come up with a joke that would tame his ire, but I was so flustered, nothing humorous came to mind. Fortunately, he quickly regained his usual carefree attitude.

With a lighthearted lilt in his voice, he said, "Well, babe, Mrs. Cranshaw doesn't know you the way I do. Give me ten minutes with that misguided woman, and I'll have her convinced that you are the finest of the fine."

"Not necessary, Kevin, but thanks anyway. Thanks, too, for listening to some of the details of my rather weird morning at Elsbury Place."

"There will be no bill for my services. My pep talk was my charitable work for the day."

"In appreciation for your charitable work, Kevin, how about coming over for dinner some night soon? I know you'll be leaving for New York tomorrow to spend a couple of days with your mother. You're still planning to see the new year in with her, right?"

"Yes. I don't want Mom to be alone when the new year arrives."

"Are you still planning to be back in Massachusetts on Monday afternoon?"

"I sure am. I plan to get an early start for my drive home. I'll leave at the crack of dawn."

"Then, why don't you come here for dinner Monday night? It would be nice if we could spend the first evening of 2018 together."

I was a bit surprised that Kevin did not respond to my invitation right away. A good thirty seconds passed before he spoke.

"Linzie, you know how I recently started reserving Monday nights to meet with clients who are not free during the daytime hours of the week?"

"Yes. You started reserving Monday nights about six weeks ago."

"Well, even though this coming Monday is January first, I still have to meet a client that evening. She needs some guidance on buying stocks and bonds. There is no way I can postpone the meeting because she is leaving Boston on Tuesday to go to France for two months. I'm free on Tuesday night. Would that night be okay with you?"

"Yes," I replied.

"Instead of your cooking for me, let me take you out to dinner."

"Are you sure? I don't mind cooking one bit."

"I'm sure. You pick the restaurant, Linzie, and I'll pick you up on Tuesday at six o'clock."

"Okay. Thanks, Kevin."

"By the way, I want to be at the head of the line when you sign and pass out copies of your first best seller."

"The first copy will be yours," I said giggling. "Even Mrs. Cranshaw will not be allowed to cut in front of you when that long line forms."

"She better not even try, Miss Linzie, or she'll have me to reckon with," he said in a rather good imitation of a Western drawl.

Laughing, I said, "Personally, Kevin, I think you should be a volunteer at Elsbury Place. The facility desperately needs a stand-up comedian. You'd fill that role quite well."

"Babe, I might get people laughing so loudly that I would be kicked out for disturbing the peace."

Kevin's comment was not as far-fetched as he thought. It set my mind adrift for a moment. I visualized Kevin cracking jokes in front of a group of Elsbury Place residents. Then, suddenly from nowhere, appears the infamous Bonnie Tulley. She grabs Kevin by the ear and ushers him out the door for the crime of spreading humor throughout the halls of the facility. The sound of Kevin's voice snapped me out of my reverie.

"Linzie, my other phone is ringing. I'll call you later on, probably before dinnertime."

"Okay, Kevin."

"Bye, babe."

"Bye."

When I hung up the phone, I felt like a new person. Kevin had a knack for lifting my spirits. With my mind now feeling a lot less muddled, I considered working on my manuscript. However, a different thought suddenly popped into my head —to take the rest of the day off. Rarely did I treat myself to some R&R, but on that Friday, I felt that a little downtime would do me a world of good. So, I put all my winter "armor" back on and descended the staircase for the second time that day. I was heading for Harrud's, a favorite restaurant of mine that was located two streets over from my apartment.

It was not only the good food that attracted me to Harrud's. During the two years that I had been frequenting the restaurant, I had grown quite close to the owners, Rudolf and Harriet, a married couple. Rudolf was one of the most upbeat people I had ever met in spite of the fact that life had not always been good to him. Born in Hungary in 1948, he lost both his parents at a young age. Raised by his aunt, he lived in his native country, behind the Iron Curtain, until 1991, when the Cold War ended. Then, at the age of forty-three, he came to the United States to carve out a new life. Grateful for the freedom he enjoyed in this country, he was determined to face every day with a positive attitude. Shortly after settling in the United States, he met the love of his life, Harriet, a warm, bubbly woman. Eight months after their meeting, Rudolf and Harriet got married, settled in the Boston area, and entered the restaurant business. By combining the first three letters of his wife's first name and the first three letters of his own first name, Rudolf came up with the name Harrud's for the restaurant they established. Although Rudolf was approaching the age of seventy-one, he still ran Harrud's with unquestionable gusto.

When I entered Harrud's around noontime, Rudolf spotted me in the lobby and hurried over to greet me. Tall and thin, he had to stoop a bit in order to grasp my left hand with his right one. He then raised my hand to his lips and kissed the top of it. That was his usual way of welcoming me. It was an old-world custom that I found to be charming. As always, his appearance was flawless. Every strand of his somewhat thinning white hair was in place. His black suit was neatly pressed and was complemented by a white shirt, red tie, and a boutonniere in his lapel. Rudolf always wore a boutonniere. It was more than just a fashionable touch. It was something that called attention to the fact that he was involved in the operation of the restaurant. If a customer had a complaint, Rudolf wanted that customer to approach him and voice what was wrong. He ran a top-notch operation. The loyal clientele of Harrud's was proof of that.

"My Linzie has arrived," he said with his distinctive Hungarian accent. "Harriet and I missed you so much on Christmas Day. Our home seemed empty without you."

"Believe me, Rudolf, I missed both of you. I guess the weather just wasn't going to cooperate."

"The weather is working in your favor today, Linzie. The cold snap is keeping people away, so I can seat you wherever you like."

"That's good for me, but not so good for you," I said sympathetically.

"You lead the way, dear. Choose a table to your liking. I have a pretty good idea where you are going to head."

Rudolf knew that I loved to sit by the large fieldstone fireplace that was situated at the far end of the dining room. The fire not only provided warmth but also stimulated my creative juices when it came to my writing. It was a habit of mine to bring a pen and a small notebook with me whenever I went to Harrud's so that I could jot down new ideas for my stories.

As I walked over to my favorite table in front of the fireplace, I could not help but notice that of the twenty-five tables in the dining room, only three were occupied. Harrud's was usually booming with business at that hour. After removing my outerwear, I sat down in the chair that faced the fireplace.

"Summer seems far away," Rudolf commented as he placed the menu on the table.

"I hope for your sake, Rudolf, that Old Man Winter starts to take some pity on us poor New Englanders. This weather must be hurting your business."

"It is, but I can't complain. Life is good. By the way, Linzie, my better half has some news for you. I'm sure that she will be joining you in a moment."

"Do you know if it is good news?"

After the crazy morning I had experienced at Elsbury Place, my ears did not want to hear any bad news.

"Potentially good news," he cautioned. "To Harriet's way of thinking, it is indeed good, but you know my Harriet. She is on a mission to make your life as happy as possible. What she considers to be good, you may not. In any case, she wants the very best for you, just as I do. We think of you as the daughter we never had."

"Thank you, Rudolf. I think of you and Harriet as family too."

"Enjoy your lunch, dear."

With that, he turned and started to head for the reception area. There was little doubt in my mind that Harriet would soon be paying me a visit at the table. Although she helped Rudolf manage the restaurant and constantly surveyed it with an eagle eye, she always found time to sit with me and chat. A close friendship had evolved from all the chats we had enjoyed together. We were so close that I felt quite comfortable calling her by her nickname, Harri.

Harriet's male-sounding nickname was deceiving, for she embodied all the qualities of a true lady. She was kind, tender, and loving. Twenty-six years my senior, she had become a mother figure to me. While I was grieving over the loss of my mother, who passed away during the winter of 2016, Harri reached out to comfort me. She started to include me in all her holiday celebrations as if I were one of her family. Always interested in what was going on in my life, there was never any hesitation on her part to try to give me some guidance when she felt it was necessary. I always thought of Harri as an angel that my mother sent my way to fill a void in my life after her passing. Once my mom passed, I had no immediate family. My father died fifteen years before my mother, and I was an only child.

Before I had a chance to open the menu, I saw, out of the corner of my eye, a person sit in the chair to my right. It was Harri. She was so bubbly that she started to speak before I had time to greet her.

"Linzie, I have good news."

"Hi, Harri. Rudolf mentioned you had news."

As a gesture to herald the good news she was about to impart, she reached over and squeezed my right hand with her left one. Harri was short and a bit on the plump side. Her fingers felt stubby, and her palm, fleshy. The warmth that radiated from her hand matched her personality.

"My son, Joseph," she said, "is moving back to Boston from Europe next month. His engineering project in London is finally coming to an end."

"That's wonderful."

I touched her on the shoulder in order to accentuate how pleased I was. Joseph was her adopted son and her only child. I knew how she longed to have him nearby.

"That's not all, Linzie. My news involves you."

"Me?"

"Yes, you. Allow me to explain. While Joseph was traveling through Switzerland three years ago, he met a nice man at a ski resort. The man lives in Cambridge, Massachusetts. He and Joseph became friends and have stayed in touch with each other. At Joseph's coaxing, his friend came to eat dinner here the night before last. He introduced himself to me, and he and I had a long chat. Linzie, guess what Joseph's friend does for a living."

Shrugging my shoulders, I replied, "I have no idea. I'm quite sure you are not going to tell me that he is a ski bum."

"No. He is not a ski bum. He is a successful publisher. I told him all about you and your writing career. He wants to meet you."

Before I could verbalize any response, Harri continued to speak enthusiastically.

"Joseph's friend's name is Adam. Adam is very handsome and only several years older than you. Thanks to Joseph, I can give you some background information about him. Adam has never been married. During the last five years, he was dating a woman that he wanted to marry. Time after time, his marriage proposals were rejected by her. She was married before, unhappily, and is not willing to give marriage a second try. It was a difficult thing for him to do, but he broke up with her recently. Apparently, perpetual dating is not his thing. He wants a permanent relationship. Although he is still suffering from a broken heart, he is now willing to try to move on. After I told him about you the other night, he suggested that he invite you out to dinner to get to know you and to hear about the stories you have written."

After releasing my hand, she banged the palms of her hands on the table to indicate that this news was truly good. My reaction to Harri's good news was one of silence. Too much had come at me too quickly. It was as though a whole ball of wax had been thrown at me, a ball in which aspects of both my professional life and my personal life were intertwined. Fearing that my silence would lead Harri to believe that I was unappreciative of her good intentions, I managed to think of a question—a very basic one.

"So, Harri, what is the man's full name?"

"His name is Adam Proctor."

Waiting for some feedback from me, she sat back in her chair and started to fiddle with a few of the many tight curls of her light-brown hair. Her dark-brown eyes had a look of hopeful anticipation in them. It was obvious she wanted me to feel overjoyed, and perhaps I would have felt overjoyed if such news had reached my eardrums two years earlier. The thought of meeting a nice single man attuned to my writing career would have been exciting then, but not now. I loved Kevin. Our relationship seemed solid and was built upon a foundation of true friendship. That friendship, in my opinion, was developing into something special with each passing day. I dated no one but Kevin, and Kevin dated no one but me. There was no way I was going to jeopardize my relationship with Kevin in order to begin one with Adam Proctor. The last thing I wanted to do was hurt Harri's feelings, so I knew I would have to let her down as gently as possible.

"Harri, I want to thank you for all your efforts, but I don't think it would be fair on my part to encourage any kind of meeting with Adam. As you know, I've been dating Kevin Conway for two years now. You have seen me in here a number of times with Kevin. In fact, you and he have had a few short conversations. I don't want to do anything that would hurt Kevin or Adam, and I—"

"Hold on now, Linzie. Just listen to your second mom for a moment. As a companion, I'm sure Kevin is great, but I do not believe he is husband material. He strikes me as a guy who is not eager to commit himself to any real future with you. I'm just curious. Has Kevin ever told you that he loves you?"

"Well, not exactly."

"Has he ever mentioned that marriage is in store for the two of you?"

"No, not really, Harri, but he obviously has deep feelings for me."

"You, my dear Linzie, are not getting any younger. I don't think you should close the door to other prospects."

Harri was not shy when it came to voicing her opinion on any subject. I never took offense when she expressed her feelings because I knew she spoke from the heart. Blessed with an uncanny ability to accurately size people up, she reminded me of an archer whose arrows never miss the bullseye. Somehow, her opinions were always right on target. When it came to her opinion about Kevin, however, I believed she had shot an arrow that was way off course. In fact, that stray arrow had struck me in the heart. Sad and baffled, I sat there wondering why she was so negative about my future with Kevin. She barely knew him.

"Where is the harm in meeting Adam?" she asked. "Even if you two decide not to go out socially, he may be able to give you some pointers on how to succeed in the writing business. He may even be interested in publishing your work. You owe it to yourself to seek all the available avenues."

Kevin's habit of tapping his fingers when he was perplexed and in need of time to think had apparently rubbed off on me. As I searched for a proper response, I was tapping my fingers on the white linen tablecloth. My fingers may have been hard at work, but my mind was at a standstill. Harri must have realized that I was in a quandary, for it was she who resumed the conversation.

"Linzie, take a look at that painting on the wall to your left."

I turned my head in the direction of the light-green wall on which the large framed oil painting hung. The scene was not a stranger to me. It had drawn my attention many times when I sat in that area of the dining room.

"What do you see in that painting?" she asked.

"I see a fox surrounded by hounds."

"And how would you describe the emotion that is in the eyes of the fox?"

"I would describe it as fear," I replied.

"And why fear?"

"Well, the fox has no place to run. He is cornered."

"Exactly, Linzie. I'm afraid the same thing is happening to you. My gut feeling is that Kevin is cornering you into a relationship that is a dead-end street. I bet he has no intention of offering you a future that goes beyond dating. You deserve a guy who truly loves you and wants to marry you. It's the end of the line for that poor fox in the picture, but it doesn't have to be the end of the line for you. You should feel free to move on."

My head was spinning from all that Harri had said about Kevin. I knew that my eyes were now mirroring the look of fear that was in the fox's eyes, and for a brief moment, I tried to avoid eye contact with Harri. After regaining my composure, I was able to look into Harri's eyes and ask her a question or two about her not-so-promising prediction of my future with Kevin.

"Harri, did Kevin say anything to you that caused you to believe that I'll never be anything more than a girlfriend to him?"

"No, Linzie, he did not."

"Then, why do you feel the way you do about him?"

She reached for my right hand again and squeezed it gently.

"Let's just say that it is a second mom's intuition."

Harri's feelings about Kevin perplexed me. My mind was in such a state of upheaval that I did not wish to pursue the topic of Kevin's intentions any further with Harri. The issue of whether I should or should not meet Adam Proctor now had to be addressed.

Taking a deep breath, I said, "It sounds as though Adam has had his share of heartbreak when it comes to romance. What happens if I meet Adam and he wants to start dating me, but I don't want to date him? I don't want to hurt the guy, and I certainly don't want to use him as a stepping-stone when it comes to my writing."

My remark about not wanting to use Adam as a stepping-stone carried my mind back to the unpleasant meeting I had with Mrs. Cranshaw that morning. I was still reeling from her near accusation of my using her as a stepping-stone into the literary world. A trancelike state came over me as I began to relive the disturbing moments of my visit at Elsbury Place. Harri transported my mind back to Harrud's when she responded to my concerns about meeting Adam.

"Linzie, your writing career gives you the perfect opportunity to meet Adam without feeling any pressure to go out with him socially. Maybe you two will hit it off, and maybe you won't. As for your career, to simply let Adam ask you about your writing is not to use him. Don't forget. I have read your stories and believe that you have been blessed with the gift to write. Has it occurred to you that Adam Proctor, the publisher, may be darn glad to meet you, Linzie Cole, the writer? Please don't underestimate your talent, dear. If you do, you may be doomed to failure."

Harri was dead right about one thing. I did indeed have the tendency to downplay my ability to write even though those who had read my works had given me encouraging praise. When it came to my writing, humility was not a virtue that worked in my favor.

Harri got back on her feet. It was typical of her to voice her opinions and then back off in order to give me time to digest what we had discussed.

"Think things over, Linzie. Let me know what you decide about Adam. I truly believe that as a mate, he is a good catch, and that as a publisher, he is a good contact. Naturally, the decision to meet him or not meet him is entirely up to you."

"Thanks, Harri. I'll let you know soon."

As she walked by my chair, she tapped the back of my neck with her right hand as a sign of affection. A moment later, she disappeared into the kitchen to dutifully perform her job as manager.

Shortly after Harri left my table, a waiter came over to take my order. Normally, I would have asked for a few more minutes to look over the menu. This time, however, the thought of scouring it was too much for my tired brain. I opened the menu and chose the first offering that met my eyes. Then I handed the menu to the waiter and thanked him.

As I sat waiting for my meal, I was in a reflective mood. The day had been a strange one, one that had offered some possible avenues for my writing career, but one that had forced me to question the solidity of the avenue on which my personal life was traveling. Harri's assessment of my relationship with Kevin was preying on my mind. Although I did not want to accept her assessment, I knew deep down that I could not dismiss it either. Perhaps if Kevin had at least once said the words *I love you* to me, I could have begged to differ with Harri about Kevin's intentions. Marriage was what I wanted, but did Kevin really share my sentiments on that matter? He had never said. Harri's reminder that I was getting up there in age was indisputable. Although Mr. Rockfeld had flattered me that very morning by saying that I looked as though I were on the sunny side of thirty, I knew only too well that I was on the shady side of that number. Kevin was too. He was five years my senior.

As I sat by the fireplace on that Friday, I knew there was no point in reaching into my bag to take out the pen and the small notebook I used to record new ideas for my stories. I suddenly felt incapable of developing the lives of my fictional characters, for I had no idea where my own life was going.

When I returned to my apartment after lunch at Harrud's, it was about 2:00 p.m. What a horrid day it had been! Nothing had gone right! I was tempted to peek at my calendar to see if the date was really Friday the 13th rather than Friday the 29th. The twists and turns of the day had zapped my energy.

Very seldom did I take a nap, but I decided to do just that upon my arrival home from the restaurant. Once I put my head on the pillow, it did not take long for me to enter a deep sleep. Had it not been for the ringing of my phone around 5:00 p.m., I believe I would have slept until a late hour of the night. I clumsily reached for the phone and almost succeeded in knocking it off the nightstand. Kevin had said he would probably call me before dinnertime. I was in such a groggy state that I assumed it was Kevin calling. Without checking my caller ID, I started to speak to the person on the other end as though it were Kevin for sure.

In a voice that sounded as though I had been sedated, I said, "Hello, honey."

My greeting was met with silence, which led me to believe that a glitch had prevented Kevin's call from coming through to my line. I was just about to hang up and dial his phone number when I heard a voice on the other end.

"Is this Miss Linzie Cole?"

"Yes. Who is this?"

"This is Constance Cranshaw. Miss Cole, I do not appreciate being called 'honey.' "

Embarrassed, I quickly shot out of bed and headed for the boudoir chair on the other side of the room. As I sat down, I coughed to clear my throat of any raspiness. Once I felt that I could speak clearly, I found myself to be at a loss for words. I had just called a very sour woman honey and now had some explaining to do. I did not dare tell Mrs. Cranshaw that I had been sleeping. Such a confession would have doubtlessly led her to believe that I was a lazy person, which I certainly was not. With the exception of holidays, my computer and I were practically married. I tirelessly worked on my stories in an effort to produce high-quality work. It was just my luck that Mrs. Cranshaw would call me at a time when I needed to recharge my battery.

"Mrs. Cranshaw," I finally said, "please forgive me. I was expecting a call from my boyfriend, Kevin. He was supposed to call me around this time."

"Miss Cole, your voice sounds quite different over the phone. I certainly hope you are not getting a cold. I want to see you next week in my apartment, but if you are carrying germs, we'll have to put our meeting off until you are well. I do not wish to get sick."

How typical of Constance Cranshaw! All she seemed to care about was her own well-being. The heck with me!

"I assure you, Mrs. Cranshaw, that I am well. I simply have a frog in my throat."

For some reason, there was a strong urge inside of me to

tack on a little humor to my last statement. My better judgement told me not to act on that urge, but I defied my better judgement.

"Can't you tell, Mrs. Cranshaw, that the frog has already jumped out?" I asked with a chuckle.

My hope was that Mrs. Cranshaw would return my chuckle with a chuckle of her own. That hope was dashed when she quickly let me know that my frog joke did not exactly tickle her funny bone.

"Miss Cole, I do not have the time or the desire to discuss the frog that had been trapped in your throat and that just managed to escape. I would like to see you in my apartment on Wednesday, January third, at ten o'clock. Do not be tardy."

"Please hold on," I said in an efficient tone of voice. "I'll have to check the calendar in my office to make sure I am free."

I knew darn well that I was free at that time, but my self-respect would not allow me to kowtow to Constance the Great. What a nerve she had to assume that I could be at her beck and call on a day and at a time that was convenient for her! So, I did something that was uncharacteristic of my honest nature. I sat as still as a mummy in the boudoir chair for a couple of minutes while she thought I was checking my "busy" schedule. I suppose such behavior on my part should have caused me to feel guilty, but I must admit that the opposite was true. It did my heart good to keep her waiting. Her cold and self-centered personality was beginning to take a toll on my temperament. I had to wonder just how vindictive I would become if my relationship with her were to continue.

"Good news," I said when I resumed speaking. "It just so happens that I am free on Wednesday at that time."

"Very well, Miss Cole. I shall see you on Wednesday at ten."

Before she had a chance to hang up, I was determined to extract from her the purpose of our upcoming meeting. Based on our meeting that morning, I knew that any attempt on my part to encourage her to unveil her purpose would be as foolish as sticking my hand into a bee nest. However, I felt I had been kept in the dark long enough and was willing to subject myself to any venomous remarks she might mouth over the phone.

So, in a firm voice, I said, "Mrs. Cranshaw, you have not said why you want to see me on Wednesday."

That statement fared even worse than my frog joke. The firmness in my voice was outmatched by the loud, harsh-sounding response that her vocal cords produced.

"Miss Cole, did I not tell you that I would call you if I found your writing to be satisfactory?"

"Yes, you certainly did."

"Now, use your head, Miss Cole. Why do you think I am calling you?"

"Because you found my writing satisfactory."

"And just what do you think our meeting on Wednesday is all about?"

"My writing."

"Good work. Take a bow for all your intuitiveness."

The good news that my writing had received her approval was overshadowed by her insolent attitude. There was no way I was going to be a passive target of her rudeness. Making my voice sound sterner, I fought back.

"Mrs. Cranshaw, I realize that you would not have phoned me unless you had found my writing satisfactory. That is a no-brainer for me. However, you still have not explained what your purpose is when it comes to my writing. I think I have a right to know."

Expecting to hear some screaming on the other end, I was quite surprised to hear her respond in a much calmer tone of voice.

"When you meet with me on Wednesday, I shall make my intentions clear, Miss Cole. Then we shall see where we go from there."

The fact that she remained tight-lipped about her intentions did not please me, but at least her temper had cooled down. Before it heated up again, I thought it best to bid her adieu, so I hurried to do so.

"Mrs. Cranshaw, thank you for calling. I'll see you on Wednesday. Goodbye."

I did not expect her to say goodbye—good thing, because she did not. The click of her phone told me the conversation was over. A very strange woman she was indeed—humorless, demanding, and demeaning. Why she was that way was an enigma to me, but one thing was becoming increasingly clear: Anyone who wanted to deal effectively with Constance Cranshaw could not be among the faint of heart.

Shortly after my conversation with Mrs. Cranshaw ended, the phone rang. My caller ID revealed that it was Kevin calling. I picked up the phone.

"Hi, Kevin."

"Hi, babe. I tried to get you a few minutes ago, but your line was busy."

"Oh, I was talking to Mrs. Cranshaw," I said in a voice that was devoid of feeling.

"From the sound of your voice, I take it she did not think too much of your unfinished manuscript."

"Actually, Kevin, that's not the case. The manuscript met her approval. I am supposed to be at her place next Wednesday morning at ten o'clock."

"You don't sound happy. I thought you would be pleased if your work received her blessing."

At that point in the conversation, I asked Kevin to hold on. I rose from the boudoir chair and headed for my bed. Feeling weak, I needed to lie down. Once settled under my blanket, I was able to share with Kevin some of the reasons for my depressed state of mind. Little did he know that he, too, was one of the causes of my sadness. This, however, was not the time to test the soundness of Harri's belief that Kevin was not husband material, so I decided to keep the conversation focused on my feelings about Mrs. Cranshaw.

"Kevin, Mrs. Cranshaw is such a difficult person. She

talks down to me. I'm sure she is not the type to praise anybody's work, but she could have at least said something to me about my manuscript other than she found it to be satisfactory. Plus, the reason of her interest in me as a writer remains a mystery. I have to wait until Wednesday to find out what's on her mind."

"You are taking this woman way too seriously, babe. When she does make her intentions clear on Wednesday, just remember that you're in charge of your own welfare. If you don't like what she is proposing, tell her so and leave her apartment, never to return. My real concern is that her bitter disposition will wear you down if you get involved in whatever she has planned. You have known this woman less than one day, and you are already in a stew over her."

"I know, Kevin. I am in a stew."

"Don't drown in that stew, Linzie. Crawl out of it if you have to and move on. Speaking of stew, have you had your dinner?"

"No."

"I made some chicken soup. Do you want me to bring some over?"

"No thanks, Kevin. In a little while, I'll make some scrambled eggs and then go back to bed. I'm looking forward to our dinner date on Tuesday night, though."

"Me too. Have you decided where you want to go, babe?"

"Not yet."

"Dinner Tuesday night will be our first date of 2018, so pick a special restaurant. There will be plenty of new years ahead of us. I think we should make it a tradition that our first date of each new year should be a humdinger."

I got teary-eyed when Kevin said those words. Those words were practically a confirmation of what Harri had said about Kevin—that he had no intentions beyond dating me. To discuss that matter with Kevin would have been too much for me to handle at that moment. I wanted to end our conversation, so I hurried it to its conclusion.

"Thanks for your patient ears, Kevin. Have a safe trip to New York. Happy New Year to both you and your mother."

"Thanks. I'll call you shortly before the new year arrives, okay?"

"Okay. Bye, Kevin."

"Bye, babe."

It was with a heavy heart that I hung up the phone. It had finally dawned on me that at some point, I would have to question Kevin about his plans, or lack of plans, for our future.

Kevin's advice regarding my future dealings with Constance Cranshaw struck me as being quite sound. Now reconciled to the probability that my future without Mrs. Cranshaw in it would be a better future for me, I was able to eradicate the uncongenial woman from my mind. However, I would soon discover that Mrs. Cranshaw was like a stubborn weed that refuses to be eradicated. In no time, thoughts of her replanted themselves in my mind, where they took center stage.

Chapter Three

The old year was out, and the new year, in! January 1, 2018, had arrived. Unfortunately, it appeared that for me, the new year was going to begin in the same lackluster way that the year 2017 had ended.

I had spent Sunday night, New Year's Eve, alone. Receiving Kevin's phone call was the highlight of my evening. His call came around 11:30 p.m. We chatted for about ten minutes, and then I went to bed. At the stroke of midnight, I was dead to the world. What a downer the last day of 2017 had been!

The thought of now spending New Year's Day with me, myself, and I was not a cheery one. As I rose from bed on that Monday, the people that were dearest to me were all out of town. Harri and Rudolf were visiting relatives in Concord, Massachusetts, and would not be back in Boston until late afternoon. Kevin would be returning home from New York later in the day, but due to that evening appointment with his client, I would not be seeing him at all on the first.

I found myself missing Kevin terribly on that holiday. In spite of Harri's attempt to open my eyes to the dead-end relationship she believed I shared with Kevin, I let my heart, not my head, do my thinking for me. As the seconds of New Year's Day ticked by, I tried to justify Kevin's hitherto noncommittal behavior. To do so, I had to turn the clock back to his childhood.

Kevin's parents divorced when he was only seven years old. Their breakup wounded him emotionally. When his parents' marriage crumbled, his childhood did too. His father, whom he adored, rarely came to visit him after the divorce. There was constant fighting between his parents over many issues, not the least of which was financial support for him. His childhood was not a time in his life that he liked to discuss, but it was certainly a time that had left its mark on how he viewed the institution of marriage. He often voiced his opinion that it was an institution that should be entered with extreme caution, for once the door of that institution slams behind you, you might have a heck of a time finding a window that can provide an escape.

Harri knew nothing about Kevin's past. I wondered whether she would have been more understanding of Kevin's reluctance to tie the knot if she had known about his traumatic childhood. I tried to encourage myself to be patient with Kevin. To push him towards marriage might push him away from me. Then a bunch of *perhaps* infiltrated my noggin. In time, perhaps Kevin could let go of the pain his parents' divorce had caused him. In time, perhaps he would be able to express his love for me in words. In time, perhaps he would feel comfortable about proposing. Perhaps, perhaps, perhaps!

In an effort to stop torturing my mind with all those *perhaps*, I chose to shift my attention to my make-believe characters, whose words and thoughts I could control with the taps of my fingers on my keyboard. Through much of the afternoon and early evening of January 1, I sat at my computer and developed their lives according to my own whims. How I wished that I could have exerted the same control over my own life! It was about 7:00 p.m. when I called it quits with my writing.

After eating a dinner that was prepared with a gourmet touch in honor of the holiday, I watched television. When I turned the set off, I retired for the night, with joyful anticipation of my dinner date with Kevin that would take place the following evening.

The next morning, I awoke around 7:00 a.m. to the

sound of the wind rattling the bedroom windows. I rose from bed and wrapped the warmest bathrobe I owned around my body. Boston was still in the clutches of the brutal cold snap. Despite the nasty weather, I was in an upbeat mood. The man I loved would be at my door in about eleven hours.

As I sat at my kitchen table, enjoying my first cup of coffee, it dawned on me that I should go the extra mile and look as attractive as possible for my date that evening. Kevin had said that it was important to make our first date of the new year a humdinger, and I believed that sprucing myself up would help make it so. A couple of thoughts entered my mind as to how to improve my appearance. The first thought was to call my hairdresser and ask her—beg her if necessary—to squeeze me into her schedule. The second was to take a trip to the mall and buy an elegant-looking cocktail dress.

Luck was on my side that Tuesday. Due to a cancellation at 11:00 a.m., my hairdresser was able to see me and spend ample time styling my hair. When I left the salon, I was so pleased with the hairdo she had given me that I felt like a Broadway star who was on her way to the Tony Awards. My trip to the mall was also successful. At a boutique, I found a stylish black cocktail dress that looked as though it had been made for me. The cost of it was a blow to my budget, but this was not the time to worry about my lack of wealth.

It was approaching 3:30 p.m. when I returned home. I was famished, so I grabbed a small snack to sustain me until 7:00 p.m., the time of the dinner reservation I had made. After snacking, I rummaged through my jewelry boxes with the hope of finding the right earrings, necklace, and bracelet that would complement my new dress. When I was satisfied with my choices, I proceeded with the final steps of "Operation Spruce Up"—applying nail polish and makeup. Then it was just a question of getting dressed, which was a snap compared to all the other preparation to which I had subjected myself.

When I opened the front door to Kevin at 6:00 p.m., I was extremely happy to see him. Had he not been holding a bouquet of flowers in his hands, I would have thrown my arms around him the moment he entered the downstairs hallway. We kissed, being careful not to crush the flowers between us. It was not unusual for Kevin to bring me flowers, but he had always done so to celebrate an occasion such as my birthday or Valentine's Day.

"Oh, Kevin, the flowers are beautiful. As far as I know, it isn't my birthday. Are the flowers for some other special occasion?"

"If you want to call your appointment tomorrow morning a special occasion, then the answer to your question is *yes*. Are you still planning to see Cranky—I mean Mrs. Cranshaw—at ten o'clock?"

I burst out laughing when I heard the nickname Kevin had conferred upon Mrs. Cranshaw. Kevin's great sense of humor was one of the things I loved most about him.

"Yes, I am still planning to see Cranky at ten. Let me just add that I shan't be late if I know what's good for me."

Although I said those words amusingly, I firmly believed that if I did not arrive at Mrs. Cranshaw's door at the stroke of 10:00 a.m., there would be hell to pay. The nickname Kevin had given to Mrs. Cranshaw was not a complimentary one, but it was, unfortunately, a fitting one.

"In view of what you'll be facing tomorrow, methinks your spirits need bolstering," Kevin said in one of his many comical voices.

"Methinks you are right," I said. "I am not looking forward to tomorrow."

"Then, babe, let's just focus on having a good time tonight. I must say that you look stunning."

"Thanks, Kevin. In honor of our first date of the year, I wanted to look nice for you."

"You sure succeeded."

"I made the reservation for seven, so we really do not have to rush. We can go upstairs and chat while I put the flowers in water."

"Lead the way, babe."

We ascended the staircase and entered my apartment. After removing his hat, scarf, and gloves, all of which he placed on the small wooden chair in the foyer, he took off his coat. Tan, wool, and three-quarter length, it was the coat he wore on special occasions. As he struggled to find a spot in the foyer closet to hang it, I noticed how nicely he was dressed. He was wearing a handsome navy sport coat, a white shirt, a red and blue striped tie, and khakis. Of average height and fit build, he sported the clothes as well as any model in a men's fashion magazine.

"Kevin, you're all dressed up tonight," I remarked. "You must have gone on a shopping spree."

"I haven't yet been enlightened as to where we are going for dinner, so I had to be prepared in case you chose a five-star restaurant. In honor of our first date of the new year, I paid a visit to a barber in New York on Saturday afternoon. He cut my hair and trimmed my mustache. After leaving his place, I took myself to the men's clothing shop around the corner from my mother's apartment. Charles, the owner, helped me pick out this sport coat, these slacks, and this tie. You know me, babe. I'm a guy who wears jeans and sweatshirts all the time, but tonight I wanted to look nice for you. It appears that buying these duds was a good move on my part. You're wearing what I assume is a new dress, and your hair looks beautiful. I think I can deduce that the hamburger joint down the street will not be seeing us tonight."

"I'll keep you in suspense as to where we are going until I get these beauties that I'm holding into some water."

"Fair enough," he said chuckling.

It warmed my heart to learn that Kevin had gone to great lengths to look nice. His efforts made me feel even closer to him.

As he kicked his boots off, he remarked, "You better brace yourself. Tomorrow, the temperature is supposed to climb above twenty degrees. There is a real heat wave on the way."

Kevin, of course, was being his usual funny self, but in truth, a temperature reading in excess of twenty degrees would indeed feel balmy to us Bostonians, who had been in a deep freeze since December 27. In fact, December 27 through January 2 would prove to be the longest cold snap that had hit the Boston area in one hundred years.

As Kevin placed his boots on the mat in the foyer, he said, "Now for the bad news. There is a snowstorm that is expected to hit us on Thursday. It is going to be a bad one."

"Yes, I heard about the storm that's coming. I like your news about tomorrow's heat wave a lot better."

We exited the foyer and walked into the living room. From there, we turned left into the dining room, which led us to the kitchen. Kevin took a seat at the kitchen table while I looked for a vase for the flowers. It did not take me long to find one. I then put my hands on my trusty scissors, which were necessary for the snipping of the stems.

"While you're hard at work arranging those flowers, I'm going to try to guess where we are going tonight," Kevin said.

"Good luck with that," I said laughing.

He ran his hands through his thick blond hair in order to clear any strands from his forehead. He then placed the fingers of his right hand just above his right temple as if he were deep in thought.

"Oh, I feel a premonition coming on," he said. "Aha, aha, aha, it's quite clear now. I see us walking into Harrud's. Rudolf is right there at the door to greet us. Suave and sophisticated, he is reaching for your left hand. Now that it is within his grasp, he seems reluctant to let it go. In fact, he is kissing it repeatedly. Finally, Rudolf releases your hand. He is now seating us at your favorite table. Harriet has spotted us and is making a beeline for our table. She can barely wait to sit with us and chew the fat for a few minutes. No, hold on. It appears that Harriet is going to chew the fat with us for an hour or two. How am I doing, babe?"

Laughing almost hysterically, I answered, "Not well at all."

"Are you saying that my premonition has taken a wrong turn, that maybe Harriet will spend the whole evening with us rather than an hour or two?"

"I'm saying that your premonition was never on the right course. I chose a restaurant that I think you'll like. It isn't Harrud's."

"Hard to believe," he commented while shaking his head. "I was looking forward to a delightful evening with Harriet. You better not tell her she was cast aside in your decision-making process."

Kevin's sense of humor was a very fine attribute, but it was an attribute that he had hidden from Harri. He always seemed so quiet and reserved when Harri chatted with us at Harrud's. My mind began to drift to the notion that if Kevin had humored Harri a bit, she would have better understood my attraction to him and thought of him as a warm human being who was a good match for me.

As I began to fill the vase with water, an idea struck my mind with the speed of a bolt of lightning. Wanting to prove that Harri's judgements about Kevin were wrong, I was going to make a bold move. I was going to tell Kevin that I love him to see how he would react. I knew that such a move on my part would be going out on a limb. Perhaps I would fall off the limb and land on my posterior. It was my hope that Kevin would not let me fall, that he would take me into the safety of his arms and verbally express his love for me. It was not without taking a deep breath that my perilous journey down an untraveled path began.

"Kevin, thank you for all your moral support. Your sense of humor is so special to me. In fact, you are special to me. I love you."

While speaking those words, it was too difficult for me to look at Kevin. The flowers provided me with a good excuse to keep my back to him. As I trimmed the stems, I anxiously awaited his reaction.

My expression of love was met by silence on Kevin's part. The prolonged silence forced me to finally turn around and look at him. He was tapping his fingers on the table, so I knew he was perplexed and needed time to figure out what to say. I had never seen Kevin blush before, but he was certainly red in the face at that moment. Feeling guilty for making him emotionally uncomfortable, I struggled to find words that would soothe his nerves, but no such words came to mind. It was Kevin who found the words to continue our conversation.

"Well, babe, each one of us has been blessed with a gift, and I suppose I was blessed with the ability to make people laugh. Maybe I really should volunteer at Elsbury Place as a stand-up comedian," he said with a nervous chuckle.

Kevin had chosen to zero in on my comment about his sense of humor and to ignore my words *I love you*. It was a clever tactic on his part, one that had enabled him to avoid expressing any feeling for me. My attempt to disprove Harri's judgements about Kevin had failed miserably. The thought that I might well be spending the rest of my life without a true partner sent my mind on a roller-coaster ride. My head was spinning. Too upset to address Kevin's inability to reciprocate my expression of love, I chose to change the subject while turning to face the kitchen counter. I did not want him to see my eyes, which had quickly filled with tears of disappointment.

"So, Kevin, do you want to guess where we are heading tonight?"

"No, Linzie. I think it's time that you enlighten me."

His voice sounded strained, and his cheerful demeanor had vanished. It was obvious that my words of love had hit him with the destructive force of a torpedo.

"How does a newly opened restaurant that overlooks Boston Harbor sound?" I asked.

"Sounds okay," he mumbled.

"Don't you want to know the name of it?"

"No. If it's new, the name won't ring a bell. Do you have directions?" he asked half-heartedly.

"Yes. They are in my evening bag. If we want to get there by seven, I guess we better leave now."

Kevin rose from the chair and followed me into the living room, where I placed the vase of flowers on the coffee table that was situated in front of the sofa. Once again, I thanked him for the flowers. He seemed to have lost his ability to speak; all he did was nod to acknowledge my expression of gratitude. My reaction to his silence was to become silent myself.

We walked over to the foyer closet. I removed Kevin's coat from the rod and handed it to him. There were at least six winter coats of mine hanging in the closet. I grabbed the first one that met my eyes. It was not the fancy coat I had planned to wear, but that no longer mattered to me. Without Kevin's usual assistance, I put on the coat. Once boots, gloves, and all other winter protection were on us, we exited my apartment and entered the exterior hallway. The silence between us continued as we descended the staircase, exited the house, and headed for the driveway, where his maroon SUV was parked. As we approached the vehicle, I hoped that he would at least open the door for me, which was a courtesy he had always exercised. He did open the door. That kind gesture on his part gave me the courage to try to reopen the line of communication between us once he got settled in the driver's seat.

"Kevin, you have not commented much about my choice of restaurants. Would you prefer to go somewhere else?"

"No, babe. I trust your judgement. Besides, it is always fun to try new places," he said with a renewed enthusiasm.

It seemed as though he had suddenly erased from his mind all the awkwardness that my words *I love you* had created for him. I, however, did not have an eraser big enough to clear from my mind his noncommittal attitude. However, to avoid spoiling the evening, I decided to remain silent about the whole matter. In fact, I steered the conversation towards something to which we had both been looking forward—Valentine's Day.

"Kevin, I was thinking about something you mentioned a few weeks ago. You told me to put on my thinking cap and come up with some ideas on how we could celebrate Valentine's Day together. You do remember telling me that, don't you?"

"Sure, babe," he replied as he turned the key in the ignition.

"Well, one idea of mine is to go to a show in the Boston Theater District and then have dinner at a nice restaurant. What do you think?"

As Kevin was letting the SUV warm up, he was tapping the fingers of his right hand on the steering wheel, all the while remaining quiet. That darn tapping was not a good sign. I was bewildered as to why he needed time to respond to my suggestion about Valentine's Day. My patience was ebbing away. I did not wait for his careful thinking process to complete its cycle.

"Is there a problem with our spending Valentine's Day together?" I asked.

"Ah, Linzie, I've been meaning to talk to you about that. We cannot celebrate Valentine's Day on the fourteenth. You see, I have to go to Bangor, Maine, on that day for business reasons. I'll be back the following day. How about we celebrate on the fifteenth?"

I was livid. Kevin's job had never required any traveling. I found myself doubting that there really was a trip in store for him on the fourteenth. Up to that point in our conversation, I had not wanted to rock the boat, but now I was ready to capsize it. The time had come for Kevin to sink or swim.

"Kevin, I think it's time we have a serious conversation."

"What do you want to talk about?" he asked as he was about to put the vehicle in drive.

"I want to talk about us and in which direction this relationship is going."

"Well, I can't drive and carry on a serious conversation at the same time. Let's talk about what's on your mind at a later time, okay?"

"No, Kevin. I think we need to talk now. Please turn the engine off."

He sighed and did what I asked.

"Okay, Linzie, you have my attention. You better do the talking because I'm not sure what this is all about."

"I think you do know what this is all about. Let me ask you a question. When I told you I love you a little while ago, why did you choose to ignore those words? Those words came from my heart."

He grasped the steering wheel with both hands, perhaps to brace himself before answering. When he did answer, he chose to look straight ahead rather than at me.

"Well, Linzie, when you said those words, you sort of crossed a line. To me, those words are a hint that you want something more permanent than what we have now. I'm a free spirit. I like the kind of relationship we have. Neither one of us is legally tied to the other. It's a nice, easy association that is not going to cause us any headaches."

"Kevin, I need to know something. Do you love me?"

"Linzie," he said slowly while keeping his eyes focused straight ahead, "there are different kinds of love. There is the love between a husband and a wife. There is the love between friends. There is the love between a brother and a sis—"

"What kind of love do you think exists between us?"

"Babe, why do we have to put a label on our love? We enjoy each other's company and get along well. Why ruin a good thing? We don't need to cage ourselves in by defining our relationship."

"So, are you trying to say that there is no possibility of marriage for us?"

"Linzie, we have been seeing each other for some time now, and in all that time, I never once led you to believe that I am the marrying kind. In fact, I have done my best to tell you how leery I am of marriage because of my parents' breakup. Believe me when I say that once you lose your freedom, life gets pretty sticky. We are both in our forties and not used to compromising."

"So, you consider our relationship to be nothing more than a companionship?"

"Sure, what's wrong with companionship? Chances are that a good companionship will last longer than most marriages do today. If companions decide to part company, at least there are no legal hoops to jump through. My parents went through a very messy divorce, financially and otherwise."

"Kevin, you and I are not your parents. If you were to decide to get married, am I the person you would ask?"

"I have no intention of ever getting married," he said with more than a hint of irritation in his voice. "So, your question is senseless."

"Then, please answer just one more question. Would it bother you if I accepted an invitation to go out with another man?"

"Now listen to me," he said angrily as he finally turned his head in my direction. "We have a good thing going. Why can't you appreciate that and accept me for the person I am. If another man comes into your life, then you can just forget about me."

His words revealed a side of him that I had never seen before—a selfish side. He would not commit to me, yet he was incensed by the idea of my dating another man. He wanted it all. His attitude triggered a reply from me in which I held no punches back.

"I think the time to forget about you is already here, Kevin, whether or not another man comes into my life. What you're really telling me is that I am not worth any effort on your part to make a commitment. You want me without any strings attached. What a convenient arrangement for you! You get tired of being a companion to Linzie Cole, and all you have to do is push her aside without having to cut one single string! And what becomes of poor Linzie Cole, who never had the chance to forge a solid relationship with anyone else?"

"It's time to call it a night," he yelled.

"It certainly is time," I said in a very firm tone of voice. "It's time not only to call it a night but also to call it quits. Goodbye, Kevin. Have a good life."

I got out of the vehicle and closed the door. While remaining behind the steering wheel, he made sure I got inside the hallway on the first floor safely. That was the first time he did not escort me to the door.

I was a wreck as I ascended the staircase to my apartment. My nerves were so shot that my legs were weak and shaky. Harri had been right on target when it came to her assessment of Kevin. For two years, I had dated him and him alone. After two years of an exclusive relationship, the words *I love you* should have been words that he welcomed. Instead, they had turned him off just as quickly as the flick of a light switch. I knew that the time had come to end the relationship, but I also knew that I would be in emotional pain for some time. Kevin and I shared many good memories. His sense of humor had been a source of cheer in my life. His sage advice had guided me through tough decisions. His absence was going to leave a hole in my life, a hole the size of a crater! When I went to bed that night, I cried myself to sleep.

Chapter Four

When I woke up the next morning and looked in the mirror, my heart jumped. The person staring back at me looked like a creature from another planet! I was not a pretty sight. My usual rosy cheeks were as pasty as bread dough. My eyes were red and puffy from all the crying I had done thanks to my breakup with Kevin.

The thought of facing a new day depressed me. The thought of facing Cranky Cranshaw depressed me even more. How I wished I could have picked up the phone and asked her to reschedule our meeting! That, I knew, was not feasible. Mrs. Cranshaw had demanded that I be at her apartment at 10:00 a.m. sharp unless I were ill. I was not ill, at least not physically, so I had no choice but to go to Elsbury Place.

Rather begrudgingly, I took a shower and dressed for the meeting. I then drank a couple of cups of coffee, hoping that the coffee would give me a jump start. The coffee did give me a boost, but I was afraid that little could be done for my puffy eyes. My crying had left its mark, one that makeup could not mask completely. Having no desire to eat, I skipped breakfast. After putting on all my outerwear, I headed for the front door.

Once I exited the house, it became obvious that the temperature was tolerable. It was still cold but not as cold as it had been during the cold snap. The weather on that January 3 was really a tease because Mother Nature was not going to give us much of a break from nasty weather. The snowstorm that Kevin and I had discussed the night before seemed certain to hit Boston and to hit it hard. The forecast called for about a foot of snow along with high winds and possible power outages. To make matters worse, the temperature was expected to plummet after the storm. We would once again be subjected to a frigid blast of air for several days after the snow stopped falling from the sky. The forecast was a gloomy one for sure. Nevertheless, as I began my trek to the bus stop that morning, I was grateful that Mother Nature had extended an olive branch to us poor Bostonians for at least one day.

I arrived at the bus stop right on schedule, but the bus did not. It was delayed by about ten minutes. The delay did not rattle me. I had adopted the attitude that if I failed to knock on Mrs. Cranshaw's door on the dot of 10:00 a.m., so be it. That nonchalant attitude was a new one for me, one that had been shaped by the emotional blows that had hit me during the course of the last five days. Mrs. Cranshaw's rude behavior and Kevin's callousness had led me to the conclusion that sometimes caring too much for others can backfire on the one who does the caring.

Upon entering the reception room of Elsbury Place, I glanced at the clock that was hanging on the wall behind the counter. The time was 9:52 a.m. Hooray! At least Constance the Great could not banish me from the kingdom for the reprehensible act of being late. As I approached the counter, it appeared that another *hooray* was in order. Bonnie Tulley was nowhere in sight. A young woman, whose name tag displayed the name Rebecca, was managing the counter. Bouncy and sweet, she actually wished me a good morning and asked me how I was. I thanked her for asking and fibbed that I was fine.

After I entered information in the guest book, Rebecca phoned Mrs. Cranshaw to let her know I had arrived. By that time, it was 9:54 a.m. Upon hanging up the phone, Rebecca informed me that Mrs. Cranshaw said that I was too early and that she needed six more minutes before she could see me. Her annoying preciseness did not shock me, nor would any further strange behavior on her part do so.

As I headed for the sitting area to reclaim the spot on the sofa I had occupied on Friday, I was hoping that Norbert Rockfeld would make an appearance. My down-in-the-dumps mood was sorely in need of a pleasant conversation with that kind man, who had such a soothing way about him. When I sat down, the fireplace had an audience of one—me. However, that soon changed. Two women, perhaps in their seventies, entered the area and sat on the sofa that was perpendicular to the one on which I was sitting. They did not acknowledge my presence. There was little point in my acknowledging theirs because they were in their own little world. Deeply engrossed in gossip that I had no desire to hear but could not help but hear, they were chatting about a Mrs. McKinney, who resided in Room 306. Their chitchat revealed that Mrs. McKinney was widowed less than a year and that rather than being steeped in grief, she was having a wild fling with a gentleman sixteen years her junior. As they dragged the poor woman's name through the mud, they shook their heads in utter disgust. My feelings were so raw due to my breakup with Kevin that I wanted to jump to my feet and defend the condemned victim of their privately held "court session." It was tempting for me to scream out that an age difference has nothing to do with anything and that if Mrs. McKinney and the younger man are truly committed to each other, that is all that matters. It, of course, was not my place to make such an outburst, so I sat there with my lips buttoned. When 9:58 a.m. arrived, I got on my feet to head for Mrs. Cranshaw's apartment. I must say that it was with sheer relief that I left the company of the two gossipers, who were continuing to smear that poor soul in Room 306.

It was 10:00 a.m. sharp when I arrived at Room 243. I knocked on the door. Mrs. Cranshaw promptly opened it.

"Come in, Miss Cole. Then take your boots off and put them on the mat."

I greeted Mrs. Cranshaw with a friendly *hello*, entered her apartment, and then performed a balancing act as I slipped the boots off. Just as last time, my hostess did not offer to hang my coat, so I did not bother to remove it. I tucked my hat, scarf, and gloves into my coat pockets and, with my briefcase in hand, followed Mrs. Cranshaw down the hallway that led to the living room.

"Sit in the same armchair you occupied last Friday," she instructed as we entered the living room.

I obediently headed for my assigned French provincial armchair, placed my briefcase next to it, and sat down. Mrs. Cranshaw sat smack-dab in the middle of the sofa, just as she had done during my first visit on December 29. She was just as impeccably dressed as she was on that Friday. This time, she was wearing a handsome-looking red wool blazer with a matching skirt. The brown leather pumps on her feet were just as stylish and probably just as expensive as the black pair she had sported during our first meeting. No strand of her neatly coiffured hair was out of place. Our second meeting was beginning to feel like a repeat performance of our first. I could only hope that I was not going to witness a re-enactment of the explosive behavior she had exhibited before.

"Miss Cole, as promised, I want to return your manuscript to you."

"Thank you. I appreciate your reading it and returning it to me so promptly."

The shallow box that contained my manuscript was lying on the coffee table between us. Mrs. Cranshaw stood up, picked up the box, handed it to me, and sat down. Then she struggled to properly position one of the sofa pillows behind her back. It was my expectation that once she got nice and comfy, she would make some comments about my work, but her silence continued even after her struggle with the pillow had ended. To make matters worse, while her mouth was in an apparent state of self-imposed paralysis, she turned her head towards the picture window and gazed at the rolling hills. An unconscionable amount of time was passing without any verbal or visual communication from her. I was in no mood to be ignored. I picked up my briefcase, placed it on my lap, and released the latches. As I put the box into the briefcase, I had one goal in mind—to fabricate an excuse to leave. Mrs. Cranshaw broke her silence before I could come up with a sensible reason to part company with her.

"Miss Cole, may I make a comment?"

Assuming she was finally going to say something about my manuscript, I nodded my head and replied, "Yes, of course you may make a comment."

"You look terrible," she said. "Your eyes are bloodshot, and your voice sounds hoarse. I suspect you have a cold. I thought I made it clear that I do not wish to be on the receiving end of your germs. Did I not tell you that we would have to postpone this meeting if you were ill?"

"Yes, Mrs. Cranshaw, you made it perfectly clear that if I had any germs, you wanted to be nowhere near me. Since I am feeling just fine, I came, and I came on time. In fact, as you well know from the call you received from Rebecca, I was ready to report for duty six minutes before our scheduled time—not a bad feat for someone who has to depend on a bus."

My remarks were somewhat caustic, but I had done my best to say them in a tone of voice that was calm and controlled. There was a reason for my wanting to keep my cool. Although Mrs. Cranshaw continued to be an enigma to me, I was beginning to believe that she derived pleasure from making others feel miserable, probably because she was so miserable herself. I was determined not to give her the satisfaction of knowing she had gotten under my skin.

"All right then, Miss Cole, let's get to the business at hand. A few years ago, I started to author a book. I never got beyond the first chapter. It is important to me that the book I have in mind get written, but I no longer want to try to write it. I would like to hire you to ghostwrite the book. Now, Miss Cole, tell me what your understanding of a ghostwriting arrangement is."

Astonished that she wanted me to write a book on her

behalf, I said with some hesitation, "As a ghostwriter, I would write the book, but you, Mrs. Cranshaw, would get the credit as being the author."

"That's right, Miss Cole. My name would appear as author on the cover, but you would be compensated for all your hard work. Naturally, I know you want to have a good idea as to what is involved before you even think of accepting my offer to hire you. So, the purpose of our meeting today is to discuss some of the matters related to the ghostwriting job. If after this meeting, you think you would be interested in the job, my lawyer can draw up an agreement that would spell out all the conditions. You can review the conditions with a lawyer of your own. If the agreement is satisfactory to all involved, both of us would sign it. That being said, Miss Cole, I do not want to waste your time or mine if there is no hope that you would be interested in ghostwriting the book. Is there any point in my continuing to discuss some of the issues involved?"

Still in a state of disbelief, I replied, "I would certainly like to hear more about what you have in mind, Mrs. Cranshaw."

"Good," she said.

Leaning towards the coffee table, she reached for her gold-rimmed spectacles and a piece of paper that appeared to have notes on it. Once her spectacles were on, her eyes were riveted on the paper, which she had placed on her lap.

"Let's begin with the matter of your pay. I believe the amount I have in mind is quite generous. Some ghostwriters are paid by the hour, some by the number of words, and so forth. I would pay for the project as a whole. I am prepared to offer you twenty-five thousand dollars to write a novel. I would pay you five thousand dollars at the beginning of the project, ten thousand around the midway point, and ten thousand upon its completion."

I was flabbergasted by Mrs. Cranshaw's offer, which truly was generous. My financial situation was such that I desperately needed to make some money, but oddly enough, the money to be made was not the major issue on my mind at that moment. To me, the major issue was her desire to hire me in the first place. Nothing made sense to me. Why would she want to hire me when the only thing on which she had based her decision was my unfinished, unpolished manuscript? My sense of professional integrity demanded that I ask her a few questions at the risk of leading her to believe that I was an incompetent writer.

"Mrs. Cranshaw, why me? Why are you asking me to write this book? I'm sure you know many capable and proven writers that would jump at a chance like this. All my submissions to publishers have been rejected. The three books of mine that have been published have all been self-published, and the sales of my books have been sporadic. The truth is that I am an unknown author who is struggling to stay afloat financially."

She looked at me intently and asked, "Do you think that I was an instant success? If that is what you think, then allow me to set you straight. It was such a struggle for me to become known that it almost did not happen at all. Fed up with all the rejections I had received from publishers, I almost threw in the towel several times. The thing is, Miss Cole, I stayed the course because writing was my passion. Only a fool walks away from a passion."

Constance Cranshaw was no fool, but she had, at least according to Elsie, done what she just said only a fool does. At some point, she had walked away from her passion and had never returned to it. Why she had walked away at a time when she was enjoying the sweet taste of success continued to mystify me. It was unclear to me as to whether or not Elsie knew the reason for Mrs. Cranshaw's abandonment of her writing career. I realized it would have been way too forward on my part to interrogate Elsie about that matter, so I had asked no questions.

I appreciated Mrs. Cranshaw's willingness to tell me

that her road to success had been a bumpy one. Her honesty prompted me to express some more of the apprehension I was feeling in regard to her job offer. Deep down, I doubted my skill as an author would meet her expectations. Harri had warned me that my underestimation of my writing ability could lead me to failure, but I could not heed Harri's warning as I sat there with Mrs. Cranshaw. I feared that my humility might make me look weak in her eyes, but my desire to be honest outweighed that fear.

"Mrs. Cranshaw, your interest in hiring me to write your book concerns me because you are basing your interest on one thing—my unfinished manuscript. You may think that I have been blessed with the gift to write when, in fact, that may not be the case. Aren't you afraid that your hiring me would be quite a gamble for you?"

She rose from the sofa without saying anything and walked across the room to the large mahogany bookcase. My words, I believed, had somehow offended her. Baffled, I got to my feet in anticipation of an exit that would be painfully awkward.

"Go ahead, Miss Cole, and stretch your legs. Just give me a minute or two to put my hands on a few things here."

Relieved that I had not upset her, I walked over to the picture window to gaze at the tree-covered hills. My curiosity caused me to cast a glance or two in Mrs. Cranshaw's direction. She appeared to be systematically eyeing the spines of the books that were neatly arranged on the shelves of the bookcase. When she finally started to head back to the sofa, I, in turn, headed for the armchair. As I did so, I noticed that several books were in Mrs. Cranshaw's hands. The books remained in her hands as she sat down.

"Miss Cole, I want to show you these books."

After I settled into the chair, she laid the books on the coffee table. My earlier assumption that Mrs. Cranshaw could do nothing further that would shock me was totally faulty. I was stunned when I looked at the books on the table.

"These three books should not be strangers to you, Miss Cole."

In a very faint voice, I said, "Why, those are my books, Mrs. Cranshaw. Why do you have—"

"Why do I have your books in my possession? I simply ordered them from an online bookstore that carries them."

"Yes, but why?"

"Miss Cole, I'm no dunce. It would have been an idiotic move on my part to offer you a job as a ghostwriter if I had not checked out your ability to write. Elsie told me about your self-published books and how I could go about ordering them. I had read all three of them before I even met you. When I read your unfinished manuscript on Friday, it only confirmed what I already knew—that you do have the gift to write."

Her words touched me deeply. I did not think there were any tears left in me after all the crying I had done the night before, but that very special moment evoked some.

"It should be obvious to you by now," she continued, "that I was never in need of a volunteer companion. My only need is for a ghostwriter. Elsie knew that. She and I have been friends for years. When she read on your application for volunteer work that you are a writer, she ordered one of your books and read it. Impressed with your work and knowing that I needed a writer, she suggested I read what you had published. As you now know, I did just that. It was really a ploy on my part and Elsie's to ask you to come here last Friday as my companion and to make you think that you were going to read your manuscript to me as a means of entertainment. The truth is, Miss Cole, I not only wanted to get my hands on your manuscript but also wanted to meet you. This book that is to be ghostwritten is important to me. Therefore, I am fussy as to who will be creating the words that tell the story. I begged Elsie not to say anything to you about the possibility of my offering you a job as a ghostwriter in case the chemistry between us was not good."

It appeared that I had been misled by Elsie but in a good

way. I knew her intentions had been honorable, for she had made a heartfelt effort to give my writing career a push forward. Whether or not I would be creating the words for Mrs. Cranshaw's book, I knew I would always be grateful to Elsie Wyman for what she had attempted to do for me.

"Miss Cole, if you do decide to work for me, the ghostwriting job will not begin until the beginning of June. That should give you plenty of time to work on your own novel that is in progress and to focus on any other matters related to your writing career. Assuming you take the job, I want it understood that my book will be your only focus until it is finished. All other writing projects and opportunities would have to be cast aside until its completion. Would you agree to that condition?"

"Yes, I would."

"Good. Now please listen carefully as I talk about some of the other issues regarding the job offer."

She reached for the piece of paper on which her notes were listed. She then grabbed her pen and put check marks next to the issues she had already addressed.

"To give your career a boost," she said, "your name would appear in the acknowledgements section of the book along with a description of your contribution to the work. Generally, ghostwriters are not given any credit, but I assure you that you will be given credit. Now, when it comes to this ghostwriting project, Miss Cole, I want it understood that I am in charge. It is imperative that I work closely with the one doing the writing. I also intend to make an outline as to how the book should begin, progress and end. I fully expect my ghostwriter to adhere to the plot I create. I reserve the right to fire the one I hire should things go awry."

She removed her spectacles and looked at me quite earnestly.

"Miss Cole, have I said anything yet that has displeased you?"

"No," I replied.

"That may soon change. Pay good attention to what I am about to say."

While she returned her spectacles to their rightful spot on the bridge of her nose, I brought my hands together and started to twiddle my thumbs. I was not bored; I was nervous. Nothing Mrs. Cranshaw had said so far seemed unreasonable, but I feared that some crazy condition was about to be mentioned that would torpedo the whole offer.

"Are you familiar with Rockport, Massachusetts?" she asked.

"Somewhat familiar. Over the years, I have visited Rockport a few times."

"I own a cottage in Rockport," she said. "During the spring, fall, and winter, I rent the cottage to a couple who spend the summer months in Vermont. During June, July, and August, I live in the cottage. So, here comes one of the major conditions of my job offer, a condition that would not be listed in the ghostwriter agreement but that would be understood between us. I want you to stay with me at the cottage during June, July, and August, during which time we would work on the book. The book may not be completed by the end of those three months, but great progress could be made on it. Your stay with me would not be all work and no play. You would have some free time to do whatever you like, and naturally, you would be staying at my place free of charge. Your quarters would be on the second floor. That floor consists of a bedroom, bathroom, office, and sitting room. The kitchen and the laundry room are on the first floor but would be at your disposal anytime you need them. So, tell me, Miss Cole. How do you feel about that condition?"

That condition was so unexpected that I knew it was going to take time for it to penetrate my noggin. I was speechless. As the seconds ticked by, I felt more and more mortified by my inability to make a comment about staying in Rockport. The pace of my thumb twiddling accelerated.

"Perhaps, Miss Cole, you would feel more comfortable

driving to Rockport and driving back to Boston each day. The drive each way would be about forty miles."

Shaking my head, I replied, "No. Driving is out of the question. I do not own a car."

"I understand. You have my apology for even suggesting you commute. I was worried that you would turn down my offer simply because the idea of staying with me would be repugnant to you. Getting along with me, I admit, is a challenge. My friend Bertha, who used to stay with me in Rockport, could attest to that if she were still with us, but she is not. She died three months ago."

As Mrs. Cranshaw made those comments, her voice quivered, which caused me to look more closely at her. It appeared that she was now the teary-eyed one. She turned her head in the direction of the picture window. I surmised she was embarrassed by her show of emotion and was trying to avoid eye contact with me.

"Does that mean, Mrs. Cranshaw, that if I decline your offer, you will be living in the cottage by yourself this summer?"

"Yes."

"How do you feel about that?"

"I do not relish the thought of being alone. The house will seem so empty without Bertie."

"Bertie was your friend's nickname?"

She nodded while keeping her head turned towards the rolling hills. The sound of a few sniffles led me to believe that she was being overcome by more and more grief. Although Mrs. Cranshaw had come across as a rather tough cookie who valued her independence, her sudden display of emotion sparked some speculation on my part. Maybe, just maybe, she needed more than a ghostwriter. Maybe she needed a companion after all.

When Mrs. Cranshaw resumed eye contact with me, she remarked, "Miss Cole, I am not an unreasonable person. I just want to say that I would understand perfectly well if you want your boyfriend to stay at the cottage once in a while. There is a sofa bed in the living room that he could use. As long as his visits do not interfere with the work we have in store for us, I would not mind at all. I was young once. I know how it is."

Her words, which were intended to be kind, only served to deepen the emotional wound Kevin had inflicted on me. I could not control my sadness. Tears formed in my eyes and started to roll down my cheeks. I scrambled to find a tissue in one of my coat pockets and then in the other. When neither pocket produced a tissue, I unbuttoned my coat and started to search the pockets of my slack suit. As I became more and more flustered, Mrs. Cranshaw came to my aid. She got up and walked over to the end table to her left. There was a box of tissues on top of that table. She picked up the box and handed it to me.

"I am terribly sorry, Mrs. Cranshaw. I must be suffering from some kind of allergy."

"Yes, you must be," she said softly as she sat down.

I pulled several tissues out of the box and then mopped up the tears on my face. My next task was to try to pull myself together in order to stop the waterworks that my emotions had turned on.

"Miss Cole, I suggest you go home and relax for the rest of the day. Think about what we discussed so far and let me know on Monday if it would be worthwhile for my lawyer to prepare an agreement that you could review. If an agreement is drawn up, at least you could study its terms. Seeing things in black and white may help you decide what to do. As I said before, if the job interests you, I recommend that an attorney of your own look over the agreement before you sign your name on the dotted line."

Her suggestions were music to my ears. Too much had come at me too fast. I needed time to think.

"Thank you, Mrs. Cranshaw. I appreciate your advice."

She stood up and headed for the hallway. I rose from the armchair and followed her. As we approached the mat on which my boots were placed, she did something that surprised me. She picked up a kitchen chair and then placed the chair in front of the boots so that I could sit and slip them on comfortably.

Before she opened the door to let me out of the apartment, she said, "There is one other thing. Please promise me that you will not say one word to anyone in this retirement community about the book I want written. There is no shortage of gossipers here. I want my business to be my business and nobody else's."

Having witnessed the verbal attack on Mrs. McKinney of Room 306, I could understand Mrs. Cranshaw's request.

"I promise," I said. "Believe me. I am not a fan of gossip."

"No, I do not believe you are, Miss Cole."

"What time would you like me to call you on Monday?"

"Anytime on Monday would be fine," she replied as she opened the door. "Goodbye, Miss Cole."

"Goodbye."

As I walked to the elevator, I walked to it with the realization that Constance Cranshaw did, in fact, have a soft side. It was a side that did not manifest itself too readily, but it was there, shrouded by the many sides of her complex personality.

Chapter Five

Upon the conclusion of my second appointment with Mrs. Cranshaw, I went directly home. Knowing that I was in no condition to work on my manuscript, I changed into some casual clothes with the intention of heading for Harrud's. My emotional state was in such an uproar over Kevin that I felt a strong need to talk to Harri. As disappointed as I was in Kevin, thoughts of him were tugging at my heartstrings. I was beginning to have doubts about my decision to completely close the door on our relationship. The desire to see him again was taking root in my heart.

I locked my apartment door with the hope that my walk to Harrud's would take my mind off my troubles. As I approached the block of which Harrud's was a part, I glanced at my watch. It was 11:15 a.m. The restaurant would not open for another fifteen minutes. There was a bookstore located three doors down from Harrud's. Touring the aisles of the bookstore would, I felt, be the perfect way to kill some time.

Such a vast array of books greeted my eyes when I entered the store that it made me wonder how a new writer can possibly hope to swim in such a sea of competition. The sight of all those books made me realize that Mrs. Cranshaw's job offer might prove to be the life raft that would rescue me from drowning in that sea. The ghostwriting offer was a darn good one in my opinion. Yet, it was going to require a lot of careful thinking on my part, and that thinking would have to be done in a very short period of time. There was no question that I had come to a fork in the road. The road I had been traveling had not led me to success, but at least it was a road with which I was familiar. Now I faced the possibility of following a new route on which only the unexpected could be expected. Perhaps it was the uncertainty of that route that caused me to stroll over to the aisle where the self-help section was situated. A little book about having courage to embrace change in one's life drew my attention. It appeared to be the ideal book for me to read, so I purchased it. Then I left the bookstore and began my very short walk to Harrud's.

When I entered the lobby of the restaurant, I noticed that Rudolf was standing near the maître d' station. He was talking to one of the busboys. Upon seeing me, he abruptly ended his conversation and came over to me. He reached for my left hand and was about to kiss the top of it. However, his lips never touched my hand. A troubled look came over his face. Instead of kissing my hand, he patted it in a consoling way.

"Linzie, are you all right? You look as though you have been crying."

With a slight shrug of my shoulders, I replied, "My love life hit a rough patch. Not to worry, Rudolf. I'll be okay."

"Go, dear, and take your favorite seat by the fireplace. Harriet is in the kitchen. I'll let her know you are here."

After handing me the menu, he scurried towards the swinging doors that led into the kitchen. He obviously sensed that whatever was troubling me could best be handled by his better half. In the meantime, I headed for the chair in which I had sat on Friday. No sooner had I taken off my winter coat than Harri appeared by my side.

Doing my best to smile but failing miserably at it, I said, "Hi, Harri. How are you doing?"

Harri ignored my question and whispered, "Let's sit down and talk. Rudolf said you looked upset, and Rudolf was sure right about that."

As I sat down, I pulled some tissues out of my coat

pocket and held onto them with my left hand. Harri took the seat to my right. Then she gently placed her left hand on my right shoulder and looked at me sympathetically.

"Tell me what's happening, Linzie, and please don't worry about robbing me of any time. Rudolf has everything under control in the restaurant. I can lend you my ears for as long as you need them."

In an effort to show my appreciation, I once again tried to smile, but my smile was a pathetic one. In spite of Harri's willingness to listen to me patiently, I was determined, for her sake, to try to get right to the point.

"I don't know how you do it, Harri, but you always hit the nail on the head with that imaginary hammer of yours. Do you remember the opinions you expressed about Kevin when I was here last Friday?"

"I sure do. Basically, I told you that there was no real future for you with Kevin."

"Well, you were right. He and I were supposed to go out to dinner last night. While we were in the car getting ready for our drive to the restaurant, I asked Kevin to turn the engine off so that he and I could have a serious talk about our relationship. That talk did not go well at all. In fact, when Kevin finally backed out of the driveway to leave my place, I was no longer in the car."

"In other words, Linzie, you two had a fight?"

"Yes. It was a humdinger of a fight. What led to that fight was something that happened just a little bit earlier in my apartment. While Kevin and I were in the kitchen, I told him that I loved him. He went into panic mode. He could not even return my verbal expression of love. So, while we were in the car, preparing to leave for the restaurant, I decided to question him about his intentions in regard to our future. What I found out is what you already told me. Kevin has no intention of ever marrying. He likes being footloose and fancy-free."

"So, where do things stand now?"

"We broke up. To put it more precisely, I broke up with

him."

The news of my breakup with Kevin did not appear to surprise Harri one bit. In fact, the expression on her face was interpreted by me to be one of sheer relief.

"I'm glad you called it quits with Kevin. He was all wrong for you, Linzie."

"Harri, I am very perplexed about something. How could you have possibly known that Kevin is so noncommittal? You spoke to him only a few times, and those conversations amounted to nothing more than chitchat. How do you do it? Are you some kind of x-ray machine that can see through people?"

Just at that moment, Peppi, one of the waiters, was passing by our table. Harri gestured to him to come over to us.

"Peppi, please bring Miss Cole a glass of white wine and please make sure that she is not billed for the wine or her lunch today."

"Yes, ma'am," Peppi said with a slight bow of the head.

As soon as Peppi was out of earshot, I wasted no time in saying, "Harri, you and I are supposed to have a clear understanding about my eating here. As I have told you so many times, I insist that you bill me. We are constantly fighting over that issue. Sometimes you let me win; sometimes you don't."

"Today, let me win that fight, Linzie. I think you are going to need that glass of wine when I tell you what I must tell you."

Surprised by Harri's comment, I took a deep breath and clutched the arms of the chair. It was apparent that whatever she was about to say was not going to cheer me up.

"Linzie, perhaps I have a certain ability to see through people, but when it came to Kevin, I did not have to utilize my so-called x-ray vision. All I had to do was observe his behavior."

"His behavior?"

"Yes, his behavior. Rudolf and I are friendly with a couple that owns a Greek restaurant, located about ten miles from here. We go there to eat on Monday nights. Guess who we saw eating there three times during the course of the last six weeks."

"Kevin?"

"Yes, Kevin. He was not alone. On the three occasions we saw him, he was with a woman, the same woman each time. The last time we saw the two of them was this past Monday night. I'm afraid he has been cheating on you, Linzie."

I unclutched the arms of the chair and breathed a sigh of relief.

"I have an explanation for what you saw, Harri. You see, Kevin sets aside Monday nights to meet with clients. As you know, he is a financial advisor. The woman you saw with him is a client. Even though this past Monday night was a holiday, Kevin had to meet with her because she was leaving for France the next day and is not planning to return to this country for two months. Before she left, Kevin had to give her advice about investing in stocks and bonds."

Shaking her head, Harri said, "Stocks and bonds have nothing to do with the meetings Kevin has been having with that woman. The only bond that is of interest to them appears to be a romantic one. All three times, they were sitting in the same booth. My guess is that they reserve that booth because it is in an alcove of the restaurant—a quiet, somewhat secluded spot. The first time I saw them, they were sitting across from each other. The last two times, they were sitting side by side and were holding hands. This past Monday night, things progressed beyond hand contact. I saw Kevin give the woman a kiss on the cheek every so often, and she did not hesitate to return his show of affection."

Harri's claim that Kevin had been two-timing me was simply too ridiculous for me to accept. Nothing Harri had said about the man she saw at the Greek restaurant fit the profile of the Kevin I knew. It was Kevin who had insisted that our relationship be an exclusive one. It was Kevin who lost his temper just the night before when I asked him how he would feel if I were to date another man. Surely, that outburst of anger was not the reaction of a man who had strayed into the arms of another woman.

Harri, of course, was not the type to fabricate lies. I realized that what she said she saw was absolutely true in her mind, but I also believed that what was true in her mind was simply false. Therefore, I had to uncover some kind of flaw in her observations of Kevin and the woman in question. That would require that I interrogate her without hurting her feelings.

Before I was able to pose my first question, Peppi appeared and placed a glass of wine in front of me. I raised the glass to my lips and took a few gulps rather than the dainty sips I normally took. Then, figuratively speaking, I called Harri to the stand in an effort to exonerate Kevin. He was certainly guilty of the charge of noncommitment, but I had to clear him of the charge of unfaithfulness.

"Harri, are you sure it was Kevin you saw? Maybe it was a man that looks like him. You know the saying that everyone has a twin."

"Does Kevin have an identical twin brother?" she asked.

"No. He has one sister. There are no other siblings."

"Then, it was Kevin. Rudolf also saw him. Two pairs of eyes simultaneously recognized Kevin."

Harri's claim that Rudolf had also recognized Kevin was not helping my case, but it was still my belief that the man they had seen was not Kevin. I continued my questioning with steadfast resolve to clear Kevin's name.

"Do you recall what Kevin was wearing on any of those three nights you saw him?" I asked.

After dating Kevin for two years, I doubted there was any part of his wardrobe that I had not seen. To ask Harri about his attire was, I felt, a clever move on my part.

"The first two times I saw Kevin at the restaurant, he was dressed pretty casually," she replied, "so I did not take much notice of his clothes. I do remember what he was wearing this past Monday night because he looked so sharp. He was wearing a navy jacket, a light-blue shirt, and a striped tie. As for his slacks, they were a yellowish-brown color."

"Khaki?"

"Yes, khaki."

"Did you notice the colors of the tie?"

"The stripes were either red and black or red and blue."

My heart started to sink. Harri had blown a big hole in my defense of Kevin. With the exception of the light-blue shirt, her description of Kevin's attire matched what he wore on Tuesday night during his short-lived date with me. My blood pressure was going in a different direction than my sinking heart; it was skyrocketing. The tissue, still in my left hand, was not going to be needed after all because instead of crying, I felt like screaming. Kevin had boasted that he had bought that jacket, pair of slacks, and tie in honor of our going out, but he had failed to mention that another woman had seen him in his new duds first, and just the night before my date with him! Although my defense of Kevin was coming apart at the seams, I felt obliged to proceed with it.

In a much-weakened voice, I said, "Harri, you mentioned that on each of the three occasions that you saw Kevin and the woman, they were sitting in a booth in an alcove of the restaurant. Were you and Rudolf dining in the same alcove?"

"No. Our friends that own the restaurant always reserve the same table for us in the main dining room."

"Then, isn't it possible that your view of the booth was not a clear view and that this is merely a case of mistaken identity?"

"No, dear. We had an unobstructed view of that booth from our table. You see, the alcove is set apart from the main dining room by a wall, but the wall has a large opening in it. From where we sat, we could see clearly through the opening."

"So, if Kevin was sitting down, how did you know that his slacks were khaki?"

"He walked by our table twice, once to go to the men's

room and once to return to the booth."

"And Kevin did not see you sitting there?"

"No. We made sure of that. Each time Kevin was about to pass by our table, we grabbed two dessert menus and shielded our faces with them. When we were not in danger of his seeing us, we lowered the menus and took a good look at him."

"Harri, how tall would you say Kevin is?"

"I would say about five feet ten inches," she replied.

Her answer was correct. Feeling desperate, I made a pathetic attempt to trick her with my next question about Kevin's appearance.

"And you would say that Kevin's hair is light brown, right?"

"No, it is blond."

"Was the man you saw wearing glasses?"

"No."

"What about a mustache?"

"The man had a blond mustache."

Kevin's innocence was now hanging by a thread. It was time to dismiss poor Harri from the witness stand.

"Thanks," I said. "No more questions."

Harri, however, would ask a question of her own before stepping down from the stand.

"Linzie, Kevin owns a maroon SUV, doesn't he?"

Too distraught to speak, I nodded my head.

"Rudolf," she continued, "saw Kevin drop you off at the front door of Harrud's a few times and remembers that Kevin was driving a maroon SUV with bumper stickers. When we were exiting the parking lot of the Greek restaurant on Monday night, Rudolf noticed that a maroon SUV with bumper stickers was parked in one of the spaces."

Kevin's innocence was no longer hanging by a thread. The thread had been severed by Rudolf's sighting of the SUV. As far as I was concerned, the case was closed, and Kevin was guilty beyond a reasonable doubt. My mind was reeling from the realization that Kevin could not be trusted.

A final question popped into my head. It took me a minute or so to find the courage to ask Harri that question.

"Harri, why didn't you say something to me before now about seeing Kevin with that woman?"

Although Harri had proved to be an unwavering witness in her testimony against Kevin, my final question unnerved her. It was a question that she could not answer right away. When she finally did respond, it was with a shaky voice.

"I simply did not want to hurt you, Linzie. Perhaps I should have told you right away, but you have been through so much lately. You're still grieving over the loss of your mother. I was afraid that news of Kevin's misbehavior would send you into an emotional tailspin. However, last Friday, when your loyalty to Kevin caused you to resist my suggestion that you meet Adam Proctor, I began to feel that I should tell you about Kevin and that woman. Due to the upset Kevin caused you last night, I could not hold my tongue today about his deception."

"I am sure it was hard for you to tell me about Kevin's deceitful behavior, but I am grateful that you did, Harri. I am also grateful that, last Friday, you voiced your opinion that my relationship with Kevin was a dead-end street. It was your opinion that prompted me to tell Kevin last night that I love him in order to see what his reaction would be. Thanks to you, I learned that my relationship with him was a dying one. His two-timing behavior is simply the final nail in the coffin."

"Linzie, don't let Kevin sour your attitude towards the opposite sex. There are some good men out there. I know. I married one."

"You certainly did marry a good one. They don't come any better than Rudolf."

"I hope you will think about my suggestion that you meet Adam Proctor. Adam strikes me as being a fine man and someone whose company I believe you would enjoy."

"I don't have to think any longer. I want to meet Adam."

She squeezed my right hand with her left one to show

her approval of my decision.

"Then, it's okay with you if I call him and give him your phone number?" she asked.

"Yes, it's okay."

"Please try not to grieve over Kevin," she said as she rose from the chair. "It's time to move on. If you need to chat before you come to Harrud's again, pick up the phone and call me at home."

"Thanks for being such a good friend, Harri."

"We're more than friends, honey. We're family."

She gave me a pat on the shoulder. Then she headed for the maître d' station, where her services were needed due to the arrival of quite a few customers.

Shortly after Harri parted company with me, Peppi came over to the table to inquire if I was ready to order. I had not had the opportunity to study the menu, so I asked Peppi to come back in a few minutes. He told me to take my time and then headed for the kitchen. It was with a half-hearted effort that I glanced at the day's offerings. I soon concluded that trying to choose one meal over another was an exercise in futility. News of Kevin's unfaithfulness had embittered me to the point that any food entering my mouth could taste only sour, so I ordered an appetizer instead of a meal.

After eating, I exited Harrud's and headed for the gift shop that was on the corner of the block. The blizzard would be arriving the next day, and I wanted to take advantage of the calm before the storm. I also wanted to take my mind off the storm that was brewing within my very soul. Any doubts about ending my relationship with Kevin had suddenly vanished. What would not be vanishing anytime soon was the emotional pain he had caused me.

Chapter Six

My gift shopping adventure on the afternoon of January 3 had not been fruitful. Not one single purchase had been made by me. The good news was that I did not have any bags to carry during my walk home. I was, however, carrying a lot of emotional baggage now that Harri had opened my eyes to the devious side of Kevin.

As I turned onto the street where I lived, it appeared that even more rattling was in store for my nerves. There was a police car parked in front of the house I called home. The sight of the car caused me to quicken my step as I walked on the sidewalk that was opposite the side of the street where my residence was located. Once the front of the house was fully visible to my eyes, I could see that its front door was wide open. Parked about ten feet in front of the police car was an unmarked white truck, the back doors of which were also fully open.

I raced to the conclusion that a burglary had been in progress, that someone had noticed the crime taking place, and that the witness to the crime had called the police. There was not a doubt in my mind that the apartment I occupied was the target of the alleged crime. The tenant who had been renting the downstairs apartment had moved out two weeks earlier, taking all her belongings with her.

As I timidly crossed the street and drew closer to the vehicles, it became obvious that no one was inside either one, nor was anyone on the grounds in front of the house. With shaky legs, I inched my way towards the front walkway.

Two men suddenly exited the house. Each of the men was wearing dark clothes, a black knit cap, and sunglasses. One man had a scraggly beard that extended halfway down his chest. The other had a mustache that was in dire need of a trim. The bearded man closed the front door while his comrade spat over the railing. After descending the staircase, they traveled down the walkway lickety-split and then headed for the truck. I was convinced that those two men had perpetrated the burglary and were now trying to make a getaway. My impulse was to make a getaway of my own, but my legs were paralyzed by fear. My fear was fueled by the thought that the cop or cops who had arrived at the scene of the crime had probably been overpowered by the two thugs.

When the men came within six or seven feet of the spot where I was standing, I asked in a quavery voice, "What is going on here?"

They both gave me a rather vacant look.

"Speak to Officer Grumey," the bearded one finally said. "He can explain our being here."

"Officer Grumpy?" I asked.

"No, lady. Officer Grumey."

He chuckled and then walked to the back of the truck, where he slammed the rear doors in a manner befitting a ruffian. Then he got behind the wheel and started the engine. His partner entered the truck and sat in the passenger seat. When the truck left the premises, I was in a quandary as to what to do next. The bearded man was such a scruffy-looking character that I found myself doubting that there really was an Officer Grumey inside the house. The thought occurred to me that the police cruiser may have been stolen and then abandoned in front of the house by the two men. The thought also occurred to me that some of my possessions may have left the premises via that unmarked white truck.

I decided to venture up the walkway but with great caution. I approached the front door with the realization that I should not rush into the house. My common sense told me to stand quietly behind the door for a while and keep my ears open for any strange sounds. As I did so, I nervously searched through my bag for some sort of weapon to protect myself. The best thing I could come up with was a nail file. No strange sounds were detected by my ears, so I figured it was time to enter the house.

Armed with my trusty file, I slowly turned the front door handle and then pushed the door open. Once in the hallway, I noticed that the first door to my right, which was the door to the downstairs apartment, was ajar. There was a noise—a ripping sound—coming from the living room. Keeping the front door of the house fully open, I knocked on the apartment door. It was my intention to run like the wind if whoever came to that door did not appear to be one of the boys in blue.

"I'll be with you in a moment," someone called out.

The voice of the person who said those words was deep. It was obviously the voice of a man.

A white-haired man of medium build soon appeared at the door. Although the color of his hair was white, his face was youthful looking. He was dressed in blue jeans and a red sweatshirt. In his left hand was a box cutter. That cutter did not do my nerves any favors as I stood there concealing my flimsy nail file in my right hand. However, the fear the box cutter instilled in me was allayed when a pleasant smile appeared on the man's face.

"Good afternoon, ma'am," he said. "How may I help you?"

"Hello. I live in the apartment upstairs. When I saw the police cruiser and the truck parked outside, I became concerned that something was wrong."

"I'm terribly sorry," he said, "if the sight of the cruiser scared you. I am a police officer here in the city. My name is Jack Grumey. A couple of days ago, I signed a lease agreement to rent this apartment from John Pritchard, who is obviously your landlord too."

When I heard the name John Pritchard, I was very much relieved. Mr. Pritchard had been my landlord for a little over five years.

"Because of my move to this apartment," he continued, "I'm taking a few hours off from work today. I'll be back on duty at three o'clock. There are so many boxes I have to tackle that I changed out of my uniform the second I got here and went right to work. As for the truck you saw outside, it belongs to two brothers who are helping me transport my belongings from my prior home to here. I think they will have to make at least two more trips here this afternoon. The two brothers are former neighbors of mine. I guess you're my neighbor now. I apologize for greeting you at my door with a box cutter in my hand," he said with a wide grin on his face and a twinkle in his dark-blue eyes.

He placed the cutter on a nearby box so that he could shake my hand. Before his hand reached mine, I quickly and stealthily transferred the nail file from my right hand to my left one.

"It's nice to meet you, Mr. Grumey," I said as I shook his hand. "My name is Linzie."

"Please call me Jack. I'll bet my bottom dollar, Linzie, you have a last name too. May I ask what it is?"

"My last name is Cole."

"Linzie Cole," he said rather reflectively. "I like it."

"It's a good thing I like it too," I said giggling, "because that's the name I've had since day one."

"So, there is no Mr. Cole as in husband?" he asked.

"No. I'm single."

"Same here," he commented. "Well, Linzie Cole, new neighbor, after I get a bit more settled, let's chat some more."

"That would be fine, Jack. In the meantime, if you need anything, let me know. I work at home, so I'm here a good deal of the time."

"Thanks, Linzie. You're very kind."

"Good luck with the unpacking."

"It will take more than good luck to get through this jungle of boxes," he said as he comically wiped his forehead with the back of his right hand. "I may have to trade in my box cutter for a machete."

I laughed and said, "I hope it doesn't come to that."

"Bye, Linzie."

"Bye."

With that, he turned and disappeared into his "jungle." I closed the front door. As I started to ascend the staircase, I could not help but think what a pleasant man Jack appeared to be. However, I had to caution myself not to etch my initial opinion in stone. My relationship with Kevin had taught me a valuable lesson—that people we think we know well can turn into strangers in the blink of an eye.

Upon entering my apartment, I immediately walked over to the coffee table in the living room. The flowers Kevin had given me the night before were still on that table but not for long. The cheerful arrangement, which had failed to give me any cheer, would have to be moved to an inconspicuous spot. I picked up the vase, carried it over to the kitchen sink, removed the flowers, and threw them into their new home—the garbage container under the counter.

After removing my outerwear and putting it all in the foyer closet, I glanced at my watch. It was approaching 2 p.m. I needed to unwind. The problem was that I did not know how to accomplish that. As I re-entered the living room, I suddenly realized that the solution was staring me in the face. That solution was the television set, which could transport my mind to other places via soap operas. The soaps might even teach me a thing or two. Realizing I had not been too savvy when it came to analyzing Kevin's personality, I figured I could pick up a few pointers from some of those television characters who were smarter than I.

I sat on an end section of the sofa and put my feet up on an ottoman, fully intending to be a lady of leisure for the rest of the afternoon. Before I had a chance to turn the television on, the phone on the end table next to me rang. I looked at the caller ID display. It showed the name of Kevin Conway, the one person that I wanted to avoid. I refrained from picking up the phone but kept my eyes fixed on the display to see if my ex-companion would leave a message. He did not. Good, I thought. Let him monopolize the time of his new lady friend. My time was precious.

With the push of a button on the television remote, I began my journey out of my own world into that of others. As I watched the first soap of my choice, my attention was captured by all the emotions that were at play among the various characters. When it came to their love lives, it became evident that there is often a fine line between love and hate. I could certainly relate to that. As I sat there becoming more and more engrossed in the problems of the characters, the phone rang, causing me to jump. I was suddenly back in my own world. I glanced at the caller ID display and discovered that it was Kevin calling. This call came about twenty minutes after his first call. Once again, I did not answer the phone, and once again, he left no message. It was my hope that he would assume I was not at home and would stop calling. That hope was dashed when he called yet again, twenty minutes after his second call. Thoroughly annoyed, I disconnected my phone from the electrical outlet in the living room and connected it to an outlet in the den. I closed the den door and settled back on the sofa in the living room.

It was 4:00 p.m. when I turned off the television. I remained seated on the sofa awhile and thought about all the characters I had observed that afternoon, particularly the ones who were dealing with stormy relationships. I did not know whether to extend my admiration or my sympathy to the ones who were struggling to ride out the storms that had darkened their love lives. All I knew was that I was not capable of battling the storm Kevin had sent my way. For me, it was time to seek shelter from the storm.

Harri's news about Kevin's disloyalty had ruined my

appetite at lunchtime, but I was determined to eat a good dinner. On my way to the kitchen, I heard a knock at my apartment door. A knock at my door was highly unusual. John Pritchard had installed a doorbell intercom system at the front door of the house so that I would hear the voice of anyone who came calling for me. The person who had knocked on my apartment door had obviously been able to enter the house without using the doorbell intercom system. My new neighbor, Jack, had told me he would be back on police duty at 3 p.m., so I assumed it was not Jack at the door. As quietly as possible, I walked over to it and looked through the peephole. Standing on the other side of the door was the person who had been irritating me all afternoon with those darn telephone calls.

I crouched behind the door and remained silent. All I wanted was for Kevin to leave, but as the minutes passed, my hope for his departure was turning into despair. He would knock, wait a minute, and then knock again. His knocking became more frequent and louder. Things then progressed to the point that he was calling my name between knocks.

Finally, in a very cross tone of voice, he hollered, "Linzie, I know you're in there. When I arrived behind your door, the television was on. Then you turned it off. I've been trying to reach you all afternoon. I think we should talk."

The television, which had been a source of comfort to me, had betrayed me in the end. I stood up, turned the door handle, and slowly opened the door.

"What the heck is going on?" he asked. "Why didn't you open the door right away?"

Trying to appear unfazed by his demanding attitude, I firmly replied, "I thought I made it quite clear to you last night, Kevin, that I was calling it quits on our relationship."

"So, you're just going to pull the plug without any more discussion," he muttered while placing his hands on his hips in a bullylike manner.

Nodding, I said, "Yes. Based on the conversation we had

last night, it is obvious that you have already eliminated the possibility of any kind of permanent future for you and me."

"May I please come in for a moment, Linzie?"

"No, Kevin. I think it's best for both of us that you leave. Just accept the fact that things did not work out for us."

He stood there quietly. Although I could have mentioned his lady friend, I chose not to. The reason I had just given him for terminating our relationship was reason enough. To engage in a discussion about his roving eye would have led to a heated argument, and a heated argument would have led to nowhere.

As he continued to stand there in silence, I searched for a few final words to say to him. The words that came to my mind were short and sweet.

"Goodbye, Kevin. I wish you happiness in the future."

I started to close the door. The door was about a foot away from the strike jamb when Kevin placed his left foot between the two and started to speak rapidly.

"Linzie, you know I'm squeamish about marriage because of my parents' divorce. Maybe I have been too slow to express my feelings for you. I do love you. It's just hard for me to say it. Please be patient with me. You know you're the only woman for me. The fact that I wanted us to be exclusive should have convinced you of that."

Kevin's left foot was still between the door and the jamb, so it must have been his right foot that he had just put in his mouth. The man on the other side of the door was not only a cheater but also a liar.

"Kevin, this conversation is over, just as our relationship is. Now, take your foot away from the door so that I can close it."

I was afraid that Kevin would refuse to obey my order. To my relief, he did withdraw his foot. The second he did, I shut the door and engaged the security chain. Thankful that I had avoided a major altercation with him, I headed for the kitchen. Unfortunately, I never made it to my intended destination. The pounding on the door recommenced, and it was louder than before. It caused me to do an about-face. Although I headed back to the door, I had no intention of opening it.

"Kevin," I shouted, "stop banging your fist on the door. You'll damage it."

This time, my ex-boyfriend did not obey me. He continued to pound on the door, with only a few seconds between poundings. The more he pounded, the more my heart did too. He was turning me into a nervous wreck.

"Open this door right now," he screamed.

"Kevin, leave now. If you don't, I'll call the police."

Completely ignoring my warning, he yelled, "Did you not hear me say that I love you and that you are the only woman for me? Now, let me in and let's talk."

There was no way I was going to open the door. There was something that needed to be opened, though. It was time for me to open Kevin's eyes to the fact that I knew I was not the only woman in his life. I was hoping that revelation would transform his aggressiveness into defensiveness and cause him to back off and leave.

Trying to speak calmly but firmly, I said, "I heard you, Kevin. You claim you love me and that I'm the only woman for you."

"So, those remarks are what you want to hear, aren't they, Linzie?"

"No, Kevin. Not when they're not true."

There was silence on the other side of the door, and that silence said it all. He had no comeback because he knew he had been dishonest with me. I waited patiently for some kind of response, which he took a considerable amount of time to give.

"You can't possibly deny I love you, Linzie," he finally said in a weak voice. "I've always been there for you through all your ups and downs. Isn't that what love is all about?"

Sly-as-a-fox Kevin was focusing on the "I love you" part of his earlier comment and avoiding the "you are the only woman for me" part. With the locked door separating the two of us, this was the perfect time for me to confront him on that little matter.

"Kevin, how can you say that I am the only woman for you when you have been keeping company with at least one other woman?"

"What other woman?" he asked in a barely audible voice.

"The one you've been entertaining at the Greek restaurant on Monday nights."

This time, the silence that ensued lasted so long that I began to think that he had finally left. A look through the peephole, however, proved otherwise. Kevin was pacing up and down the hallway outside my door. He, no doubt, was preparing his defense. Although I knew his defense would be pure rubbish, I was relieved that his yelling and pounding on the door had ceased. Thankfully, the rate of my heart beat was slowing down.

Finally, in a matter-of-fact tone of voice, Kevin said, "Linzie, I told you that I reserve Monday nights to meet with clients. Sure, I went to the Greek restaurant with a woman, but that woman is a client of mine. Did you see me there with her?"

Having no intention of revealing my source of information, I simply replied, "It makes no difference if I or someone else saw you with that woman. Do you deny that you were sitting side by side with her in one of the booths? Do you deny that you were holding her hand and kissing her?"

Kevin's goose was cooked, and he knew it.

"That woman means nothing to me," he said sheepishly.

"Then, why did you date her?"

"I don't know. I'm a man. Sometimes men do stupid things."

His comment about the stupidity of the members of his own sex was a far cry from the apology I felt I deserved. To make matters worse, he proceeded to try to place some blame on me.

"Last night," he said, "when we were in the car, you said you wanted to date another man. How do you think that made me feel?"

"Kevin, you know very well that you are twisting what I said. When you told me you never intend to marry, I asked you how you would feel if I were to date another man. I never said there is another man in my life. I have dated no one since I met you. By the way, I know you have been dating your lady friend over the course of at least six weeks."

At that point, I thought he might make an effort to provide me with an apology, but no such effort was made.

"So, what do you say we wipe the slate clean?" he asked. "I promise never to date that woman again or to date any other woman."

"I have no desire to rekindle our relationship," I said. "As for that woman you have been dating, she did not really cause our breakup. You did. The simple fact is that our relationship was going nowhere. I wanted it to go somewhere, but you did not."

"Linzie, I'm not ready to call it quits when it comes to us. Please let me come in so that we can negotiate."

"This is not a business deal, Kevin. There will be no negotiation. I'm going to ask you one more time to leave."

"And if I don't leave, what then?"

"I already told you. I'll call the police."

"You have no intention of calling the police. Now, stop this foolishness and open the damn door."

The audacity of the man caused my heart rate to start escalating again. I could feel sweat forming on my forehead.

"If I have to call the police, Kevin, believe me, I will. Now, for your own good, go. I have work to do, so I am not going to spend the rest of the day standing behind this door."

It was my hope that my latest threat to call the police would make him disappear, but disappear he did not. His loud pounding on the door resumed, but this time, it was nonstop.

As his maniacal behavior continued, I shook from fear and prayed that I would not be forced to dial 911. Although I had threatened to call the police, I was doing my best to hold back from doing so. I did not want to cause any harm to the man I had once loved. On the other hand, if his temper did not cool down and cool down soon, I knew calling the police would be my only recourse.

Suddenly, the pounding stopped. It took me a minute or so to regain enough composure to once again look through the peephole. Kevin was still in the hallway, but another person had joined him—a uniformed policeman. I immediately opened the door and discovered that Jack Grumey had handcuffed Kevin and was in the process of frisking him. I cringed when I saw the scene that was taking place.

After frisking Kevin, Jack turned his head in my direction and asked, "Are you all right, ma'am?"

"Yes, I'm all right," I replied in a voice that was so shaky that it contradicted my response.

"I am Officer Jack Grumey. I would like to ask you a few questions, ma'am. Is that okay with you?"

"Yes, Officer."

"This man claims to be your boyfriend. Is that true?"

I cleared my throat and said, "He is my ex-boyfriend."

"Did he harm you in any way, ma'am?"

"No, Officer."

"He said that you invited him to come here today. Is that correct?"

Incensed by Kevin's latest lie, I replied in a much stronger voice, "No, that is not correct. He invited himself to come here today. I broke off my relationship with him last night, and he seems to be having a hard time accepting that. He lost his temper because I would not let him into my apartment so that we could hash out our differences. I do not want to cause him any problems with the police department. All I want is for him to leave the premises and not to bother me in the future."

Jack looked intently at Kevin and said, "You heard the lady. You are not to return here or bother her in the future. Understand?"

A bewildered-looking Kevin nodded his head. Jack uncuffed Kevin's hands and then escorted him down the staircase and out the front door. My legs felt as strong as straw, so it was with some difficulty that I walked over to one of the living room windows to observe what was happening outside. I saw Jack standing on the sidewalk and Kevin opening the door to his SUV. Jack remained on the sidewalk until Kevin drove off. Then Jack sat in the driver's seat of the cruiser, which was parked in front of the house. He continued to sit in it so long that I finally stopped looking out the window and headed for the kitchen to make dinner. Even though my appetite was now shot to hell, I needed to try to focus on something other than Kevin's disturbing behavior. I chopped a whole head of lettuce and then mixed the lettuce with shredded cheese and several types of vegetables. Then I put two large pieces of chicken and two potatoes into the oven.

I was in the midst of rounding up pieces of lettuce that never made it into the salad bowl when there was a knock at my door. I glanced at the stove clock. It was 4:50 p.m. About thirty minutes had gone by since Kevin had driven away. I assumed that Jack was now behind the door and that he wanted to learn more about Kevin. However, this was not the time to assume anything. The possibility that Jack was no longer on the premises and that Kevin had returned entered my mind. That possibility caused my heart to gallop. Trying to be as quiet as a mouse, I headed for the living room, where I peered through one of the windows. When I saw that the cruiser was still parked in front of the house, I was very much relieved. I approached the door that Kevin had pounded on so furiously during his disruptive visit. Upon looking through the peephole, I saw Jack standing in the hallway. I opened the door.

Before I had the chance to express my thanks to him for his help, he asked, "Linzie, are you okay?"

"I am still quite shaken," I replied. "Kevin somehow got into the house without using the doorbell intercom system. I asked him to leave several times, but he would not. He was so angry, he kept pounding on my door. It's a miracle it's still intact."

"Actually, Linzie, I feel somewhat responsible for what happened. Now that I know that you did not let Kevin into the house, I suspect that those two brothers that have been helping me move failed to lock the front door when they last left the premises. I know I locked the front door when I left the house to go back to work this afternoon. At that point, the brothers had one more delivery of boxes to make to my place. I loaned them a key to the front door and told them to lock it when they left. They obviously did not. Kevin was able to walk right in."

"Don't blame yourself, Jack. The unlocked door was not your fault. I am very grateful that you showed up when you did."

"I had been out patrolling," Jack explained, "and came home to pick something up. When I opened the front door, I heard a lot of commotion in the hallway up here. I ran up the stairs to find out what was going on. As I approached Kevin, he started to make some threatening remarks to me. He also kept reaching into his jacket pocket, making me suspicious that there was a gun in it. For safety reasons, I handcuffed and frisked him. Fortunately, there was no gun on his person. He assumed you called the police, which really heated up his anger. Has he lost his temper with you before, Linzie?"

"No. He got aggravated with me last night when I told him our relationship was over, but today is really the first time I've seen him lose his cool in a big way. It is hard for me to believe that the Kevin I observed today is the same Kevin I dated for the past two years."

"After I escorted him out of the house and watched him drive away, I sat in the cruiser and stayed in it for a while in case he tried to come back."

"I realized that you were in the cruiser. I was watching what was happening outside through one of the living room windows until my nerves got the best of me. At that point, I started to prepare dinner just to try to calm down."

"Linzie, I have to leave in a few minutes to return the cruiser to the station. Then I'll return here in my own car. I should be back very shortly. Keep your door locked. I'll lock the front door downstairs too."

"I don't think Kevin will attempt to come back here," I remarked. "I'm sure he will calm down and eventually accept that it is over between the two of us. He has always been level-headed. As I say, the way he acted today was so out of character."

"I understand, Linzie, but I think it would be a good idea if we chatted about Kevin when I return from the station. Your safety is important to me."

"Jack, would you have dinner with me? There are two pieces of chicken and two potatoes baking in my oven right now. I also made enough salad to feed an army."

He smiled and said, "You don't know how tempting your invitation is. The boxes downstairs kept me so busy that I never stopped to eat lunch."

"I hope that means you are accepting my invitation."

"I gladly accept," he said as he glanced at his watch. "It is about five o'clock. If I come back at half past six, would that be good timing for you, Linzie?"

"Perfect timing."

"Is there anything I can bring?"

"Do not bring a thing," I replied. "You earned your dinner here tonight. I'm so sorry about the rumpus here today."

"Linzie, don't be sorry. I'm on the receiving end of a good deal here—a home-cooked meal, which is such a rarity for me. You're talking to a single guy who eats out a lot. I'll see you a little later. Thanks for the invite."

"You're welcome, Jack."

As I watched Jack head for the staircase, I felt terrible

about all he had gone through on my behalf. Yet, he had remained good-natured throughout it all and totally concerned about my safety.

Chapter Seven

Jack knocked on my apartment door at exactly 6:30 p.m. that evening. When I opened the door, I immediately noticed how nice he looked. He was wearing a gray sport coat, a white shirt, and black slacks.

"Come in, Jack," I said. "You're right on time. I hope you did not have to rush to get ready after you returned from the station."

"No, not at all," he said as he entered the foyer. "I had plenty of time to take a shower and to put on some respectable clothes. Just think, Linzie, you have known me less than a day, and you have seen me in casual clothes, in my uniform, and now in my more fashionable attire. I think you have seen at least half of my wardrobe."

"I doubt that," I said giggling.

He handed me a gift bag that contained two bottles of wine—one red and one white.

"For you, Linzie. After the day you had, I think you could use some wine."

"Thank you, Jack, but honestly, you should not have brought one thing. You are my guest."

"My mother did her best to raise me as a gentleman. Some of what she taught me actually stuck. I never go to anyone's home for dinner empty-handed."

"I'm grateful to your mother," I said with a respectful bow of the head.

"I must pass on that gratitude to her when I see her. She

never turns down a compliment."

"She sounds like a smart woman to me," I commented. "What about your dad? Are you lucky enough to still have him?"

"No. Dad passed away four years ago. He was a great guy. My mother misses him terribly, so I do my best to visit her often. At the age of eighty-three, she is still a bundle of energy. Going out to eat is one of her favorite things, so I take her out for lunch or dinner several times a month."

"Does she live nearby?"

"She lives in Somerville, in the same house I grew up in. I had actually planned to see her tomorrow because I'm not working. That snowstorm that's on its way is going to postpone my plans with her. It's going to be a wild one."

"I'm sure anyone who can stay home tomorrow, will," I commented. "I'm so lucky. Unless the power goes out tomorrow, I can proceed with my work."

"So, what kind of work do you do, Linzie?"

"I am an author of fiction."

"No kidding. Do you specialize in a particular genre?"

"Yes, romance. After what you witnessed outside my door today, you're probably thinking that I'm the last person in the world who should be writing about love."

"Don't be silly. I don't think that at all."

"Jack, rather than stand here and chat in the foyer, let's sit in the living room. Would you like a glass of wine before dinner?"

"I have no objection to that," he said grinning.

He followed me into the living room and took a seat on the sofa. I took the two bottles of wine out of the bag and placed them on the coffee table in front of him.

"Which wine do you prefer, Jack? Red or white?"

"You choose, Linzie. I'm really happy with either."

"Your mother really did do a great job raising you as a gentleman," I said laughing. "Your manners are definitely polished."

Returning my laugh with a hearty one, he said, "Let me caution you. Our evening together is just beginning. You're bound to uncover a few flaws in my manners before the night is over. If you meet my mother someday, please don't tattle on me."

Jack's sense of humor put me at ease with him. It also helped to dissipate some of the tension that had built up inside of me due to Kevin's disturbing visit that afternoon.

I brought the bottles of wine into the kitchen and opened the bottle of red. After pouring the wine into the glasses, I returned to the living room and placed the glass for Jack on the coffee table. After placing my glass on the little table next to my favorite armchair, which was situated across from the sofa, I sat down.

As Jack reached for his glass, he said, "So, Linzie, do you want to tell me about your failed relationship with Kevin? I don't mean to pry. I just want to feel that he is not going to be a menace to you in the future."

I took a couple of sips of wine in order to give myself a few seconds to think.

"Well, let me start by saying that I met Kevin at a New Year's Eve party two years ago. From the moment I met Kevin, I liked him. He had a certain charisma about him and a great sense of humor. He was so easy to talk to. During the party, he asked me if I would consider going out to dinner with him the following weekend. Without any hesitation, I accepted his invitation. Our first date went so well that a second one quickly followed. Before I knew it, we were seeing each other several times a week. Kevin became my soul mate. He was always so supportive of me and always eager to give me advice when I faced tough decisions. Although he warned me that he was not keen on the idea of marriage, he rather quickly concluded that our relationship should be exclusive. He claimed he wanted to date no one but me and expressed his hope that I felt the same. I wanted to date no one but Kevin, so I agreed to his wish that we be exclusive."

"Linzie, it did not bother you that Kevin resisted the idea of marriage?"

"I guess I assumed his attitude towards marriage would change, but I realize now that it was wrong of me to make that assumption. Kevin always claimed that his fear of committing himself to marriage stemmed from his childhood. His parents divorced when he was seven years old. Their breakup left him very fearful of tying the knot with anyone. I really never confronted Kevin about his lack of commitment until last night, which led to his angry outburst today."

Jack had an inquisitive look on his face and asked, "What happened last night?"

"I suspected that my two-year relationship with him was going nowhere, so I questioned him on his plans for our future. Basically, he told me he had no intention of marrying me. To add insult to injury, he wanted us to continue dating each other on an exclusive basis. I could see nothing positive in that for me, so I told him I wanted out of the relationship, which really angered him last night. Today, he came to my door to try to patch things up, but I told him it was all over between us."

Jack scratched his head and said, "So, that explains his screaming in the hallway and pounding on your door earlier?"

"Well, partly. There is more to the story. I just found out this afternoon that Kevin has not been honoring the exclusive relationship he insisted we have. He has been cheating on me. Two friends of mine saw him dating a particular woman on several occasions. While Kevin was behind my door ranting and raving about my breakup with him, I let him know that I was quite aware that he was dating another woman. At first, he tried to deny his two-timing, but at least his anger subsided a bit. When he finally admitted to dating the other woman, he tried to convince me that she meant nothing to him and that I am the one he loves. When I stuck to my position that we should part company, he became downright belligerent. Then you appeared on the scene."

Jack appeared to be deep in thought and remained quiet for a few moments. I, too, remained silent in order to give him time to digest all I had said.

Finally, Jack said, "It seems that Kevin wanted everything to go his way. I must say, Linzie, it sounds as though you have been more than fair to Kevin. I believe you absolutely did the right thing by closing the door on that relationship. There is no chance, I hope, that you will reopen that door."

"There is no chance of that. I'm forty-two years old. I'm not about to give Kevin a second chance. The love I had for him was obviously not appreciated, and I don't believe that a round two in our relationship would fare any better than round one did."

I reached for my wine and took a generous gulp of it.

As I placed the glass on the table, I said, "I thought I knew Kevin as well as I know myself. Within the past twenty-four hours, he has become a complete stranger to me."

With a sympathetic look in his eyes, Jack said, "Linzie, I've been a cop for twenty-five years and have witnessed the irrational behavior of some people when a breakup occurs. Kevin may calm down, but if he doesn't, you need to protect yourself. I want you to feel free to call on me if you feel threatened. If I'm not on the premises, and you feel as though you're in jeopardy, just call the police station. If Kevin becomes a real threat, you may be able to obtain a restraining order against him."

The thought of obtaining a restraining order seemed so absurd that I could not help but blurt out, "Oh, I don't think things will get to that point. Kevin will calm down. I'm sure he will."

"Let me ask you this. Did you expect Kevin to exhibit such anger after your breakup with him?"

"No," I replied reluctantly.

"Linzie, I've done more than just witness the irrational behavior of jilted lovers. Ten years ago, I was a victim of such behavior. While responding to a call that involved a domestic dispute, I was shot in the chest by a man who was outraged that his wife was having an affair with another guy. If that bullet had hit me a few more inches to the right, you and I would not be sitting here chatting."

A lump formed in my throat when I heard the news of Jack having been shot. I was unable to verbalize any emotion right away.

"Oh, Jack, I'm so sorry," I finally said.

"Me too. A hospital room was my home for several weeks after I underwent emergency surgery. While I was recuperating, my wife begged me over and over to leave the force and find a safe job, but I was born to be a cop. I could not find it within myself to stop being a cop."

His mention of a wife astonished me just as much as the news of the shooting. He had said he was single, and I had wrongfully assumed that he had never married. With another leap of my mind, I reached the conclusion that the strain of his being a cop had finally gotten to be too much for his wife and that they had divorced. That assumption would soon prove to be just as faulty as my first one.

"I often feel guilty that my wife worried so much about me while I was on duty," he continued. "She was a good woman and deserved to have a peaceful life. When she was diagnosed with cancer five years ago, the tables were turned. It was I who worried about her every single day. She passed away three years ago."

Jack's eyes were not free of tears as he spoke of his wife. He had obviously loved her deeply, and she, him.

"Jack, you have my deepest sympathy about your wife. I don't know why I jumped to the conclusion that you had never married."

"It's okay, Linzie. You opened up to me about your relationship with Kevin, so I felt comfortable telling you a little bit about myself."

"Thanks for sharing," I said. "Suddenly, my problem with Kevin seems more like a molehill than a mountain."

"No, Linzie. This afternoon, you were quite justified in feeling threatened by Kevin. He, by the way, does not know I live here. It may be a good thing that he believes you called the police. That may deter him from showing up here again."

I nodded and said, "Yes. I'm sure he thinks that if I called the police once, I would call the police again if necessary."

Jack and I sat silently for a moment, almost out of respect for the serious topics we had just discussed.

To break the silence, I said, "Enough of such gloomy talk. Let's shift our attention to something pleasant, namely dinner. While I get things ready in the kitchen, enjoy your wine, Jack. The remote is on the end table next to you if you want to watch television."

"May I join you in the kitchen, Linzie? I'd much rather chat with you than sit here by myself. Who knows? I may even be of some assistance. Although I'm living the life of a bachelor now, I like to think of myself as a reformed bachelor—one who has learned to fend for himself in the kitchen in order to ward off starvation."

Laughing, I said, "Join me in the kitchen if you want, but I'm not going to put you to work. The only thing I'll let you work on while we chat is that glass of wine."

"Okay, it's a deal," he said as he rose from the sofa with his glass in hand. "How about your glass of wine? Do you want to sip it while you're getting dinner ready?"

"No. My wine can wait till we're seated in the dining room."

Jack picked up my glass. On the way to the kitchen, he placed it on the dining room table. After entering the kitchen, he sat in the same chair that Kevin had occupied the evening before. The irony of the situation did not escape me. Kevin had been my protector, so to speak. The man now sitting in that chair was trying to protect me from my former protector.

The oven had been keeping the chicken and the potatoes warm. Using a couple of potholders, I moved the food to the top of the stove.

"I love to watch other people work," Jack said in jest. "While I'm relaxing, I would like to hear more about your work as a writer, Linzie. By the way, I am quite a reader. You may turn out to be one of my favorite authors."

As I searched for a large fork in one of the drawers, I said, "You're probably into action and adventure stories. Being a cop, I imagine that is what you favor. My latest love story does have some nail-biting moments in it, but do you really think you would enjoy a love story?"

"Now, Linzie, please don't assume that just because I'm a man and a cop that a love story would not appeal to me. Believe it or not, there is a sensitive side to me. You must have faith in your writing and not assume that certain readers won't appreciate what you have to offer."

His advice about having faith in myself as an author was similar to Harri's, which made me feel that he was not a stranger to me.

"How do you go about getting your works published?" he asked.

"I self-publish."

"And how many books have you put out?"

"Three novels."

"That's great."

"To be honest, Jack, I cannot crow about the number of sales my novels have generated."

"I think if you persevere, success will eventually come."

"I hope you are right."

"So, Linzie, are all three novels in the romance genre?"

"Yes. Each book is quite different from the others, though. My first novel is humorous. My second has a touch of mystery in it, and the third has a spiritual overtone."

"It sounds as though you're not afraid to experiment with your writing. That's great. Before I leave here tonight, please write down the titles and where I can buy them."

"Jack, please don't feel obligated to buy my books."

"You're my new neighbor and friend, Linzie. I truly am interested in reading what you've written."

"Then, let me order the books and give them to you in appreciation for what you did for me today."

"How are you going to get ahead if you give your books away? I insist on paying for them. Besides, this great dinner you're about to serve me more than compensates for my actions today. Also, do not forget that I am a cop. It was my duty to come to your rescue."

Such a kind man he truly appeared to be. Never before had I felt so comfortable with a newcomer in my life. A sense of peace was beginning to come over me. Unfortunately, that peace came to an abrupt end when a loud, crashing noise reached our ears. The noise came from the living room.

I was so startled that a plate flew out of my right hand and made a crash landing on the kitchen floor. The plate broke into many pieces. Jack practically jumped out of the kitchen chair and said, "Linzie, stay here in the kitchen and stay away from that window over the sink. Okay?"

I nodded and in a faint voice said, "Okay."

Jack cautiously made his way through the dining room and into the living room. As he did, my nerves were once again on edge. My hands started to shake. After a minute or so, I tried to holler to him in order to inquire what had caused the noise, but I was so rattled, no words could escape my lips.

"Linzie," Jack finally called out, "someone threw a rock through one of the living room windows. I'm going outside to investigate. I'll lock the door behind me. Keep it locked until I knock and give you my voice. I'll be back as soon as possible. Please stay in the kitchen."

It took all my strength to say, "Okay, Jack. Please be careful."

As I awaited his return, I nervously swept the pieces of the broken plate. I then paced back and forth in the kitchen, doing my best to stay away from the window. As I paced, I speculated that some kid, with little else to do on a weekday night, had weirdly entertained himself by committing an act of vandalism.

Roughly thirty minutes after Jack had gone outside, there was a knock at the door. I exited the kitchen, passed through the dining room and the living room, and entered the foyer.

"It's okay to open the door, Linzie. It's Jack."

I wasted no time in letting him in. He entered with a fairly large piece of cardboard in his left hand and a camera in his right hand. He rested the cardboard against a wall in the foyer.

In a high-pitched voice that sounded as though it belonged to someone else, I asked, "Who would throw a rock through the window? Who would do such a thing?"

"At this point, Linzie, I'm afraid I have to say that I don't know. By the time I made it into the front yard, the culprit was nowhere in sight."

I sighed deeply and remarked, "My guess is that a kid threw the rock, just for kicks."

"That may not be the case," Jack said. "While I was roaming around the front yard, Sam, the neighbor across the street, came over to talk to me. He said he knows you."

"I met Sam the day I moved into this place," I commented.

"Well, as I say, Sam came over to me. He explained that he was in the process of taking Christmas lights off his front porch railing when he saw a fairly tall person in dark clothes throw the rock. Sam is convinced that the perpetrator is an adult and—"

"How can he be convinced of that?" I interrupted. "It was dark outside when the rock came crashing through the window. Maybe the thrower was a tall kid."

"According to Sam, whoever through the rock ran down the side street that abuts Sam's yard. Sam tried to follow the vandal in order to get a better glimpse of him. Just before Sam made it to the side street, he heard a car door slam, followed by the sound of a car engine being started. The car was gone by the time poor Sam reached the side street. He swears that the person who drove off is the person who threw the rock. If he's right, it appears that the culprit is old enough to drive."

Befuddled, I asked, "Do you think the rock was deliberately thrown through the living room window because I, Linzie Cole, live here?"

"If what Sam believes happened is accurate, I'm afraid there is a real possibility that the vandal knows you."

"I don't understand," I muttered. "I have no enemies."

"Are you sure of that, Linzie?"

"You're not thinking that Kevin threw the rock, are you, Jack?"

"I have no evidence to say that he did. I asked a few of the other neighbors if they saw anything suspicious. They said they did not."

As long as there was no proof that Kevin had thrown the rock, my mind was not even going to entertain the possibility that he had. I simply refused to believe that Kevin would stoop that low. Nevertheless, someone had thrown the rock, and the idea that my apartment may have been targeted sent chills up my spine.

"I checked all around the house, Linzie. Everything other than the window appears to be undisturbed. I also made two phone calls. The first was to the police station. There is a cruiser patrolling the area because of my reporting of the incident. My second call was to John Pritchard to inform him of the vandalism. He was far more concerned about you than the broken window. He said he would contact a handyman to replace the glass pane as soon as possible. I think we can safely assume that the pane will not be replaced tomorrow due to the snowstorm."

All I could do was nod. I believed that Jack was doing his best to calm my nerves, but my nerves had a mind of their own.

"Linzie, I'm going to take a few pictures of the broken

window and shattered glass. Then I'll clean up the mess and board up the window with the cardboard I just brought in. Would you prefer taking a seat in the den, away from all the debris?"

"I'd rather stay with you, Jack."

On wobbly legs, I walked over to my favorite armchair in the living room and sat down. The window that was the victim of the senseless act was the window behind the seat on the sofa that Jack had occupied earlier. Many small pieces of glass were now lying on the sofa and on the floor. The thought that Jack could have been injured by the rock or the glass gave me goosebumps.

"Before I start taking pictures, Linzie, let me get you your glass of wine. You look as though you could use something that will calm you down. Today, I'm sure, has not been your best day ever."

"It has been a hellish day. I don't know what I would have done without you."

"I'm glad I was here for you, Linzie."

He went into the dining room and picked up my glass of wine that was on the table. When he returned to the living room and handed me the glass, it was with a shaky right hand that I grasped it. Jack then walked over towards the broken window. He proceeded to take pictures of it and the shattered glass from various angles.

When the final shot was taken, he said, "I've put my photographic skills to the test. Now comes the fun part. I need to gather up all this broken glass. Do you have a broom and dustpan handy?"

"Yes. They are in the kitchen closet. I'll get them."

"It's okay, Linzie. You stay where you are. I'll find them. Might you have an empty cardboard box as well?"

"There are several empty boxes in the back of the closet," I replied. "Take any one you want."

"Will do," Jack said as he exited the living room.

A couple of minutes later, the phone rang. The phone

was still plugged into an outlet in the den. As I rose from my armchair to go answer it, my attempt to steadily place my glass on the little table next to the chair was unsuccessful. At least one-quarter of the wine splashed onto the tabletop. Mopping up the spill would have to wait, for I felt that the phone call might be important. Perhaps it was the police calling with some sort of news about the rock thrower, or perhaps it was a neighbor who had witnessed something before, during, or after the vandalism. My curiosity caused me to walk to the den as quickly as my wobbly legs could take me.

As I approached the desk on which the phone was sitting, I glanced at the caller ID display. The phone number that appeared was not familiar to me. I put the handset to my ear and said, "Hello." My greeting was not reciprocated, but there was someone on the other end, someone who was breathing heavily. The sound of breathing was then replaced with another sound—the sound of tapping fingers. My heart sank, for Kevin often tapped his fingers when I carried on phone conversations with him.

"Who is calling?" I finally asked.

The caller, in a very deep voice, said, "I bet the temperature in the phone booth I'm calling from is warmer than the temperature in your apartment. Don't you find your apartment to be on the drafty side?"

The caller then hung up. With a trembling left hand, I did the same. In a state of shock, I held onto the chair behind the desk for a few moments. It did not take much wisdom on my part to conclude that the person who had made the call was the rock thrower and that it was Kevin who had made the call. What I had refused to believe was now believable. The sound of the finger tapping was, I surmised, his clever way of letting me know that he was the culprit, without really incriminating himself. Calling from a public phone booth was another touch of genius on his part.

I walked over to the brown vinyl love seat that hugged the wall across from the desk and sat down. I was in a trancelike state when I heard Jack's voice. He was standing in the doorway of the den.

"Linzie, I was looking for a box in the kitchen closet when I heard the phone ring. I just wanted to make sure everything is okay."

Although I believed it was Kevin who had called, I had no hard evidence to support that belief. Certainly, the sound of finger tapping was not going to prove Kevin's guilt. So, I decided to simply relay to Jack what the caller had said.

"When I picked up the phone, there was some heavy breathing on the other end. Then the caller said that he bet the temperature in the public phone booth he was calling from was warmer than the temperature in my apartment. Before hanging up, he asked if I found my apartment to be on the drafty side."

Jack said, "I'm sure you have deduced that the caller is the person who threw the rock."

"Yes."

"Did you recognize the voice?"

"No. The caller spoke in a deep voice, so deep that I am sure he was trying to disguise his normal speaking voice."

Jack walked into the den and stood in front of the love seat. The look on his face was one of concern. I knew darn well that Kevin was his number one suspect but that due to lack of evidence, he was not in a position to accuse Kevin.

"Linzie, I'm uneasy about your being alone in this apartment tonight. Is there anyone in the area that you can stay with?"

I shook my head and replied, "No. My only living relatives are two cousins who live in California. I have a couple of close friends who would gladly let me come stay with them, but I don't want to burden them with my situation. They own and manage a restaurant so have enough to deal with. Not only that, I have to think about the storm that's coming. If I were to leave here tonight, I might not be able to return for a couple of days. I've taken some time off from my writing lately and don't want to take any more time off. It's better that I stay here."

Jack folded his arms across his chest and said, "Hmm, how would you feel if I stayed with you in your apartment tonight? I could sleep on the sofa in the living room. As far as my intentions go, I assure you they are honorable. If you need a reliable reference when it comes to my honor, feel free to call my mother," he said with a slight chuckle. "I'll gladly give you her phone number."

With a hint of a smile on my face, I said, "I know your intentions are honorable, but I cannot have you lose a good night's sleep because of me. You have had a hectic day of moving and unpacking. You need the comfort of your own bed."

"Linzie, what bed? I have no bed. In fact, I have very little furniture—just a rocking chair and a night table. I was planning on buying new furniture, including a bedroom set, sometime this weekend. If I sleep in my apartment tonight, my bed will be my sleeping bag, So, you see, that sofa in the living room is very inviting. May I stay tonight?"

"Now that you put it that way, I don't feel quite so guilty. Yes, of course you can stay. The good news is that the sofa in the living room is a sofa bed. It's quite comfortable."

"I thank you, and my back especially thanks you. After all the bending and lifting I've done today, that sofa is going to be a blessing."

"Jack, your apartment has the same floor plan as mine. So, as you know, at the end of the hallway that runs parallel to the dining room and the kitchen, there is a second bathroom. Think of that bathroom as yours while you stay here."

"Thanks."

"Don't thank me. It is you who is doing me a favor. Having you here with me makes me feel safer."

"I'm glad, Linzie, that I'll be staying here tonight. Well, I must get back to the window situation. The sooner I board up that window, the better. The apartment is getting chilly."

"What time is it?"

Jack glanced at his wristwatch and said, "It is quarter to eight."

"I just want to rest my eyes for about fifteen minutes," I said. "Then I'll get that long-awaited dinner on the table. You must be famished."

"I'm fine, Linzie. I had a snack after I returned the cruiser to the station earlier."

"Oh, good. I was getting worried about the delay in dinner because you skipped lunch today."

"After I sweep the debris and board up the window, I'll go to my place to pick up a few clothes and some toiletries. I won't be gone long. Nevertheless, I want to lock the door behind me."

I pointed to the desk and said, "There is an extra key to the apartment in the second drawer on the right."

He walked over to the desk and opened the drawer. After moving a few papers around, he found the key.

"I'll make sure the key gets returned to its usual spot, Linzie. Get some rest."

After Jack exited the den, I curled up on the love seat. Although it was my intention to simply rest my eyes, sleep came quickly, transporting me out of a world of harsh reality and into one of sweet dreams.

Chapter Eight

While I was sound asleep on the love seat, the phone rang, waking me up. Groggy, I got on my feet and managed to walk to the desk without falling. With one eye shut and the other eye open, I glanced at the caller ID display on the phone. It revealed the name of Adam Proctor. For a few seconds, the name Adam Proctor did not ring a bell. When a bell finally did ring, I was faced with the decision to either let voicemail do its job or pick up the phone and try to carry on a coherent conversation with Adam. After taking a few deep breaths, I picked up the phone.

"Hello," I said in a voice that did a fairly decent job of disguising my drowsiness.

"Hi. This is Adam Proctor calling. Am I speaking to Linzie Cole?"

"Yes. Hello, Adam."

"Hello, Linzie. I did not want to interrupt your dinner, so I waited until nine o'clock to call."

His mention of the time snapped me out of my foggy state of mind and led me to the crystal clear realization that my intended resting of the eyes for fifteen minutes had turned into a deep sleep of one hour and fifteen minutes. Worried that the dinner I had prepared was unsalvageable, it was difficult for me to carry on a conversation with Adam. All I wanted to do was get off the phone as quickly as possible and put some kind of meal on the table.

To give Adam a polite hint that I did not have much

time to talk, I said, "Oh, I'm eating later than usual tonight. In fact, I was just about to take chicken out of the oven."

"In that case, Linzie, I won't keep you. Harriet tells me that you are an author. As you know, I am a publisher. I would really like to meet you and talk about your books. Would you like to go out to dinner some evening?"

"Sure, I would enjoy that," I replied.

"How about getting together this coming Wednesday night, January tenth?"

"That would be fine, Adam."

"What kind of cuisine do you like?"

"Oh, I'm not fussy. You pick the restaurant, Adam."

"There is a quaint little Italian restaurant in Medford that I frequent. The food is excellent, and the atmosphere will make you feel as though you're dining in Rome. Would you want to give that place a try?"

"Yes. I like Italian food."

"Great. I'll come to your place at half past six, okay?"

"Okay, Adam. Thanks so much for the invitation. I look forward to meeting you. Goodbye."

I did not give the poor man a chance to say one more word. I simply hung up the phone and began to make a dash for the kitchen. However, my feet never reached the threshold of the den door because the phone rang again. Back to the desk I went and glanced at the caller ID display, which showed Adam's name.

I picked up the phone and said, "Hello, Adam."

"Hi, Linzie. You hung up just as I was about to ask for your address."

Perhaps I had not come across as a rude person during my first phone conversation with Adam, but I was willing to bet that I had come across as a scatterbrain.

"I'm terribly sorry, Adam. I'm afraid today, for a number of reasons, has been a stressful one for me."

"Please don't apologize, Linzie. We all have those days."

Harri, not surprisingly, appeared to be on the mark

when it came to her judgement of Adam's personality. He did indeed sound like a kind gentleman. After I provided him with my address, he expressed his hope that things would go more smoothly for me. Then he graciously wished me a goodnight, and I, him.

I hung up the phone and turned around with the intention of making another dash for the kitchen. This time, I took only a few steps forward before coming to a halt. In the den doorway stood Jack, with a kitchen towel draped over his left arm.

"I was just about to wake you, Linzie, but I guess the phone did that for me. Was that another public phone booth call?"

"No. The call was from a man who is a publisher. He wants to meet me to discuss my books."

"So, the day hasn't been a total disaster. That publisher may give you the break you need."

"That could be, but I don't want to get my hopes up too high."

"You certainly don't want to keep your hopes down too low either."

"I guess you're right, Jack. When it comes to dinner, though, I have to confess that my hopes for it are close to rock bottom. I never intended to sleep. The dinner I prepared must be dried up and ready for the trash. We may be eating bologna sandwiches tonight. I apologize."

"As far as the dinner goes, Linzie, everything is under control. I had a feeling that you would fall asleep and would be out like a light for some time. So, after I bordered up the window, I covered the chicken and potatoes and put them in the refrigerator to be on the safe side. I must say, I'm getting to know my way around your kitchen quite well. Fifteen minutes ago, I reheated the food."

"Thank you, Jack. Once again, you have come to my rescue."

With a bow of his head, he said, "Dinner awaits you, my

lady. The first course is on the table. I'll show you to your seat."

I laughed. It felt so good to laugh. I followed Jack to the dining room. The chandelier lights had been adjusted to the dimmest setting, and the candles on the table had been lit. The salad plates were filled, and the glasses were brimming with red wine. Jack pulled out a chair for me. I sat down, feeling as though I truly were a lady of privilege. He took the seat across from me.

"If you keep this up," I said, "you're going to spoil me."

"It is I who is being spoiled, Linzie. I have been surviving on snacks lately. This home-cooked meal is like manna from heaven. Not only that, tonight I have been given the opportunity to carry on a conversation with a dinner companion. Eating by myself can get pretty boring."

"I know what you mean. After I broke up with Kevin last night, one of the first thoughts that entered my head was that I would be eating my meals all alone."

"See how wrong you were," Jack said. "I suddenly popped into your life. I hope we can enjoy many meals together in the future."

"Me too, Jack."

"Now, before that nasty rock made its way into your apartment, we were discussing your writing. I want to remind you to jot down the titles of your books and the stores that carry them."

"Please let me repeat that I would like to give you my books as a gift."

Jack smiled and said, "Please let me repeat that I want to pay for them."

"Okay, Jack, you win. Thanks to you, my sales report will look a little rosier this month."

"Linzie, I know how hard it is to succeed in any of the arts. The oldest daughter of my friend Doris is a fantastic artist, but every month, the proceeds from the sales of her paintings cannot cover the rent for her apartment. As a result, she works part-time as a waitress."

"I can certainly sympathize with your friend's daughter. Right now, I'm able to survive financially thanks to the savings I accumulated from my prior job as an accountant. Those savings won't last forever, though. It was looking more and more probable that I would eventually have to find a good-paying job somewhere. Today, however, a ray of sunshine did peep through some very dark clouds. A retired author has offered me a job to ghostwrite a book for her. She has offered me a decent pay. I have to let her know on Monday if I'm interested in having her lawyer draw up a ghostwriter agreement that I and a lawyer of my own could review."

"That sounds promising, Linzie. That ghostwriting job may be your salvation if you decide to take it."

"Yes, maybe."

"Writing is not one of my talents, so after I read your books, I promise to be a very kind critic."

"Feel free to be as tough as nails, Jack. I learned early on that writers cannot be sensitive when negative criticism comes their way. One reader may give a book an excellent review while another reader may torpedo the same book with bitter words. It simply goes with the territory."

"I'm sure."

For a few minutes, we stopped chatting in order to focus on our salads. It was not a silence that made either one of us feel ill at ease. Although we were strangers, we sat there like a longtime married couple, not feeling the need to fill every second with conversation.

When the last piece of lettuce had disappeared from each of our plates, I said, "I better go get the chicken and the potatoes."

"Absolutely not, Linzie. I took it upon myself to be the waiter tonight. Once I start a job, I finish it. Mother trained me not to shirk my responsibilities," he said laughing.

"Oh, I have no doubt about that," I said with a giggle.

He stood up, removed the salad dishes from the table,

and entered the kitchen. He soon re-entered the dining room with two plates that contained our main entrée and placed the plates on the table.

"You see, Linzie, the dinner looks as good as it did when you first took it out of the oven."

"I'm so sorry that it took forever to finally get on the table. I regret all the commotion that Kevin's visit caused you today."

"Now, Linzie, you must stop apologizing. What happened here today was not your fault. Not only that, Kevin, in an unintentional way, did us a favor. Had it not been for him, we would not be enjoying each other's company tonight. I'm sure we would have eventually become friends, but Kevin's behavior hastened the whole process."

"You certainly are looking at today's disturbing situation in a positive light," I commented.

"A positive attitude sure beats a negative one."

"Please tell me more about yourself, Jack."

"I'll be happy to tell you the story of my life, but would you like more wine to kill the boredom that I may inflict on you?" he asked jokingly.

"Come on now. I'll bet your life has been anything but boring."

"Don't place too much money on that bet."

"Someone here tonight told me I must have faith in myself. I would like to tell that someone to heed his own advice."

"Your point is well taken," he said nodding his head. "Well, here comes my story. As I mentioned before, I grew up in Somerville. I was lucky to have great parents. My mother was an elementary school teacher. My dad was a cop for thirty-two years, right in our hometown. He had such a positive influence on me that I followed in his footsteps. As for siblings, I have one brother, George, who is three years older than I am."

"How old is George?" I asked.

"George just hit the big five-oh last July."

"That makes you forty-seven. Feel free to correct my math."

"I'm happy to say that your mathematical skills are flawless. I turned forty-seven last August."

"Happy belated birthday. Please continue with your story."

"At the age of twenty-four, I married Irene. Oddly enough, we met at a wedding. It was love at first sight for both of us. Our twenty-year marriage was a good one. We had no children. Irene was unable to give birth. As you already know, she passed away three years ago."

He paused and took several sips of wine. Fearing that his mention of his wife's passing had put a damper on his spirits, I decided to try to shift his focus back to his brother.

"Tell me more about George," I said.

"George and I have always had a close relationship. I'm proud to say that there was never any sibling rivalry between us. That's a good thing because of the two of us, George is the one who got all the brains. He studied hard and became a brilliant lawyer. His practice used to be in Boston, but a few years ago, he moved to Gloucester and opened an office there. As for his home, it's a beauty. It overlooks Gloucester Harbor. To make good use of the harbor, George bought a twenty-eight-foot cabin cruiser last year. I spend as many weekends as possible with him during the summer. When I visit him, we practically live on the boat."

"And his wife doesn't mind?" I asked half-jokingly.

"There is no wife. George has always been a bachelor. He was madly in love with a woman he met in college, but the woman married one of George's best friends. My brother never quite got over losing that woman."

"Oh, I'm sorry."

"Don't be sorry. Bachelorhood and George get along very well. He can come and go as he pleases. The boat has become the object of his affection."

"It's funny you should mention Gloucester," I commented. "The author who offered me the ghostwriting job owns a cottage in that neck of the woods—in Rockport. If I accept the job, she wants me to live with her at her cottage during June, July, and August. That way, we can work on the book together."

"Hey, that's great. Rockport is next to Gloucester. May I visit you when I'm staying with George?"

His question caught me by surprise, but I found myself to be quite pleased that he had asked it.

I looked into his eyes and replied, "I would be happy to have you come visit me."

"I know a number of excellent restaurants in Rockport," he remarked. "We can have a nice lunch together. Then we can take a ride to Gloucester. George will be happy to take us out on his boat."

"It is possible, of course, that I'll decide against accepting the ghostwriting job and stay here this summer."

"Well, Linzie, the nice thing about Rockport is that it isn't on the other side of the world. It's only about forty miles from here. So even if you don't take that writing job, we can still visit Rockport and then head for Gloucester. As for George, I guarantee that you will like him. I'm not the only son my mother raised to be a gentleman."

"Your mother is truly a remarkable woman," I said amusingly. "I must meet her someday."

"I'll make sure you do. So, tell me. How did you like my life story?"

"It was interesting but a little sketchy here and there. As I get to know you better, I'll be able to fill in some of the blank spots."

He laughed and said, "I have nothing to hide. You can ask me anything you want."

"Well, for now, I'll just ask you if you would like some coffee."

"I would love some coffee," he said.

"Good. While I'm making a pot of it, you can catch up to

my bites. I was able to put a big dent in my dinner while you were talking. You have barely touched your food because of my request to hear all about you."

"That's true," he said. "I never try to talk and eat at the same time."

"Another lesson from your mother?"

He roared and said, "Of course."

"As far as the coffee goes, you have two choices—regular and regular."

"I guess I'll take the regular," he said grinning. "That brings up another exciting fact about my life. I drink only regular coffee."

"Will the coffee keep you awake, though?"

"I can sleep quite well after drinking coffee at night."

"Jack, I just thought of something. What if another rock gets hurled through the window tonight?"

"I don't think that's going to happen, Linzie. I don't think the perpetrator will want to return to the scene of the crime tonight. Nevertheless, after I bordered up the broken window, I pulled down the venetian blinds and closed them. The closed blinds make me feel a bit safer about sleeping on the living room sofa."

"If you prefer, you can sleep in the den. The problem is, the love seat in that room does not have a pullout bed."

"It's okay. The living room sofa will be fine. My five-foot-ten-inch body is too long for the love seat. Not only that, I prefer to bed down in the living room. It is more centrally located in the front of the house than the den is. If any strange sounds occur during the night, I am more apt to hear them if I am in the living room."

His remark about strange sounds made me feel edgy, so much so that a worried look came across my face. It was a look that Jack noticed.

"Linzie, I'm sorry. I did not mean to scare you. Please do not worry. I am well trained in situations like this."

"I feel very fortunate," I said, "that the new tenant in

this house is a cop."

"It seems that fate brought us together today," Jack said. "I moved in just at the right time to be of help to you."

"That's for sure. I'm very grateful to you, Jack. Now let me do something for you by getting that coffee I promised you. Enjoy the rest of your meal while I'm gone. It's going to take a little while for the coffee to perk."

"When you come back, Linzie, I expect to hear the story of your life. We have pretty well covered your writing career, and you can skip the part about being a great cook. That's something I already know. I'm sure, though, that there are many more things about you that I'd like to learn."

"I must keep you in suspense for a few minutes," I said as I rose from the chair.

He smiled and said, "I shall await your return with bated breath."

I chuckled as I exited the dining room. Once in the kitchen, I started to think about what I was going to tell Jack about my life. The truth is, I did not think of my life as a terribly exciting one. As a cop, Jack had led a daring life, never knowing what each day would bring. I feared that my life story would sound boring. However, being an honest soul, I was not about to embellish the highlights of my life in any way.

When I re-entered the dining room with two mugs of coffee, Jack's plate was no longer in front of him. He had neatly stacked all the empty dishes and placed them on one end of the table.

"Okay, Linzie, you have my complete attention. The floor is now yours. Let me hear about you."

"Do you want any sugar or cream?"

"No. I just want to hear about you."

I placed the two mugs on the table and reclaimed my seat. Jack reached for one of the mugs and then sat back in his chair.

"Let me start my story by saying that I was born in

Nashua, New Hampshire. When I was five years old, my dad, who worked as a welder in that city, found a better-paying job in Boston, so my parents and I left New Hampshire and moved to Roslindale, Massachusetts. Dad did not make a big salary, which may explain why I am an only child. To help keep us solvent, Mom worked as a secretary in a library near our home. My parents were very kind people. They were quite religious. They volunteered much of their free time at our parish church and insisted that I attend parochial school for both my elementary and my high school years."

"Did you ever think of becoming a nun?" Jack asked.

"No. I never even entertained that thought. Now, on with my story. After graduating from high school, I went on to college and majored in accounting. I figured that was a field that would always be in demand. After graduating from college, I managed to find an accounting job rather quickly in an auto parts company and—"

"Allow me to interrupt yet again, Ms. Linzie. I bet you graduated from college with honors."

"Why yes, as a matter of fact, I did."

"I'm going to take a wild guess here. I bet you graduated magna cum laude."

"Mr. Jack, you are forcing me to brag about myself. I graduated summa cum laude."

"I'm very impressed but not surprised. Continue with your story."

"This is beginning to sound more like your story than mine," I said giggling.

"Ms. Linzie, I apologize. I'll try to stop interrupting. My curiosity simply got the best of me. By the way, so far your story is quite fascinating."

"Jack, I recognize a tongue-in-cheek remark when I hear one. You are quickly turning the story of my life into a comedy."

We both had a good laugh. I laughed so hard that tears were rolling down my cheeks.

After mopping up my tears with a napkin, I said, "Once again, on with my story. Due to a couple of promotions, I did fairly well financially at the auto parts company, that is, until it went out of business a couple of years ago. After working there for eighteen years, I found myself without a job. Instead of looking for a job with another company, I made a daring move. I decided to focus on my passion, writing. So, for the past two years, I have been doing what I love, but I have also failed to come out ahead financially."

Jack put his right elbow on the table and propped his chin on his folded right hand. There was a look of admiration in his eyes.

"Not everyone can claim to be a writer," he said. "It is quite an accomplishment. Although I joked with you while you were giving me some of the details about your life, I admire you for following your dream. In view of your financial situation, it has taken a great deal of courage on your part to keep trying to succeed."

"Some might call it courage, and others, stupidity," I commented.

"Thank you, Linzie, for not letting your gift go down the drain. Think of all the countless hours of pleasure your current and future works will give to readers. I wish I had that kind of talent. They say we are all blessed with a gift, but mine has not shown up yet."

I leaned forward in my chair, looked at him closely, and said, "You do have a gift, Jack. You have the ability to calm people down when they are in crisis mode. I can attest to that. I was a wreck until you soothed my nerves. In spite of all the bad things that happened here today, you managed to make our evening together very enjoyable."

"It has been enjoyable," he said with a sincerity that warmed my heart.

"Would you like more coffee, Jack?"

"No thanks. If you wouldn't mind, though, would you keep some in the coffee pot in case I decide to have another cup later?"

"Sure."

"Thank you for a great dinner, Linzie. It was well worth the wait."

"You're welcome. I'll just bring the dishes into the kitchen, clean them off a bit, and put them in the dishwasher."

"I think I hear Mother's voice. She is insisting that I help you, Linzie."

"I'll let you help. I would not want to cross your mother," I said facetiously.

After all the kitchen duties were completed, Jack and I sat in the living room and watched television until 11:30 p.m. We then wished each other a good night sleep.

When I got under the covers of my bed that night, I realized that January 3, 2018, had proved to be a day of contradictions for sure. I had felt frightened by Kevin's aggressiveness but calmed by Jack's protectiveness. Possible new avenues for my writing career had presented themselves, but I had to ask myself if those avenues might prove to be detrimental to my personal life. Mrs. Cranshaw had exhibited a soft side to her personality that very day, but would that soft side disappear if I were to work as her ghostwriter? Adam Proctor was a publisher, but was he truly interested in me as a writer or as a replacement of his ex-girlfriend?

For a good hour, I tossed and turned over all those issues. Then sleep finally came.

Chapter Nine

When I woke up the next morning, the smell of coffee permeated my apartment. I promptly got out of bed and put on my bathrobe and slippers. Then I headed for the kitchen, thinking that Jack would be seated at the table. When I entered the kitchen, I discovered that Jack was not there. It occurred to me that he might have returned to his own apartment. I was about to call out his name when I heard his voice.

"Good morning, Linzie."

Upon passing through the archway that led to the dining room, I was pleased to see Jack sitting at the dining room table, in the same chair he had occupied the night before. He rose to his feet when I entered the room. Unlike me, he was already dressed to meet the challenges of the day. He was wearing tan slacks and a black turtleneck pullover.

"Good morning, Mr. Jack," I said in a cheerful tone of voice. "When did you get up?"

"About an hour ago. I took the liberty of making a pot of coffee. I hope you don't mind."

"Mind? Why should I mind? I like the feeling of being a lady of leisure."

I glanced at the table. On it had been placed the coffee pot, two mugs, two plates, a creamer, and an oval dish that held six doughnuts.

"Did you make all those doughnuts during the hour you have been up?" I asked grinning.

"I'd like to take credit for that, but I'm afraid I can't. Yesterday afternoon, I took a break from my unpacking and walked to the market down the street. News of the snowstorm made me realize that I would starve if I did not stock up on a few things. I saw these doughnuts in the bakery. They jumped off the bakery rack and into my carriage, insisting they come home with me," he said with a hearty laugh.

He picked up the coffee pot and poured coffee into my mug. Then we sat down.

"I confess I have already enjoyed one cup of coffee," Jack continued, "but I kept my hands off the doughnuts. I was waiting for you to help me tackle them."

"Thank you, Jack. This is a treat I was not expecting."

"Well, dig in. As you can see, there are three kinds of doughnuts and two of each kind."

I reached for one of the chocolate-covered doughnuts and put it on my plate. Jack followed suit by choosing its mate.

"What time is it, Jack?"

He glanced at his wristwatch and said, "It is half past seven."

"I'm usually up by six," I said.

"You had a rough day yesterday, Linzie. You needed that sleep."

"What about the storm? Is any white stuff coming down yet?"

"It is snowing lightly right now," he replied, "but according to the weather report, the snow will soon be coming down heavily. This will be a perfect day for me to make some more headway on my boxes."

"Do you need any help?"

"Thanks, Linzie, but I think I can manage just fine on my own. You said last night that you had to get back to your writing. I think you should do just that."

"I suppose you're right. My current plot seems a bit dull to me. It needs some exciting twists and turns. Maybe if I gaze out the window every so often today, the turbulence of the storm will energize my thinking."

"This blizzard is definitely going to give us a good punch, Linzie. We can expect a foot or more of snow and plenty of wind and ice. Power outages are expected."

"If the power goes out, I'll be lost without my computer."

"A power outage won't be a plus for me either," he commented. "Opening boxes by candlelight sounds romantic, but I doubt it really is."

Jack became quiet for a moment. I sensed he had something to say and was collecting his thoughts before opening his mouth. When he finally did speak, it was not in a lighthearted tone of voice.

"Linzie, I want you to know that I am still concerned about your safety. Promise me that if you receive any strange phone calls or if anything out of the ordinary happens that you will let me know immediately. Do you promise?"

"Yes, I promise."

He reached into the right front pocket of his slacks and pulled out a slip of paper. He leaned forward and handed it to me.

"This is my cell phone number. I won't have a landline phone until the middle of next week. Also, if you need me, you can always knock on my door. I'm just a staircase away from you when I'm home. Today, by the way, is not the only day I'm taking off from work. I'll be off the rest of this week and all of next week."

"Oh, that's great," I said.

"Before I go downstairs, would you give me your cell phone number and your landline number, too, in case I have to call you?"

"Yes, of course."

"Today, I obviously will not be going anywhere, but what are you going to do if, some other day, I am not here, and there is some trouble brewing because of Kevin?"

"I am going to call the police station."

"Good," he said as he nodded approvingly.

We sat there quietly for a few minutes, eating the doughnuts and drinking the coffee. Just as the night before, we felt totally at ease with each other, not feeling a need to fill every second with chatter. While I remained silent, I thought about Kevin and how the snowstorm was, in a way, a godsend to me. The storm would eliminate the possibility of his showing up at my door that day and would also give him time to cool off. In spite of my belief that he was the rock thrower, I did not want any harm to come his way. I knew that my breakup with him had hurt him deeply, but I also could not lose sight of the fact that my feelings and expectations had been crushed by him, so much so that there was no chance of a reconciliation between us.

My thoughts about Kevin were interrupted by the sound of Jack's voice. Whatever Jack had just said did not penetrate my noggin.

"I'm sorry, Jack. Would you mind repeating what you just said?"

"I'll be going downstairs shortly," he said. "I want to thank you for the dinner last night and for letting me sleep on the sofa bed."

"Jack, I encourage you to continue sleeping here until you get your new bedroom set."

"Are you sure, Linzie?"

"Absolutely. Plan to use the sofa bed and to have dinner with me every night until you get settled. As for dinner tonight, I have plenty of canned goods in the pantry closet that will come in handy if we lose the power."

"Thank you, Linzie. I also have nonperishable food we can share."

We both rose from the table. I went into the den to write my phone numbers on a piece of paper while Jack headed for the foyer. After I jotted down my numbers, I walked to the foyer and handed the piece of paper to Jack.

"Thanks, Linzie. What time would you like me to come back?"

"Six o'clock would be fine. If you need more time for your unpacking, just give me a call."

"Okay. Good luck with your writing."

"Good luck with your jungle of boxes," I said smiling.

Jack opened the door and exited the foyer. As I closed the door, I was relieved that he had accepted my offer to continue sleeping in my living room, not only because I was still anxious about Kevin's present state of mind but also because I wanted to enjoy some more of Jack's companionship.

When Jack left my apartment, the time was approaching 8:00 a.m., and the rate at which the snow was falling was still fairly light. When I took a seat in front of my computer around 9:30 a.m. to begin my writing session for the day, the snow was coming down with a vengeance. As I looked out the den window, which was rattling from the howling wind, all I could see was a sheet of white. Conditions were so bad that I decided to turn the radio on and leave it on. According to the reports, heavy snow bands could cause the snow to fall at a rate of one to three inches per hour. The foot or more of snow that Boston was expected to receive was not the only concern. What was going to make this storm particularly bad was the wind, which, in some areas, was expected to rival hurricane force. To make matters worse, another nasty cold snap was on the way. It was expected to arrive the following day and to linger awhile. The drop in temperature—to single digits—was going to create dangerously icy conditions.

Returning to my writing made me feel that I was returning to some normalcy in my life, and knowing that Jack was downstairs made me feel secure. Oddly enough, the sound of the howling wind, the rattling window, and the radio did not detract my attention from my story. The opposite was actually true. The excitement that the storm generated put me in the mood to write, and before I knew it, I was introducing situations into my story that I had not previously imagined.

With the exception of a few short breaks, I wrote feverishly all day. Around 5:00 p.m., I turned my computer off. It was time to focus on preparing dinner. I entered the kitchen and decided that my first task would be to make a fresh pot of coffee, so I cleaned the pot, put fresh grounds into the coffee basket, and plugged the pot into an outlet. The room was beginning to get filled with the aroma of coffee when suddenly the sound of the perking ceased, and the light over the kitchen table went out. That which I had feared had finally happened—no power!

Within a few minutes of losing power, my cell phone rang. The apartment was dark. I carefully but steadily made my way into the den, where my cell phone lay on the desk. Jack's phone number was appearing on the caller ID display.

I flipped open the cover of my phone and said, "Hi, Jack."

"Hi, Linzie. The inevitable finally happened. I'm without power, so I assume you are too."

"Yes. It just went out while my coffee pot was perking."

"What do you have as an alternative to electric power?" he asked.

"I have candles stuck in a drawer somewhere. If I had been smart, I would have put my hands on them before the storm got started. I also have a flashlight in my foyer closet."

"Linzie, I have four battery operated lamps, which I just found in one of my boxes about an hour ago. May I come up and bring a couple of them to you?"

"Thanks. I would appreciate that. I guess you won't be opening your boxes by candlelight after all."

"No. There will be no romantic candlelight tonight. Actually, there will be no more unpacking tonight. I'm pooped. Losing the power did me a favor. It forced me to call it quits."

"When do you want to come up?"

"I'll be there in a few minutes."

"Okay, Jack. I'm going to fetch my flashlight to help light your way up the staircase."

"Not to worry, Linzie. I also have a flashlight."

"I'll still get mine out of the closet in case we need it."

After my phone conversation with Jack, I took baby steps to travel from the den to the foyer. The rooms were so dark that bumping into or falling over something seemed like a sure bet. Miraculously, I managed to make it to the foyer without any mishaps and opened the closet door. I knew that the flashlight was on the bottom shelf of the closet, but it was buried under a pile of blankets. After struggling to pull it out, a rather practical question popped into my mind. Were the batteries dead? A push of the switch revealed that they still had life in them. I heaved a sigh of relief but also silently reprimanded myself for not being better prepared for a blackout.

With my flashlight in hand, I opened the apartment door and stepped out into the hallway. Shortly thereafter, Jack appeared at the bottom of the stairs, holding a bundle in one hand and a flashlight in the other. He safely made it up the stairs.

As he approached my door, he said, "Long time no see."

"Welcome back, stranger," I said chuckling. "Come on in."

We entered the foyer. Jack immediately removed two battery operated lamps from the bag, turned them on, and then walked into the living room, where he placed both lamps on the coffee table. I turned off my flashlight and placed it on the small desk in the foyer.

"This storm has taught me a lesson, Jack. In the future, I won't be such a dunce when it comes to storm preparation. I had all day to locate my candles but did not. I'm afraid there are times when my brain is running low on common sense."

"Now, don't be so hard on yourself. As it turned out, you don't really need the candles. You should give yourself a little pat on the back for having a flashlight handy."

"I suppose I have at least a thimbleful of common sense."

"Speaking of common sense, I better check the cardboard I put in the broken window yesterday. I'm sure by now, it is completely saturated."

He walked over to the damaged window with the aid of his flashlight. After pulling up the venetian blind, he felt the cardboard.

"The cardboard is soaked. I should cut another piece."

"Jack, the cardboard can wait. Please sit down and relax."

"I must admit that sitting down sounds good. I really am tired."

He turned off his flashlight and placed it on the coffee table. Then he took a seat on the sofa, the same seat as the night before.

"Jack, are you sure you want to sit on the sofa? Aren't you worried that another rock will be thrown through one of the windows behind you?"

"No. I'm not worried about sitting here. There is probably a foot of snow on the ground and more on the way. It is windy, icy, and foggy outside. I doubt any vandal would want to venture outdoors on such a miserable night."

"I suppose you're right."

"By the way, Linzie, does John Pritchard do the shoveling here himself or does someone else do it?"

"John has a contract with a company that is quite reliable."

"That's good. I was thinking of shoveling the front stairs and the walk before the snow becomes frozen solid. Now I know I won't have to."

"You have earned some downtime," I said. "Would you like a glass of wine?"

Nodding, he replied, "Right now, there is nothing I would like better."

"Me too. I'll go get us some."

He got up from the sofa and said, "Tonight, getting the wine is a two-person job. I'll help you."

He picked up one of the lamps and led the way into the kitchen. Then he handed me the lamp so that he could grab a couple of glasses off the second shelf of one of the cupboards.

"Learning my way around your kitchen, Linzie, was a snap. You have things well organized. My kitchen is a disaster area right now."

"This kitchen was, too, when I moved in five years ago."

"Maybe there is hope for mine, but being a single man, I have my doubts," he said with a chuckle. "Now, as far as wine goes, shall we finish the bottle of red wine, or would you prefer that I open the bottle of white?"

"Red is fine with me, Jack."

He put both glasses in his left hand and reached for the wine bottle that was on the counter with his right hand.

"Since you are holding the lamp, Ms. Linzie, would you lead the way back to the living room?"

"Don't you want me to free your hands of some of that glass? I can carry the lamp and that bottle quite easily."

"Not necessary," he said. "I guess I forgot to tell you that once upon a time, I was a professional juggler. I traveled with the circus all over the country. My hands have been trained to handle difficult tasks, such as carrying a bottle of wine and two glasses during a power outage."

"Were you a clown as well?" I asked laughing.

"Yes. I was a circus clown in addition to being a juggler. In fact, I was born a clown. Just ask my mother."

"I'll do that the second I meet her. In the meantime, please don't trip over me on the way back to the living room."

"When I worked for the circus, tightrope walker was not part of my job description. I'll do my best to watch my footing but cannot make any promises that I won't trip over my own feet."

"In that case, keep some distance between you and me," I said jokingly.

"Will do, Ms. Linzie. Lead the way."

We slowly walked back to the living room. I placed the lamp on the table while Jack did the same with the glasses and the bottle. He then poured wine into the two glasses and handed one to me. As he reclaimed his seat on the sofa, I reclaimed mine in my trusty armchair.

"Linzie, I think we should make a toast to Old Man Winter. Do you want to do the honors?"

"No, not me. If I make the toast, there will be some anger in it. He has not been overly kind to us lately."

"Come now. When you live through a rough winter, you appreciate spring all the more when it finally comes."

"I'm afraid, Jack, that I am asking myself why I subject myself to a rough winter in the first place. I could be in Florida right now, sitting on a beach, drinking a pina colada, and watching the palm trees sway in the breeze."

"Well, Linzie, I like to think that there are two types of seasons. There are the seasons outside ourselves. Mother Nature is in control of those. Then, there are the seasons within."

"The seasons within?"

"The seasons within our hearts," he said. "We have a lot more control over those seasons because our attitudes shape them. Today, for example, is a stormy, dismal day outside, but the season within my heart is not winter. Being here with you makes the day sunny and happy for me. It is springtime in my heart."

I smiled and said, "I admire your point of view, but I am not quite ready to adopt it. Old Man Winter has been so nasty lately that the season within my heart is definitely winter."

"In that case, Linzie, I agree that you should not make the toast. You might insult the old man. So, leave the toast to me." Raising his glass, he said, "Thank you, Old Man Winter, for covering the ground in a beautiful blanket of white. And thank you for sending us the power outage, which made it possible for me to come see Linzie an hour earlier than we had planned. That extra hour means a lot to me because I truly enjoy Linzie's company. She is a charming, talented, and witty woman."

He took a sip of wine. I was laughing so hard that I did not dare raise my glass to my lips.

"I believe, Jack, that you may have hurt the old man's

feelings. Most of your toast was about me."

"Ah, he won't mind," Jack said while waving his hand in a downward motion. "He has shared all this snow with us. I'm sure he is more than pleased to share the compliments I just made in my little toast."

"Thank you for your compliments about me. I just want you to know that I enjoy your company too. So, here's to you, Jack," I said as I raised my glass.

I was about to give Jack a few compliments when we both heard a noise—a thump. It sounded as though something had hit the front of the house. That thump was followed by three more.

Bewildered, I said, "I wonder if someone is at the door and trying to get my attention. The doorbell intercom system is hardwired, so it is obviously out of commission due to the power outage."

"Who would come to the door on a night like this?" Jack asked.

"I imagine there are kids in the neighborhood looking for a shoveling job," I replied.

"The storm isn't over yet. If there are kids at the door, they are calling on you prematurely."

"They're probably trying to beat any competition for the job," I commented.

I rose from the chair and walked to the foyer to retrieve my flashlight. Jack put his glass of wine down and stood up.

"I'll go to the door, Linzie. You stay here."

"How about we both go to the door? You take your flashlight, and I'll take mine."

"All right, but stay behind me and hold onto the railing tightly."

We exited the apartment and headed for the staircase. Before we reached the top step, we heard knocking at the front door. The knocking continued off and on as we slowly descended the steps.

When Jack opened the front door, the sound of the

howling wind greeted our ears. Snow was blowing in every possible direction. With the help of our two flashlights, we could see someone standing on the other side of the storm door. The unexpected visitor was wearing a heavy winter jacket. The hood was so tightly drawn around his or her face that the facial features were barely visible. As I looked more closely, I suddenly realized that I did not have to see the person's face to realize who it was. I had seen that jacket many times before. The person wearing that jacket was Kevin.

Before Jack had a chance to open the storm door, I blurted out, "That's Kevin behind the door."

No sooner had I said those words than Kevin quickly turned and started to descend the front steps. He made it to about the second step down from the top when he tripped and landed face down on the snow, which was coated with ice. His body slid down the rest of the steps. Once at the bottom of the stairway, he struggled to get up. When he got back on his feet, he turned his head in our direction and hollered, "Damn you, both of you. You'll pay for this, Linzie." Then he trudged through the deep snow on the walk. After climbing over a snowbank that hugged the sidewalk, Kevin made it onto the recently plowed street, which offered him the opportunity to move faster.

Kevin's appearance at the front door stunned me. I started to shake. Jack closed the door and put his arm around me in an effort to comfort me.

"Let's go back upstairs, Linzie."

Silently, we retraced our steps to my apartment. When we entered the foyer, I felt so cold that I immediately removed a heavy winter sweater from the closet. Then, on trembling legs, I entered the living room and proceeded to sit down in my armchair. Jack sat on the sofa. After giving me a moment or two to collect my thoughts, he spoke to me in a soft voice.

"Linzie, I feared that Kevin might try to pay you another visit. Seeing him at the door was a shock to you, I know. I'm quite surprised that he would come out in such horrific weather. He is obviously a very determined man."

I took a couple of sips of wine not only to warm up but also to calm down. When I thought I could speak coherently, I expressed my concern to Jack.

"What troubles me, Jack, is that Kevin has now seen you here with me twice. When you approached him yesterday in the hallway, you were in uniform, so I'm sure that in his eyes you were simply a cop performing your duty. Now that he has seen us together here tonight, in a situation in which you were not acting as a cop, I am afraid he is going to think that there is a romantic tie between us. My fear is that you are now in danger. Kevin is a jealous man."

"I certainly understand your concern, Linzie. As I told you yesterday, I did not tell Kevin that I live here. He was obviously outraged to see us together a few minutes ago, so it may well be that his mind is running wild right now as to what kind of relationship you and I have."

Jack moved his left hand towards one of the lamps on the coffee table so that he could read the time on his wristwatch. Then he looked up at me and continued talking.

"We don't know what Kevin's motive was for showing up at the door this evening. What we do know is that he ignored my warning not to return here and that he also threatened you. I'm going to report to my lieutenant what just happened and find out what advice he can give in regard to the possibility of your seeking protection against Kevin. I'm convinced that Kevin hurled the rock through the window last night. It's too bad we have no proof that he did. Will you be okay here alone for just a few minutes? I need to go downstairs. While I'm in my apartment, I'll phone my lieutenant. Then I'll grab some cardboard for the window and pack a few things for my stay here tonight."

"I'll be fine here," I replied in a voice that did not sound terribly convincing.

"I promise to be as quick as possible," Jack said, "and I'll lock the door on my way out."

"Please don't hurry. I'm fine."

"Do you have your cell phone on you now, Linzie?"

"No. My phone is on the desk in the den."

"I'll go get it."

Jack grabbed his flashlight, got on his feet, and headed for the den. When he returned, he put my cell phone into my right hand.

"Call me if you need me, Linzie."

"I will."

After Jack closed the door behind him, I flipped open the cover of my phone and glanced at the time. It was 5:35 p.m. As I sat in my favorite chair, I wondered whether my life would ever return to the tranquility it had once enjoyed. My breakup with Kevin had caused a wave of chaos to flood my life. I was drowning in questions to which I had no solid answers. I found myself second-guessing the way I had handled Kevin's unexpected visit the day before. Had I been wrong, I wondered, to ignore Kevin's plea to discuss our differences, or had I done the right thing by ordering him to leave? I swayed back and forth on that issue, leaning more towards the course of action I had taken. After all, it was Kevin who had been adamant that marriage was out of the picture for us. It was Kevin who had been so selfish that he would not hear of my dating anyone else in spite of his stance on marriage. It was Kevin who had cheated on me. It was Kevin who had lied to me.

As I carried on an internal debate about the way I had ended my relationship with Kevin, it suddenly dawned on me that Jack had been gone for much more than a few minutes. I flipped open my cell phone cover and looked at the time. It was 6:12 p.m. More than half an hour had gone by since Jack had left my place to go downstairs. Concerned, I called his cell phone number and got his voicemail. After calling his number several more times and getting the same result, I decided to go downstairs to make sure everything was all right. I parted company with my chair, grabbed my flashlight, and exited my apartment.

When I reached the staircase, I began to slowly and carefully descend the steps. Just as I reached the bottom step, I heard the sound of a creaking door. Jack then appeared in the downstairs hallway with his flashlight in one hand and an overnight bag in the other.

"Linzie, are you all right?" he asked as he pointed his flashlight in my direction.

"Yes. I was worried that something had happened to you. I called your cell phone number several times and got your voicemail message each time."

"I was talking to my lieutenant to tell him about Kevin's appearance at the door and his threatening behavior. Ten minutes after we concluded our conversation, he called me back with a report he had just received. Why don't you and I go upstairs and talk?"

From the sound of Jack's voice, I suspected that some sort of bad news was about to reach my ears. I turned around. Jack accompanied me up the staircase.

Upon entering the apartment, I silently headed for my armchair while Jack made his way to his usual spot on the sofa. When we sat down, there was a very somber look on his face.

"I am afraid that what I am about to tell you, Linzie, is very unpleasant news. When my lieutenant called me back, it was to tell me about an accident report that he had just received. He knew the report would be of interest to me because the person injured in the accident is the same person he and I had just been discussing."

I turned white. My hands began to tremble uncontrollably.

In a very weak voice, I asked, "Are you telling me that Kevin has been injured?"

"Yes, Linzie. His injuries are severe."

I became numb, so numb that I could not speak, or cry, or react in any definitive way.

"Kevin was ambulanced to the hospital," Jack continued, "and is in the emergency room right now. He sustained various fractures, and he has lost a lot of blood. He lapsed into a coma. Things are in the hands of the hospital right now, so we don't have a complete report on the injuries yet."

I leaned back in the chair and stared at the ceiling. Any attempt on my part to speak at that moment would have been utterly useless.

When I regained some composure, I asked, "Do they expect him to pull through?"

"I wish I could answer that question, Linzie. We'll just have to wait."

"What on earth happened to cause such an accident?"

"Apparently, Kevin walked here on foot and was returning home the same way. As he was walking down a winding road that was pitch-black due to the power outage, a vehicle skidded and hit him."

I could no longer hold my emotions in. I burst out crying. Jack got up from the sofa and, with his flashlight in hand, headed for the bathroom that I had given him permission to use during his stay with me. He returned with a box of tissues and laid the box on my lap. He then went into the dining room, picked up a chair, and carried it into the living room. After placing it next to my armchair, he sat on it.

"I know," he said, "that you wanted no harm to come to Kevin and that this news is a terrible jolt to you. It's good to cry, Linzie. Let your emotions out. You'll feel better if you do."

There was no shortage of tears. I wept bitterly. All the while, Jack did his best to console me. As the tears flowed down my cheeks, he tenderly held my hand.

Chapter Ten

January 8, 2018, arrived. It was the day I was supposed to call Mrs. Cranshaw to let her know if I was interested in her ghostwriting job offer. Kevin's accident had turned me into an emotional mess, so I was at a loss as to what to do about Mrs. Cranshaw's offer. Had it not been for the fact that Kevin was in such tough shape, reaching a decision would have been much easier. Kevin was still in a coma, and his chance of survival was questionable. He had suffered internal bleeding. His two legs, one arm, and his collarbone had been fractured.

I felt guilty about what had happened to Kevin. I simply could not rid myself of the idea that if I had been a bit more understanding, he would not have ventured out into the snowstorm on January 4. Adding to my feeling of guilt was an item that was found in Kevin's jacket pocket by one of the hospital attendants on the night of the accident. That item was an engagement ring. Apparently, it had been Kevin's intention to propose to me.

Kevin was not the only man on my mind. Jack had quickly become my soul mate, and the thought of not having him nearby during June, July, and August was a gloomy one for me. Ironically, it was Jack who encouraged me to seriously consider accepting the ghostwriting job. Such an opportunity might not come again he said. Jack was not happy about the fact that I would be absent from the apartment for three months. However, he assured me that he would be spending as many summer weekends as possible at his brother George's home in Gloucester and that the close proximity of Gloucester to Rockport would allow us to spend a lot of time together.

Jack had spoken to George in regard to the matter of my needing a lawyer to review the ghostwriter agreement that would be drawn up by Mrs. Cranshaw's lawyer should I express interest in the job offer. According to Jack, George was more than happy to perform that service for me and insisted on doing so free of charge. I was very grateful to George for his willingness to help me out.

As the hours passed by on January 8, I became more and more frustrated with myself, for I could not reach a decision about the ghostwriting job. Finally, around 3:00 p.m., I adopted a course of action. I picked up the phone and dialed Mrs. Cranshaw's number. After the fourth ring, I heard a rather faint *hello* on the other end.

"Hello, Mrs. Cranshaw. This is Linzie Cole. I told you I would call you today in regard to the ghostwriting job."

"Yes, Miss Cole. I have been expecting your call."

Her voice sounded so weak that I was tempted to ask her how she was, but I decided it was best not to ask. Some of my past experiences with Mrs. Cranshaw had taught me that it did not take much to rouse her ire, and I feared that a simple inquiry about her health might do just that.

"I'm calling, Mrs. Cranshaw, to let you know that I am interested in your job offer."

"That's good, Miss Cole. As the day wore on, I was beginning to think that you were going to tell me otherwise," she said in a much stronger voice.

"I'm sorry. I did not mean to keep you waiting for my decision. I'm afraid that I almost did pass on your offer due to something terrible that happened last week during the storm."

Why those words escaped my lips I'll never know. Perhaps it was due to my needy emotional state.

"May I ask what terrible thing happened during the

storm?"

In a shaky voice, I replied, "My friend Kevin was hit by a car during the storm and is badly injured."

After a short pause, she asked, "Is that the Kevin you have been dating?"

"Yes."

"How badly injured is he?"

It took all my might to hold back from bursting into tears as I said, "He is in a coma and has multiple injuries. He may not survive."

"I'm terribly sorry, Miss Cole. I truly mean that."

"Thank you, Mrs. Cranshaw."

"Let me just say that if Kevin does survive and you need to leave Rockport at any time to pay him a visit, I shall understand. We can certainly take a break now and then from working on the book."

I became quiet because I could no longer keep a stiff upper lip in our conversation about Kevin. It was my belief that Mrs. Cranshaw sensed that I was emotionally drained, for she quickly changed the subject.

"I shall contact my lawyer and ask him to draw up an agreement," she said. "When I receive the agreement from him, would you like me to mail it to you, Miss Cole?"

"That would be fine," I replied.

"Do you have a lawyer in mind to review it?"

"Yes, I do. His name is George Grumey."

"Excellent. I want you to feel that I am treating you fairly."

"I appreciate that."

"If Mr. Grumey has any questions or issues in regard to the agreement, please tell him to give my lawyer a call. I shall attach my lawyer's business card to the agreement before mailing it to you."

"Thank you, Mrs. Cranshaw."

"I do hope things will improve in regard to Kevin's condition."

"I appreciate your concern."

"Goodbye, Miss Cole."

"Goodbye."

When my phone conversation with Mrs. Cranshaw ended, I was deep in thought. The concern she had just expressed about Kevin's condition reaffirmed for me that she did indeed have a soft side to her personality. My initial opinion of her as a hostile, egotistical woman now seemed harsh to me, and I realized I had been wrong to have judged her so quickly.

My thoughts about Mrs. Cranshaw were interrupted by the ringing of my cell phone. When I flipped up the cover of the phone, I discovered that it was Jack calling. He had been working on organizing his apartment since early morning. Eager to hear how much progress he had made, I wasted no time in answering his call.

"Hi, Jack. How are things going?"

"I'm happy to report that I just emptied my last box. Now it's just a question of putting a lot of things in their proper places."

"That's great," I commented.

"How about you, Linzie? Did you make a decision about the ghostwriting job?"

"Yes. A few minutes ago, I phoned Mrs. Cranshaw to tell her I was interested in her offer."

"Good for you. I think you made the right decision."

"I sure hope so."

"Linzie, I have a question for you. Would you like to go to the mall with me? I'd like to treat you to dinner at a nice restaurant there and then go shopping for some furniture."

I was in such a blue mood due to Kevin's accident that I did not know how to respond to Jack's invitation. Fortunately, Jack did not wait for me to answer.

"Now, Linzie, you haven't left your apartment since the blizzard last week. I think it would be good for you to get out and enjoy a change of scenery. Not only that, I need a woman's advice on what kind of furniture I should buy for my place. We can start by looking at bedroom sets. I'm afraid if I spend too many more nights sleeping on your living room sofa, I'll feel obligated to pay you room and board."

For the first time in four days, I laughed. Jack returned my laugh with one of his own.

"I guess you're right, Jack. Getting out of the house probably would do me a world of good. As for your sleeping on my sofa, I don't mind one bit. Don't hurry to buy a bedroom set on my account. You can sleep here ad infinitum."

"Oh, you writers! You do have a way of tossing out fancy terms," he said laughing. "You wouldn't really be happy if I slept on your sofa ad infinitum, would you, Linzie?"

"Sure, I would."

I was not being polite when I said that to Jack. I was being truthful. Although I had known him a mere five days, I felt that a special bond had developed between the two of us.

"Linzie, I'm going to take a shower and put on some decent-looking clothes. How about I come upstairs at half past four? Then we can take off for the mall."

"That sounds good. If you want, I can spare you the trip up the staircase and come to your door."

"No. A gentleman always escorts a lady out of her home and to the car."

"Another lesson from your mother?"

"You should know the answer to that one by now, Ms. Linzie," he said chuckling. "See you later."

"See you."

I had almost an hour and a half to kill before leaving for the mall and decided to spend part of it writing. My computer had not seen me since I finished my writing session on the day of the blizzard. As I got settled in front of the screen, I feared that the stress I had been under would retard my creativity. However, the opposite proved to be true. Many of the emotions I was feeling inside stimulated my writing ability. Words flowed easily and new ideas quickly entered my mind. When I was done writing, I saved my work and proceeded to get ready.

This was my first outing with Jack and although we were not going to a fancy place, I wanted to look nice. I put on a black velvet slack suit, a red blouse to complement it, and a pair of black boots. Then came the final touches—makeup and some pieces of casual jewelry.

At 4:30 p.m., I heard a knock at my door. I looked through the peephole and saw Jack. I opened the door, and he entered the foyer, holding a bouquet of red roses. Smiling, he handed the bouquet to me. I returned his smile, but my lips were quivering.

"Something is wrong, Linzie. What is it?"

"I'm sorry, Jack. It's just that the roses remind me of the last date I had with Kevin. He came to the door with a bouquet of flowers. The evening started just fine but ended up with my telling him we were through."

"Linzie, I understand, but you must try to stop feeling guilty about what happened to Kevin. From what you have told me, Kevin never really valued the love you had for him. I'm sure he was fond of you, but common sense tells me he was not capable of completely giving you his heart. The engagement ring that was found on his person on the night of the storm was, to my way of thinking, not a symbol of love. It was a symbol of panic. He apparently was going to propose to you, but you must ask yourself if that proposal stemmed from love or from the fear of losing you. If he had to compromise his position on marriage so that he would not lose you, do you really think such a marriage would have withstood the test of time?"

I looked into Jack's eyes and shook my head.

"Linzie, what happened to Kevin was not your fault. Kevin is responsible for his own actions, and to put it frankly, his actions were not those of a gentleman. Let me ask you a few questions. Which one of you insisted on an exclusive relationship?"

"He did," I said softly.

"Which one of you violated that agreement to be exclusive by romancing someone else?"

"He did."

"Which one of you lied in an attempt to cover up the cheating?"

"He did."

"Which one of you was unwilling to commit to marriage?"

"He was."

"Linzie, your conscience should be clear. You deserve a lot better than what Kevin was willing to offer. The fact that he was too selfish to let you go is not your problem. It is his problem."

"Thank you, Jack. I actually feel a lot better now. It was not my intention to belittle your very kind gesture of bringing me these roses. They are beautiful, and I am grateful."

"So, Ms. Linzie, after we put the roses in water, grab your coat. Let's go out and kick up our heels for a change. It's time for us to have a little fun. We don't have to restrict our browsing to furniture. If there are stores you want to visit, we can make time for them too."

We left the foyer and made our way to the kitchen. To prove to me that he knew my kitchen well, Jack opened the cupboard that held my vases. I chose a vase other than the one I had used for the flowers Kevin had given me. Once the roses were in water, we returned to the foyer. With a greatly eased conscience, I opened the closet door and grabbed the stylish coat I had intended to wear on the night of my last date with Kevin. Jack took the coat from my hands and helped me put it on. Then we exited the apartment and headed for his car.

Our drive to the mall was a pleasant one. Jack talked about Gloucester and Rockport quite a bit. The more he talked, the more excited I got about exploring the many places of interest that both Gloucester and Rockport had to offer.

When we arrived at the mall, it was packed. The snowstorm of January 4 and the subsequent cold snap had, for several days, prevented people from descending on the stores to return or exchange their Christmas gifts. The weather on January 8 was decent. The sky was clear, and the temperature, bearable. Many took advantage of the good weather and headed for the mall.

After enjoying an early dinner at a seafood restaurant, Jack and I decided to make the furniture store our first stop. As luck would have it, a handsome bedroom set caught Jack's eye. I agreed with Jack's opinion that the other sets the store had to offer did not quite measure up to the one he fancied. The salesman informed Jack that the set was not in stock and that there would be a two-week wait for delivery. After I convinced Jack that he should continue to use my sofa bed for the next two weeks, he proceeded to make his first purchase of the evening.

Jack also spotted a dining room set that was to his liking. Upon receiving my nod of approval, he purchased it. The right living room set, kitchen set, and den furniture were yet to be found, so we agreed that a trip to another store on another day was in our near future. Our hunt for furniture was challenging but fun. Although I could not claim to be an interior decorator, I believed I had a good sense of color coordination, so I offered to help Jack decorate his apartment. He gladly accepted my offer, claiming that when it came to choosing colors, he might as well have been born color-blind.

After we left the furniture store, Jack insisted that we go to a store of my choice. There was a large bookstore in the mall that I wanted to visit. So, off we went to the bookstore, which was a fairly short walk from the furniture store.

While we were roaming the aisles of the bookstore, I came to realize that Jack was far more talented than he had claimed. Books on carpentry immediately drew his attention. As he flipped through the pages of one of the books, he informed me that some of his free time was devoted to making small pieces of furniture. When we strolled through the aisle where art books were shelved, he modestly mentioned that he had been painting landscape scenes for years.

As he pored over pictures of paintings in one of the large art books, I said, "You lied to me the other night when you told me that you had not been blessed with any kind of gift. It sounds as though some of your talents slipped your memory."

He laughed and said, "You better not call my pastimes 'talents' until you see the products of my labor."

"I am eager to see your work, Jack."

"I'll be happy to show you what I have on hand. A lot of the furniture I made and pictures I painted have been sold at craft shows."

"So, you're not only a carpenter and an artist but a business entrepreneur as well."

"I would hesitate to call myself a business entrepreneur. I'm still a cop, so it isn't as though I have all the time in the world to devote to my hobbies. Let's just say I enjoy dabbling in them and that I have been able to make a few bucks from my efforts."

"I've made a few bucks from my writing—very few bucks."

"Don't get discouraged, Linzie. Keep trying. Now that you have expressed interest to Mrs. Cranshaw about the ghost-writing job, it sounds as though things may turn around in your favor."

"Yes. I guess there is some hope for my career."

"You are still planning to meet with that publisher who phoned you last week, right?"

After hemming and hawing a bit, I said, "I actually thought of postponing my meeting with him."

"Now, why on earth would you want to do that, Linzie?"

I sighed and said, "I guess I just feel so deflated over Kevin's accident that I doubt I would make a good first impression."

"As your friend, I advise you to seize every opportunity that comes your way. If you postpone your meeting with the publisher, he may lose interest in what you have to offer."

"That's true," I mumbled.

What I did not tell Jack was that my meeting with Adam Proctor was probably not strictly business in Adam's mind. I did not share with Jack the fact that Adam was recuperating from a broken heart and was making an attempt to move on with his personal life. I suspected that Adam was looking upon my upcoming date with him to be as much or more of a social date than a business one. Before Kevin got hurt, I was more willing to meet Adam and entertain the possibility that our meeting could lead to dating. Kevin's accident had soured me on beginning a new relationship. I feared more than ever that if Adam developed feelings for me that I could not reciprocate, Adam would get hurt. That thought convinced me that I had not completely rid myself of the guilt I felt over Kevin's accident. My hope in regard to Adam was that once we met, he would not care one bit about dating me and that my writing would be the only focus of his attention.

"Do you feel like paying a visit to the ice-cream parlor?" Jack asked. "It's on the other end of the mall. The walk to the parlor will give us the chance to burn some of the calories from the dinner we ate earlier."

"That sounds like a great idea," I replied. "I might even indulge in a hot fudge sundae. I haven't had one in about two years."

We exited the bookstore and began our fairly lengthy walk to the ice-cream parlor. As we were reaching the halfway point to our destination, I heard a woman call out, "Jack, Jack." Seconds later, I heard the woman holler, "Jack, wait up." I tried to locate the woman who had called out, but doing so was almost an impossible task. The hallways were jammed with people who were on the move.

I looked at Jack, who had apparently not heard the woman's voice, and said, "Jack, I think I heard your name being called."

"Was it only my first name you heard?"

"Yes. Then I heard, 'Jack, wait up.' "

After stopping and looking around, he said, "I don't see anyone I recognize. It's most likely a different Jack that was being called, not yours truly."

"I guess so," I said. "Jack is a pretty common name."

"In this case, it is a pretty common name for an extraordinary person," he said chuckling.

"Ah, Mr. Jack, your modesty is extraordinary too."

"Linzie, it does my heart good to hear you joke again."

"I can thank you for that. You have helped me free myself of a lot of the blame I was carrying on my shoulders due to Kevin's accident."

"You should not be burdened by any blame, Linzie. Rid yourself of all of it."

"I'm trying, Jack. I'm trying."

We arrived at the ice-cream parlor. It was crowded, but Jack managed to find an empty table. After he and I took seats across from each other, he removed two menus from the holder on the table and handed me one of the menus.

Although I took a good look at all the offerings of the parlor, my mind was set on a hot fudge sundae with all the works. Jack decided to order the same. As we waited for our order to be taken, we let our eyes roam around the parlor, which was reminiscent of the 1950s. There was a jukebox in the corner of the room playing hits of that decade and pictures of movie idols of that time period hanging on the walls.

As Jack and I were engaged in conversation about some of those movie idols, a woman appeared out of nowhere and sat in one of the two empty chairs at our table. I was startled not only by her unexpected appearance on the scene but also by her physical appearance. Her bleached blond hair, thick makeup, and giant earrings gave me the willies. I looked at Jack inquisitively. I wondered whether he knew this uninvited guest.

"Jack," she said, "I saw you in the hallway and hollered to you. It's so noisy out there that you did not hear me. I did my best to catch up to you, but I could not pass through the crowd."

Jack looked at the woman. The look on his face was interpreted by me to be one of disappointment.

"Hello, Doris. I want you to meet my friend Linzie. She has been helping me shop for furniture."

Doris glanced at me and gave me an unenthusiastic *hello.*

"It's nice to meet you," I said.

She immediately turned her head back in Jack's direction and in a scolding tone of voice said, "Jack, I thought you were going to call me and give me your new address once you got settled in your apartment."

"I'm not settled, Doris. Linzie can tell you that. I've been up to my eyeballs in boxes."

Doris apparently did not want me to tell her anything, for she kept her eyes focused on Jack.

"My daughter," she said, "will be more than happy to help you decorate your place."

Jack looked at me and said, "Linzie, do you remember I told you about Doris's daughter, the artist?"

"Yes, I remember. Doris, I understand your daughter is a terrific artist."

Doris responded to my comment about her daughter with silence.

"Doris's daughter, whose name is Beth, does a little interior decorating on the side," Jack explained.

"When should I have Beth give you a call so she can look over your place and decide how to decorate?" Doris asked.

The look on Jack's face was no longer one of disappointment. It was one of annoyance. I felt uncomfortable, for I sensed that he was about to say something to Doris in a not-too-kind way.

In a firm voice, he replied, "I won't be needing Beth's help. I have already engaged someone to help me with color coordination and so forth."

I knew that Jack was referring to me, but I did not dare open my mouth to say so.

"Beth is a real professional," Doris said. "Is the person that is going to help you a professional?"

"To my way of thinking, she is one of the best," Jack replied.

Jack looked at me and winked while Doris started to rummage through her bag.

"I don't know if I have a pen with me," she said. "I would like to write down your new address, Jack."

After a thorough search that involved emptying most of the contents of her bag on the table, she concluded that she had no pen with her.

"Do you have a pen, Jack?"

He lightly patted his shirt pocket and said, "No."

Doris then turned to me, for the first time since we were introduced, and said, "How about you, Lucy? Do you have a pen?"

"I'm afraid not."

"Doris, her name is Linzie, not Lucy."

"Oh, you know me," she said. "I'm not good at remembering names. Maybe I should go up to the counter and ask the cashier if he has a pen."

"Doris, I know your phone number," Jack said. "There is no need for me to give you my address at this moment."

"Very well," she said snippily. "I'll expect to hear from you."

She rose from the chair and said, "Goodbye, Jack."

"Goodbye, Doris," he said.

During her stay at our table, Doris had treated me as though I were an invisible third party, and her departure from the table was equally unimpressive. I expected that she would acknowledge me with some sort of parting statement, but my expectation was too high. Without saying one word to me, she turned on her heel and headed for the door. I found her behavior to be inexcusable and would soon learn that Jack shared my sentiment.

"I'm sorry, Linzie. Doris can be very rude at times. She

should have been more respectful towards you."

Shaking my head, I said, "All I can say is that she seemed resentful of my being here with you."

"I'm sure she was. Ever since I lost my wife, she has been trying to claim me for her own. At my old place, she would sometimes show up at my door without giving me any warning that she was coming."

"How did you meet her?"

"Oh, a friend—or, rather, ex-friend—set me up on a blind date with her about a year after my wife died. He was afraid I would be too lonely without a partner. When it comes to my relationship with Doris, I consider loneliness to be bliss."

"Can't you just tell her that you're not interested in having a relationship with her?"

"I have told her that, Linzie, but she prefers not to listen to what I'm saying. It's sort of like what happened between you and Kevin. You told him you wanted out of the relationship, but he refused to accept what you were saying."

"Yes, I can see the comparison."

"I don't call Doris. She just pops into my life when she darn pleases. I have no intention of phoning her to give her my new address."

"I don't blame you, Jack."

Jack's frustration over Doris earned my empathy, and it also led me to the conclusion that I truly was blameless for what had happened to Kevin. The realization that we can be responsible only for our own actions and cannot always curb the actions of others finally hit home. I relived the moments when Kevin came to my door unannounced and banged on it in a bullylike fashion, all the while demanding that I let him in. Kevin had invaded my territory. He had crossed the line. I could finally say to myself that I was sorry about Kevin's accident, but I was in no way responsible for it.

My unpleasant memories of Kevin were interrupted when a waitress came over and took our order. When she left, Jack and I did our best to return to pleasant conversation, but I could not help but feel that he was still disturbed by Doris's invasion of his privacy.

When the sundaes arrived, he seemed more relaxed and started to joke with me again. We thoroughly enjoyed the sundaes, and after consuming them, we both agreed it was time to return home. With the exception of one fly in the ointment—a fly by the name of Doris—my first outing with Jack had been delightful.

Chapter Eleven

When Adam Proctor came to pick me up for our date on the evening of January 10, I had to agree with Harri's opinion of his good looks. Tall, trim, black-haired, and blue-eyed, he looked as though he belonged on stage or screen. Harri had boasted about his gentlemanly manner, and I would soon realize that her boasting was not exaggerated. In fact, his politeness manifested itself before he even entered the house.

"Good evening, Linzie," he said. "I believe I am ten minutes early. I hope that is all right."

"That's fine, Adam. Please come in."

He entered the downstairs hallway, shook my hand, and then wiped his boots on the mat. In his left hand was a fancy gift bag.

"This is for you, Linzie," he said as he handed me the bag.

"Oh, thank you, Adam. Shall I take a peek at the contents?"

"Please do."

I placed the bag on top of the small maple table that was situated to the left of the front door. The first item I removed from the bag was a bottle of Italian white wine.

As I studied the label on the bottle, I said, "This bottle found the right home. I tend to favor white wines over other kinds."

When I removed the other item from the bag, I discovered it was a box of fine chocolates from Switzerland.

"Thank you, Adam. I hope we can enjoy the wine and the chocolates together when we come back here."

"I am not one to eat sweets," he commented, "but I would enjoy having a glass of wine with you later."

"Good," I said. "Let's plan on that."

I headed for a chair over which my coat was draped. Adam made it to the chair before I did in order to help me put the coat on.

"Thank you, Adam. Chivalry still exists."

"I hope it never dies," he said in a serious tone of voice.

"My apartment is on the second floor," I explained. "Rather than have you walk up all those stairs, I felt it was easier to meet you here in the hallway."

"I don't mind climbing a flight of stairs, Linzie. In fact, I make it a point to spend at least one hour every day at the health club that I joined several years ago."

I wanted to tell him that he appeared to be in excellent shape, but he seemed so stiff and formal that I was afraid to extend such a personal compliment to him.

"Are you ready to leave, Linzie?"

"Yes."

He opened the storm door and gestured for me to precede him outside. Then he firmly closed the front door while holding the storm door open.

"I imagine you want this door locked, Linzie."

"Yes. I do."

I fumbled about in my pocketbook for the key, which was doing an excellent job of hiding at the bottom of the bag. Once I managed to find it, Adam took it.

"Allow me, Linzie."

After the door was secured, he returned the key to me. As we descended the staircase to the walkway, he held onto my left arm, a gesture which seemed to be in tune with his obviously protective nature. He continued to hold onto my arm until we approached his car, which was parked in front of the house. Although I knew zilch about vehicles, the luxuriousness of Adam's car did not escape my attention. It was a handsome four-door silver sedan with a plush red interior. Adam opened the front passenger door for me. Once I was settled in the seat, he closed the door and then got behind the wheel of the car. After starting the engine, he turned on the radio, which was set to a station that was playing easy listening music.

Once Adam pulled away from the curb, he and I engaged in conversation that amounted to nothing more than small talk. After five minutes or so of that small talk, the conversation turned in a direction that I was not quite expecting.

"Linzie, this is such a pleasure to be going out to dinner with you. I don't know if Harriet told you that I was in a five-year relationship that I recently ended."

"Yes. Harri—I mean Harriet—did mention that. I'm sorry things did not work out for you."

"Don't be sorry. I should have walked away from my girlfriend a long time ago. She refused to commit to a serious relationship. I wanted marriage; she did not."

It was tempting to tell Adam that I could relate to that type of situation, but I did not want to interrupt his apparent need to vent some frustration over his failed romance. I also believed he was trying to give me an honest account of his past love life. I appreciated his honesty.

"To tell you the truth, Linzie, you are the first person I have dated since Evelyn and I split up three months ago."

It was now perfectly clear to me that Adam considered our going out that evening to be a personal date. The bottle of wine and the chocolates had put that suspicion in my head, and now his remark that I was the first person he had dated since his breakup left no doubt. I began to wonder if we were going to spend much time or any time discussing my books.

"Evelyn is a wonderful person," he continued, "but her disastrous first marriage ruined any prospect of our getting married. No matter how hard I tried to convince her that a second marriage could be a happy one, she would not entertain the possibility of tying the knot again."

I did not know what words of comfort to offer him other than *I'm sorry*, and I believe I said those two words about ten times during our drive to the restaurant. Evelyn's name was mentioned so many times that I began to feel that she was with us in the car. As Adam pulled into the restaurant parking lot, I heaved a sigh of relief. Maybe now, I thought, he would leave Evelyn in the car and focus a little more on me.

Once the sedan was parked, I waited for Adam to open the passenger door. To do otherwise would have insulted his prim and proper manner. He also put out his right hand to help me out of the seat.

"Thank you, Adam," I said as I stepped onto the lot pavement. "I'm not used to such courteous treatment."

That statement actually led him to focus on me—for about twenty seconds.

"When Harriet called me to give me your phone number," he said, "she mentioned that you just broke up with your boyfriend. She felt that he was not a good match for you."

"My situation was similar to yours with Evelyn. My ex was very noncommittal."

That was the wrong thing to say. Rather than ask me any questions about my relationship with Kevin, he continued with his tale of woe about Evelyn. She was once again the star of the show, and she remained the star from the time we walked into the restaurant through our completion of the main entrée. When our plates were removed from the table, I felt it was time to remove Evelyn from our conversation, so I proceeded to steer the conversation away from personal relationships.

"Adam, I know you are a publisher, but do you write?"

"I used to write. In fact, that is how my publishing business began. I self-published my own books. As time went on, I expanded the scope of my business by publishing the works of other authors. From what Harriet told me, you write romance novels and self-publish them. Is that correct?"

"Yes. After I wrote my first novel, I tried to find a publisher who would accept my book, but it was an uphill battle, so I decided to publish the book myself. I followed the same route with my next two books."

"Do you have a copy of each of your books that I could borrow? I would like to read them."

"Yes, I do have a copy of each. I'll be glad to give them to you when we go back to my apartment."

"After I read them, I'll have my editors look them over. Who knows? There may be a publishing contract in our future."

"Even if a contract never comes about," I said, "I do appreciate your willingness to read my novels."

"You're very welcome, Linzie. It may take some time before I can get back to you about your novels. My editors are buried in work, but I'll do my best to push things along."

"Thanks."

"Would you like some dessert?" he asked.

"Oh, I don't think so. I want to keep my girlish figure," I said laughing.

He did not return my laugh. All he did was nod.

"All right then," he said, "I'll ask for the bill, and we can go back to your place and enjoy that bottle of wine."

Out of the corner of his eye, he noticed our waitress. He beckoned to her and requested the bill. In no time, she complied with his request. Once Adam paid the bill, he helped me on with my coat. We exited the restaurant, and we were soon on our way to my place.

During the drive back to my apartment, I was grateful that our date was no longer a threesome. Rather than talk about Evelyn, Adam talked about himself. I learned that he had majored in English literature in college and then, a few years after graduating, returned to college to get a second degree in business. He informed me that his publishing business had grown dramatically in a matter of a few years. I definitely got the impression that he was doing quite well financially.

When he asked me a few questions about my writing business, I told him the truth—that writing was my passion, but it had not provided me with a decent living. I was not looking for any favors from him. I was merely trying to be honest.

When Adam parked in front of the house, I noticed that Jack's apartment was in darkness. That did not surprise me because Jack had told me that he was going to pay a visit to his mother and take her out to dinner. He did not expect to be back at his place until around 11:00 p.m. I glanced at my wristwatch. The time was 9:15 p.m.

"Well, Adam, let's go in and take the cork out of that fancy bottle of wine you gave me."

For the first time that evening, I heard Adam laugh.

"I have never tried that kind of wine before, Linzie, but I thought the bottle was rather attractive. You can save it and put a few flowers in it. That's what my mother used to do with her wine bottles."

"Good idea. I may just do that."

We got out of the car. I, of course, got out with Adam's helping hand. When we arrived at the front door, I did not have to fumble about in my bag for the key. My prior search had prompted me to put the key in my coat pocket, thus sparing me from playing a game of hide-and-seek within my bag. We entered the downstairs hallway, I picked up the gift bag containing the wine and the chocolates, and then we proceeded to walk up the staircase.

"This old house has a lot of charm," Adam commented.

"It has a lot of charm, I agree, but there is an endless list of improvements that need to be made to it. My landlord has been very kind to me, so I am the last person who would ever complain to him."

"Have you ever thought of moving into a more modern place, Linzie?"

"Sure, thinking about it is easy. It doesn't cost a cent to think about it. Moving is a different story. My financial situation demands that I stay put for now. Actually, there are some benefits to living here. The house is within walking distance of the stores, and the bus service is excellent here. Those two benefits are invaluable to me because I cannot afford a car right now."

"Before my business took off," Adam said, "I shared an apartment with three other bachelors."

"How did that go?"

"If you like looking at a pile of dirty dishes in the sink and clothes that no one bothers to hang up, it went quite well."

I smiled. I believed Adam was beginning to feel more comfortable with me. His sense of humor was beginning to make itself known.

"Now I can afford to be king of my own castle," he continued. "I own a ritzy condo in a high-rise building that overlooks the Charles River."

As I opened my apartment door, I said, "This place is not ritzy, and I'm afraid the Charles River is nowhere in sight when you gaze out my living room windows."

"If we strike up a publishing deal, Linzie, things could change dramatically for you."

Upon entering the foyer, I turned on the light. Adam and I removed our coats, and I hung them in the closet. Then, holding the gift bag in one hand, I flicked the light switch in the living room with the other hand so that we could safely see our way to the kitchen, where a corkscrew awaited us. We were halfway through the living room when I heard Adam gasp.

I turned to Adam and said, "What's the matter?"

He pointed towards the sofa and said, "There is a man lying down over there."

I nervously cast a glance in that direction and discovered that Jack was asleep on the sofa. That was a scene I was not expecting.

Trying to make light of a rather embarrassing situation, I said to Adam, "Oh, that's not just any man on my sofa. That's Jack."

With a disgruntled look on his face, Adam asked, "Who is Jack?"

"Jack is the tenant who just moved into the apartment downstairs. As a matter of fact, he moved in a week ago today."

"So, why is he here in your apartment?" Adam asked in a demanding tone of voice.

"Let me explain the situation," I said. "When Jack moved into the apartment downstairs, he brought very few pieces of furniture with him from his prior home. It was his intention to go shopping for some new furniture, including a bedroom set, last weekend. The roads were so bad due to the blizzard last Thursday that Jack delayed shopping for furniture until this past Monday. He ordered a bedroom set, but there is a two-week delivery wait. I've been letting him use the sofa bed in my living room until he has his new bed. Otherwise, he would have to sleep on the floor in his sleeping bag."

Adam still looked upset. I was astonished by his attitude. After all, he was in my home, and there was no reason for me to have to answer to him.

"So, you have known this guy only one week, and you are sharing your apartment with him."

"Please don't put it that way, Adam. Jack has been very good to me."

"Very good in what way?" he asked while raising his eyebrows.

"In so many ways that I cannot begin to tell you."

My blood pressure was rising as I said those words. Adam, I felt, had not only overstepped his bounds but had also insinuated that there was some inappropriate activity going on between Jack and me.

Just then, Jack woke up and turned his head in our direction. He slowly changed his position so that he was sitting on the sofa rather than lying on it.

"Linzie, I'm sorry about being here earlier than expected," Jack said. "My back has been bothering me all night. After I took my mother out to eat, the pain really got bad.

I meant to rest on your sofa for just a little while, but I fell asleep. I guess lifting all those boxes finally caught up with me. I'm afraid I wrenched my back."

I thought that Jack's words would appease Adam. However, as I glanced at Adam's face, I did not see any signs of that happening.

"I'm sorry about your back," I said. "You did the right thing to come here and lie down. By the way, I would like you to meet Adam Proctor. Adam, this is Jack Grumey."

Jack rose from the sofa with the speed of a tortoise, walked over to Adam, and extended his hand to initiate a handshake. Despite his sore back, Jack heartily shook Adam's hand. Adam appeared to put no effort into the handshake.

"It's nice to meet you, Adam. Linzie told me that you are a publisher. I imagine that is a fascinating field."

"Yes, fascinating," Adam muttered.

"I told Linzie that I am going to order her three books," Jack remarked. "She verbally gave me a little summary of each one the other night. Each book is quite different from the other two, and I must say that they all sound very interesting."

Adam simply stared at Jack and said nothing. The situation was getting so tense that I feared that Adam would say or do something stupid.

"Adam," I said, "Jack is on the police force here in the city. He has been a cop for twenty-five years. To tell you the truth, I think Jack should write a book about his experiences. It might just turn out to be a best seller," I said with a chuckle.

No one else was chuckling. I believed that Jack was beginning to catch on to the fact that Adam was not a happy camper because there was another man in my apartment.

"Well, Linzie and Adam, I'm sorry I interrupted your time together. As I said, I meant only to rest on the sofa for a while but ended up falling asleep. I'm going to return to my apartment now and let the two of you enjoy the rest of the evening."

"That won't be necessary," Adam said haughtily. "I am

going to leave. Please give me the copies of your books, Linzie."

I went into the den and took my three books out of one of the desk drawers. The evening was ending on such a sour note that handing the books over to Adam now seemed more like a duty than a hopeful act. I seriously doubted that Adam would even open the cover of any of the three novels. Nevertheless, I had told him that I would give him a copy of each, and I intended to keep my word.

When I re-entered the living room, Jack was still there, sitting on the sofa. Adam was standing in the foyer, looking as though he wanted to make a quick escape from my place.

"Here you are, Adam," I said as I handed him the books. "You don't have to return these. I can order others easily enough."

"Fine," he said. "May I have my coat?"

"Yes, of course. In fact, please take the bottle of wine with you."

Looking quite indignant, Adam said, "I would not dream of doing such a thing. I'll leave the bottle here so you can toast your anniversary."

"Anniversary? What anniversary?" I asked.

"Yours and Jack's. Your one-week anniversary."

I turned and looked at Jack, who returned my look with a shrug of his shoulders. I then walked over to the foyer closet and removed Adam's coat. After handing it to him, I opened my apartment door.

"Goodbye, Adam," I said.

He exited my apartment without saying one word. I closed the door and walked over to Jack.

"I'm sorry, Linzie. I think I destroyed any hope of Adam's publishing house taking on your work. I have to say, though, that he was acting like a jealous lover. Was this really a business meeting tonight or was it a date?"

I looked into Jack's eyes and said, "I was never really sure what tonight was meant to be. I am certain of one thing, though."

"What's that?"

I smiled and said, "That we should take Adam's advice and toast our one-week anniversary."

Jack rose from the sofa, kissed me on the cheek, and said, "I'm all for that. Let's go open that bottle of wine."

Chapter Twelve

On January 26, the ghostwriter agreement that Mrs. Cranshaw's lawyer had drawn up arrived in my mail. It was accompanied by a note from Mrs. Cranshaw. In it, she expressed her hope that Kevin was improving. I was touched by her note and responded to it with a note of my own, in which I thanked Mrs. Cranshaw for her concern. Unfortunately, I was not able to pass along any good news to her about Kevin. He was still in a coma, and his situation continued to be touch and go.

Upon my receipt of the ghostwriter agreement, Jack phoned George to inform him that I was in possession of the agreement, which George had graciously offered to review for me. The brothers decided that Wednesday, January 31, would be a good day for Jack to drive me to Gloucester to meet with George at his home. George insisted that Jack's and my visit with him be just as much a social one as a business one. He invited us to join him for lunch at his place. We accepted his invitation.

At 10:30 a.m. on Wednesday morning, Jack pulled into the circular driveway in front of George's residence, which was a large white brick two-story house with black shutters.

It was such an impressive-looking home that I turned to Jack and said, "I would say this place is a mansion."

Jack nodded and said, "As I told you, Linzie, one of my parents' kids got all the brains. I was not that kid."

I laughed and said, "Judging from the looks of this property, George must have done something right. He has obviously been quite successful."

"He is a very smart guy," Jack commented. "Not all of his money came from his job, though. He is a whiz when it comes to choosing the right investments."

"The front of the house is so pretty," I remarked.

"Wait till you see the back of the house. There are sliding doors in the living room that lead outside to a huge elevated patio. Sit on that patio and you will be enjoying a spectacular view of Gloucester Harbor. Walk down the patio stairs towards the water and you will find yourself heading for the dock that George had built for his cabin cruiser."

"Is it difficult for George to keep such a big place under control?" I asked.

"No. He has a crew of workers who take care of just about everything here. The one chore he reserves for himself is cooking. He is practically a gourmet chef. When he asked us to have lunch here today, I suspected that he wanted to show off his culinary skills."

"In any case," I said, "it was nice of him to ask us to dine with him."

Jack laughed and said, "Oh, my big brother is nice, for sure, but is also a bit of a ham."

"Are you sure there isn't just a touch of sibling rivalry going on between you two?"

"Not even a touch, Linzie. George has worked very hard to attain success. I'm quite proud of him."

"I'm sure he is proud of you too, Jack."

"I believe so. When I got shot, George was beside himself and never stopped praising me for my courage to be a cop. He stayed at a hotel near the hospital until it was certain that I was on the mend. Well, enough about that. We better get out of the car and head for the front door."

Jack got out of the driver's seat and walked to the passenger side of the car to open the door for me. His courtesy brought to mind my date with Adam Proctor, a date I was trying hard to forget. After I exited the car, Jack and I began to follow the granite walkway that led to the front door. The closer we came to the door, the more uptight I felt. The grandeur of George's property had taken me by surprise, and I worried that I would feel out of place in such an environment. When Jack rang the doorbell, I fully expected that a maid would greet us at the door. That expectation proved to be unfounded when the door was opened by a gentleman, who was neatly dressed in casual clothes.

"Hello, little bro," the gentleman said laughing. "Come on in."

After we crossed the threshold, Jack said, "George, I want you to meet Linzie Cole, my friend and fellow tenant."

"It is so nice to meet you, Linzie," George said as he shook my hand. "Jack has told me so much about you that an introduction barely seems necessary."

I smiled and said, "I guess I could say the same. Jack talks about you all the time."

George laughed and said, "If what Jack told you about me is nasty, just let me know. I'll tell Mother, and she will quickly straighten him out."

George's sense of humor was so akin to Jack's that the uptight feeling I had been experiencing quickly vanished. There was also somewhat of a physical resemblance between the two brothers, which put me at ease with George. George's dark-blue eyes were dead ringers for Jack's, and just as Jack's, they twinkled when he laughed. Although George was a little leaner and a bit taller than Jack, and although his hair was brown as opposed to Jack's white hair, one could easily assume, based on appearance, that they were brothers.

"Let me take your coat, Linzie," George said. "I'll hang it in the closet here."

"Thanks," I said as I allowed him to help me remove my coat.

"I don't see anyone helping me with my coat," Jack whined comically.

"Oh, Jack, you're such a girl," George said in an equally amusing tone of voice.

"George, you have an impressive piece of property here," I said.

"Thanks, Linzie. You'll have to come back here in the spring. This time of year doesn't do the beauty of the grounds justice. Come when the shrubs and the flowers are in bloom and when the snow is not hiding the fountain and the statues that are on the section of the lawn enclosed by the circular driveway. When it comes to the statues, you will see everything from sea creatures to sea captains."

"Linzie, when you come back, you truly will see an aquatic fairyland," Jack remarked.

"I'll look forward to it," I said.

"Today," George said, "I can at least give you a decent tour of the interior of the house. Before I show you around, let's get the business of the day behind us first. We'll go upstairs to the library, and I'll review the ghostwriter agreement. Follow me."

Beyond the front door was a large circular vestibule. Hanging on its white walls were six oil paintings of maritime scenes. The navy-blue tile floor contributed to the nautical ambiance of the vestibule. Towards the back of the vestibule was a spiral staircase that led to the second floor.

Jack and I followed George up the spiral staircase and into the library, which was located at the end of a long corridor. The bookcases in that room were chock-full of law books, the sight of which made me realize how challenging a lawyer's job is. As George stood behind the large cherry wood desk, I took the agreement out of my pocketbook and handed it to him.

"Linzie, please take a seat over there," George said as he pointed to the brown leather sofa that faced his desk.

As soon as I sat down, George sat in the swivel chair behind the desk.

"Maybe I should leave and let you two discuss the agreement privately," Jack said. "I can watch television or—"

"Please stay, Jack," I interrupted. "I really want you to stay."

"Is that okay with you, George?" Jack asked.

"Oh, I guess so, if you promise not to cause a rumpus," George said with a grin on his face.

"I promise not to say a word," Jack said as he cupped his hand over his mouth and took a seat next to me on the sofa.

While George read the agreement, I fixed my eyes on the tropical fish that were swimming in the large aquarium that was situated in a corner of the room diagonally across from me. Watching the fish was an attempt on my part to try to relax. I was nervous as to how George would react to the agreement. I realized only too well that Mrs. Cranshaw's offer might be my only salvation when it came to my writing business, and I could only hope that George would find the agreement to be fair and satisfactory. Otherwise, I would have to face the growing possibility that my retirement from writing was in my not-too-distant future.

After George studied the agreement, he laid it on the desk. Then he looked at me and proceeded to ask me a few questions about my writing experience and my sales history. He took everything into consideration and reached the conclusion that the agreement was fair. Believing that Mrs. Cranshaw's offer to hire me as her ghostwriter was a terrific opportunity for me, George urged me to accept the terms of the agreement. He pointed out that Mrs. Cranshaw or I could terminate my services at any time and if termination should occur, I would be compensated for any work I performed up to that point. The fact that there was an escape clause in the agreement made me feel a lot more receptive to signing it, which I proceeded to do right then and there.

George rose from his chair and said, "I'll take care of sending the agreement back to Mrs. Cranshaw's lawyer."

"Thank you, George," I said. "I appreciate your help."

"It is my pleasure," George said. "Feel free to call on

me anytime you need some guidance in legal matters. I truly mean that, Linzie. Now, let's get down to serious business. I promised you a tour of the house, and I never go back on my word to a pretty lady. I'll do my best to be a gracious tour guide. Since we're on the second floor, I'll start the tour with the upstairs rooms."

As I would soon discover, there seemed to be no end to the rooms on the upper floor. In addition to the library, the upper floor was home to a barroom, a billiard room, an entertainment room, and a gym. The tour of the first floor was no less spectacular. On one end of that floor was a master bedroom suite that boasted elegant furniture fit for a king. Situated on the other end of the first floor were guest quarters. Located between the master bedroom suite and the guest quarters were a kitchen, a living room, and a dining room. The kitchen was roomy and modern and provided every convenience imaginable, including a laundry area. The dining room and the living room were of considerable size and tastefully decorated in earth tone colors. On the walls of those two rooms hung original oil paintings of European scenes that George had purchased during one of his many trips abroad. During his last trip, in the spring of 2016, George spent some time in Paris, where he met a renowned interior decorator. George asked the decorator if he would be willing to come to Gloucester and redecorate every room in his house. The decorator accepted the challenge and was given the use of the guest quarters while he meticulously gave each and every room a fresh and attractive appearance. I suddenly felt great sympathy for Jack, who was relying on unprofessional me to help him decorate his humble apartment.

Upon completion of the tour, our gracious guide asked, "How does a glass of wine sound to you two?"

"Oh, I don't know about a glass of wine for the two of us," Jack said laughing. "Can't you be generous, George, and offer each one of us a glass? After all, Linzie is a connoisseur of wines. She deserves a glass all to herself."

George folded his arms across his chest and muttered, "Very funny, Jack, very funny."

I grinned and said, "I don't claim to be an authority on wines. I just know that I haven't tasted a wine yet that I disliked."

Jack winked and said, "Any kind is her favorite. She drinks anything and everything."

"George, your brother is quite the kidder. Don't believe a word he says."

"Not to worry, Linzie. Don't forget. I grew up with this guy."

"Is it true he was born a clown and eventually joined the circus?" I asked while trying to keep a straight face.

George roared and replied, "I don't recall that he actually joined the circus, but I think there were times when my parents would have gladly encouraged him to follow that route. He would have been right in his element."

With a rather witty look on his face, Jack said, "George, please stop clowning around. Where is that wine you promised us?"

"We'll have to go back up the staircase and head for the barroom," George said.

"Brace yourself, Linzie, for another two-mile hike," Jack said with a lilt in his voice.

"Linzie," George said, "I'm beginning to think that Jack should leave the police force and fulfill his childhood calling to join the circus."

"Those are my thoughts too," I said giggling.

We ascended the spiral staircase, turned left, and began to follow the red carpet that led to the barroom.

"Tell me something, Linzie," George said as he walked beside me. "Do you think that it is crazy for a bachelor like me to live in a large house like this?"

"Oh," I replied, "I don't think it is my place to give you any advice on that issue. What's good for one person may not be good for another."

"Wise answer," George said, nodding his head approvingly. "I sometimes think—"

"If you're finding this place to be too big, George," Jack interrupted, "I can solve that problem for you. I'll gladly reside in half the house. My ride to work will be longer, but I'll make that sacrifice."

"If I ever get so desperate that I want you to be my housemate, Jack, I'll let you know," George said kiddingly. "In the meantime, don't hold your breath on that one."

We entered the barroom. With its red tile floor, black leather furniture, and dark wood walls, it was quite cozy. Adding to its homey ambiance were the photographs hanging on the walls, all of which were related to one activity—fishing.

"Please take a seat, Linzie," George said. "I know you don't claim to be a connoisseur of wines, so let me try to match your taste buds to the right wine. Do you prefer red or white today?"

"White sounds good," I replied.

"Sweet or not so sweet?"

"Not so sweet."

"Pinot grigio might be a good choice for you," George said. "If not, we can try another kind of wine. And how about you, Jack?"

"Pinot grigio sounds good to me."

George walked behind the bar to remove a bottle from the wine rack while Jack took a seat next to me on the sofa that faced the bar.

"Based on the photos on the walls," I said, "I think it is safe for me to assume that you are quite a fisherman, George."

"I am a fisherman, sometimes a good one and sometimes not so good. Have you ever gone fishing, Linzie?"

"Yes, a few times. When I was a child, my parents rented a cottage on Cape Cod one summer. My dad and I used to try our luck fishing at various spots on the Cape."

"How would you like to go out fishing on my boat sometime?"

"Sure," I replied. "I won't know what I'm doing, but I'm willing to give fishing another try."

"I can teach you the basics in no time," George said.

Jack pointed to the large barracuda that was mounted on the wall to our right and said, "Just think, Linzie, if that big guy had won the tug-of-war with George, George might still be swimming in the ocean somewhere, trying to find his way back home."

I laughed and said, "I'm certainly glad he won the battle."

George looked up from the bottle of wine he was in the process of opening and said, "I, too, am glad I won the battle. Otherwise, I never would have had the chance to meet you, Linzie."

I suddenly felt like a shy schoolgirl who had just been told by one of the boys in her class that he had a crush on her. I suspected that my cheeks were going to turn as red as the red tile beneath my feet. Jack came to my rescue when he attracted everyone's attention to the ship model that was on one of the glass shelves behind the bar.

"I want you to know, Linzie, that George spent countless hours on that ship model that is on the glass shelf behind his head."

I was grateful that George's eyes were no longer on me. He had turned around to look at the model.

"That is a model of *Flying Cloud*, a beauty of a clipper ship," George commented.

"I imagine you need a good deal of patience for a project like that," I said.

"Yes, it does require patience," George agreed, "but I enjoyed every minute of working on that model. If my law practice did not keep me so busy, I believe I would have a roomful of ships to show you. I've been in love with boats since I was a boy."

"Was a career in the navy something you ever considered?" I asked.

"Yes. I actually looked into such a career, but my analytical mind steered me in a different direction—to the study of law. Also, my grandfather on my mother's side of the family was a lawyer, and he encouraged me to go for a law degree."

"Your mother must be quite proud of you two," I commented. "You both have done so well in your chosen careers."

Laughing, George said, "I think Mom is at least relieved that Jack did not join the circus. She managed to talk him out of it."

"She sounds like a remarkable woman," I said with a chuckle. "I hope to meet her someday."

"I'll make sure you get the chance to meet Mom," George remarked as he removed two wine glasses from a shelf behind him. "Are you usually free on Sundays?"

"Usually," I replied.

"Good. I'll make plans to pick Mom up on some Sunday in the near future. Then I'll swing by your place and pick you up. We can all go out to eat."

"Excuse me, George," Jack piped up. "I certainly hope I am included in the 'all' that you just mentioned. It has been my intention to introduce Linzie to Mom."

Jack's reaction to George's invitation made me uncomfortable. It was obvious that Jack was no longer in a comical mood. He truly felt slighted that George had not explicitly included him in his invitation. Not knowing what to say, I remained quiet.

George rather sheepishly said to Jack, "Now, why would you think that you were being left out?"

"I guess because you made no mention of my coming," Jack replied.

George was tongue-tied for a moment. He cleared his throat before speaking.

"I suppose, Jack, you were right to take offense. I apologize."

George poured the wine into the two glasses. Then he walked over to the oval table in front of the sofa and placed the glasses on top of it.

"I better leave you two for a while," George said, "so that I can get lunch on the table."

He exited the barroom. I suddenly felt awkward being alone with Jack because of that moment of unpleasantness that the two brothers had just experienced. Not knowing what to say to Jack, I prayed that he would initiate some conversation. It appeared that Jack did not know what to say either because he remained quiet for a minute or so.

Finally, he said, "I know you must have felt uneasy a little while ago, Linzie. I'm sorry. It would have been better if I had talked to George privately about that invitation, which, I truly believe, excluded me. I think he is quite smitten with you. I can't say I blame him. You are an attractive, kind person, and I must tell you that even though you and I recently met, I have developed some special feelings for you. Forgive me for saying that so soon in our relationship, but if I don't make my feelings known, I'm afraid George will try to fill a spot in your life that I want to fill. Am I scaring you, Linzie, with all my chatter?"

I was not scared, but I was taken by surprise by Jack's revelation of his feelings for me. So much had happened to me emotionally due to my failed relationship with Kevin that I had not attempted to put a label on the type of relationship I was enjoying with Jack. Without a doubt, I had very warm feelings for him and truly appreciated all the efforts he had made to protect me. The moments I had spent with him were moments that brought me happiness and peace. Yet, I knew I was simply not ready to even think of giving my heart to another man so soon after Kevin. I proceeded to try to verbalize those feelings to Jack with the hope that I would not offend him.

"Jack, you are very special to me, but I must admit that I am not ready to commit myself to anyone right now. I'm still reeling from all the commotion that Kevin caused me. What also concerns me is that you are letting the feelings you suspect George has for me hurry you in your thinking. We need to take our time and get to know each other well. As time goes on, you may even discover things about me that you will not like."

He looked at me lovingly and said, "I doubt that there is anything about you that I won't love. When I lost my wife, I never believed that I would be attracted to another woman. You have certainly changed my view on that. Let me just say that it was not my intention to rush you in any way, but George's behavior forced me to tell you how I feel about you. I am willing to go as slowly as you like when it comes to our relationship. Please know that I am fully sympathetic about the hurt you still feel due to your breakup with Kevin."

Too emotional to speak, all I could do was squeeze Jack's hand. He gave me a kiss on the cheek, picked up one of the glasses in front of us, and handed it to me. Then he picked up the other glass, clicked it against mine, and said, "To us."

"To us," I said.

It was quite ironic that in a matter of twenty minutes or so, the words *to us* would once again reach my ears. As George, Jack, and I sat at the dining room table, it would be George who would say those words as he clicked my glass and Jack's glass with the glass he held in his own hand. What George would say immediately after the clicking would lead me to believe that he was feeling guilty over the invitation incident that had clearly annoyed Jack.

"Jack," he said, "I want you to understand that *to us* includes you."

Jack made no comment. He merely raised the glass to his lips and took a sip.

There was tension in the room during the meal. Jack was in a melancholic mood and had little to say. George made more of an attempt to converse, but it was clear that he, too, was no longer feeling chipper. I tried to ease the tension by complimenting George on the dinner he had prepared, which was duck with orange sauce accompanied by a medley of fresh vegetables. In an attempt to get Jack to join in the conversation, I brought up a number of general topics, but not one of those topics elicited much of a response from Jack.

When we finished the dessert—peach cobbler—Jack announced that it was time for us to go. George retrieved our coats from the closet. While I expressed my thanks to George, Jack said a quick goodbye to him, exited the house, and waited for me outside.

I left George's house with a heavy heart, for I could not help but feel that I had quite innocently created friction between the two brothers. That was the last thing I had ever wanted to do, for they were both such fine men.

Chapter Thirteen

Upon arising at 7:15 a.m. on May 31, 2018, I headed for the kitchen to gaze out the window. What a relief it was to realize that the nasty winter months were now ancient history! A green carpet of grass had replaced the white blanket of snow that had been so reluctant to leave. The shrubs and flowers were in bloom, birds were chirping to their hearts' content, and the warmth of the spring season was something I was truly relishing.

My kind thoughts about spring were interrupted by the ringing of my landline phone. I exited the kitchen and walked to the living room to peek at the caller ID screen, which displayed Harri's name. Eager to talk to her, I immediately picked up the phone.

"Hi, Harri," I said in a fairly strong voice that defied the early morning hour.

"Hi, Linzie. I hope I'm not calling too early, but I was anxious to learn how things are going. Are you up to your neck with packing and what not?"

"It has been a busy week, but things are under control," I replied as I sat down on the sofa. "I was going to call you before I leave for Rockport on June second."

"I was sure of that, dear. I just wanted to tell you how much Rudolf and I are going to miss you. Sometime during your stay in Rockport, we'll try to break away from Harrud's and spend a day with you."

"That would be wonderful." With a hint of a laugh, I

then added, "Who knows? I may be back here sooner than planned. There's always the possibility that Mrs. Cranshaw will dismiss me in the blink of an eye."

"As much as I'm going to miss you, Linzie, I do not wish for that to happen. This ghostwriting job is a godsend to you. It will give you the financial cushion you so desperately need."

"That's true, Harri."

"I have a feeling that another opportunity will soon come knocking at your door."

"How so?" I asked.

"My hunch is that Adam Proctor will eventually call you. I bet he read your three books. If I am right, he cannot help but realize that you produce quality work. It would be to his benefit to strike a publishing deal with you."

"Oh, Harri, I don't think I'm going to hear from Adam. Almost five months have gone by since he stormed out of my apartment because he saw Jack sleeping on my sofa."

"Give him time, Linzie. My judgement of Adam as a person is still quite positive. Adam was probably so frustrated with his former girlfriend that he took his anger out on you. I think it is possible that his ex-girlfriend had a roving eye. If she did and Adam was aware of that roving eye, it might explain why he got mad when he saw Jack in your apartment. Adam probably assumed that you, too, have a roving eye. In any case, when you went out with Adam back in January, I believe he needed more time to heal. I still believe he is a good catch for you."

"It is obvious that Adam was badly hurt by that woman," I remarked. "Jack's presence in my apartment that night was such an innocent thing, but Adam chose to read too much into the situation. The thing is, Harri, since that night of my date with Adam, my relationship with Jack has, in fact, blossomed into something quite special."

"I have never met Jack, so I won't make any comments about him. My advice is not to write Adam off just yet. He has many good qualities, and when it comes to your careers, you certainly have a lot in common."

"Jack, too, has many good qualities. One of those qualities is patience. The darker side of Kevin's personality took me by such surprise that I just want to let my relationship with Jack proceed at a comfortable pace. Jack has been fully supportive of my feeling about that."

"I tried to warn you, Linzie, that Kevin was all wrong for you. Have you received any more news about his condition?"

"Yes. Kevin's sister keeps me informed about his progress. As you know, Kevin came out of the coma four weeks after the accident. According to his sister, who called me two nights ago, Kevin still has an uphill battle in front of him. Due to the severe injuries to his legs, there is still a good deal of rehabilitation in store for him. With the help of therapists, he is currently able to get on his feet and take a limited number of steps."

There was a pause on the other end, and then Harri said, "I don't mean to sound cruel, but if and when he is able to take a lot more steps, I hope those steps won't be heading in your direction."

"Do not worry, Harri. I have no intention of renewing a relationship with Kevin. I wish him a good recovery, but if he tries to come near me, I'll have to send him walking in a different direction."

"Did Kevin's sister ever talk to you about the engagement ring that was found in Kevin's pocket the night he was rushed to the hospital?"

"Yes. She told me that Kevin confided to her that the ring was meant for me and that it had been his intention to propose to me on that stormy night."

My voice shook when I said those last few words. Neither Harri nor I spoke for a moment. I was grateful that it was Harri who would continue the conversation.

"Linzie, do not feel guilty about what happened to Kevin. You tried to nicely end your relationship with him, but he simply would not abide by your decision. What happened on the night of January fourth was not your fault. My big worry is that Kevin is going to prey on your sympathetic nature in the hope that he can re-enter your life."

"I understand what you're saying, Harri. I truly believe that the sense of guilt I had over the accident is gone. Jack, as a cop and as a companion, has helped me to overcome my guilty feeling. Nevertheless, I cannot help but feel bad for Kevin."

"Keep following Jack's advice, Linzie. I wish Kevin no harm, but I also wish him to be nowhere near you. I hope you did not tell his sister that you are going to be living in Rockport for the next three months."

"No, I did not."

"Good girl."

"That's one big plus about my three-month absence from here. If Kevin becomes physically able to come to my door, I won't be here to face him."

"That ghostwriting job may be a godsend in more than one way, Linzie. Well, dear, I'll give you a call when Rudolf and I can spend a day with you. In the meantime, call me if you want to chat. Good luck with everything."

"Thanks, Harri. Bye."

"Bye, dear."

When I hung up the phone, I had mixed feelings about leaving my apartment for three months. Going to Harrud's, where I could enjoy a good lunch and the company of Harri and Rudolf, would not be feasible until September, which suddenly seemed centuries away. Then, too, the thought of not being in the same house as Jack was a sobering one for me. Although he promised to come to Rockport to visit me as often as possible, I knew I would miss seeing him each and every day.

With Jack very much in my thoughts, I exited the living room to return to the kitchen. The coffee pot on the counter was faithfully waiting to perform its perking duty. The day was warm and sunny, so the thought of enjoying my coffee out on the second-floor balcony grew increasingly appealing. As I plugged in the coffee pot, my cell phone rang. It was Jack.

"Top of the morning, Ms. Linzie," he attempted to say with an Irish accent.

"Top of the morning to you too, Mr. Jack. Unless you took a plane to Ireland after you left here last night, I assume you are somewhere in these parts."

"That I am, my sweet colleen. In fact, I'm still in my apartment. I don't have to be at the station until nine o'clock this morning. My taste buds were wondering if they could come upstairs and enjoy one of your great cups of coffee."

"Of course, they can come up. You're welcome to come too," I said giggling. "The coffee is perking right now, and I thought I would enjoy drinking it out on the balcony this morning. How does that sound?"

"Super. I'll be there in fifteen minutes, okay?"

"Okay."

As the coffee continued to perk, I hurried into the bathroom to comb my hair and put on some decent-looking clothes. Then I rushed back into the kitchen, took two coffee mugs out of the cupboard, and placed them on the counter. Before I had a chance to search the refrigerator for a suitable morning snack, I heard Jack's unique knock at the door. I walked to the foyer, looked through the peephole, and opened the door. Jack was standing there with a box in his hands. He handed me the box and then kissed me tenderly on the lips.

"This is a nice surprise," I said. "Until you phoned me a little while ago, I did not expect to see you until tonight, and I certainly did not expect to see you arrive here bearing a gift."

"It's an edible gift," Jack said, "and based on our eating habits, I believe it will be gone in no time."

I raised the lid of the box and discovered that Jack's gift was a delicious-looking Danish coffee cake.

"Thank you, Jack. This cake is so big, it's going to take us more than one morning to eat it all. You'll have to help me finish it off tomorrow morning."

"I want to spend every possible minute with you I can,"

he commented. "Before you know it, Saturday will be here, and I'll be dropping you off at Mrs. Cranshaw's cottage. I'm dreading that moment."

"I'm dreading it too. I'm afraid that the next three months will prove to be the longest in my life."

"I'm going to spend as many weekends as I possibly can at George's place so that I can be just a hop, skip, and a jump away from you, Linzie."

I was grateful that I could breathe a sigh of relief when it came to the relationship between Jack and George. The visit Jack and I had paid to George's home in January had caused an unusual strain between the two brothers, and I knew I had been the cause—the innocent cause—of that strain. Fortunately, the brothers had a heart-to-heart talk a week after Jack's and my visit to George's house and were able to repair their strained relationship. Jack willingly shared with me what he and George discussed in their heart-to-heart talk. What I learned was that George had admitted to Jack that he had been attracted to me and that in order to get to know me better, he had extended the invitation to me to have lunch with him and his mother. George also admitted that Jack was quite right when Jack assumed that he was not included in the invitation. Jack, in no uncertain terms, explained to George that his feeling for me surpassed that of a mere friendship. Once George understood that, he apologized profusely to Jack for overstepping his bounds. So, by talking things through, the rough waters between the two men had been calmed. In fact, George still insisted that Jack and I enjoy the boat with him during Jack's stays in Gloucester.

"Let's go into the kitchen, Jack. There's a mug for you on the counter. While I'm cutting the coffee cake, pour yourself some coffee."

As Jack followed me into the kitchen, I said, "It's a gorgeous day, perfect for sitting out on the balcony."

"Ah, that balcony," Jack said with a sigh. "For the next three months, I'm not going to be able to sit out there with you and gaze at the stars while we sip wine."

"Now cheer up," I said. "You can use the balcony while I'm gone."

"Linzie, I want no part of that balcony while you're gone. The stars and wine mean nothing to me if I can't enjoy them with you. He comically wiped his forehead with the back of his right hand and said, "I just don't think I'm going to survive here while you're in Rockport."

"Well, you better survive. The police force needs you," I said smiling.

"And I need you," he said in a tone of voice that was suddenly no longer of a jesting sort.

I quickly looked away from him and said, "I better go get the key to the deadbolt so that we can enjoy the balcony before another winter sets in."

Before I could move one inch, Jack stepped squarely in front of me and placed his hands on my shoulders. He looked as though he wanted to say something but was hesitating to do so.

Finally, he said, "Would you forget about the key for a moment, Linzie? I want to talk about us."

I nodded nervously. He looked straight into my eyes before continuing.

"We have been taking our time with this relationship, and I can certainly understand your feelings for wanting to go slowly. Kevin did a job on you emotionally. I would, however, like to hear you say that there is a good chance that our relationship will develop into something permanent. I love you, Linzie, and cannot imagine my life without you."

I was speechless. What Jack had just said was too much for me to digest at that moment. I felt as though I already had too much on my plate. The very thought of leaving my apartment for three months to live with a woman whose behavior might prove to be difficult and volatile was, in my mind, challenging enough. I did not want to try to shape my future beyond the three months that were immediately ahead of me.

Flustered, I said, "You're going to have to be patient with me right now, Jack. Too much is coming at me too quickly."

He kept his hands on my shoulders. A troubled look appeared on his face.

"Linzie, do you love me?"

Suddenly, I thought of Kevin, who had never been able to freely say the words *I love you* to me. I could certainly commiserate with Jack. I had so desperately wanted to hear those three words from Kevin, and now Jack wanted to hear those three words from me.

In a weak voice, I replied, "Of course, I love you, Jack. I just don't think this is the right time to talk about our future. My life is in a state of flux right now."

He released his hands from my shoulders and asked, "Are you still in love with Kevin?"

My cheeks turned red. I was not sure if it was anger or embarrassment that caused me to blush.

"Absolutely not," I blurted out. "How can you possibly think that?"

"I don't want to think that, Linzie. All I want to think is that we truly love one another and that our love will move us beyond the lifestyle we share now."

"Jack, do we have to talk about our future at this very moment when the thought of just the next three months is nerve-racking enough for me? You promised me you would not hurry me when it came to our relationship."

He folded his arms across his chest and looked down towards the floor. The silence that ensued was uncomfortable for both of us. Though it lasted only a short time, it seemed to last an eternity.

"I'm sorry, Linzie," Jack said as he kept his eyes fixed on the floor. "I should not have pushed you. You have enough to contend with right now."

"Please don't apologize. I understand where you are coming from. I've been there myself."

"I do think, though, that it is better if I go along," he said. "There are a few things I need to handle at the station. Getting there a little early can do no harm."

Quite distraught, all I could say was, "Will you call me later?"

He finally looked into my eyes, nodded, and then headed for the door. I followed him. Without saying a word, he opened the door and left.

Jack's sudden departure from my apartment upset me. As I tackled various chores that day, my mind was in a battle with itself, entertaining two opposing points of view in regard to my relationship with Jack. On one hand, I could not help but feel that I had exhibited the same noncommittal behavior that had been so typical of Kevin during the two years of our dating. I could understand Jack's obvious disappointment in my noncommittal stance on his and my future. On the other hand, I felt quite justified in telling Jack that I needed more time before I could make a decision about committing my future to him. After all, Kevin had strung me along for two years, and Jack and I had known each other for only five months. I rationalized that I had in no way been stringing Jack along; I was simply being cautious. As my mind tortured itself with those opposing points of view, I became emotionally weary. Finally, I decided that the battle within myself must come to an end and that whatever was meant to be between Jack and me would simply be. I could only hope that he could find it in his heart to continue to be patient with me.

Jack was supposed to phone me at 6:00 p.m. that evening. We had planned to order Chinese food and then watch television. When 6:20 p.m. arrived and no phone call from him had come, I decided to call him. He did not answer right away. His phone rang about eight times before he picked up.

"Hello," he said in a groggy tone of voice.

"Jack? Is that you?"

He said, "Hi, Linzie. Yes, it is me."

"You don't sound like yourself. Are you all right?"

"No. I've had a terrible headache all day. I got home around five o'clock and put my head down. I guess I fell into a deep sleep. What time is it?"

"It is twenty past six. I was concerned because I was expecting a call from you at six. You are always so punctual."

"Never say 'always,' " he said with a chuckle that sounded forced. "What one expects does not always turn out to be."

There was not a doubt in my mind that he was referring to his disappointment that stemmed from my hesitation to commit to the future he had anticipated for us. At that moment, I had a choice to ignore what he had just said or to face it head on. I decided to ignore it.

"So, are you still planning to come upstairs for Chinese food? I have not phoned in an order yet."

"It may be better if I don't come tonight, Linzie. I want to stay in bed and try to get more sleep. Hopefully, this headache will take a hike soon. I usually don't get them this badly."

I had looked forward to spending the evening with Jack. The news that he would not be joining me for dinner was a real letdown for me. I decided to ask him a point-blank question.

"Jack, are you upset because of the discussion we had this morning?"

"Linzie, don't give that brief moment of tension between us a second thought. I was being too pushy, and once again, I apologize."

"I not only gave that moment of tension between us a second thought," I said, "I gave it countless thoughts throughout the day. I want you to know that you mean the world to me. I just cannot commit myself to anything permanent right now."

"Linzie, I understand, and I promise that I'll never rush you on that matter again."

"Will you reconsider coming upstairs tonight, Jack? After tonight, I have just one more night here in the apartment till September."

"I'm feeling so lousy that I'm sure I would be awful company tonight. I tell you what. Why don't we plan to order the Chinese food tomorrow night? I'll bring a bottle of pinot grigio, which seems to have become your favorite wine."

The fact that Jack seemed eager to come the following evening gave me a sense of assurance that our relationship would once again be on an even keel.

"Okay, let's plan on tomorrow night. I'll miss you tonight, Jack. Please let me know if you need anything."

"Will do, Linzie. I'll call you when I get home from work tomorrow. It will be around five o'clock."

"Okay, Jack. Bye."

"Bye."

After hanging up the phone, I made my way to the kitchen. The thought of not seeing Jack that night had soured my appetite, so I decided to delay having dinner. There was a bottle of white wine sitting on the counter. Using my trusty corkscrew, I opened it. Then I poured myself a generous glass of wine. Due to the strained conversation between Jack and me early that morning, I had abandoned my plan to sit out on the balcony. Now seemed like a good time to execute that plan. After unlocking the kitchen door that led to the balcony, I stepped onto the balcony and headed for one of the two lounge chairs that faced the backyard. My wine glass was filled to the brim, so I carefully lowered my body onto the chair.

Although I lived in a highly populated area, the tall evergreen trees planted around the perimeter of the backyard gave me the feeling that I was living in the country. Sitting on the balcony was a favorite activity of mine, for it gave me the opportunity to communicate with nature. I particularly enjoyed watching the many kinds of birds that made use of the bird bath that was situated in the center of the backyard. As I sat sipping my wine that evening, I soon had company. A male and a female cardinal stopped by to take a rather prolonged bath. It was fascinating to watch them as they splashed about in the water. Being outside and enjoying the beauty of nature was doing wonders for my psyche. There was suddenly a feeling inside of me that both my personal life and my professional life were going to turn out just fine.

About half an hour after my arrival on the balcony, I discovered that the backyard was about to be enjoyed by not only me and my feathered friends but also by two other people. Directly below my balcony was a patio of equal size, the use of which was intended for the occupant of the first-floor apartment. I quickly recognized Jack's voice. There was a female voice, too, that was reaching my eardrums. The female voice was on the loud side. Although Jack was speaking more softly than the woman, I was able to hear every word he was saying. Their discussion revolved around using the gas grill to cook hamburgers.

"I'm going to pull the grill away from the house and put it over here," the woman said.

I heard Jack say, "I'll do it."

"No. You sit right there. Men are meant to be pampered."

I rolled my eyes. Then I heard a few squeaks from the wheels of the grill as it was being pulled across the cement patio floor.

"How do you want your hamburger cooked?" the woman asked.

"Medium rare," Jack replied.

There was a lull in the conversation, which I assumed was due to the woman's focusing on getting the grill started. She obviously succeeded, for in a matter of minutes, the aroma of the hamburgers cooking on the grill reached my nostrils.

"Well, the grill seems to be doing its job," she said. "Honey, will you keep an eye on the burgers? I have to go out to the car and get the potato salad and coleslaw I made."

"Yes, I'll keep an eye on the burgers."

"Good. How about wine? Do you have a bottle of white?"

"Yes," Jack replied. "There is a bottle of white wine in

the fridge. When you come back, I'll go inside and open it."

"Honey" was soon alone, for there was silence. How I wanted to break that silence by leaning over my balcony railing and telling him off! I was livid. The one man I thought I could always trust—the one who had professed his love for me that very day—was seeing another woman behind my back! He was just another Kevin. How stupid of Jack to invite that woman to his place when I lived right upstairs! It made no sense, but then again, I was coming to the conclusion that men were never going to make any sense to me.

A few minutes later, the woman returned to the patio. I could hear the rattling of dishes.

"I'll go open the wine," Jack said.

"When you come back, bring a towel with you," the woman said in a rather demanding tone of voice. "The table is dirty."

Jack mumbled something and then apparently went into his apartment. During his absence, the woman obviously plugged a radio into an outdoor electrical outlet, for the chirping of the birds was now drowned out by the sound of jazz music.

Upon Jack's return to the patio, he said a few words, but I could not make them out due to the music. The woman's voice was still coming through loud and clear. I could hear every word she was saying.

"This wine is so good. What kind is it?" she asked.

I heard the words *pinot grigio* come out of Jack's mouth. That really irritated me. How dare he serve my favorite wine to that woman!

"Jack, let me know when you're planning to go to Gloucester because I want to go out on George's boat," the woman said. "Maybe George will let me stay overnight at his place so that you and I can spend two days together."

The only words I could make out of Jack's response were *not sure*.

Then I heard the woman say, "Oh, honey, let's make it

happen. It would be so great."

That was all I could take. I gulped what was left in my wine glass and hurriedly went inside my apartment. My thoughts about men were not terribly complimentary at that moment. I realized that my instinct to take my relationship with Jack at a slow pace had been quite wise.

Upon entering the kitchen, I poured myself a second glass of wine, which was just as generous as the first glass I had consumed. For the next fifteen minutes, I roamed around my apartment with the glass in my hand, all the while taking gulps of wine, not my usual ladylike sips. As I wandered aimlessly from one room to another, my thoughts ran wild and questions filled my head. I found myself doubting that Jack had suffered from any headache that day. Had Jack invited that woman to his place out of vindictiveness because I had been so noncommittal that morning? Was he trying to make me jealous, or was he simply giving up hope for any solid future with me? Then my thoughts drifted to George, who had struck me as being such a kind and caring gentleman. Would George have been a better match for me? Thanks to Jack who had blocked George's attempt to get to know me better, I would never have an answer to that question. My mind was in such an uproar that I knew I had to calm down. I sat on the sofa to try to get a hold of myself.

Whether I regained complete control over my emotions was questionable. I did, however, regain enough control to come to the conclusion that I must eat. Since Jack was enjoying a dinner with that brazen woman, I saw no point in denying myself a decent meal. I picked up the phone and ordered some Chinese food to be delivered to my apartment. I did not know when I would be eating Chinese food again. All I knew was that I would not be eating it the following evening as I had planned and that never again would I be eating it with that Casanova who occupied the first-floor apartment!

Within forty minutes of phoning in my order for Chinese food, a polite teenager was at the front door, holding a brown paper bag that contained my meal. After I paid him, he handed me the bag and said, "Enjoy."

As I ascended the staircase, I had serious doubts that I could really enjoy the meal. I did, however, realize that I must eat in order to keep up my strength. The temporary move to Rockport was, I feared, going to be a bumpy transition for me. I had to retain my good health in order to deal with all the bumps that might come my way.

To make the meal as appealing as possible, I set the dining room table and turned the chandelier lights on. I even turned the radio on and set the dial to a station that was playing instrumental music. After filling my plate with food, I poured myself half a glass of wine. I cannot say that I savored every bite of my meal, but at least I finished everything on my plate as well as every drop in my wine glass. After eating, I rinsed the dishes and put them in the dishwasher. Feeling tired, I decided to take a nap. I went into the living room and stretched out on the sofa. Sleep came quickly.

Sleep ended when the landline phone on the end table next to the sofa rang. I clumsily turned my body so that I could look at the caller ID display. I was shocked to see Adam Proctor's name. I almost let voicemail do its job but suddenly decided to pick up the handset.

"Hello," I said in a firm voice.

"Hi, Linzie. This is Adam Proctor."

"Hello, Adam. What can I do for you?"

"Actually, Linzie, I am hoping I can do something for you. My editors and I read your three books. All of us agree that publishing them would be a smart business move. They are excellent novels."

When I heard Adam say those words, I immediately thought of Harri. Her prediction that Adam would find value in my books and contact me had come true. Adam's favorable opinion of my books was such a surprise that I was unable to articulate any kind of response right away. I did not know whether to be happy that my books had been received well or to be angry that I had not heard one word from Adam since his hasty departure from my apartment on January 10.

"Adam," I finally said, "I had abandoned any hope that you would even read my books. You were so angry when we parted company in January."

"Linzie, I apologize for my behavior. I really had no right to even ask you out on a date in January. The truth is, at that time, I had not gotten over Evelyn. You remember that I told you about Evelyn, don't you Linzie?"

"Yes, I certainly do remember your telling me about Evelyn," I replied. "How is she?"

"I assume she is okay. I have not talked to her since I saw you, Linzie."

"She may call you when you least expect it."

"No, that is not going to happen," he muttered.

I surprised myself when I mustered enough courage to ask, "Why not?"

"Evelyn got married two months ago. I recently found out that before I even broke up with her, she was dating her future husband behind my back. I was suspicious that she was cheating on me."

Now I was convinced that Harri was a clairvoyant. During my phone conversation with her that very morning, she had not only predicted that Adam would call me about my novels but also suggested that Adam's former girlfriend might have had a roving eye. Once again, Harri's intuition was on the mark. As for Adam, I truly felt sorry for him. I knew what it felt like to be deceived by a lover.

"I am sorry, Adam."

"Thank you, Linzie. I am not just calling to let you know that I am interested in publishing your books. I am also calling to ask you if you would be interested in going out again. I enjoyed your company in January even though Evelyn was still stuck in my mind. Would you give me a second chance and let me take you out to dinner?"

Even though I believed Adam was being quite sincere, I

was hesitant to accept his invitation. Tired of being hurt by men, I was not willing to expose myself to another kick in the shins. I was most grateful that I could give him an honest excuse to turn down his request to take me out.

"Adam, I appreciate your invitation, but I am actually leaving Boston for a few months. I won't be returning to my apartment until September."

"May I ask where you are going, Linzie?"

"I'm going to Rockport."

"Oh, you're taking a vacation for yourself?"

"No. I'm going to be a ghostwriter for a woman who no longer writes but who was quite successful during the days that she did. She has asked me to stay with her in her cottage in Rockport so that we can confer with each other on the book that she wants me to write."

"When are you leaving?"

"Saturday," I replied.

After a short pause, he said, "My recollection is that you did not have a car back in January. Do you have one now?"

Adam's question was a wake-up call that my brain needed. Jack's date with his lady friend had upset me so much that I had lost sight of the fact that it was Jack who was going to drive me to Rockport on Saturday. How awkward a ride that was going to be!

"No, I still do not own a car," I replied. "A friend of mine has offered to drive me to Rockport."

I was not about to tell Adam that Jack was going to be my driver, for I feared that the mere mention of Jack's name would anger Adam.

"How would it be if I took you to Rockport, Linzie? I'm free on Saturday. Even if you don't want to see me again socially, and I can't say I blame you if that is the case, the ride to Rockport would give us the chance to discuss the possibility of a publishing deal. Think of our getting together as strictly business if that is what you prefer."

It was tempting to accept Adam's invitation to drive

me, especially since he had based his invitation on a potential business deal. Yet, I was still hesitant to accept.

"I appreciate your willingness to drive me, Adam. I'll find out if it is still convenient for that friend of mine to take me."

"Whether it is convenient or not for your friend, I really would like to drive you to Rockport. It is one of my favorite places. I have not been there for a while, so the thought of going there on Saturday really appeals to me. What time are you due at the cottage?"

"Mrs. Cranshaw, the woman who hired me, expects me around two o'clock."

"If we leave fairly early," Adam said, "we could roam through some shops and art galleries. Then we could enjoy a leisurely lunch, preferably at a restaurant that overlooks the water."

My bitterness towards Jack was making Adam's offer sound sweeter and sweeter by the second.

"Would it be all right, Adam, if I call you after I talk to that friend of mine?"

"Of course," he replied. "Let me just say that I hope I'll be the one driving you."

"Thanks. I'll talk to you later."

"I'll look forward to hearing from you. Bye, Linzie."

"Bye."

After hanging up the phone, I pulled the ottoman over to the end of the sofa on which I was sitting and rested my legs on it. Then I turned on the television and started flipping through stations. I stopped flipping when I found a movie about the Old West. In terms of choice, the Old West would do just fine, I thought. I certainly was in no mood for a love story that night. Although the movie was action-packed, I fell asleep within the first fifteen minutes of my watching it. It was not the sound of guns or galloping horses that eventually woke me up. Rather, it was the sound of my landline phone ringing. Half-asleep, I picked up the handset without looking at the caller ID display.

"Hello," I said in a voice that sounded anything but friendly.

"Hi, Linzie. How are you doing?"

The receiver and my ear did not quite match up, so I did not recognize the voice on the other end.

"Who is calling?"

"This is Jack. Are you okay?"

Doing my best to sound alert, I replied, "I'm fine. How is that pounding headache of yours?"

"It is gone, thank goodness."

"Miracles really do happen," I said sarcastically.

I was not sure if Jack detected the sarcasm in my voice. If he did, he made no comment about it.

"I know you were not expecting me to call you until I got home from work tomorrow, but I wonder if I could come upstairs now with a bottle of pinot grigio and enjoy a glass or two with you."

His mention of pinot grigio added fuel to the fire that was raging inside of me. Why would he want to share a bottle of pinot grigio with me when he had already shared one with his date earlier that evening?

"What time is it?" I asked.

"It is twenty minutes to ten."

"It's too late, Jack. I want to go to bed soon."

"Okay, Linzie, I understand. I'll bring the bottle tomorrow evening for our Chinese dinner, just as we had planned."

"Actually, Jack, I'm going to have to cancel our plans for tomorrow night. I have too much on my plate. There's no room for Chinese food on that plate."

"Oh," he said bewilderedly. "How about I come upstairs tomorrow evening just to enjoy the bottle of wine with you? Will you have time for that?"

"No, I don't think so."

"Linzie, I want to spend time with you. Tomorrow night will be your last night here until September."

I remained silent. He did, too, for a moment.

"Look, Linzie, I bought a nice bottle of your favorite wine. Why can't we enjoy it together?"

I took a deep breath and said, "Why don't you offer it to your friend who dined with you this evening?"

My question was met by silence on Jack's part. When he resumed speaking, he sounded flustered.

"Okay, okay, I understand why you're upset," he said hurriedly. "Were you sitting out on the balcony while she was here?"

"I certainly was."

"Linzie, the way things appeared are not the way things are."

"All I know, Jack, is that we had a date, and you pushed me aside to accommodate her."

"Linzie, you don't understand. I know it looked that way but—"

"I don't know how it looked, but I know how it sounded. She called you 'honey.' "

"Did you hear *me* call her that, Linzie?"

"Once the music started to play, I did not hear every word you said, but I sure heard every syllable that came out of her mouth. A demolition project would be no match for the volume of her voice. Her desire to spend more time with you, as in spending two days with you at George's home, came through loud and clear."

"Linzie, are you going to listen to my explanation or not?"

"Not," I replied.

"Fine," he said angrily. "I promised to take you to Rockport on Saturday, and I'll keep that promise."

"When it comes to men," I said, "I fully expect promises to be broken. I have a ride to Rockport, so your Saturday is free of Linzie Cole."

Without allowing him the chance to say another word, I hung up the phone. I then called Adam Proctor and told him that I gratefully accepted his offer to take me to Rockport. Upon terminating my conversation with Adam, I phoned Harri to inform her that her predictions about Adam had come true—that he was interested in publishing my books and also wanted to date me. She was elated and even more elated when I told her that it was Adam who would be driving me to Rockport on June 2.

Chapter Fourteen

June 2, 2018, finally arrived. After getting out of bed, I headed for the kitchen to perform my usual ritual of peeking out the window and glancing at the outdoor thermometer. Just as the weathermen had predicted, it was a partly sunny day and pleasantly warm.

Once I was dressed, I ate a good breakfast and then carried, one by one, all four of my bags down the staircase and into the hallway on the first floor. I wanted to be ready to take off as soon as Adam arrived. He and I had agreed that 8:30 a.m. would be a suitable time to leave Boston.

Adam arrived in his silver sedan right on schedule. When I saw his car, I opened the front door of the house and stepped onto the platform outside. As he got out of the car, I noticed how nicely he was dressed. He was wearing white Bermuda shorts, a blue short-sleeve shirt, and white athletic shoes. He looked quite attractive as he made his way up the front walk.

"Good morning, Linzie," he said cheerfully as he spotted me on the platform.

"Hello, Adam. It's so nice of you to take me to Rockport. Thank you so much."

"Don't thank me," he said as he began to ascend the outdoor staircase. "I have been looking forward to this little trip since I talked to you on the phone Thursday."

After reaching the top step, he approached me and grasped my right hand with his. For a moment, I thought he was going to give me a kiss on the cheek, but he did not. Perhaps he thought such a move would have been too presumptuous on his part.

"Well, this is a big day for you, Linzie. You are beginning a new adventure."

"I am both excited and nervous. The ghostwriting job is a good opportunity for me, but what if my writing does not live up to Mrs. Cranshaw's expectations?"

Adam gazed into my eyes and said, "Don't worry, Linzie. Think of me as your safety net. I love your books. Whether or not things work out with Mrs. Cranshaw, you certainly have a future with me, professionally speaking, if you want that future. However, I do not feel that today is the day for you to make any decisions regarding publication of your books through my house. You have enough on your mind. So, rather than devote all our time today to a lot of chatter about publication, I thought it would be better if I simply gave you material to read that would cover a wide range of issues regarding publication through my house. Read the material whenever you have time. Then feel free to ask me questions. How does that sound?"

I nodded my head and said, "That sounds reasonable. After I read the material, I can at least start to mull things over. You are quite right, though. Today is not the day to look too far ahead. I promised Mrs. Cranshaw that until I complete the ghostwriting job for her, I am not going to be sidetracked by any other writing jobs or opportunities. The possibility of my signing a contract with you would have to be put on hold until I fulfill my commitment to her."

"I understand, Linzie. Let's just enjoy each other's company today. By the way, after you gave me Mrs. Cranshaw's address Thursday night, I looked up directions to her cottage. Her street is within walking distance of Bearskin Neck. Have you ever been to that area of Rockport?"

"I have been there a few times, not recently, though."

"How would you feel if we made Bearskin Neck our

destination spot today? The shops there are interesting, and the views of the ocean are impressive. As you probably know, Bearskin Neck is an art colony. There are plenty of art galleries to visit."

"Going to Bearskin Neck sounds like fun."

"So, Linzie, I assume you have some bags in your apartment that need to be carried out to the car."

"They are in the hallway here on the first floor."

Adam followed me inside and then carried my bags out to the platform.

"These bags are pretty heavy for a woman. Did someone carry them down the stairs for you?"

"No. I carried them myself. I like to think of myself as an independent woman."

"I have no doubts about that," Adam said with a chuckle. "I'm just curious. Does the guy I met on the night of our date still live in the downstairs apartment?"

"Yes."

"I do not remember his name," Adam remarked, "but I do know that I owe him an apology for the way I acted when I saw him lying on your sofa. I cringe when I think of how I lost my cool that night."

"Trust me. You do not owe him an apology," I said with more than a touch of irritation in my voice.

The anger in my voice caused a perplexed look to come across Adam's face. I feared that Adam would wrongly think that my anger was directed towards him. Jack's deceitful behavior on Thursday evening was still grating on my nerves, and the thought of Adam apologizing to Jack was too much for me to bear. I had practically snapped at Adam and knew I had to say something to dispel any notion in his head that I was displeased with him.

"I suppose, Adam, if I were a guy who had just wined and dined a woman, I would not be too happy to see another man sleeping in her apartment upon taking her home. Please do not feel bad that you got upset that night. I can certainly understand why you acted the way you did."

"Thanks, Linzie. That makes me feel a lot better. Now, I know you just said you like to be independent, but I hope you will let me carry these bags to the car."

Grinning, I said, "I like to be independent but not to the point of being a fool. I have to admit that when I lugged the bags, one by one, down the staircase this morning, I had to hold onto the bannister for dear life and almost took a tumble or two along the way."

"Then it's settled. I appoint myself carrier of Linzie Cole's bags."

Adam seemed much less stiff and formal than he was during our date in January. His relaxed manner caused me to feel quite at ease with him. He picked up two of the bags as if they were as light as feathers and headed for the car, where he gently placed them in the trunk. In no time, he was back for the other two bags. I locked the front door. Together, we walked to the car. Adam put the remaining two bags on the sidewalk and opened the passenger door for me. I glanced at the house before getting into the car. Once I was settled in the seat, Adam closed the car door, picked up the two bags, and put them in the trunk. The slamming sound produced by the closing of the trunk made me realize that there was no turning back now.

"Any regrets about leaving?" Adam asked as he lowered himself into the driver's seat.

I shook my head, but that gesture was a bit of a lie. A few tears had formed in my eyes. I was afraid that if I looked at the house again, I might see Jack and that a lot more tears would follow. I had not seen hide nor hair of Jack since Thursday morning. Our phone conversation on Thursday night had ended so acrimoniously that I was trying hard to convince myself that it was better that our paths had not crossed since that conversation.

Adam started the engine and said, "All systems go. If traffic isn't too heavy, we should be in Rockport within an hour."

As Adam pulled away from the curb, I searched for my handkerchief in my pocketbook. My bag was so packed with all kinds of items that my search was a challenging one.

"There is a small box of tissues in the glove compartment," Adam said. "Please help yourself."

It seemed logical to assume that Adam had noticed my tears. It was a kind act on his part not to question why my eyes were becoming little pools of water. He turned on the radio and selected a station that was playing soft music.

"Linzie, when we went out together in January, I talked so much about my former girlfriend that I really did not tell you much about myself. Will I sound obnoxious if I talk about myself for a few minutes?"

"No," I replied. "I would like to hear all about you," I said as I tried to inconspicuously wipe a few tears from my eyes.

I was grateful that Adam was taking charge of the conversation. My attempts to eradicate Jack from my thoughts had failed miserably. I was feeling too blue to be chatty. My state of mind was such that I doubted Adam would be able to capture my complete attention.

"Well, I started out as a hoodlum. No, not really," he said laughing.

He succeeded in evoking a hearty laugh from me, much to my surprise.

"From the time I was four years old, my mother was faced with the challenge of raising me, her only child, all by herself."

"Did something happen to your father?" I asked.

"Yes. He was killed in a train accident."

"Oh, Adam, I'm terribly sorry. I had no idea."

I suddenly stopped pitying myself. He now had my full attention.

"In spite of the loss of my father, I had a good childhood. My mother was a kind person who did her best to guide me in the right direction. She was a firm believer in a well-rounded education and made sure that by the time I was ready to enter the first grade, I could read and write well. At the age of six, I was reading and writing at the third-grade level. I must say, the nuns at the parochial school I attended were quite impressed with me."

"Is your mother still alive?" I asked.

"No. She died three years ago at the age of seventy-four. When she was diagnosed with cancer a couple of years before her death, I insisted that she live with me. I wanted to make sure she received the best care possible. We were extremely close right to the very end."

"You were obviously a very good son, Adam."

"I did my best to be a good son. Anyway, Mom instilled in me the love of books. Going to bed when I was a young boy was always fun because she would pull up a chair next to my bed and read all kinds of stories to me. As I got older, she would have me read aloud to her while she was knitting or engaged in some other activity. By the time I was ready to enter college, there was not a doubt in my mind what my major would be. I believe that during our first date, I told you that I chose English literature as my major and eventually returned to school to get a second degree in business. From the moment I entered college, I was considering a career in the publishing business. Journalism was another idea I had in my head, but publishing won out in the end."

"Is publishing a hectic business?" I asked.

"It can be at times. I turn to golf to escape the pressures of the job. Maybe it's a good thing I never got married. If I had, my wife would have been a golf widow."

I laughed and said, "I've never played, but my mom did. I inherited her golf clubs."

"Will you play golf with me sometime, Linzie?"

"I know nothing about the sport, only that you whack that little ball all over the place until it lands in a hole."

He chuckled and said, "The trick is not to whack it all over the place. I'll teach you how to play if you like. We can start at a driving range and then graduate to a par-three course. You'll be a pro before you know it."

"I'll be willing to give golf a try, but please keep your expectations low. My first attempt at golf may prove to be my last."

"Come on now, Linzie. You need to have more determination than that. Giving up too fast is not the way to go. Just think. If you had given up on your writing before you finished your first book, there would be no Mrs. Cranshaw to greet you at her cottage this afternoon, and there would be no Adam Proctor reaching out to you as a publisher."

"You're right, Adam. You're absolutely right."

Laughing, he said, "Stick with me, my dear, and you will beat down the barriers to success."

Thanks to Adam's jovial personality, my spirits were improving by the minute. The more we talked, the more I liked him.

"Linzie, in the glove compartment, you will find a manila envelope with your name on it. Inside the envelope are some papers about my publishing house. There are also sheets about terms and conditions should we engage in a publishing contract. What my house can offer you in terms of payment is also included in the envelope."

I reached into the glove compartment and pulled out the envelope. It was fairly thick.

"Thanks, Adam."

"I deserve no thanks," he said. "I was selfish enough to want to spend our time today in a personal way. Talking business would have robbed me of the pleasure of getting to know you better. I think I would like to hear more about you. Our first date was really all about me. Actually, it was all about Evelyn, which was so unfair to you. Tell me about yourself, Linzie."

For the next few minutes, I gave Adam some of the highlights of my life, from birth to the present. I dared not speculate about my future, for I had no idea where my life was headed.

Upon the conclusion of the rather brief summary of my life, I turned to Adam and said, "Sorry to say, Adam, but my life has not been all that exciting."

"I disagree," he said. "You have a special gift that others would love to have. You transform a blank computer screen into a world that is a product of your imagination. You breathe life into characters that you create—characters that must face the situations that you have envisioned for them. You have the power to control their emotions. What could be more exciting than that?"

Grinning, I said, "Well, now that you have put it that way, I guess my life has been a lot less boring than I thought."

"Harriet told me that you are forty-two years old. I'm surprised that you have managed to stay single. You're so pretty, pleasant, and gifted that I don't understand it."

"Well, Adam, the same can be said of you—not the pretty part, of course. You are attractive, nice, and ambitious, but you are still a bachelor."

"I guess we were both tied up in relationships for a while that were going nowhere," he commented. "I recall that back in January, you had just broken up with your boyfriend. Am I being too bold to ask if you ever hear from him?"

I did not consider Adam's curiosity about Kevin to be bold, but it did catch me off guard, causing me to satisfy his curiosity in a roundabout way.

"No, you are not being too bold to ask about Kevin. I have not seen him since January fourth. I recently heard from his sister, who informed me about his progress."

"His progress?" Adam asked.

"Yes. Kevin was hit by a car during the snowstorm on January fourth. He lapsed into a coma and was badly injured. A month later, he came out of the coma. His legs, though, are still in bad shape. I'm afraid that there is a long road of rehabilitation ahead of him."

"You must feel terrible about his accident even though

your relationship with him has ended."

"Yes, I do feel terrible."

I had no desire to engage in further conversation about Kevin. Fortunately, Adam changed the subject.

"So, Linzie, you say that Mrs. Cranshaw was a successful author in her day. Did she specialize in a particular genre?"

"She was a romance novelist."

"How old is she now?"

"Seventy-eight unless she had a birthday since my last visit with her, which was on January third."

"She no longer writes?"

"No. For some mysterious reason, she stopped writing at the pinnacle of her career."

"That's strange," he commented. "What is her first name?"

"Constance."

"Hmm. Constance Cranshaw. That name does not ring a bell."

"I can understand why her name is not familiar to you. She stopped writing many years ago."

"Any ideas, Linzie, on what publishing house handled her books?"

"I have no idea, Adam."

He asked no more questions about Mrs. Cranshaw. Our conversation drifted to a different topic—politics. For the remainder of the ride to Rockport, Boston politicians and national leaders were the focus of our discussion. Although Adam's and my point of view on various issues did not always agree, I considered him to be an intelligent man who kept abreast of newsworthy events.

Upon arrival at Bearskin Neck, we began to stroll through its quaint streets. Gift shops and art galleries alike attracted our attention. While in one of the galleries, Adam noticed an oil painting of the Thacher Island Twin Lighthouses.

"Linzie, are you at all familiar with the history of these two lighthouses?"

I took a good look at the painting, shrugged my shoulders, and replied, "I can't say that I am."

"These lighthouses have a remarkable history," he said.

"I guess I can assume they are located on Thacher Island, but I have no idea where Thacher Island is," I admitted.

"Thacher Island is a small island one mile off the coast of Rockport. The two lighthouses depicted in this painting were built in 1861 and replaced the original lighthouses that were built in 1771. Would you believe that the original lighthouses were the last ones built under British rule in this country?"

I smiled and said, "I'll take your word for it. I'm beginning to think that you are a walking encyclopedia."

Adam laughed and said, "I won't share all the nitty-gritty details about the history of the lighthouses. I'll just add that the Twin Lights on Thacher Island are also known as the Cape Ann Light Station, which is now considered a national historic landmark. The lighthouses have served as a navigational blessing to sailors for many, many years."

"You are a bit of a navigational blessing to me right now, Adam. I really don't know my way around here."

"In that case, let's take a little tour. Would you like to walk over to T Wharf?"

"Sure, as long as you lead the way. For all I know, walking to T Wharf could mean walking all the way back to Boston."

"It's a short walk, Linzie. I have a feeling you won't be huffing and puffing by the time we get there."

Adam was right. In a matter of minutes, we had reached our destination.

"After that very long journey to the wharf here, you must be near exhaustion," he said facetiously. "Let's walk to the end of the wharf and sit on a bench. Do you think you can make it to the bench?"

"I think I can make it," I said laughing.

As we proceeded down the wharf, the beauty of the area

did not escape me. To me, the view that greeted my eyes was a harbor scene at its finest. The mélange of water, jetties, quaint structures, and boats immediately endeared me to T Wharf. At the end of the wharf, we found an unoccupied bench and sat down. As we gazed at Rockport Harbor, we enjoyed the comings and goings of boats of all kinds.

Pointing towards the left, Adam said, "That is Bradley Wharf, home to Motif Number 1."

As I gazed at Motif Number 1, I said, "I know a bit about that landmark. It is famous."

"Okay, Linzie, it's time for you to give me a history lesson. What do you know about Motif Number 1?"

"Well, let me see. I believe it originally served as a fishing shack."

"Very good. What else can you tell me?"

"It is a structure that many artists have painted."

"That's for sure," Adam agreed. "In fact, do you know that it may well be the most painted building in the world?"

"I know that now," I said with a girlish giggle.

"So, share some more of your knowledge with me, Linzie."

"You mean about Motif Number 1?"

"Yes."

"Well, it is red," I said laughing.

Grinning, he said, "I won't give you any points for that little piece of knowledge."

"I'm quickly running out of knowledge about Motif Number 1," I admitted, "but I do know that what we're looking at right now is a replica of the original structure. I remember that during the Blizzard of 1978, the original structure was destroyed and that the replica was constructed the same year as the storm."

"Wow, I am impressed."

"Thanks. Coming from you, a history guru, that is quite a compliment."

"Linzie, do you know when the original Motif Number 1

was built? You don't have to give me the year. I'll settle for the century."

"You're all heart," I said kiddingly. "I'm going to say twentieth century."

"Subtract a century from your answer."

"Really? It was built in the eighteen hundreds?"

"It was," he replied.

"I think those nuns that taught you in grammar school were quite right to be impressed with you. How do you know so much?"

"I read constantly. I particularly like to read historical books. Since Rockport is full of history, I have read a lot about this place. I meant it when I said that I was excited about coming here today."

"How do you retain all those historical facts in your head?" I asked.

"I was blessed with a good memory, which is invaluable when you are a history buff."

We remained quiet for a few minutes as we watched a man hoist the mainsail and then the jib of his sloop. Then Adam broke the silence.

"I think you are going to enjoy your three-month stay here, Linzie. Rockport is one of the most unique places I have visited, and I have to say that I have traveled through many parts of this country."

"I don't believe that Mrs. Cranshaw is one to leave the confines of her home very much. I may become a homebody too. I don't know anybody in Rockport."

Adam gave my right hand a little pat and said, "It sounds as though you are afraid that you may be lonely here. Am I right?"

Nodding my head, I replied, "You are quite right."

"May I come and visit you, Linzie? There is plenty to do and see in Rockport. We can explore the town together when both of us find free time from work, and you won't even have to consult a history book. You will have a competent, although not humble, historian right by your side."

"I would love to explore Rockport with you," I said quite joyfully.

Adam looked at his wristwatch and said, "Speaking of things to do, how about we have some lunch? It's quarter to twelve."

"That's a good idea. Two o'clock is fast approaching."

"There is a restaurant on Bearskin Neck that I have eaten at before," he remarked. "It has a great view of the water. Want to try it?"

"Sure."

Fortunately, there was a table available when we arrived at the restaurant, and our order was taken fairly quickly. As we waited for our meals, Adam talked enthusiastically about his plans to visit me in the future.

"One of the places in Rockport that I would like to visit is Halibut Point State Park," he said. "There is a massive abandoned granite quarry at the park that is now filled with water. Did you know that once upon a time, the quarrying of granite was a huge business in this area?"

"I think you already know the answer to that question, Adam."

"Well, it was a business that really thrived during the nineteenth century and into the early part of the twentieth century. I thought it would be interesting to follow the trail around the quarry. There are also trails in the park that lead to the ocean. The views, I understand, are spectacular. We can pack a picnic lunch. Do you think you would be interested in spending a day there, Linzie?"

"Yes, I would. If I'm going to be an inhabitant of Rockport for three months, I might as well get to know the territory."

Shortly after our discussion about Halibut Point State Park, our waiter placed our meals on the table. As I ate lunch, I enjoyed not only the water view but also the pleasant conversation that flowed so easily between Adam and me.

After we finished eating, Adam said, "It's quarter past one. Would you like to sit on Front Beach for half an hour or so? Mrs. Cranshaw's cottage is on a side street not far from the beach."

"That sounds like a good way to spend the time we have left together," I said.

"Good. Let's go."

It was a very short drive to Front Beach. After parking the car, Adam removed two beach chairs and a portable sun shade umbrella from the back seat.

As we walked towards the water's edge, he said, "Years ago, I stayed at a bed and breakfast in this area. You will be living in a convenient location, Linzie. You will be within walking distance of not just this beach but also Back Beach, where I gave scuba diving a try during my stay here. In a matter of minutes, you can get to downtown by foot. Bearskin Neck is practically around the corner. When I think of where I am going to retire, this area comes to the forefront of my mind."

"Harriet said you are a few years older than I am, so let me take a guess and say that you are forty-five."

"I'm forty-six, Linzie. I just celebrated my birthday in May."

"Happy belated birthday. I think you have quite a few years ahead of you before retirement enters the picture."

"I may fool you and walk away from the publishing business sooner than you think in order to try my hand at writing again. I'm not bragging, but my publishing business is booming. If it continues to be successful, I'll be able to purchase a home here someday, preferably with a water view. I picture myself writing up a storm as I sit in an office that overlooks the ocean."

"That's a great dream to have. Have you considered writing historical novels?"

"I sure have," he replied. "I would be in seventh heaven writing historical fiction."

"It is so important to be happy at what you are doing. I

can honestly say that I love the challenge of writing."

"We have a lot in common, Linzie. In fact, I think I relate to you far better than I did to Evelyn. She and I were worlds apart in our thinking. I really don't understand why I was so attracted to her for so long. Well, there I go again. She was practically with us on our first date. There will be no more said about her today."

"It is good to vent your frustration, Adam. The good news is that Evelyn is finally out of your system."

"I am glad that she is. The guy that married her did me an enormous favor. I had no choice but to move on with my life."

"When do you think you can come up to Rockport again so that we can begin our exploration of other areas in the town?" I asked.

"Weekends are the best time for me, Linzie. The weekdays I take off are few and far between because of my business. Once you are settled, please give me a call so that we can figure out which weekend would be a good one for us to get together. I hope it will be the first of many weekends."

"I do too," I said sincerely. "Adam, I have really enjoyed your company today."

"Same here, Linzie. I hope I did not bore you with all the history-related tidbits I shared with you today."

"No, you did not. I want to learn more."

Adam unfolded the two chairs and placed them on the sand. Then he positioned the sun umbrella between the two. Once seated, we began to enjoy the view of Sandy Bay, and I began to look forward to those weekends when Adam would come to visit.

Chapter Fifteen

It was exactly 2:00 p.m. when Adam parked his car in front of Mrs. Cranshaw's cottage. The street on which Mrs. Cranshaw lived was quite picturesque thanks to the quaint cottages and colorful gardens that lined both sides of it. The towering oak trees that were visible in the background added a touch of rusticity to the residential area.

Mrs. Cranshaw's cottage, a gray two-story house with white shutters, was modest in size. A white picket fence ran along the perimeter of the front yard. Hugging the section of fence that bordered the town sidewalk were rugosa roses of a lovely pink shade.

Adam turned to me and said, "Linzie, before we get out of the car, let me ask you a question. Do you want me to stay in the cottage with you awhile before I bring your bags inside?"

"I would like that, but I'll have to ask Mrs. Cranshaw's permission. She is a prim and proper lady who enforces her own rules of etiquette that I do not want to violate. I do hope she will let you stay. I have butterflies in my stomach. Your staying here awhile may help chase them away."

Adam and I got out of the car and began our walk on the gray pavers that led to the front door. As we admired the lavender and the white rhododendrons that bordered both sides of the house and the petunias and the impatiens that were planted in the flower beds in the front, not a single weed met our eyes. We ascended the three-step cement stairway leading to the front door. Once on the platform, I took a deep breath and rang the doorbell. It did not take long for Mrs. Cranshaw to open the front door.

"Hello, Miss Cole," she said. "Please come in."

"Hello, Mrs. Cranshaw. Would it be all right with you if my friend also comes in and stays here awhile before he brings my bags in?"

"Yes," she replied. "That would be fine."

Adam opened the screen door. We crossed the threshold and entered the hallway.

Mrs. Cranshaw looked at Adam and said, "You must be Officer Grumey."

Adam appeared confused and rightfully so.

"Mrs. Cranshaw, this is my friend Adam Proctor. Jack Grumey had offered to drive me here, but as it turned out, I accepted Adam's offer to drive me instead. I am very appreciative to Adam for all he did for me today."

I was surprised that Mrs. Cranshaw then took the initiative to shake Adam's hand.

"I am Constance Cranshaw. Thank you for driving Miss Cole to my cottage."

"You're welcome," Adam said. "It is very nice to meet you."

I was greatly relieved that Mrs. Cranshaw had received Adam so well. Discourteous and cold when I first met her, she now seemed so polite and warm that I wondered whether she had gone through some kind of emotional metamorphosis. Even her manner of dress had drastically changed. As we stood in the hallway, I noticed that she was not sporting an elegant-looking suit or expensive leather pumps. They had apparently been cast aside for casual wear—blue jeans, a white sweatshirt, and black sneakers.

"I would like to serve you iced tea out on the porch. How does that sound?" Mrs. Cranshaw asked.

Adam nodded his head to indicate that he was in favor of the idea while I replied, "I think a glass of iced tea would hit the spot right now."

"Good," she said. "Follow me."

She walked towards the white staircase in the hallway that led to the upstairs. As she neared the base of the staircase, she turned left and led us into the living room. A red brick fireplace, colonial furniture, and oil paintings of countryside scenes contributed to the cozy ambiance of the living room. Covering a good part of the floor was a large oval brown and white braided rug, which not only complemented the pale-yellow walls of the room but also hinted that the age of the cottage was not young.

The living room led directly to our destination—a square-shaped screened porch that overlooked the large backyard. With its yellow tile floor and white wood, the porch looked like a cheerful place to relax. Four lime-green padded armchairs surrounded a round white table that was ample enough in size to serve as a dining table.

As I gazed at the backyard, a vegetable garden caught my eye. I turned around to make a comment to Adam about the spacious size of the garden, only to discover that Adam was not on the porch. I returned to the living room, as did Mrs. Cranshaw. Adam was standing in front of a table that was situated about eight feet to the left of the fireplace. A ship model on that table had claimed his attention, so much so that he had put his eyeglasses on to study every detail of it.

"Adam," I said laughing, "I thought you had taken off for Boston, and I could only hope that you left my bags behind."

"Linzie," he said, "this is an amazing piece of work. It is a model of PS *Portland*."

"I don't want to appear ignorant, Adam, but what is PS *Portland*?"

"PS *Portland* was a large steamship with paddlewheels that were side-mounted. Her purpose was to transport passengers between Boston and Portland, Maine."

I walked over to the model to take a look because Adam seemed so enthralled by it.

"Do you know roughly when she was built?" I asked.

"She was built in 1889," he replied.

It did not surprise me one bit that Adam had the exact year in his noggin.

"Did you ever hear of the Portland Gale of 1898?" he asked.

"No," I replied.

"Well, it was a horrific storm that hit the New England Coast. It took the lives of over four hundred people and sank over one hundred fifty vessels. PS *Portland* was one of its victims. It was off of Cape Ann that the ship went down. There were no survivors."

"You certainly know all about the ship, Mr. Proctor," Mrs. Cranshaw commented. "My father, who left me this house and all of its contents, was fascinated by the history of this area. That ship model was one of his prized possessions."

Adam looked at Mrs. Cranshaw and said, "It is a beauty, ma'am. I can understand why your father valued it so."

"Adam is quite a history buff," I remarked. "He knows all about the history of Rockport."

"That's wonderful," Mrs. Cranshaw said.

"As I mentioned to Linzie earlier," Adam said, "I think Rockport is one of the most unique places I have visited. Not only is it a quaint seaside town, but it is also rich in history."

"I agree," Mrs. Cranshaw said. "Rockport is a special place. I feel like a new person when I come here for three months every year. If it were not for the harsh New England winters, I would be living here all year long. By the way, did you two have any lunch?"

When Mrs. Cranshaw asked that question, I believed that she had found Adam to be quite acceptable. I began to feel more at ease.

"Yes, we did," I replied.

"Then, let's get settled out on the porch and have iced tea," she said.

She led the way back to the porch, this time with Adam following.

"Please make yourselves comfortable," Mrs. Cranshaw said. "Sit wherever you like."

Adam and I sat across from each other, in chairs that provided an excellent view of the backyard, which was somewhat similar in looks to the yard behind my apartment. Tall evergreens, planted here and there along the perimeter of the yard, provided some shade without robbing the vegetable garden of the sun it needed. Between the patio, which was located directly behind the house, and the vegetable garden, which was about twenty-five feet beyond the patio, was a bird bath, the sight of which made me feel at home. I envisioned myself sitting on the porch after a long day of writing and watching all kinds of birds stop by to enjoy a dip in the water.

"You young people relax and enjoy the view of the yard. I'll get the iced tea," Mrs. Cranshaw said.

"Do you need any help?" I asked.

"No. I can manage."

As soon as I felt confident that our hostess was out of earshot, I whispered to Adam, "Mrs. Cranshaw really seems to like you. You don't know what a compliment that is to you."

"I take it," he said softly, "that you have witnessed a gruff side of her personality."

I nodded my head.

"Not to worry, Linzie. I have a feeling you two are going to develop a compatible relationship."

A couple of minutes later, Mrs. Cranshaw entered the porch with a tray that held three glasses. Adam rose from his chair, relieved her of the tray, and placed it on the round table. He then pulled a chair away from the table so that she could sit.

As he reclaimed his seat, Adam said, "You certainly have a nice place here, Mrs. Cranshaw. It is in such a convenient spot. There are beaches nearby, and you can walk to the downtown in a matter of minutes."

"Yes, my house is conveniently located," she agreed. "That is a blessing for me. I do not drive anymore, and most things I need are close by. Whenever I need to travel outside the area, my neighbor Randy drives me. I pay him, of course."

Adam wasted no time in saying, "I am planning to visit Linzie during some of the weekends she is here, so if I can be of any help to you in terms of transportation, please feel free to ask me. There will be no charge."

"I appreciate your offer, Mr. Proctor, but I think Randy needs the money, so I do not want to take any business away from him."

"I understand," Adam said.

Adam reached for his glass and proceeded to take a few sips of the iced tea. While his mouth was occupied, I attempted to carry on the conversation.

"Adam has put Rockport way up on his list of potential retirement spots. He just loves it here."

Mrs. Cranshaw looked at me and said, "Why, Miss Cole, the man does not have one gray hair on his head. I think he is at least two decades away from retirement. Am I right, Mr. Proctor?"

Adam put his glass down on the table and shrugged his shoulders slightly. Before he had a chance to respond to Mrs. Cranshaw's question, she asked him another one.

"What is your line of work, Mr. Proctor?"

"I am in the publishing business, ma'am. I started out as a writer who self-published my own works and then expanded my business to publish the works of others. In fact, I have read Linzie's three novels that she self-published and have suggested that I take over publication of them."

"Adam's publishing house has been very successful," I added. "He says it has been growing by leaps and bounds."

Adam reached into one of the pockets of his Bermuda shorts and took out his wallet. He then opened the wallet and pulled out his business card.

"Allow me to give you my business card, Mrs. Cranshaw. If you know of any authors who are looking for a good publishing house, I would appreciate your referring them to me.

Linzie told me that you used to be a writer. If you have any unpublished works that you would like to get published, I would be more than happy to look at them. In fact, when Linzie completes ghostwriting the novel for you, would you consider choosing my house as the publisher of that novel?"

Looking disgusted, Mrs. Cranshaw said in a tone of voice that definitely revealed the gruff side of her personality, "Mr. Proctor, I do not wish to discuss the future publication of the novel that Miss Cole is going to ghostwrite."

I do not know if my jaw dropped lower than Adam's or if it was the other way around. We were both so astonished at her reaction to Adam's seemingly innocent question that we were speechless.

Finally, I said, "Mrs. Cranshaw, Adam meant no harm by inquiring about the publication of the book I am going to ghostwrite. I am sure he was just trying to be helpful."

I was sitting to the left of our now not-so-gracious hostess, who began to lean in my direction. As she leaned towards me, I leaned back in my chair, as far back as I possibly could. My body language said it all. I was trying, though futilely, to avoid the full impact of the wrath she was about to unleash.

"Miss Cole, I believe I told you that I am the one in charge of the ghostwriting project. I do not wish to receive any input from your friend—a total stranger to me—as to how I should go about publishing the book when it is completed."

I had no comeback to her snide remark. I glanced at Adam, who looked horrified. The silence that ensued was almost unbearable. Adam would be the one to finally speak.

"I do apologize, ma'am. There was no intention on my part to insult you in any way or to pry into your business."

Adam's apology seemed to have fallen on deaf ears, which made the situation even worse. Mrs. Cranshaw sat there silently, gazing at the backyard. Her behavior reminded me of my meetings with her at Elsbury Place when she stared out her picture window at the rolling hills behind her apartment and ignored me until she was darn well ready to reacknowledge my presence.

Adam gulped the rest of his iced tea, placed his empty glass on the table, and lightly slapped his hands on his thighs. He then cleared his throat, probably in an effort to regain Mrs. Cranshaw's attention.

"Well, it has been a long day. I should be on my way. Thank you, Mrs. Cranshaw, for your hospitality."

She looked at him and simply nodded. Adam rose from the chair.

"Linzie," he said, "I have to get your bags out of the trunk. Will you come with me to the car?"

"Yes, Adam. I think you could use my help."

When I stood up, Mrs. Cranshaw finally opened her mouth.

"Mr. Proctor, please carry Miss Cole's bags upstairs to the bedroom. They may be too heavy for her."

Her concern for me was something I was not expecting. What an enigma Mrs. Cranshaw was! One moment she was insensitive, and the next moment, caring.

"It is a good idea that I bring the bags upstairs," Adam remarked. "They are heavy."

Adam extended his hand to Mrs. Cranshaw as a gesture to shake hers. She hesitated to extend her hand but finally did.

"Goodbye," Adam said.

She said nothing. Adam and I exited the porch and then retraced our steps through the living room and the hallway. As soon as we made it outside to the stairway, Adam took me by the arm and escorted me down the three steps. As we scurried down the walkway, he continued to hold my arm and did not release it until we were at the car. Then he stood squarely in front of me.

"Linzie, I want you to come back to Boston with me. Your own apartment is where you belong, not here with that crazy woman."

Adam's point of view on the situation made perfect sense to me, but I had made a commitment to Mrs. Cranshaw.

I had signed the ghostwriter agreement. There was no way I could get back into the passenger seat of Adam's car and return to the sanity and peace of my own apartment. I certainly wanted to do just that, but I could not.

"Adam, I cannot go back with you. I signed the ghostwriter agreement that Mrs. Cranshaw's lawyer drew up."

"Linzie, please do not stay here. You will not be able to put up with the strange behavior of that woman."

"The good news," I said, "is that Mrs. Cranshaw, according to the agreement, can discharge me at any time. I have a feeling that she will, in the very near future, find fault with my writing and tell me to pack up and leave. Also, per the agreement, I can call it quits at any time, but I certainly cannot quit before I even start writing."

Adam stared at the ground and said, "I'm worried about you."

I was touched by his compassion. There was not a doubt in my mind that it was genuine. I gently placed my hand on his shoulder, which caused him to look into my eyes.

"Please don't worry," I said.

"I can't help it. I am not happy that you are staying here."

He leaned forward and gave me a tender kiss on the lips. I welcomed his kiss and fully returned it.

"Will you promise to call me if you run into any problems?" he asked.

I nodded and replied, "I promise."

"What I want to stress," he said, "is that if you need me at any time and for any reason, call me. I'll get in my car and come right away. Don't worry if you need me on a weekday. There are times when work has to take second place."

"Thank you, Adam."

"Linzie, if a miracle happens and you are able to endure the next three months here, I still want to visit you on weekends whenever possible. When I come to visit, I'll stay at an inn or a motel here in town so that we can spend the whole weekend together."

Adam reluctantly took a key ring out of his pocket and opened the trunk. Then he carried the bags, two-by-two, into the front hallway. When all four were waiting to be carried up to the second floor, he picked up two bags and followed me up the staircase. The staircase curved to the right as it neared the second floor, and the bedroom I was to use was directly across from its final step.

As we entered the bedroom, I was impressed by the size of it. It extended all the way from the front to the back of the second floor. The white French provincial bedroom set and the pink wall-to-wall carpet gave the room a cheerful look. On the queen-size bed was a box of candy. I walked over to the box and saw that there was a small piece of white paper taped to the top of it. On that paper were written the words *Welcome, Miss Cole.*

After Adam placed the two bags at the foot of the bed, he remarked, "This bedroom was obviously decorated with a female in mind. I cannot imagine any male feeling at home in this room."

"Mrs. Cranshaw's friend Bertie used to stay with her in the cottage," I explained. "I imagine that this was Bertie's room."

"I hope Bertie was not a bird or a man," Adam said chuckling.

"Bertie was a woman friend of Mrs. Cranshaw. Her first name was actually Bertha. She died last year."

"It's encouraging to know," Adam whispered, "that at least one person was able to endure Mrs. Cranshaw's personality. On second thought, maybe it was Mrs. Cranshaw's personality that finally did poor Bertie in."

I was unable to laugh at Adam's last comment, for I knew how heartbroken Mrs. Cranshaw had been over the passing of Bertie. I felt obligated to say something in Mrs. Cranshaw's defense.

"Adam, Bertie's death was a terrible blow to Mrs. Cranshaw. They were very close."

He shrugged his shoulders and left the room to retrieve the other two bags. During his brief absence, I wondered whether Mrs. Cranshaw now regretted that little note of welcome that she had attached to the box of candy left on the bed. One thing was for sure. Things had gotten off to a rather bumpy start.

Adam entered the bedroom with the other two bags and placed them next to the first two arrivals. Then we walked down the staircase, out the front door, down the walk, and to his car.

"Well, Linzie, I guess this is it until we meet again. Please call me when you want me to come back to Rockport, no matter what the circumstances are."

"I certainly will, Adam. I look forward to seeing you again. Thank you for such a nice day. I'm sorry that your visit with Mrs. Cranshaw ended on such a sour note."

"It's okay," he said. "You were gracious. That's all that matters."

He gave me another gentle kiss on the lips. Then he got in the driver's seat and started the engine.

As I stood on the sidewalk, facing the passenger side of the car, he lowered the window and said, "By the way, Linzie, if you have any questions about the publishing information I gave you, feel free to call me."

"Will do," I said.

After he drove off, a sadness came over me that I could not quite define. For a minute or two, I stood on the sidewalk, feeling all alone.

When I re-entered the cottage, I headed for the porch. I assumed that Mrs. Cranshaw would still be there sipping her iced tea. That assumption was wrong. Both she and her glass of iced tea were gone. A further search revealed that she was nowhere to be found on the first floor. The living room, dining room, kitchen, laundry room, master bedroom, and bathroom were all unoccupied.

Surely, she is upstairs, I thought. I walked up the staircase and peeked inside the bedroom. She was not there, nor was she in the office, sitting room, or bathroom on that floor. One of the bedroom windows and the one window in the office overlooked the backyard. It was not until I peered through the office window that I spotted Mrs. Cranshaw. She was working in the vegetable garden. With a hoe in her hands, she was tilling the soil and doing it quite vigorously for a woman her age.

My first impulse was to head for the garden and confront her about the rude way she had treated Adam and me. Upon reflection, however, I decided I better cool off and that she, too, should be given the chance to calm down. For the next hour, I focused on unpacking. I was grateful for the tall bureau and for the two large closets in the bedroom, all of which had apparently been emptied to accommodate my clothes.

When my unpacking was completed, I decided to take a more thorough look at the other rooms on the second floor. Midway between the two ends of the floor was a bathroom. With its combination of white and floral tiles, it was a pretty room that I assumed had been remodeled in the not-too-distant past. The large walk-in shower was something I looked forward to using. Just beyond the bathroom was an office, in which I knew I would be spending much of my time. Compared to the small den that served as my workplace in my apartment, the office in Mrs. Cranshaw's cottage was a writer's delight. All the pieces in the room—the large oak desk, the tables, the bookcases, and the cabinets—had ample room to co-exist peacefully with one another. The final stop on my self-guided tour was the sitting room, which overlooked the front yard. That room was home to an off-white leather sofa, a matching recliner, a television set, and a bookcase.

Naturally, the bookcase was like a magnet that immediately drew me over to the books on its shelves. As I studied the spines of the books on the top shelf, I realized that they had all been written by the same author—Constance Cranshaw! My curiosity caused me to remove one of the books from the shelf and to start reading the first chapter. Immediately drawn into the story, I did not notice that the book's author had entered the room.

"Well, Miss Cole, you appear to have made yourself right at home."

I jumped and looked up, in absolute horror, at Mrs. Cranshaw, who was standing just inside the doorway, wiping her hands with a paper towel. Now there will be hell to pay, I thought. The great author, who had exploded over Adam's question about her route to publication, had caught me in the act of an even more heinous crime—reading one of her books without her permission! With trembling hands, I hurried to put the book back in its proper place on the shelf. My mind raced to come up with an apology that would appease Mrs. Cranshaw.

Before I could come up with any words, she asked, "How do you like your quarters here?"

Astonished at her lack of anger, I replied to her question in a voice that was just as shaky as my hands.

"The rooms are lovely, Mrs. Cranshaw. Thank you for the box of candy."

"You are quite welcome, Miss Cole. Yesterday, shortly after I arrived here from Boston, Randy drove me to a candy shop so that I could pick out a gift in honor of your coming here. I hope you like assorted chocolates."

"I do. It was very kind of you to welcome me with that box," I said as I stood there with my knees knocking.

"Randy also took me to the grocery store. There is plenty of food in the refrigerator and in the pantry closet. Please help yourself. As for the laundry room, it is off the kitchen. Use the washer and dryer whenever the need arises."

I did not dare tell Mrs. Cranshaw that I had discovered the laundry room earlier during my search for her throughout the house. I was now most grateful that I did not come face to face with her during that search. If I had, I undoubtedly would have vented some anger over the rude way she had treated Adam and me. The steps she had gone through to make me feel at home in her cottage now made me regret the anger I had felt earlier.

"Tomorrow morning, we begin our work on the novel, Miss Cole, so relax and enjoy the rest of the day. Let's plan to begin our work at ten. That will give you time to shower and have a good breakfast."

"That sounds perfect, Mrs. Cranshaw."

She exited the room, leaving me in a quandary. I wondered whether the ghostwriting job would prove to be an emotional roller-coaster ride. If so, would I be able to endure it? I simply did not know.

Chapter Sixteen

When I rose from bed the following morning, I did so with the intention of keeping a positive attitude towards the ghostwriting job. Mrs. Cranshaw's outburst of anger the day before had rattled my nerves, but I was determined not to let that outburst affect my writing ability.

After getting washed and dressed, I walked downstairs and headed for the kitchen. On the counter was a pot of hot coffee, so I knew that Mrs. Cranshaw was up and about. I searched the pantry closet and the refrigerator for breakfast items and then prepared a bowl of hot cereal and a boiled egg, a breakfast which I felt would give me the strength to face the challenge of the first day of writing. Upon finishing breakfast and one cup of coffee, I glanced at my watch. A half hour remained before Mrs. Cranshaw and I were to begin our literary adventure together. To fill that free time, I decided to sit on the porch and enjoy some outdoor scenery. If a bird or two stopped by to take a dip in the bird bath, that was all the better.

As I was about to descend the step between the living room and the porch, I heard Mrs. Cranshaw say, "Good morning, Miss Cole. Please join me."

Upon her request, I walked over to the table and sat in the chair across from her, the same chair I had occupied during the horrid iced tea incident the day before.

"How are you this morning, Mrs. Cranshaw?" I asked.

"I am fine," she replied. "You, however, are not dressed warmly enough. There is a nip in the air."

She grabbed a gray cardigan sweater that was draped across the back of the chair to her left. She then pushed her coffee cup aside, leaned forward, and handed the cardigan to me.

"Put that on, Miss Cole. Do not let that sun in the sky fool you. It is a bit on the chilly side this morning."

I had to admit that she was quite right. In her red sweatshirt and tan slacks, she was dressed more sensibly than I, who was wearing a white short-sleeve blouse and light-blue Bermuda shorts.

After I slipped the cardigan on, I said, "Thanks. The sweater feels good."

"Did you have breakfast, Miss Cole?"

"Yes, I did."

"What about coffee?"

"I had one cup," I replied.

She looked at her watch and said, "We have twenty-five minutes to relax before getting started on the book project. Feel free to have another cup of coffee."

"Thank you. I would like another cup."

I eagerly rose from the chair and headed for the kitchen. Mrs. Cranshaw's suggestion that I help myself to another cup of coffee was music to my ears. My usual consumption of coffee in the morning was two cups. It had been tempting for me to pour myself a second cup while I was eating breakfast, but I had refrained from doing so. My fear was that I might rob Mrs. Cranshaw of enough coffee for herself. I truly was walking on thin ice, fearing that any words or actions on my part might ignite her temper.

As I reclaimed my seat on the porch, I said, "Thank you, Mrs. Cranshaw. I look forward to that second cup of coffee in the morning."

"You must not feel like a stranger in this house," she commented. "The more at home you feel here, the more your heart will be in your work."

I did not know how to interpret that comment. Was she being kind to me so that I could write more effectively for her, or was she being kind simply for the sake of being kind?

She leaned back in her chair and had a pensive look on her face. I was certain she wanted to say something, so I remained quiet. After a few moments, she was ready to express what was on her mind.

"Tell me, Miss Cole. How well do you know Adam Proctor?"

Suddenly, I felt as though only one of my feet was on thin ice and that the other foot had broken through the ice and was dangling in the water. If one wrong word came out of my mouth about Adam, I knew that the foot on the ice would quickly join its partner.

"I do not know Adam all that well," I said. "A friend of mine, Harriet, encouraged him to ask me out on a date back in January. She got my permission, of course, before she gave Adam the okay to call me. Because he is a publisher and I am a writer, Harriet thought we had a lot in common and that we might hit it off both socially and professionally."

"So, Miss Cole, is your friend Harriet some kind of psychic?"

"I'll just say that Harriet possesses an uncanny ability to accurately assess the character of a person. She considers Adam to be a person of fine character."

"I think that assessing Mr. Proctor's character should be your job, Miss Cole. How many times have you been out with him?"

"Only twice," I replied. "There was that date in January. The second time was yesterday."

Mrs. Cranshaw looked at me closely and asked, "Does Mr. Proctor consider your relationship to be a personal one or a business one or both?"

I was floored that Mrs. Cranshaw, who had practically accused Adam and me of prying into her business the day before, now felt entitled to ask me questions about my personal life. To my tender set of ears, her questions sounded downright intrusive.

With as much tact as I could muster, I replied, "My relationship with Adam is in its infancy. For all I know, it could end tomorrow. At this point, he does seem interested in me both personally and professionally."

Her gaze shifted from me to the backyard for a moment. She looked troubled when she returned her gaze in my direction.

"So, Miss Cole, if he is interested in you in a personal way, why did so many months go by before he saw you a second time?"

Flustered, I said, "Adam had been dating another woman for quite some time, and things did not work out for them. When he took me out in January, he was still trying to get over her. I guess he realized that after our first date, he needed more time to heal. I did not hear from him again until this past Thursday, when he volunteered to drive me here."

I had no intention of telling Mrs. Cranshaw about Adam's angry exit from my apartment in January when Jack was lying on my sofa. Such a disclosure would have been way too personal. What I had already told Mrs. Cranshaw was personal enough.

"What about Kevin, your boyfriend who was in that terrible accident that caused him to lapse into a coma? Did he come out of the coma?"

"Yes. He came out of the coma four weeks after the accident. The injuries to his legs were so bad that he continues to need a lot of therapy."

"So, Miss Cole, is Kevin no longer your boyfriend?"

Mrs. Cranshaw's questions about Kevin made me feel uneasy. I wondered whether she entertained the notion that I had abandoned Kevin because of his serious injuries. It was important to me that I set the record straight.

"I broke up with Kevin in January, before his accident," I

explained. "Kevin was angry at me for ending the relationship, but in my opinion, he was responsible for the breakup. He was cheating on me behind my back, all the while insisting that we be exclusive."

Nodding, she said, "I see, Miss Cole. In that case, you were quite justified in ending your relationship with Kevin. Yesterday, Mr. Proctor mentioned that he is interested in publishing the three novels you wrote."

Although I felt that Mrs. Cranshaw was still prying, I was relieved that her focus of attention now seemed to have shifted from my personal life to my writing business.

"Yes, Adam is interested in publishing my three novels. That was one of the main reasons he called me last Thursday."

It finally dawned on me that the most probable reason Mrs. Cranshaw was so inquisitive about Adam was that she did not want my time during the next three months to be devoted to anyone other than her, at least in a business sort of way. Now I knew what to say to eliminate Adam as a threat in her mind.

"Mrs. Cranshaw, when I visited you at Elsbury Place in January, you made it quite clear that the writing of your novel would have to be the only business item on my plate until I complete the book. I assure you that I intend to honor that condition. I have already told Adam that any possibility of his house publishing my books would have to be put on the back burner until I have fulfilled my commitment to you."

I believed that I had chased away Mrs. Cranshaw's concerns about Adam, for she looked into my eyes and said, "Thank you, Miss Cole." She then looked at her watch and reported, "It is quarter to ten. I'll meet you in the office in fifteen minutes."

I finished my coffee and then headed for the office. It was 9:57 a.m. when I sat in the chair behind the table on which the computer was situated. Mrs. Cranshaw entered the office at exactly 10:00 a.m. with various items in her hands.

"Miss Cole, why are you sitting at the table?" she asked

as she approached me. "You are the author. You should be sitting behind the desk."

I made no comment. I simply complied with her wish and sat in the black leather chair behind the desk. Mrs. Cranshaw placed some papers on the desk and put her gold-rimmed spectacles on the bridge of her nose. She then picked up the chair in which I had been sitting, positioned it in front of the desk, and sat down.

"I made two outlines that should be guides to you in the development of the story," she explained. "The first outline should give you a general idea of what the story will be about. The second outline is far more detailed." Handing me a copy of the general outline, she said, "Let's review this outline first."

As she glanced at her own copy of the general outline, I instinctively reached for a pen and a blank piece of paper.

"If I have any questions or comments, may I express them as we review the outline?" I asked.

"Of course, Miss Cole. I encourage you to do so. Now, as shown in the first section of the outline, the main character is a woman who was born in Boston in 1939. Around the age of eighteen, she discovers that she is gifted as a writer, so she proceeds to write many imaginative stories. Writing becomes her passion. However, no matter how hard she tries, she faces roadblock after roadblock when trying to get her work accepted by publishers."

"It sounds like my story," I said with a giggle.

Mrs. Cranshaw made no remark about my comment, nor did she giggle. She simply continued with her explanation.

"As you can see in that first section of the outline, our main character refuses to give up her dream of becoming a published author. In order to pay her bills, she works at a job that is unrelated to her writing but devotes most of her free time to her literary endeavors. When she turns twenty-four, she still cannot claim to be a published author, but she continues to strive towards that goal. Her perseverance is supported by the young man she has been dating for quite some time. In fact, he and she were high school sweethearts. He is madly in love with her and wants to marry her, but he considers himself to be a pauper. Before marriage can come into the picture, he is determined to make himself financially stable. With that goal in mind, he secures a daytime job and attends college at night. He is studying to be an architect."

"Has the young man made his intention of marriage known to his girlfriend?" I asked.

"Yes, he has."

"He sounds like an admirable character," I remarked.

"They do not come any better," she said.

"What types of stories does the young woman write?" I asked.

"Fiction, mostly romance."

"It sounds as though this writer has something in common with us," I said smiling.

Mrs. Cranshaw rose from her chair and walked over to the small refrigerator in the corner of the office. She opened the refrigerator door and took out two bottles of water. When she returned to her seat, she placed one of the bottles in front of me. I twisted the bottle cap off and put the bottle aside for future consumption.

"Mrs. Cranshaw, you said that the young man is madly in love with the author. Is she just as much in love with him?"

"Let's just say, Miss Cole, that she does not fully appreciate the love he has for her. She does love him, though."

She removed a handkerchief from one of the pockets in her slacks and blew her nose. Then she took a few sips of water before continuing.

"Anyway, after receiving rejection slips from publishing houses for six years, the author becomes completely frustrated. She is not an arrogant woman, Miss Cole, but she sees the quality of her work and loses faith in the ability of others to value her literary craftsmanship."

I looked up at Mrs. Cranshaw and said, "I can certainly relate to that. After receiving quite a few rejections on my submissions to publishing houses, I followed the route of self-publishing."

"I am glad you brought up that point, Miss Cole. Today, many authors are following that route as an alternative to traditional publishing. The Internet and new technology have made the self-publishing route a good choice for many writers. It is my intention to self-publish the novel you are going to ghostwrite."

"Thanks to self-publishing, my work has not been in vain," I commented.

"So, Miss Cole, you can understand the frustration of our main character, who has failed to find a traditional publisher that will accept her work. She does indeed fear that her work has been in vain. Bursting with talent, she is going nowhere."

"Yes. She has already earned my sympathy."

"Exhausted from her fruitless efforts to get her works published," Mrs. Cranshaw continued, "the author decides to take a week off from her regular job. Her plan is to visit a female friend, who owns a cottage in Falmouth on Cape Cod. So, the author locks up her apartment in Boston and takes off for the Cape.

Early one morning, as she is walking alone along a beach in Falmouth, she spots a distinguished-looking man, walking in the opposite direction. When their paths cross, the man strikes up a conversation with her. I should mention, Miss Cole, that our main character is quite attractive and has a nice figure. After chatting for a few minutes, the man asks if she will allow him to join her in her walk. She does not mind, so they proceed to walk together along the water's edge. To her surprise, she learns that her walking companion is an editor in a publishing house. To his surprise, he learns that she is a writer. He takes an interest in her and offers to read her manuscripts, with the hope that the publishing house where he is employed might prove to be a route to publication for her. She accepts his offer to read her manuscripts but cautions herself not to let her hopes rise too high."

Mrs. Cranshaw paused to drink some water. During the brief silence, my thoughts drifted to Adam. I thought about how lucky I was that fate had brought me together with him, a publisher who valued my writing. I could only hope that fate would also be kind to the main character of the book I was to write.

"The editor and the author," Mrs. Cranshaw continued, "agree to meet the following afternoon at a restaurant in Falmouth Center. Their meeting will give them a chance to get to know one another and to discuss the author's unpublished works. When that meeting takes place, it goes extremely well. The editor and the author take to each other, so much so that he invites her out to dinner one night and to the theater another night before she is due to return to Boston. The editor recommends that upon returning home, the author waste no time in mailing him copies of her manuscripts."

"May I interrupt once again, Mrs. Cranshaw?"

"Of course, Miss Cole."

"Is the author falling out of love with her boyfriend, the aspiring architect?"

"She still loves her longtime boyfriend, but she is becoming increasingly dazzled by the charm of the editor. Also, let us not forget that the editor's job is a possible gateway to her success as a writer. Her desire to succeed makes her even more infatuated with the editor. Upon returning to Boston, the first thing on her agenda is to send copies of her manuscripts to him. Soon after, he phones her to give her his feedback on her manuscripts. He is very impressed with her work, which he refers to as 'a breath of fresh air,' and he informs her that he has delivered the copies of her manuscripts to the powers that be in the publishing house. A couple of more weeks go by, and she hears again from the editor, who is bubbling with enthusiasm. All her manuscripts have been accepted, and contracts are being drawn up for her review. Her dream to have her books published is about to be realized."

"At long last," I commented.

"Yes, at long last," Mrs. Cranshaw agreed. "The author signs the contracts. After publication, her books prove to be a great success. The publishing house is pleased with the financial rewards it reaps from her work, and the author also does quite well financially, to the point that she eventually is able to give up her regular job and devote all of her time to writing."

"That is a real success story," I commented.

"It is a success story up to that point in the outline, Miss Cole. Things are about to go downhill."

"Oh," I said with a perplexed look on my face. "I guess my congratulations for the author were premature."

"I am afraid so," she said. "It is at this point in the story that the author uses poor judgement. She lets her hunger for success cloud the feelings she has for her boyfriend, who, by this time, has attained a degree in architecture and is planning to start a small architectural firm. Time after time, the author cancels a date with her boyfriend in favor of being wined and dined by the editor, who eventually claims he has fallen in love with her. She, too, believes she has developed feelings for the editor, and of course, she is most grateful for all he did for her. Had it not been for him, she believes she would have given up writing and thrown all her manuscripts in the trash. The editor proposes and she accepts. The wedding takes place seven months after the editor and the author met on that beach in Falmouth."

"Her former boyfriend must be devastated," I remarked.

"He surely is, Miss Cole. He is beside himself."

"Does he ever marry?" I asked.

Mrs. Cranshaw shook her head and said, "No."

"This story I am going to write is sounding more and more like a tearjerker," I commented.

I looked up at Mrs. Cranshaw. Her eyes, which were watery, appeared to be supporting my comment.

"After the editor and the author marry," Mrs. Cranshaw said, "things go smoothly for a couple of years, but disaster is lurking around the corner. In spite of the fact that the couple is financially sound, the editor becomes obsessed with making more money. He starts to entertain the idea of quitting his job at the publishing house so that he can start his own publishing business. He presents such a rosy picture to his wife about his new business dream that she gives him her blessing to make his dream come true. Before quitting his job, he carefully investigates what rights his wife retains to her books that are currently published by the house in which he is employed. Any future books written by her will be published by the house he plans to establish. It is his assumption that many authors will submit their manuscripts to his house for publication and that he will make a lot of money."

"He sounds like a real risk-taker," I said. "Why rock the boat when things are going so well?"

"Miss Cole, he does more than rock the boat. He sinks the boat. His publishing business does not fare well. Any money that would have been paid to his wife for her writing is sunk right back into the business to try to keep it afloat. Things get so bad that the business approaches bankruptcy. However, the author's husband, being the clever fellow he is, finds a way to keep financial ruin at bay. Completely ignoring the fact that he is married, he starts to romance a wealthy woman behind his wife's back. When his wife learns of the affair, she is shocked. She and her husband get a divorce, after which he marries the other woman. Taking advantage of his new wife's not-so-small fortune, he pays off his debts and then closes his publishing business, with the intention of never working another day in his life."

"No way!" I exclaimed.

"The divorce was so bitter that the author's ex-husband starts to spread a rumor about her. The rumor is his way of saving face. It is his way of placing the blame for the divorce on his ex-wife."

"What rumor could he possibly spread about her?" I asked.

Mrs. Cranshaw rose from her chair and started to pace back and forth in front of the desk. She looked upset, so upset that I marveled at how deeply she could get engrossed in a story that had not even been written yet. She stopped pacing and looked directly at me.

"Miss Cole, he spreads the rumor that is ex-wife is gay and that it was his misfortune not to have discovered that fact before they were married."

I was appalled by the rumor, so much so that the pen I was holding flipped out of my hand and went flying onto the floor. Eager to hear what Mrs. Cranshaw would say next, I did not bother to retrieve the pen right away.

Mrs. Cranshaw sat down, cleared her throat, and said, "The rumor about the author spreads. Even though the rumor is false, some people jump to the conclusion that it is true. Friends pull away from her. Even some relatives whisper about her sexuality. Strangers look her up and down with suspicion, taking notice of how she dresses, walks, and talks. The publishing house that had profited from her talent finds all of her post-divorce submissions to be unacceptable. She submits her works to other houses, but they, too, reject her submissions. I am sorry to say that, in despair, the author abandons her writing career."

"That is terrible," I blurted out. "What difference does it make if she is gay or not? Talent is talent."

"Today," she said, "gay people still suffer even though the general attitude towards homosexuality has improved. They are still fighting to be recognized for the people they are and for the talents they possess. They are still fighting for the right to love the people they love. When you write this story, you will be dealing with decades past, when times for gay people were even tougher than they are now. Our main character, who has experienced the trials and tribulations of homosexuals, becomes a gay rights activist. Do you have any questions before I go on?"

"Yes, I do have a couple of questions. First, I would like

to ask if, after her divorce, the author renews her relationship with her former boyfriend who became an architect."

"No. The author, who had foolishly pushed her boyfriend aside in favor of an opportunistic marriage, now feels unworthy of him. Her horrid marriage and painful divorce have opened her eyes to the value of her former boyfriend's love for her. She is tempted to ask him for his forgiveness but can never really bring herself to do so. So, she stays clear of him, with the hope that he will eventually find a woman who appreciates his fine qualities. What is your other question, Miss Cole?"

"Is the author able to survive financially after walking away from her writing career?"

"She does manage to survive financially. A modest divorce settlement is paid to her. She is able to find temporary jobs as a secretary. What saves her the most is the inheritance she eventually receives from her father, who was widowed when he died and who had no other children."

"What does she receive from her father?"

"She receives a substantial amount of money and a healthy investment portfolio. She also receives his home."

"Where is the home?" I asked.

"The home, Miss Cole, is a cottage that is located in Rockport, Massachusetts."

Mrs. Cranshaw's last statement hit me like a ton of bricks! I now realized that the story she had just told was her own life story! The blinders that had prevented me from seeing things clearly had suddenly been removed. The woman sitting across from me was no longer an enigma. Now I knew why she had stopped writing years ago. The avarice of a devious husband, the false rumor that she is gay, and bigotry against gay people had all sabotaged her writing career. Now, too, I could understand her odd behavior. Her near reclusive lifestyle and her frequent outbursts of anger suddenly made perfect sense to me. This was a woman who had been so emotionally hurt by others that it was difficult for her to trust anyone. Her distrust obviously fueled her anger when anyone invaded her privacy. Her desire to segregate herself from her fellow residents at Elsbury Place, the invasive questions she asked me before she offered me the ghostwriting job, and her defiant reaction to Adam's suggestions about publication all reflected her distrust of people.

Mrs. Cranshaw stood up and said, "I think that we have done enough work for today. Here is the second outline, the more detailed one. You can look it over and begin to pull your thoughts together."

She started to walk towards the office door. Just before she reached the threshold, she turned around and looked at me.

"I am not gay," she said, "but over the years, I have been viewed as such. I have a good sense of what homosexuals endure. Through this book, I wish to convey that homosexuals should not have emotional pain thrust upon them by narrow-minded heterosexuals who erroneously think they have the right to cast judgement on them."

"I understand, Mrs. Cranshaw."

"By the way, Miss Cole, I want to remind you that there is an escape clause in our agreement. If you feel uncomfortable about writing this story, you are not obligated to continue."

"It is my intention to see this project through, Mrs. Cranshaw."

"One other thing, Miss Cole. If you do not want your name and contribution to the book shown in the acknowledgements section, I shall understand. Some people may jump to the conclusion that you are gay."

Without hesitation, I said, "I would feel honored to have my name and contribution shown in the book."

Mrs. Cranshaw nodded and, for the first time since we met, smiled at me. She then left the room. Once she was gone, I found myself wiping tears from my eyes, tears that had formed from my newfound respect for her. Her desire to fight prejudice against gay people was, in my opinion, worthy of the highest praise.

Chapter Seventeen

As the weeks went by, great progress was made on the writing of the novel. Mrs. Cranshaw and I attained a comfortable rhythm in our work habits. I would draft a couple of chapters, which she would then read, all the while holding a red pen in her right hand. Whenever I saw red ink on the pages of the drafts, I knew that she had either a suggestion or a revision in mind. My fear that she would be a difficult overseer proved to be unfounded. She seemed pleased with my work and even encouraged me to suggest ideas for the plot. Although the crux of the story was based on her life, the book was not intended to be an autobiography. It was meant to be a work of fiction, so, with her approval, I was able to create dinner parties and other events to make the story as interesting as possible.

I was so devoted to the writing of the novel during the month of June that I would get up early and go to bed late in order to revise a chapter or to surge forward to a new one. On several occasions, Mrs. Cranshaw scolded me for burning the candle at both ends. She even threatened to lock the office door unless I took some time to myself. In order to comply with her wishes, I did begin to set some time aside for rest and relaxation once July arrived. To my surprise, Mrs. Cranshaw expressed a desire to spend some time with me in a social sort of way, and to my even greater surprise, I found her to be good company. During the month of July, we enjoyed a variety of activities together—concerts, movies, boat rides, and dining out. On the evenings that we did not dine out, we ate dinner together in the cottage—on the porch, weather permitting. The woman who had been a loner seemed to be craving my companionship.

Early on Sunday morning, July 29, my cell phone rang. It was Harri calling.

"Hello, Harri," I said with an exuberance that reflected my joy of hearing from her.

"Hi, dear. How are you?"

"I am doing well. The writing is going better than I ever imagined, and I am really enjoying my stay here. How are you and Rudolf?"

"Fine. We miss you. We have been trying to come to Rockport to visit you, but we have been glued to our restaurant business. When I woke up this morning, I said to Rudolf that it is high time we get unglued from Harrud's and go see Linzie. This is short notice, but would it be all right if we come to see you this afternoon? It would be nice to go out to lunch together."

"I would love that," I said, "but I'll have to check with Mrs. Cranshaw. She and I had made plans to dine out this afternoon."

"I hope she will agree to our coming and will join us for lunch," Harri said. "I would like to meet her."

I had my doubts that Mrs. Cranshaw would want to join Harri, Rudolf, and me for lunch. Although she and I were enjoying an amicable relationship, I had a strong feeling that her reclusive nature would prevent her from being a member of a foursome at a restaurant table. My guess was that she would insist that I go to lunch with Harri and Rudolf and that she stay home.

"Harri, let's chat awhile," I said. "When we hang up, I'll ask Mrs. Cranshaw if she would be agreeable to the idea of the four of us going out to lunch. Then I'll call you back and let you know."

"Okay, dear. If she is agreeable to the idea, Rudolf and I

can stop by her place around one o'clock to pick you two up."

"All right, Harri."

"So, tell me, Linzie. Are you and Adam still seeing each other?"

"We sure are," I replied. "He has spent three weekends in Rockport at an inn that is not far from Mrs. Cranshaw's cottage. He is coming again next weekend. We're having a ball exploring Rockport together. A week from today, we're planning to visit Halibut Point State Park. He really is the gentleman you said he was, Harri. I enjoy his company."

"Linzie, I was definitely on the mark when I told you that Adam is a good catch and to grab him before another female does. As your second mom, I am your guiding light. There is not a doubt in my mind that Adam is the man for you."

"He really is a remarkable person," I said.

"Now, aren't you glad, Linzie, that your romance with Jack Grumey fizzled out? He was just another Kevin, seeing another woman behind your back."

I remained silent about Jack and simply let Harri continue talking.

"By the way, Linzie, do you have any more news about Kevin?"

"No. The latest news I have about Kevin is the same news I passed along to you just before I left for Rockport. As you know, Kevin's sister phoned me in late May to tell me that his legs were in bad shape and that he had a long road of rehabilitation ahead of him."

"I'm glad you did not tell his sister where you are right now. The thought of Kevin ringing Mrs. Cranshaw's doorbell unnerves me. He is such an unstable individual."

"Not to worry, Harri. I doubt very much that Kevin could even make it up the walk at this point."

"That's probably true. Well, dear, call me back after you talk to Mrs. Cranshaw. Rudolf and I are dying to see you, so I hope she will welcome our coming."

"I'll call you back shortly. Bye, Harri."

"Bye, Linzie."

Immediately after my conversation with Harri ended, I looked for Mrs. Cranshaw and discovered that she was engaged in her favorite activity—gardening. I exited the porch, crossed over the patio, and then walked to the garden. As I approached Mrs. Cranshaw, her back was towards me, so I gently cleared my throat to give her a little warning that I was behind her. She quickly turned around.

"Hello, Miss Cole."

"Hi, Mrs. Cranshaw. I have a question to ask you."

"Ask away," she said as she laid her hoe on the ground.

"I just received a phone call from my friend Harriet, who lives in Boston."

"Is that the Harriet you told me about weeks ago, the one who brought you and Adam Proctor together?"

"Yes."

"Your friend Harriet must be pleased with the results of her matchmaking efforts. You have been spending quite a bit of time with Mr. Proctor when he comes to town. I would proceed cautiously with that relationship if I were you."

I was baffled by Mrs. Cranshaw's obvious dislike of Adam. I could only speculate that she was distrustful of Adam simply because he was in the same business in which her ex-husband had been engaged.

Mrs. Cranshaw removed a tissue from a pocket in her slacks. As she wiped her brow with it, I remained quiet because I had a feeling that she had more advice to give. My feeling was correct.

"Let me give you the advice my father gave me, Miss Cole. It is advice I did not take and wish I had. The advice is this: Do not get overly enthused about any man until you have dated him winter, spring, summer, fall, and then some. You have not known Mr. Proctor very long. You should keep your guard up in spite of your admiration for Harriet's great ability to assess the character of a person. To my father's advice,

I shall add a bit of my own: Some men can be as changeable as the seasons, at least the seasons here in New England, so be prepared to bail out of a relationship when you least expect it."

"I understand," I said respectfully.

I believed there was good sense in Mrs. Cranshaw's advice and that of her father. I had known Kevin during not just one cycle of the seasons but two. I thought I knew him well until he did indeed change into a person I no longer recognized. Nevertheless, I felt Mrs. Cranshaw was being unduly harsh in her attitude towards Adam, whom she had seen only once.

"So, what is your question, Miss Cole?"

"Harriet and her husband, Rudolf, want to know if you and I will join them for lunch here in Rockport. They do not have much free time because they own a restaurant, but today they are able to drive here from Boston. Would dining with them be acceptable to you?"

I was expecting a quick negative response from Mrs. Cranshaw due to her disapproval of Harri's matchmaking efforts. To my astonishment, I received a quick positive one.

"That would be fine," she said. "I look forward to meeting your friends. When and where shall we meet them?"

"They will come here at one o'clock to pick us up."

"Tell them to plan to spend a little time here before we leave for the restaurant. Do they like wine?"

"Yes."

"Red or white?"

"Harri likes white wine, and Rudolf favors red."

"That's fine, Miss Cole. I have both in my wine rack."

She picked up her hoe and went back to work on the garden. As I headed for the house, I marveled at how wonders never cease. Perhaps there was hope for Mrs. Cranshaw after all, I thought. Perhaps she would break out of her cocoon and develop into a social butterfly.

Once I was inside the house, I called Harri and told her

that Mrs. Cranshaw and I would be able to join Rudolf and her for lunch and that wine would be served at the cottage before we left for the restaurant. Harri was thrilled.

For the next several hours, I sat in the office and worked on the novel. Around 12:30 p.m., I went to my bedroom and put on a pink slack suit, a black V-neck blouse, and a few pieces of casual jewelry. When I went downstairs to the living room, Mrs. Cranshaw was sitting on the sofa. Wearing a light-blue slack suit and a white blouse, she looked very nice.

"You must be excited that your friends are coming to visit," she said to me as I took a seat in one of the wingback armchairs across from the sofa.

"I am very excited. Harriet and Rudolf are like family to me. I should mention that I call Harriet by her nickname, which is Harri. She often refers to herself as my 'second mom' because she has been my guiding light ever since my mother died in 2016."

"You were lucky to have your mother all those years," Mrs. Cranshaw commented. "My mother died when I was ten years old."

"I'm sorry," I said. "Your childhood must have been rough without her."

"It was. I did learn, however, to be independent. It is important to form your own opinions about people and then proceed to act accordingly. If you make errors in judgement, at least they are your own errors."

Perhaps it was a good thing that the doorbell rang immediately after those words escaped Mrs. Cranshaw's lips because I did not know how to respond to the point of view she had just expressed. There was little doubt in my mind that she was encouraging me to do my own thinking rather than let Harri do my thinking for me. Upon hearing the doorbell ring, she rose from the sofa and headed for the door. I followed her. The front door creaked when she opened it. Behind the screen door stood Harri and Rudolf, with grins on their faces and with hands waving.

Mrs. Cranshaw opened the screen door and said, "Hello. I am Constance Cranshaw. Please come in."

Harri and Rudolf entered. Each of them shook Mrs. Cranshaw's hand, and each of them said how nice it was to meet her. Then, when Harri and Rudolf hurried over to me, the three of us engaged in a group hug.

"I have missed you both so much," I said.

"And we have missed our adopted daughter," Harri remarked. "Even the staff at Harrud's is eager for you to reclaim your favorite seat in front of the fireplace."

"Is Harrud's the name of your restaurant?" Mrs. Cranshaw asked.

"Yes," Rudolf replied. "Come have lunch or dinner there sometime, Mrs. Cranshaw. You will be our guest, of course."

"Thank you. Maybe after I return to Elsbury Place, Miss Cole and I will dine at Harrud's some afternoon."

"That would be wonderful," I commented.

"Let's enjoy some wine on the porch," Mrs. Cranshaw said.

She led the way through the living room. Once on the porch, Harri and I took seats across from each other while Mrs. Cranshaw and Rudolf did the same. Two bottles of wine, a corkscrew, and four glasses had been placed on the table.

"I would like each of you to choose whichever wine suits your fancy," Mrs. Cranshaw said.

In keeping with his gentlemanly manner, Rudolf asked, "May I do the honors, Mrs. Cranshaw, and serve the wine?"

Nodding, Mrs. Cranshaw replied, "That would be fine."

Rudolf stood up, took everyone's order, and opened the two wine bottles. After pouring the wine, he retook his seat.

"You certainly have a lovely spot here, Mrs. Cranshaw," he said.

"And a convenient spot as well," Harri added. "You don't have to go far to get to the stores or the beaches. Your location is ideal."

"I hate the thought of leaving here at the end of August,"

I remarked. "I'm sure going to miss Rockport. It has so much to offer."

"Just make sure you do leave," Rudolf said laughing, "or we'll have to hire a posse to escort you back to Boston."

Rudolf was sitting to my left. I turned my head in his direction and looked at him tenderly.

"No posse will be necessary," I said. "The thought of dining at Harrud's will help me come back to Boston voluntarily."

Rudolf smiled. He then gently patted my left hand with his right hand to express his appreciation for my comment.

"Speaking of dining," Harri said, "I have been trying to decide where we should eat."

"Linzie and Mrs. Cranshaw should choose the restaurant," Rudolf remarked. "They are far more familiar with the area than we are."

"I would like Miss Cole to choose," Mrs. Cranshaw said. "This is a special day for her because you two are here."

"Thank you, Mrs. Cranshaw," I said. "The day I arrived here, Adam introduced me to a nice restaurant on Bearskin Neck that has a great view of the water. The seafood dinners we ordered were delicious. I thought that restaurant would be a good choice."

"That certainly sounds like a good choice to my taste buds," Rudolf remarked. "A view of the water will make the meal even more enjoyable. By the way, Linzie, Harriet tells me that Adam has come to visit you a few times."

"Yes, he has. In fact, he is coming next weekend. As usual, he will be staying at a nearby inn."

"Mrs. Cranshaw, have you met Adam?" Harri inquired.

"Yes, I have. I met Mr. Proctor the day he drove Miss Cole from Boston to my cottage. The three of us had some iced tea out here on the porch."

"Isn't he just wonderful?" Harri asked.

Mrs. Cranshaw started to swirl the wine in her glass. She kept her eyes focused on the tiny wave she was creating. It appeared she was not going to respond immediately to Harri's question about Adam.

Finally, Mrs. Cranshaw said, "I spent about twenty minutes with the man. So, in view of that short amount of—"

"Trust me, Mrs. Cranshaw," Harri interjected, "when I tell you that Adam is wonderful and so ideal for Linzie in every way."

"How much time have you spent with Mr. Proctor?" Mrs. Cranshaw asked Harri.

"Ah, let me see. Well, I spent a good two hours with Adam when he came to dine at our restaurant one evening."

"Two hours is the total amount of time you have spent with Mr. Proctor?" Mrs. Cranshaw asked.

"Why, yes," Harri replied. "Two hours was long enough for me to get to know Adam."

"Two hours is not very long when it comes to the matter of Miss Cole's future," Mrs. Cranshaw said with conviction.

Harri looked as though she wanted to say something but could not find the right words. There was a moment of silence at the table. It was an awkward moment.

Breaking the silence, Harri said, "Well, you see, Mrs. Cranshaw, my son is a friend of Adam."

"How long have they been friends?" Mrs. Cranshaw asked.

"Three years," Harri replied.

"Are they close friends that spend a lot of time together?" Mrs. Cranshaw inquired.

"A lot of time? No, not quite," Harri admitted.

Mrs. Cranshaw shook her head disapprovingly and said, "It sounds to me, Harriet, that Adam Proctor is almost as much a stranger to you as he is to me."

There were soon telltale signs that Harri was not pleased with Mrs. Cranshaw's last comment. Mrs. Cranshaw was sitting to Harri's left, and Harri wasted no time in casting a disdainful look in that direction. That look was followed by a rolling of Harri's eyes, another not-too-subtle sign that Harri's feathers had been ruffled by our hostess.

"Linzie can tell you," Harri said defiantly, "that I have been blessed with the gift to size people up quite accurately and to make predictions that come true. I got good vibes from Adam. I firmly believe that he and Linzie are perfect for each other."

"I have heard about your psychic powers," Mrs. Cranshaw retorted, "but I do not think Miss Cole should be influenced by what you see in a crystal ball."

After taking a gulp of wine, Harri placed her glass on the table with such force that I feared that the glass would soon be leaking. Her hand that had been holding the glass was now rolled up in a fist.

"Rudolf and I want the best for Linzie," Harri said in a raised voice. "We know how hurt she was when her former boyfriend, Kevin, cheated on her. Then Kevin was followed by Jack Grumey, who also cheated on her. I see nothing wrong in my trying to match her with the right man, and I believe Adam is the right man."

I took several sips of wine to try to steady my nerves. This little get-together was definitely not going well.

"I know Mr. Grumey is a police officer and the tenant who lives downstairs from Miss Cole," Mrs. Cranshaw stated. "However, I did not know that he had also been a beau of Miss Cole."

"He was," Harri said, "but he turned out to be another disappointment. In fact, it was Jack Grumey who caused Adam to keep a distance from Linzie after their first date in January."

"How did Mr. Grumey manage to do that?" Mrs. Cranshaw asked Harriet.

"Well, after Adam took Linzie out to dinner, they returned to her apartment. Who was taking a snooze on Linzie's sofa? No one other than Jack Grumey. Adam got mad and stormed out of Linzie's apartment. At least Adam had the decency to ask Linzie for a copy of each of her three books before he left. As a publisher who was trying to take an interest in Linzie's writing, he promised her he would read her books, and he kept his promise."

"Perhaps by asking for a copy of each of her books, Mr. Proctor was merely trying to feather his own bed," Mrs. Cranshaw remarked. "After all, he is in the publishing business and is always looking for works of good writers."

Disgusted, Harri said, "Really, Mrs. Cranshaw, that is an awful thing to say about Adam. I am certain that by offering to read Linzie's books, Adam was not thinking solely of his business. I am sure he wanted to read Linzie's books with the hope that he could also help her get ahead."

Although I did not want to enter the war of words that was escalating between Harri and Mrs. Cranshaw, I felt I must. Harri, who had never met Jack, had painted a black picture of him that he did not deserve. I wanted to clarify things.

"I want to set something straight," I said. "Adam's outburst of anger the night of my date with him was not Jack Grumey's fault. It is true that Jack was sleeping on my sofa when Adam and I entered my apartment, but I had given Jack permission to use my living room as a bedroom. You see, Jack had ordered a bedroom set, but it had not arrived yet. Also, that night of my date with Adam, Jack's back was bothering him, so Jack meant to just rest on my sofa for a short time and then leave before I came home with Adam. Jack was so tired that he simply fell asleep and, therefore, was unable to leave my place before Adam's and my arrival."

"Miss Cole, was all that explained to Mr. Proctor?" Mrs. Cranshaw asked.

"Yes, it was. Unfortunately, Adam would not accept the explanation. He simply jumped to the wrong conclusion that I was in the habit of entertaining men in my place and left that night in a real huff. Almost five months went by before I heard from Adam again."

"Mr. Proctor sounds like a hothead to me," Mrs. Cranshaw commented.

I nervously looked at Harri and saw her wince. I was afraid that she would re-enter the fray at that moment, but she did not. She sat there with her mouth shut, but I worried that it would not stay shut very long.

"From the conversation at this table," Mrs. Cranshaw continued, "I gather, Miss Cole, that at some point after your date with Mr. Proctor, you began to develop feelings for Jack Grumey. What happened to your interest in him?"

I took a moment to gather my thoughts. My relationship with Jack had become so muddled that I did not want my words to follow suit and sound like gobbledygook.

"Jack," I said, "was so good to me and protective of me from the first day we met, which was January third. As time passed, we grew closer and closer. However, I wanted to take our relationship at a slow pace because I was still reeling from my breakup with Kevin. On May thirty-first, a couple of days before I came to Rockport, Jack told me that he had special feelings for me and expressed his hope that our relationship would develop into something permanent in the future. I told him that he meant a lot to me but that I wanted to continue to take our relationship at a slow pace."

"Did he accept your wish to go slowly?" Mrs. Cranshaw asked.

"Jack accepted my wish, but I think he was disappointed that I would not make a solid commitment to a future with him."

"It sounds to me as though the man had a lot of feeling for you, Miss Cole," Mrs. Cranshaw commented.

"I thought so too," I said, "until something happened later that very day. It was early on the morning of May thirty-first that Jack told me I was so special to him. That evening, he was supposed to come up to my apartment and enjoy a Chinese dinner with me. After he got home from work, I called him to make sure he was still coming to my place. He told me he had a terrible headache and wanted to go to bed early. We agreed that we should postpone our Chinese dinner until the following evening. The next thing I knew, Jack was entertaining a woman out on his patio, about a half hour after he backed out of his date with me. They were drinking wine and enjoying a barbecue. I was mad."

"So, you figured he was cheating on you?" Mrs. Cranshaw asked.

"Yes, I figured just that."

"Did you express your anger to Mr. Grumey about the matter?" Mrs. Cranshaw inquired.

"I did later that night when Jack phoned me. He said that he could explain everything—that things did not look as they appeared."

"So, Miss Cole, what was his explanation if I may ask?"

I sheepishly replied, "I do not know. I did not give him the chance to explain. I was very short with him on the phone because I felt so hurt."

"Now, Miss Cole, please use your head and think this through," Mrs. Cranshaw said. "You said just a minute ago that when Adam Proctor saw Jack Grumey on your sofa the night of that ill-fated date in January, that, in spite of your explanation regarding Mr. Grumey's presence in your apartment, Mr. Proctor jumped to the wrong conclusion. Consequently, Mr. Proctor got mad and stormed out of your apartment. Is that correct?"

"That is correct."

"You," she continued, "did not even give Mr. Grumey the chance to explain that woman's presence on his patio the evening he was originally meant to be with you. Is it not possible, Miss Cole, that you jumped to the wrong conclusion as to why that woman was present at Mr. Grumey's place that evening?"

Feeling as though I were on the stand in a court of law, I nervously twisted my paper napkin in so many directions that it is a wonder it remained intact. I looked out at the backyard briefly and then returned my gaze to Mrs. Cranshaw.

Nodding my head, I replied in a weak voice, "Yes, it is very possible that I jumped to the wrong conclusion. Actually, it is very probable. Jack was always honest with me. I had no right to refuse to listen to his explanation, especially since he had expressed his love for me that very morning. It was I who was having trouble expressing my love for him. I think I was simply afraid of getting hurt again."

Mrs. Cranshaw looked at me and smiled. Harri looked so agitated that I knew she could not bite her tongue any longer.

"Mrs. Cranshaw, you are putting all kinds of crazy ideas into poor Linzie's head. You are going to confuse her to the point that she may break off her relationship with Adam. Adam is the ideal mate for her. He is kind, smart, ambitious, and successful, and he is in a business that is related to Linzie's work. Just think of it. Adam and Linzie would not only be a husband-and-wife team but also a publisher-and-writer team."

I shuddered when I heard Harri say those words. Because of Mrs. Cranshaw's disastrous marriage to a devious publisher, I fully expected our hostess to explode over Harri's comment. Quite amazingly, she did not. In fact, she said nothing.

Due to all the tension that had been mounting between Harri and Mrs. Cranshaw, I had paid little attention to Rudolf. When I glanced in his direction, he must have interpreted my glance to be a plea to change the subject.

"Linzie, how is the novel coming along?" he asked.

"Just fine," I replied.

"Harriet and I are curious as to what the book is about," he said.

I hemmed and hawed and finally said, "Ah, it might be better if I give you a copy of the book when it is finished rather than give you bits and pieces of the plot right now. The book is really a work in progress."

Looking rather perplexed, Harri asked, "Well, can't you give us a general idea as to what the story is about?"

For some reason, I was unable to give an articulate description of the book. As I babbled on, Rudolf and Harri looked more and more confused.

"Allow me, Miss Cole," Mrs. Cranshaw interrupted. "The

story, in a nutshell, is about a female author who begins to write in the 1950s. Once her stories get published, she is quite successful. However, due to a nasty divorce, the author's ex-husband spreads a false rumor about her. The rumor is that she is gay. Although the rumor is false, many people assume that it is true. The rumor ruins the author's career, causing her to abandon her writing. The rumor also has a negative impact on her personal life. Some friends, family members, and strangers look at her suspiciously as though she has some sort of disease. She is the victim of bigotry. Bear in mind that the story deals with decades past when times for gay people were even tougher than they are now. Although the author is not gay, she experiences the trials and tribulations of homosexuals. Consequently, she becomes a great supporter of gay rights."

Harri leaned towards the left and boldly stared into Mrs. Cranshaw's eyes. Mrs. Cranshaw did not flinch one bit.

"Mrs. Cranshaw, do you mean to tell me that Linzie is writing a story about a gay woman?"

Mrs. Cranshaw leaned towards the right and stared right back into Harri's eyes.

"No," she said, "I am not telling you that Miss Cole is writing a story about a gay woman. Rather, Miss Cole is writing a story about a woman who was falsely rumored to be gay."

"What the hell is the point of such a trashy story?" Harri yelled.

All hell was about to break loose. Hoping to receive a comforting glance, I looked at Rudolf. He had no comfort to give. He appeared to be in a state of shock.

Completely unfazed by Harri's assessment of the story as "trashy," Mrs. Cranshaw replied, "This is by no means a trashy story. It is quite the opposite. It is a touching story in which a straight woman experiences the hardships that homosexuals face. Believing that no one but God has the right to cast judgement on any human being, she does her best to fight bigotry by lending support to gay rights."

"Mrs. Cranshaw, you cannot tell me that homosexuality

is normal!" Harri exclaimed.

"I am not going to tell you that it is abnormal," Mrs. Cranshaw said quite calmly.

"Why, that's the same thing as saying it is normal," Harri rejoined.

"Who are you, Harriet, to say what is normal and what is not?" Mrs. Cranshaw asked.

Harri had such an anguished look on her face that I feared that her blood pressure had skyrocketed in a matter of seconds. Rudolf must have shared my concern, for he leaned in her direction and patted her right shoulder with his left hand.

"Take it easy, Harriet," he said. "Take it easy."

"How can I take it easy?" Harri asked in a trembling voice. "This woman is corrupting Linzie. She obviously wants to wreck the relationship Linzie has with Adam. As if that's not enough, she has hired Linzie to write a disgusting story."

Harri picked up her glass and grabbed the paper napkin that had been lying underneath it. She frantically mopped sweat off her forehead.

Then she looked at me and asked, "Linzie, is your name going to appear somewhere in the book?"

"My name and contribution will appear in the acknowledgements section of the book."

"Linzie Cole, have you lost your mind?" Harri screamed. "People who see your name in the book might think *you* are gay."

"Harri, if people want to jump to the conclusion that I am gay, I refuse to feel ashamed. I support Mrs. Cranshaw's purpose in writing this book. People who are gay should not be treated as though they have some sort of disease. I feel that a gay person has the right to love that special someone in his or her life without feeling any kind of shame."

Harri thumped her fist on the table and said, "Linzie, I know you're not gay, but what you're doing is something I cannot accept. Now, I want you to pack your bags and come back to Boston with us. If Mrs. Cranshaw wants to make a fuss about your leaving, that is her problem."

"Miss Cole has the right to terminate her job here anytime she sees fit," Mrs. Cranshaw said. "If she wants to leave, I shall pay her properly for all the hard work she has done so far."

Harri rose to her feet and said, "Linzie, meet us at the car when you have finished packing."

Looking up at Harri, I said, "I am staying here. I believe in this book and want to finish it."

"In that case, we are through," Harri said bitterly.

My ex-second mom left the porch so quickly that she probably reached the front door before Rudolf rose from his chair. There was great sadness in Rudolf's eyes. I believed that his sadness did not stem from my support of gay rights. It was my hunch that his sadness stemmed from Harri's condescending attitude towards homosexuals. As he passed by my chair, he softly touched my left shoulder without saying a word. When I heard the creak of the front door, I knew that Harri and Rudolf were exiting the cottage and my life.

Teary-eyed, I looked at Mrs. Cranshaw and said, "I thought they were my true-blue friends."

With a compassionate look in her eyes, Mrs. Cranshaw remarked, "Linzie, you have just had a taste of what my life has been like."

That was the first time she addressed me as "Linzie." From that moment on, she never again addressed me as "Miss Cole."

Chapter Eighteen

On August 5, one week after Harri and Rudolf exited my life, a former acquaintance of mine re-entered it. That morning, I had just stepped out of a downtown bakery when I heard a voice call my name. I turned around and saw George Grumey hurrying towards me. Although it was Sunday, it appeared he was not taking the day off. He was dressed in a tan suit, white shirt, and red tie, and he was carrying a briefcase. The closer he came my way, the more uptight I felt. I feared that George would scold me for the bitter way I had spoken to Jack over the phone on May 31, after the woman Jack had entertained on his patio had left the premises. To my relief, when George came face to face with me, he was smiling.

"Linzie, it is so nice to see you. How are you?"

Returning his smile, I replied, "Just fine, George. How is everything with you?"

"Oh, I have been quite busy. My work is keeping me on the go. In fact, I'm on my way to Bearskin Neck to discuss business with a client during breakfast. So, what are you up to?"

"I guess you could say that I am on a mission of mercy," I said with a chuckle. "Mrs. Cranshaw has a craving for doughnuts, so I just paid a visit to the bakery."

"How is the ghostwriting job going?" he asked.

"It is going quite well," I replied. "Thank you again for reviewing the agreement for me back in January."

I wanted to ask how Jack was but felt awkward about bringing up his name. Fortunately, what George would say next would open the door to a discussion about Jack.

"Linzie, don't thank me. As you know, it was Jack who arranged for that meeting at my place in January."

"How is Jack?" I was then able to ask.

George shrugged his shoulders and replied, "To tell you the truth, I don't know how to deal with Jack these days. I keep inviting him to go out on my boat with me, but he keeps coming up with all kinds of excuses. When I last saw Jack, it was in early May. At that time, he was chipper. Ever since June arrived, he has been down in the dumps about something—something that he does not want to discuss with me. Have you heard from him, Linzie?"

Shaking my head, I said, "No."

"Now I'm convinced he is depressed. I know how much he cares for you, Linzie."

I was surprised that George was unaware of the rift that had taken place between Jack and me on May 31. The two brothers had always been so close.

"Linzie, I promised you a ride on my boat, and I intend to keep my promise. I'm going out on the boat this afternoon. A female friend of mine is coming along. Would you like to join us?"

"I'm afraid I cannot join you, George. A friend of mine, who is a publisher, is here in Rockport for the weekend. He is here to spend time with me."

"Is your friend here to discuss business with you?" George asked.

"No. The purpose of his coming is personal."

"In that case, Linzie, feel free to invite him to come out on the boat. We can make it a foursome."

I found myself wanting to accept the invitation, not so much for the boat ride but to hear more about Jack. George's belief that Jack was depressed was troubling me.

"What time are you planning to go boating?" I asked.

"Oh, around two o'clock. My friend and I are going to have lunch on my patio at one o'clock. If you and your friend decide to come out on the boat, you two should also come for lunch. I'm not going to prepare one of my famous gourmet meals," he said laughing. "Lunch will consist of hamburgers and a few side dishes."

"I have your phone number, George. May I call you to let you know one way or the other?"

"That would be fine, Linzie. Just leave a message if I do not answer the phone."

"I'll call my friend as soon as I get back to Mrs. Cranshaw's cottage. Our plan was to visit Halibut Point State Park this afternoon, but I think I can talk him into going to the park another time."

"Please try to come, Linzie."

"I'll certainly try, George. Thanks."

"Bye, Linzie."

"Bye."

As I began my walk back to Mrs. Cranshaw's cottage, the box of doughnuts I was carrying caused my mind to wander back to the morning of January 4, when that terrible blizzard hit Boston. That morning, Jack had surprised me with a half-dozen doughnuts and had made a pot of coffee for the two of us. I thought about how he had stayed in my apartment with me the night before in order to protect me from Kevin, who, we suspected, had thrown the rock through my living room window on January 3. Jack had been my knight in shining armor. Single-handedly, I had knocked him off his horse, and the reason for that self-destructive act—my fear of being hurt—was something I could no longer hide from myself. Several times, I had been tempted to phone Jack, but I was afraid that he would have nothing to do with me, so I refrained from calling him.

When I arrived back at the cottage, I wasted no time in phoning Adam. He was enjoying breakfast in his room at the inn.

"Good morning, love," he said in an upbeat tone of voice.

"Good morning, Adam," I said in a tone of voice that was far from upbeat.

"Are you all right?" he asked. "You sound a little down."

"Oh, I'm just a little tired. A little relaxation will cure me. Speaking of relaxation, how would you like to go out on a boat this afternoon?"

"Is Mrs. Cranshaw so generous that she bought you a boat?" he asked laughing.

"No," I replied without returning his laugh. "A little while ago, I was downtown and crossed paths with an acquaintance of mine. His name is George, and he lives in Gloucester. He owns a cabin cruiser that he docks behind his house, and—"

"He sounds like a rich friend," Adam interrupted.

"Whether he is rich or not, he is a great guy. Anyway, he and a lady friend of his are having lunch on his patio at one o'clock and then going out on the boat at two o'clock. He invited us to join them for both lunch and the boat ride."

"What about our plan to go to Halibut Point State Park?" Adam asked.

"I figured we could go there another time."

"Okay, Linzie. A boat ride sounds good. Do you know how to get to your friend's house?"

"Yes. I have been to his place once before."

"Great. How would it be if I pick you up at half past ten? That will give us time to see some of Gloucester before we head for George's house."

I looked at my watch. The time was 9:10 a.m.

"Half past ten sounds perfect," I said.

"Don't forget to bring a hat and a pair of sunglasses."

"I'll make sure I bring them. See you later, Adam."

"See you, Linzie."

As soon as my conversation with Adam ended, I dialed George's number and left a message that Adam and I accepted his invitation for both lunch and the boat ride. Then, carrying the box of doughnuts, I headed for the porch, where I suspected Mrs. Cranshaw would be sitting. My suspicion was correct. In anticipation of the doughnuts she was craving, she had placed a coffee pot, two mugs, a sugar bowl, a creamer, two plates, and a tray on the table.

As I entered the porch, Mrs. Cranshaw winked at me and said, "I see that your mission proved to be successful."

I laughed and said, "The mission was not only successful but also interesting. As I was coming out of the bakery, I ran into George Grumey, Jack Grumey's brother. You may recall that George is the lawyer who, on my behalf, reviewed the ghostwriter agreement your lawyer drew up."

"Yes. I certainly do recall that," Mrs. Cranshaw said. "If I remember correctly, he lives in Gloucester."

"Yes, he does. He owns a beautiful house that overlooks Gloucester Harbor. He also owns a cabin cruiser that he docks behind the house. He invited Adam and me to have lunch at his home this afternoon and then go out on his boat."

"Will Jack be going too?" she asked.

"No."

I put the box on the table and poured coffee into the mugs. Mrs. Cranshaw took the doughnuts out of the box and placed them on the tray. After I took a seat across from her, she extended the tray in my direction. Thanking her, I chose one of the objects of her craving. Then she chose one for herself.

"I am so glad George Grumey was able to review the ghostwriter agreement for you before you signed it, Linzie."

"Me too. I must admit that I am a bit of a dummy when it comes to legal terminology. In fact, if Adam and I get serious about entering into a publishing contract, I am going to ask George Grumey to review the contract before I put my name on the dotted line."

Mrs. Cranshaw nodded her head to show her approval. There was, however, a look of concern on her face.

"Mrs. Cranshaw, may I ask you a question?"

"Yes, of course."

"You do not like Adam, do you?"

She looked at me straight in the eyes and said, "No, Linzie, I do not like Adam."

"May I ask why?"

"You may ask, but I am afraid you will not be pleased with what I have to say."

Mrs. Cranshaw took a moment to grasp the sugar bowl and pull it towards her. She then proceeded to put a spoonful of sugar into her mug. That action was followed by a thorough stirring. I believed she was buying a little time to collect her thoughts before speaking.

"Unlike Harriet," she said, "who got good vibes from Adam, I got bad vibes from Adam. When the three of us were sitting on the porch, Adam struck me as being way too eager to drum up business for his publishing house. In my opinion, he was downright pushy. Do not forget, Linzie, that the day he drove you here was the first and only time I ever laid eyes on the man. That day was only the second time you laid eyes on him. To me, he was a complete stranger, and to you, a virtual stranger. I simply felt uneasy that he was zeroing in on publishing your three books and any unpublished works of mine. He even had the publication of the book you are currently ghostwriting in his sights."

"I guess I figured he was trying to be helpful," I said.

"Helpful to himself, I suspected. The conversation that took place here last Sunday, when Harriet and Rudolf came to visit you, made me even more leery about Adam. Per Harriet, Adam blew up when he saw Jack Grumey in your apartment, but he did not hesitate to take a copy of each of your three books before he went storming out of your place. That led me to believe that he is more interested in reaping the financial rewards of your work than in valuing you as a person."

"Do you really think that he is more interested in the money that can be made from my books than in me, Mrs. Cranshaw?"

"I do. I am afraid that when Harriet looked through that imaginary crystal ball of hers to foresee your and Adam's future as a couple, her crystal ball must have fogged up. Her prediction of a rosy future for the two of you is faulty. If your relationship with Adam continues, I cringe when I foresee what is in store for you, Linzie."

"I'm confused, Mrs. Cranshaw. How can *you* foresee what the future will hold for Adam and me as a couple?"

"I did not look into a crystal ball to foresee that future. I did, however, look at that future through the eyes of my accountant, who managed to gather financial data about Adam's business. Adam is not the successful businessman he claims to be. His business is floundering."

My right hand, which was holding my mug, began to shake. I quickly called upon my left hand to join forces with my right one in an effort to keep the mug steady as I placed it on the table. The news of Adam's failing business hit me hard, not because Adam was a financial flop but because he was a liar. Neither Mrs. Cranshaw nor I spoke for a minute or so. She, I believed, was giving me time to fully absorb the bad news she had just imparted. As for myself, I was so rattled that I did not know what to say.

"Is his business in very bad shape?" I finally asked.

Nodding, she said, "It is on the brink of disaster. I would hate to see you get dragged into a relationship similar to the one I had with my ex-husband. I like you, Linzie, and I do not want to see you get hurt."

Mrs. Cranshaw's father's advice about not getting overly enthused about any man until you take the time to really get to know him now made more sense than ever. The shock I felt over Adam's dishonesty was matched by my gratitude to Mrs. Cranshaw for taking the initiative and the time to check out the health of Adam's business.

"Thank you, Mrs. Cranshaw, for saving me from the clutches of a dishonest man."

"You're the last person I would want to see get hurt, Linzie."

Holding my mug with both hands, I started to drink

some coffee in order to give the wheels in my head a chance to turn. While the wheels were in motion, questions were forming in my mind. This was not the time to hesitate to ask them.

"How long have you known about Adam's failing business?"

"Not long," she replied. "My accountant called me a few days ago to relay the information."

"Was there a reason you did not break the news to me right away?"

"Yes. I knew that Adam had already made plans to come to Rockport this weekend, so I planned to tell you once the weekend was over. You were looking forward to going to Halibut Point State Park, and I did not want to burst your bubble quite yet. However, when you asked me a few minutes ago why I do not like Adam, I found it necessary to make you aware of the fact that Adam has not been honest with you."

"I appreciate your candor. You are a good friend."

"I value your friendship too, Linzie. When Bertie died, I dreaded the thought of spending the summer here alone. Thanks to you, I have not been alone. Having you here has lifted my spirits."

"Bertie was very special to you, wasn't she?"

"Yes. Bertie and I were close friends for many years. We met when we were in our twenties. After my divorce and after her husband died, we traveled a lot together. She and I enjoyed many summers here. Due to that rumor about me, it was assumed that she and I were a gay couple. We were the target of whispers and snickers, but Bertie turned a deaf ear to all of that. She never wavered in her friendship for me."

"I now realize how much such a friendship should be valued," I said sadly.

I was still trying to come to grips with the fact that Harri had disowned me and, in my opinion, for no good reason. Mrs. Cranshaw seemed to sense my sorrow.

"A true friend is so very rare, Linzie."

"I certainly agree with that."

Painful thoughts stemming from the disappearance of Harri and Rudolf from my life flooded my mind. Preoccupied with those thoughts, I began to enter my own little world.

"Linzie, there is something I would like to discuss with you."

I was in such deep thought that when Mrs. Cranshaw said those words, I jumped in my seat. Once she had my attention, I looked into her eyes. There was an unmistakable sparkle in them.

"I believe I have a rather brilliant idea," she said. "When you finish ghostwriting this novel, how would you like to work on another novel as a co-author with me? I think we make a good team. You could come to my apartment on a regular basis so that we can confer. As a co-author, your name would appear with mine on the cover of the book. We would own the copyright jointly and would split the royalties evenly."

Very touched by her suggestion, I could feel my eyes getting moist. For the first time ever, she made physical contact with me by reaching over the table and tapping my right hand gently with her left hand.

"So, what do you think?" she asked in a hopeful tone of voice.

"I cannot think of anything that would make me happier," I replied. "Thank you, Mrs. Cranshaw."

"Don't thank me, Linzie. I thank you. By the way, I think it's about time you call me by my first name."

I chuckled and said, "I'll have to practice saying *Constance*. It may not come naturally to me after calling you Mrs. Cranshaw all these months."

"Call me Connie. That has a less formal ring to it."

"Do many call you that?" I asked.

"Only true friends. In other words, very, very few."

Chapter Nineteen

After Adam's visit to the Cranshaw cottage, he swore that his first visit would be his last. He would joke that if he ever set foot in the cottage again, Mrs. Cranshaw would probably grab her broom, beat him with it, and then chase him all the way back to Boston with that broom in hand. Wanting to keep a low profile whenever he came to pick me up, he would remain in his car and wait for me to show up at the passenger door. Rather than get out of the car and open the door for me, which was his habit, he would simply stay put in the driver's seat.

When Adam came to pick me up at 10:30 a.m. for our trip to Gloucester, I was surprised to see him standing at the end of the walk when I opened the front door of the cottage. Before heading for the spot where he was standing, I took a deep breath and made a promise to myself to act as normally as possible. The news of Adam's failing business had shocked me, but I was not going to convey to him that I was aware of his financial situation. That decision was based on another decision of mine, which was not to go out with him in the future.

"Hi, Linzie," he said while giving me a hearty wave. "It's a beautiful day for a boat ride."

"That it is," I said as I began my walk on the pavers. "The temperature is in the eighties, and the sun is shining. The weather is cooperating."

As I approached Adam, he extended his right hand to me, drew me close to his body, and kissed me on the lips. Then with his right arm draped around my shoulders, we stepped onto the sidewalk. I looked for his silver sedan, but it was nowhere in sight. In the spot where he usually parked it was a much older car. Rust had obviously attacked its yellow body There were tears in the black vinyl top.

"My sedan broke down a few days ago," Adam explained. "It is in the shop right now. My friend Al lent me this car. He owns another car and hardly uses this one, so he did not mind lending it to me."

"When will your car be repaired?" I asked.

"Before any repairs are made, the mechanic is going to call me and let me know how extensive the repair job would be. If very extensive, I may look around for a new car and continue to use this one while I'm looking."

Adam opened the passenger door, and I got into the car. The stench of stale cigarette smoke was almost too much to bear.

"I better keep all four windows open," Adam said as he lowered himself into the driver's seat. "Al is quite a smoker."

"Most likely a chain-smoker," I commented while coughing.

"Once we're moving, it won't be so bad, Linzie."

Before starting the engine, Adam reached into the glove compartment and pulled out several brochures that listed attractions in Gloucester. After handing them to me, he turned the key in the ignition and pulled away from the curb.

"Linzie, if you see anything in those brochures that interests you, let me know. I thought we should first head for Gloucester Harbor. It would be fun to walk around and enjoy the water view. Overlooking the harbor is a memorial to Gloucester fishermen whose lives were lost at sea. I thought we should pay a visit to the memorial."

"Are you referring to the *Man at the Wheel* statue?" I asked.

"I certainly am. You are becoming a real history buff, Linzie."

"I have seen pictures of the statue during my stay here," I commented.

"Do you know how tall the statue is?" Adam asked.

"My guess is that it is taller than I am, but I have no idea of the exact height."

"The statue is eight feet tall. It is bronze, and it stands on a granite base. The fisherman is made to look as though he is facing stormy weather. There was a dedication in 1925, during which the statue was unveiled. Leonard Craske was the sculptor."

"Maybe you should have been a historian rather than a publisher, Adam."

"It was tempting to be a historian, but my publishing business has been so successful that I believe it was the right road for me to travel."

I made no comment about the road on which he was traveling. I suspected his luxurious sedan was now a casualty on that road.

"By the way, Linzie, have you looked over those papers I gave you in June? You know, the ones dealing with publishing your books through my house."

"I have only glanced at them, Adam. Working on the novel has kept me extremely busy, and as you know, I am not going to make any decision about having my books published by you until my work for Mrs. Cranshaw is completed."

"Well, when will that be?"

"It's hard to say. We have made great progress on the book, but I think there will be at least two more months of work ahead of us after she and I leave Rockport."

A silence ensued, which led me to believe that Adam was mad at me for not taking his offer to publish my books more seriously. When he resumed speaking, I detected anxiety in his voice.

"Time is marching on," he said. "I'm eager to draw up a contract and to have you sign it. The fact that you have not really studied the papers I gave you in June bothers me."

"Adam, even if I had studied the papers, I would not trust myself to grasp the meaning of all the legal terminology in them. I would leave that job to a lawyer."

"Are you saying that you don't trust me, Linzie?" he asked in a haughty tone of voice.

"What I am saying, Adam, can be taken at face value. I am not knowledgeable enough when it comes to legal contracts. Therefore, I would rely on the advice of one who is knowledgeable, namely a lawyer."

"And what lawyer might that be? I bet you don't even know one that deals with intellectual property rights."

"I do. I would engage the services of the lawyer who reviewed the ghostwriter agreement for me."

"What is his name?"

"His name is George Grumey, and he is the same George who owns the boat that we'll be on this afternoon."

I glanced at Adam. The expression on his face was one of sheer anger.

"Listen to me, Linzie. I know what I am doing when it comes to publishing books, and I'll treat you fairly. You do not have to discuss our business with George Grumey or any other lawyer. All you have to do is give me the okay to draw up a contract. After you sign it and give me some money to get things rolling, I'll take it from there."

"Why would you need any money from me?" I asked. "I do not claim to be an expert on publishing matters, but since you are a traditional publisher, I did not think any payment on my part was required. Also, when I glanced at the papers you gave me in June, I saw nothing that indicated I would have to give you money."

"You don't understand, Linzie. There are some fees involved—reasonable fees. I'm sure Mrs. Cranshaw has paid you something for your services. The money needed to cover the fees would certainly not drain your savings."

"Adam, do not assume I'll be publishing my books through you. George Grumey will have to advise me first."

Adam did not speak for a minute. He appeared to be deep in thought.

"The name Grumey sounds familiar," he finally said. "Where have I heard that name before?"

"You met Jack Grumey, who is George's brother, in my apartment back in January. Jack was the man sleeping on my sofa when we returned to my place after dinner. Then you heard Jack Grumey's name again when you met Mrs. Cranshaw. She thought you were Jack because Jack was originally supposed to drive me to Rockport."

"Ah, now the Grumey name rings a bell," Adam remarked. "Jack Grumey is Officer Jack Grumey, is he not?"

"Yes."

"And Officer Jack Grumey is the tenant who lives downstairs from you, right?"

"Right. Thanks to Jack, George Grumey is now my legal advisor."

Very sarcastically, Adam exclaimed, "Aren't you full of surprises! You did not tell me George's last name when you called me earlier to invite me out on the boat. Now I'm finding out that he is Jack's brother and that he is a lawyer who deals with intellectual property matters."

"Why should any of that make a difference to you?" I asked.

"It sounds as though you have a Grumey duo protecting you, Linzie—a cop to protect you personally and a lawyer to protect you legally."

The more Adam talked, the redder he got in the face, and the louder the volume of his voice became.

"As a single woman, I do not mind one bit that there are two men in my life that are willing to look after me. Why should you mind?"

Adam never answered that question. Thanks to Constance Cranshaw's insight, I already knew the answer. She had been correct in her assessment of Adam as a person who was interested in me for his own financial gain. As a writer, I was important to him. As a person, I meant nothing to him. It was now clear to me that Adam would resent any man that barred him from taking advantage of me.

During the rest of the ride to Gloucester Harbor, Adam and I did not converse, which only served to heighten the tension between us. After arriving at the harbor, we exchanged very few words as we walked around and gazed at the water. When we paid a visit to the *Man at the Wheel* statue and looked at the plaques that listed the names of the brave souls who had perished at sea, I thought for sure that Adam would not be able to resist providing me with more details about the memorial, but he did not. He remained quiet.

Once we were back in the car, Adam decided that we should head for Good Harbor Beach in Gloucester. Although we began to chat a little more during the drive to the beach, our conversation was a far cry from the easy flow of words we had always enjoyed. Upon our arrival at the beach, the communication between us improved a little more. As we walked along the water's edge, Adam reclaimed his role as my personal historian, giving me details of the history of Gloucester. I got the distinct feeling that he was making an attempt to get back in my good graces. I suspected that his efforts in that endeavor were driven by his own selfish motives.

When 12:30 p.m. arrived, we were on our way to George's house. The closer we got to George's place, the more at ease I felt. I was grateful that Adam and I would not be facing the rest of the day by ourselves.

When Adam pulled into the circular driveway in front of George's house, everything looked quite different than it did during my visit in January. The statues that had been veiled in snow were now visible. I remembered that Jack had told me to expect to see "an aquatic fairyland" when I came back after winter, and he had not exaggerated. Whales, mermaids, and sea captains were among the inanimate objects that appeared as Adam followed the curve of the driveway. Centrally located within the section of the lawn enclosed by the circular driveway was an impressive fountain. From the mouths of four dolphins, water jetted upward and subsequently traveled downward into a large scalloped basin.

The landscaping was beautifully done. Flowering shrubs bordered the sides of the house and flowers of all kinds were planted in the beds that were dispersed throughout the front yard. The elm trees that occupied the backyard were visible from the front of the house and added to the stately look of the property.

Adam parked the car behind another one in the driveway. He noticed that the other car was not in much better shape than the one in which we sat.

"I hope that car doesn't belong to George," he said. "If it does, I suspect he has fallen on hard times."

"It probably belongs to his female friend," I remarked.

"Have you met her?"

"No," I replied.

"Was George ever married?"

"No. He was madly in love with a woman when he was in college, but she married another man."

"Her loss," Adam muttered.

Adam's latest comment did not surprise me since money seemed to mean a lot to him. I wondered whether his former girlfriend, Evelyn, had been wealthy. If so, there was little doubt in my mind that the loss of her to another man was interpreted by Adam to be more of a blow to his wallet than to his heart.

"This house is really a mansion," Adam commented as we exited the car.

"It sure is," I agreed. "The interior is just as gorgeous as the exterior."

Upon arrival at the front door, I rang the doorbell. When no one came to the door within a reasonable amount of time, I rang the bell again. There was no response to the second ring.

"The maid must have fallen asleep," Adam said laughing.

"Let's walk to the backyard," I said. "George mentioned that lunch was going to be served on the patio."

As Adam and I approached the granite stairway that led to the elevated patio behind the house, George spotted us.

Waving his hand, he called out, "Linzie, we're over here. Come on up."

"Hi, George. We made it," I said as I returned his wave.

Adam followed me up the staircase. There was a woman sitting across from George at the round table that was situated in the center of the large patio. Her back was towards us. She turned to look in our direction as we approached the table. I quickly realized that I had met the woman before. She was the woman who had followed Jack and me to the ice-cream parlor at the mall back in January. I remembered that her name was Doris and that she sat down at our table in the ice-cream parlor without being invited to do so. There was no mistaking it was Doris. Her hair was still bleached blond, her face was once again covered with a heavy application of makeup, and from her ears dangled a pair of earrings that were just as huge as the ones she wore the evening I met her. Although she had paid almost no attention to me at the ice-cream parlor, she remembered me.

"I met you once before," she said. "It was in January. You were with Jack Grumey at the ice-cream parlor at the mall. How are you, Lucy?"

"I'm fine, Doris. How are you?"

"Okay."

"Doris, this woman's name is not Lucy," George said. "Her name is Linzie."

"Oh, you'll have to forgive me, Linzie. I'm not good with names," Doris confessed.

"Adam," I said, "this, as you now know, is Doris, and this is George Grumey."

George rose to his feet and shook Adam's hand.

"Nice to meet you, Adam," George said. "I'm glad you could come along today."

"It was nice of you to include me," Adam said without much gusto in his voice.

Doris sat there staring at Adam. I believed she was quite taken with his good looks. She finally put her hand out for Adam to shake it. Adam shook her hand but said nothing.

"There is plenty of food on the table next to the grill," George said to Adam and me. "Please help yourselves. In addition to the burgers I cooked, you will find Doris's famous potato salad and coleslaw. She insisted on bringing them."

"Oh, George, they are far from famous," Doris remarked, "but making them is so easy, and they fit right in at a barbecue."

When Doris said those words, a bell went off in my head. I suddenly realized that the female voice I heard that was coming from Jack's patio on the evening of May 31 was Doris's voice. Mention of potato salad and coleslaw helped me connect the dots because Doris had brought both to Jack's place as side dishes to the hamburgers they ate that evening. Another bell went off in that little brain of mine when I recalled that Jack had told me that Doris used to show up at his former house unannounced. I was now convinced that on May 31, Jack had been completely honest with me. His headache was not a phony one, and his need to rest was real. Doris, I now assumed, had shown up at Jack's place without an invitation and had disrupted his plan to sleep.

"Linzie, I remember that you liked the pinot grigio I served you in January, so I took a similar bottle out of my wine rack," George said. "Does the pinot grigio appeal to you today?"

"Yes," I replied. "Pinot grigio has become my favorite wine."

"What about you, Adam? What would you like?" George asked.

"Scotch and soda if you have it."

"I do. Help yourselves to the food. I'm going inside to get the drinks."

Adam and I walked over to the table that held the food. Doris remained seated but did not remain quiet.

"So, Linzie, how is Jack?" she asked.

"Actually, Doris, I have been temporarily staying at a cottage in Rockport since the beginning of June. I have not heard from Jack."

"So, where do you usually live?" she inquired.

"I live in the apartment upstairs from Jack."

"You live upstairs from Jack?"

"Yes, Doris."

"And you have not talked to him since the beginning of June?"

"That's right."

"Well, that's surprising," she said. "When I last visited Jack, he told me he had fallen in love with the tenant upstairs, who is obviously you, and that it would not be appropriate for me to come to his apartment anymore."

I was deeply touched by what Jack had said to Doris, but I sure wished she had not made Jack's feelings known at that very moment. Adam glared at me with such intensity that I wanted to disappear into thin air.

"When did Jack tell you that, Doris?" Adam boldly asked.

"On May thirty-first, when I dropped in on him unexpectedly. He was in bed with a bad headache, but I managed to get him up. I had made potato salad and coleslaw, thinking he and I could enjoy a nice barbecue together. We did have a barbecue, but he was not too enthusiastic about it. When I was leaving that evening, he told me not to come back because he had fallen in love with the tenant upstairs."

Doris's words confirmed that I had jumped to the wrong conclusion on the evening of May 31. Thoughts of how rudely I had spoken to Jack on the phone that evening began to frazzle my nerves. The evil eye that Adam was giving me was not doing my nerves any favors either. My right hand, which was holding my plate, started to tremble so much that my hamburger almost went tumbling to the ground.

"Let me tell you," Doris continued, "that the woman who gets Jack will be getting a gem. I was hoping he would go for me, but my hopes were in vain."

Adam looked at Doris and said, "You may have lost Jack, but you have apparently found George. I would think of the two brothers, you would favor him. He is the one with all the bucks."

I looked daggers at Adam, but he did not seem one bit sorry about his comment. He appeared to be waiting for some kind of response from Doris, who took a few sips of wine before she spoke.

"Oh, I love George too," she said, "but there is something special about Jack. Jack will always be number one in my book. George is a close second, but George is not interested in me either, at least not in a romantic sort of way."

"So, why are you here today?" Adam asked Doris.

"George invited me here today because Jack told him I wanted to go out on his boat. George begged Jack to come along, but Jack refused."

My legs felt weak, so I headed for the round table. Adam followed. We both sat down. I was praying that George would come back sooner than later, for I was in the company of two people who were making me feel most uncomfortable.

Adam looked quite at home in the patio chair. Only his shoulders touched the back of the chair. He was sitting on the tip of his spine, with his ankles crossed and his arms folded across his chest. His body language made me fear that something arrogant was about to come out of his mouth.

"Well, Doris," Adam said, "let me say something in regard to Linzie's interest in Jack. She left Boston to come to Rockport on June second and has not contacted Jack since then. Does that sound like a woman who is in love with Jack?"

Doris's eyes lit up. She quickly leaned in Adam's direction, so quickly that her earrings swung back and forth like pendulums.

"I never stopped to think that Lucy might not be in love with Jack!" Doris exclaimed.

"Adam, stop this right now," I ordered.

"Come now, Lucy, or Linzie, or whatever your name is," Adam said. "Tell Doris why you're not in love with Jack."

"Adam, I'm warning you," I said sternly. "Mind your own business."

"Oh, but this *is* my business," he said. "Doris, I have been spending all my free time with Linzie here, only to discover that she does not love me either. Do you want to know why?"

Doris, spellbound by Adam's words, nodded.

"It seems," he said, "that the object of Jack's affection and of my affection is not interested in men."

"What do you mean?" Doris asked.

"I mean that Linzie is gay. She is even writing a book on the subject."

Doris's jaw dropped a mile, but my jaw did not because I was too busy forming curse words aimed at Adam. As I was verbalizing my feelings in unladylike terms, George appeared with a glass in each hand. There was a look of shock on his face.

"What the heck is going on?" George asked.

I could not speak, Adam chose not to speak, but Doris was more than willing to speak.

"George, did you know that Lucy is gay? More important than that, does Jack know she is gay?"

Our baffled host quickly put the glasses on the table and then put his hands on his hips. He looked intently at Doris.

"Where the hell did you get that information?" he asked.

Doris pointed at Adam and blurted, "He spilled the beans."

I looked up at George and said, "What Adam said about my being gay is simply not true. He said it out of spite because I would not hurry to sign a contract that might prove financially beneficial to his publishing business. Adam has been dishonest with me. He told me his business is successful when, in fact, it is heading for the rocks. He is desperate for any business he can get, so he pretended to be interested in me romantically when all he cares about is what my books will do for him financially. George, when I told him you are my legal advisor, he had a fit and accused me of not trusting him."

"I believe you, Linzie," George said firmly. "In my law practice, I run across scoundrels all the time."

Adam, who appeared to be in a state of shock, had no comeback to what I had just said. He, no doubt, was wondering how I uncovered the secret of his disastrous financial condition.

George stared angrily at Adam and said, "You can forget about the scotch and soda. Get the hell out of here. In fact, allow me to escort you off my property."

Adam rose quickly from the chair. He headed for the car with George on his heels.

As I sat there, my heart was pounding. I took a few gulps of wine to try to calm down. I then glanced at Doris. She looked confused.

"Lucy, does this mean there's no hope for me with Jack?" she asked.

Trying hard to smile, I replied, "You'll have to ask Linzie about that one."

My answer confused her all the more. We sat there quietly until George returned and reclaimed his seat at the table.

"I'm so sorry, George, for all the commotion I caused," I said. "This was really going to be my last date with Adam. His deceitfulness was something that managed to escape me until this morning. Constance Cranshaw's accountant did some investigating into the state of Adam's business and relayed the info to her. She broke the news to me just hours ago."

George looked at me sympathetically and said, "Do not blame yourself. Just be grateful you discovered that Adam is a phony."

"I am grateful," I commented.

"And I am confused," Doris added. "All I did was mention that Jack is in love with Lucy here, and all hell broke loose."

I looked inquisitively at George and asked, "Were you aware that Jack is in love with me?"

Shaking his head, he said, "Jack never made that claim to me, but I am not surprised to hear that he is in love with you, Linzie. When you and Jack came here in January, my relationship with him became strained because I was attracted to you, and he sensed that."

"I was aware of that strain," I said. "I felt terrible about it, but Jack assured me that you and he talked things over, and after that, all was fine."

"The reason things are fine is that Jack made it clear to me, Linzie, that you are special to him and that he wanted to get to know you better without any interference from me. I did what a decent brother should do and stepped aside. He seemed so happy for a while, but as I mentioned to you this morning, he has been down in the dumps since the beginning of June."

"You can thank me for Jack's unhappy state of mind, George," I said in a self-reprimanding tone of voice. "I did not fully value his feelings for me."

"Do you have the same feelings for Jack that he has for you, Linzie?" George asked.

"I do," I said without any hesitation, "but I believe I have destroyed my relationship with Jack thanks to that imaginary hammer of mine. I broke something up that had been perfectly intact."

"Don't be so hard on yourself, Linzie," George said consolingly. "Sometimes what is broken can be repaired."

"Hey, are we going to sit here all day and talk about Lucy's love life?" Doris asked.

George winked at me. It was, I believed, his way of letting me know that Doris was not very couth.

"Linzie, you need some time to eat your lunch," George remarked. "You and Doris stay here while I bring what we need onto the boat."

"Thanks, George," I said. "Sitting here awhile sounds good."

My desire to sit at the table did not arise from any hunger pangs. Rather, I needed to stay still and calm down.

"George, I'll help you," Doris said. "I'm tired of sitting."

"All right, Doris," George said as he got to his feet. "If you would carry the bottled water onto the boat, that would be a big help. Linzie, eat well. When you're finished, meet us at the dock."

"Okay, George. Thanks."

After George and Doris left the patio, I began to eat even though I was not really savoring what entered my mouth. The food was not the only thing I had to digest. My mind was hard at work trying to absorb all that had transpired since my arrival at George's house. Thoughts of Connie Cranshaw raced through my mind. Adam's attempt, just minutes earlier, to fabricate a false rumor about me—an attempt made out of sheer spite—made me even more sensitive to the emotional pain Connie had endured through the years as the victim of a falsehood. Adam's shameful effort to hurt me, by means of a lie, made me feel even closer to Connie. My thoughts then turned to Jack. If I had only let him explain that Doris had shown up unexpectedly at his place on May 31, the argument that took place between us never would have occurred. I could blame only myself for our damaged relationship.

As I was deep in thought, I noticed, out of the corner of my eye, a person ascending the patio stairs. I cast my eyes in that direction so that I could get a good look at the stranger, who appeared to be a thin man with a beard. He had to rely heavily on a cane to make progress—very slow progress—up the steps. After the man succeeded in making it to the top of the staircase, it was with a considerable limp that he headed towards me.

"May I help you?" I asked as he drew closer.

The man did not answer. He seemed to be reserving all

his energy in order to put one foot in front of the other. When he was within six feet of the table, he finally spoke. His voice revealed that he was out of breath.

"Hello, Linzie."

I was about to ask him how he knew me when, through the forest of his beard, I noticed the hint of a mustache. That, together with his blond hair, led me to the realization that the person standing there was Kevin Conway. I did not know whether I should be happy to see Kevin up and about or if I should fear his presence. His physique was in such pathetic shape that I quickly convinced myself that he was no danger to me.

"Kevin, how are you feeling?"

With a faint smile, he said, "Better with each passing day. The doctors say that, in time, I'll be able to walk normally."

"That's wonderful," I remarked. "Do you want to sit down? These chairs are comfortable."

"I think that's a good idea," he said.

As Kevin hobbled over to the chair across from mine, I believed I recognized the slacks he was wearing to be the khakis he wore on the night of our final date. I recalled how sharp he looked that night when he came to my apartment to pick me up. He had sported those slacks and his other new duds as well as any male model. It was pitiful to see those slacks on him now. He had lost so much weight that they were baggy on him.

"Kevin, how did you know I was here?"

"Oh, after going to your place several times last week, only to find you were not at home, I decided to try again early this morning. When there was still no response after I rang the doorbell, I was about to go home. As I was walking towards my SUV, I noticed a neighbor of yours who was working in his garden across the street. I walked over to him with the hope that he could give me some information that would help me locate you."

"Do you know the neighbor's name?" I asked.

"Yes. The first name is Sam."

Oh boy, I thought. Sam was a nice guy, but he knew everyone's business in the neighborhood and did not hesitate to share what he knew with anyone willing to listen. Sam had earned the nickname Town Crier.

"I asked Sam," Kevin continued, "if he knew the name of the tenant who lives in the apartment downstairs from you. I thought if I rang that tenant's doorbell, I could get info as to where you were this morning. Sam informed me that Officer Jack Grumey is the downstairs tenant. I assumed that Jack Grumey is the name of that stupid cop who handcuffed me last January, and I was not surprised that he lives downstairs from you because when I saw him a second time—the night of the snowstorm that almost killed me—he came to the door with you. Anyway, once I found out from Sam that Grumey is the downstairs tenant, I knew there was no way I could ring Grumey's doorbell to ask about your whereabouts. Such a move on my part would have been useless anyway because Sam said Jack Grumey had driven off minutes earlier. Sam thought that my best bet in finding you today was to get in touch with Jack Grumey's brother, George Grumey, who lives in Gloucester. According to Sam, you have been temporarily living in Rockport since the beginning of June. Sam had a hunch that George would know where you are living. I thanked Sam and told him I might just take a ride to George's house today. I looked up George's name in one of the online phone books, got his address, and here I am. I figured it was better to come in person than to phone George. When I rang the doorbell here, there was no answer, so I walked to the back of the house. What a surprise to see you sitting here!"

"So, Kevin, you were able to drive here without any problems?"

"Yes. Driving is no problem. Before you know it, Linzie, I'll be physically fit to do everything I used to do. I'm starting to put weight back on too. I know I look drawn right now, but that will change soon. I'm sticking to an exercise program and a healthy diet."

"I'm sorry for what happened to you, Kevin."

"I blame Officer Grumey for everything," Kevin muttered. "What a nerve that idiot had to handcuff me the afternoon I was in the hall outside your apartment! All I wanted to do was come in and talk to you, but that jerk did not see it that way."

I did not see it that way either, but I knew this was not the time to criticize Kevin for the display of anger he had exhibited on January 3. He had suffered enough, and since there was no future for us as a couple, any criticism on my part would have been inappropriate.

"It is important that you focus on getting better, Kevin. I wish you the best."

Kevin looked earnestly into my eyes. Then he reached over and grasped my left hand with his right hand.

"As far as I'm concerned, Linzie, you are the best thing that ever happened to me. I don't know what got into me months ago when I started to see that other woman. I guess it was just a male ego thing. She meant nothing to me. I love you, Linzie."

With his left hand, he reached into the pocket of his striped blue and white short-sleeve shirt and pulled out a small jewelry box. He tightened the grip of his right hand on my left hand.

"Linzie, that stormy night in January when I came to your door, I wanted to propose to you. If it had not been for that darn cop coming to the door with you, you and I would have probably made up and gotten engaged that night. Instead, because of that buttinsky, I took off and got into that accident. I want to do now what I intended to do that night. Linzie Cole, will you marry me?"

He released my left hand and opened the jewelry box. Then he placed the box in front of me. A beautiful engagement ring was inside the box.

I was speechless but could not stay that way too long. Kevin was waiting for an answer, all the while tapping his fingers on the table, a habit that the accident had apparently not knocked out of him. I would have to choose my words carefully so that when I turned him down, he would not get agitated.

"Kevin, I cannot marry you," I said softly. "The timing is all wrong now. There was a time when I longed to hear you say that you loved me. Too much has happened since then."

"Are you saying you're in love with someone else?" he asked.

To deny that I loved someone else would only give Kevin hope, so I decided to tell him the truth.

"Yes, I am in love with someone else."

Kevin looked into the distance. He remained silent for a good minute. I felt so sorry for him that I was about to say that a new love would probably come into his life. I never had the chance to present that possibility, for he suddenly appeared to be getting angry. There was a scowl on his face that was frightening. His right hand formed a fist, and with that fist, he pounded the table three or four times.

"How can you do this to me?" he asked over and over.

"Kevin, I am no longer in love with you. It would be bad for both of us if I led you to believe I still am. I am fond of you. I can wish you the best, but that is all I can do."

Kevin was not about to accept my way of thinking. For the next few minutes, he verbally chastised me for letting him down and for not valuing the love he claimed he had for me. Although Kevin was yelling at the top of his lungs, George was not within earshot of Kevin's tirade. The dock was a good distance from the patio.

"Kevin, I have to leave now. I have been invited out on the boat," I said as I nervously pointed in the direction of the cabin cruiser.

I stood up and prayed that Kevin would do the same and then leave peacefully. He remained seated. In a further effort to encourage him to depart, I picked up the paper plate in front of me and started to walk towards the barrel that was situated on the side of the patio opposite the side where the steps were located. I suddenly heard a familiar voice. It was not George's voice, and it was not Kevin's voice. It was Jack's voice.

"Linzie, look out," Jack cried out.

I turned around to look for Jack, but before my eyes could locate him, I was shoved to the ground by Kevin, who, unbeknownst to me, had gotten to his feet and followed me. My right side hit the ground first, and then I rolled onto my back. I saw Kevin standing at my feet, holding the cane with both his hands. The cane was raised above his head. As the cane began a downward swing, I rushed to protect my face with my hands. When the blow I was expecting did not arrive, I removed my hands from my face and saw Jack kneeling at my side. Several feet in front of me stood Kevin with a police officer right behind him. The officer had handcuffed Kevin.

"Linzie, are you all right?" Jack asked.

Stunned, I did not answer Jack immediately. I remained motionless on the ground for a minute or so. Then I slowly moved my arms and legs.

"I think I'm okay, Jack. I'm going to try to get up."

"Let me help you," he said.

While Jack assisted me to my feet, the officer escorted Kevin off the patio. Once I was in an upright position, I put my arms around Jack and held him tightly.

"Are you sure you're all right, Linzie?" he asked.

"I am now," I replied.

"I'm all right now too," he said.

He looked into my eyes and then kissed me. Meanwhile, George, who had witnessed the tail end of the commotion, ran from the dock to the patio.

Once George was face to face with Jack, he said, "Good work, bro. I don't know what happened here, but I do know that you came just in time. You must have a sixth sense that told you to get here."

"Not really, George," Jack said. "Two people aided me in a bit of detective work. One person was Sam, our neighborhood town crier. After I returned from grocery shopping this morning, Sam walked across the street to tell me that Kevin had been at the house looking for Linzie. Sam said he had suggested to Kevin that he get in touch with you, George, because he believed you could tell Kevin where Linzie is staying in Rockport. Sam also mentioned that Kevin told him that he might take a ride to Gloucester today and stop by your house. The other person who aided me in my detective work was Doris. She called me this morning to get directions to your house and mentioned that you had also invited a writer friend of yours to go out on the boat this afternoon. By putting those two sources of information together, I realized that Kevin and Linzie might cross paths here today. I wasted no time in getting into my car and driving here. When I saw Kevin's maroon SUV parked in your driveway, I hurried to the front door, but there was no answer. Then I ran towards the back of the house. When I heard Kevin yelling, I feared for Linzie's safety, so I called the city police. Fortunately, the officer who arrived was within a block of your place when I made the call. He was here in no time."

"Doris called me this morning," George explained, "while I was meeting with a client at Bearskin Neck. She wanted directions to my place, but I was too busy to give them to her, so I suggested she call you, Jack. During my brief conversation with Doris, I mentioned that I had invited a writer friend of mine to come along on the boat. Thank God Doris passed on that piece of information to you, Jack. Thank God you were here for Linzie just when she needed you."

"Jack has always been by my side whenever I have needed him," I said. "I was just too dumb to fully appreciate him."

"When you come home, Linzie," Jack said smiling, "there is a bottle of pinot grigio waiting for us. It is the same bottle I was going to bring to the Chinese dinner we had planned to enjoy together before you left for Rockport. I saved the bottle in the hope that we would drink it after we make a toast."

"When we make that toast, Jack, let's not make it to Old Man Winter."

"Why not?"

"As you once said, there are the seasons outside ourselves that Mother Nature controls, and there are the seasons within our hearts that our attitudes shape. I am happy to say that winter has finally left my heart and spring has entered it. So, let's toast to springtime and to a new beginning. Let's toast to our future together if you still want a future with me, Jack."

"I certainly do, Linzie. Don't ever doubt it."

Chapter Twenty

When I woke up on Wednesday morning, November 14, almost a year had gone by since my first meeting with Connie Cranshaw at Elsbury Place. Upon getting both my feet out of bed, I headed for the kitchen and performed my usual ritual of peeking through the kitchen window at the thermometer outside. The reading of thirty-six degrees was a stark reminder that Old Man Winter was on his way.

That morning, I was to meet with Connie at 10:00 a.m. It would be an exciting day for both of us, for we were to begin work as co-authors on a new novel. The novel I had ghost-written had been self-published by Connie two weeks earlier.

Connie was not the only resident I planned to visit at Elsbury Place that day. I was finally going to dine with Norbert Rockfeld. Ever since I met Mr. Rockfeld back in December, I had thought of him quite often. I remembered how kind he had been to show me the way to Connie's apartment when I first went to visit her, and I had not forgotten that he had extended an invitation to me to have lunch with him at the facility. It had been my intention to accept his invitation much sooner, but so much had happened in my life since we met, not the least of which was my absence from Boston for three months. When I called Mr. Rockfeld to ask if I could dine with him on that Wednesday, he seemed quite excited to hear from me and was very agreeable to the idea of our getting together. We agreed to meet at the entrance to the dining hall at 1:00

p.m.

Since my return from Rockport, I had made quite a few trips to Elsbury Place so that Connie and I could complete the work on the ghostwritten novel. During each of those trips, that nice young woman by the name of Rebecca had cheerfully greeted me at the reception counter upon my arrival at the facility. On that November morning, Rebecca was not there. My heart sank as I approached the counter and saw Bonnie Tulley sitting at a small desk that was located about twelve feet behind the counter. I mentally counted to ten before opening my mouth.

"Good morning," I said rather cheerfully.

Ms. Tulley was reading something that was apparently capturing all her attention, for she did not respond to my greeting.

"Good morning," I said more loudly.

My second greeting also failed to elicit a verbal response from her, but at least it caused her to rise to her feet. As she slowly walked to the counter, she kept her eyes fixed on the paper she was holding in her right hand.

"Am I taking you from something?" I asked in a tone of voice that conveyed my irritation.

Glaring at me through her large black eyeglasses, she replied, "You're taking me from a ton of administrative work that I cannot finish because I have to take the place of the receptionist that quit. What do you want?"

"I am here to see Constance Cranshaw. My appointment is for ten o'clock."

"You should know the procedure by now," she said as she dragged the guest book across the counter until it was in front of me. "Write down the name of the resident you are to see, the time and the place you are to meet the resident, and sign and print your name."

I picked up the pen on the counter and followed her instructions. Before putting the pen down, a question popped into my head, so I proceeded to ask it.

"I am to meet with one of the other residents in the dining hall at one o'clock. Should I record that information in the book as well?"

"Of course," she replied snippily. "We have to know the whereabouts of everyone who passes through the door here."

"I understand," I said. "That's a good policy."

I recorded the information regarding my luncheon date with Mr. Rockfeld and put the pen down. She wasted no time in spinning the book around and drawing it towards her. With her gray hair pulled back in a bun and those enormous glasses resting on her nose, she looked like a stern, old-fashioned school teacher who was going to make sure that I had followed her directions properly. As she reviewed what I had written in the book, the expression on her face was similar to that of a person who was chewing a slice of lemon. I felt like a pupil who was about to be chastised for poor penmanship or some other offense. She was so upset that she was unable to speak for a few moments.

"At one o'clock, you are planning to dine with Norbert Rockfeld?" she finally asked.

"Yes."

"Whose idea was it to dine together?" she inquired in a demanding tone of voice.

My patience was dwindling fast. I was tempted to crawl over the counter, grab her by the shoulders, and tell her to mind her own business. However, my better judgement took charge, and I made an all-out effort to continue to deal with Ms. Tulley in a ladylike way.

"It is by invitation of Mr. Norbert Rockfeld that I am to dine here at Elsbury Place at one o'clock sharp," I said with more than a hint of an aristocratic air.

"I am going to check into this matter," she said huffily.

She did an about-face and walked back to the small desk, where she miraculously located a phone that had been hiding under piles of papers. She then punched in some numbers on the keypad of the phone. The callee obviously answered, for in no time, there was a heated discussion being carried on between that person and Ms. Tulley. When the conversation ended, Ms. Tulley returned to the counter with a defeated look on her face.

"Mr. Rockfeld confirms that he will meet you at the entrance to the dining hall at one o'clock," she mumbled.

I could not find it within myself to thank her, so I merely nodded. Then I headed for the elevator. As I entered it, I looked at my watch. It was 10:07 a.m., and it was the first time I had ever been late for a meeting with Connie.

As the elevator began its ascent to the second floor, I tried to erase Bonnie Tulley from my mind, but doing so was like trying to erase indelible ink from a piece of paper. It bothered me that I could not figure her out. I surmised that the reason for her bitterness would forever remain a mystery to me.

When I exited the elevator, I hurried to Connie's door and knocked. Connie greeted me warmly.

"Hi, Linzie. Come on in."

As I entered, I said, "Hi, Connie. I'm sorry I'm a little late. The check-in downstairs took longer than usual."

"Ah, don't worry about it. You got here safely. That's all that matters."

I took off my jacket and handed it to Connie. She promptly hung it in the hall closet. After she closed the closet door, she turned around and looked at me. Her eyes were gleaming with joy.

"I have something to show you, Linzie. Let's go into the living room."

As I followed her down the hallway and into the living room, there was a spring in her step. The rustle of her tan corduroy slacks accompanied the spring, making it all the more obvious she was happy about something.

"Behold the fruit of your labor," Connie said rejoicefully as she pointed to a pile of books lying on the coffee table in front of the sofa.

I approached the table. On its glass top were six copies of the book I had ghostwritten. I smiled from ear to ear. After many hours of work, the finished product—the published novel—was before my eyes.

Connie walked over to me and gave me a hug. I became so choked up that I could not speak right away.

"Congratulations, Linzie, on a job well done."

"I would call this book the fruit of *our* labor, Connie. You had a lot to do with it."

"I suppose I had something to do with it, but you, Linzie, really wrote it. I am proud of what you accomplished. Even though I had read the manuscript, there was something special about holding the story in book form and reading it from cover to cover. I could barely put the book down. Your writing touched my heart."

"Thank you, Connie."

"It is I who want to thank you, Linzie, for having served as my ghostwriter and for being my good companion. You have given me a new lease on life. You have rekindled my desire to write, and I cannot tell you how much I am looking forward to our working as co-authors on a new book. What a thrill it will be to see both our names appear as authors on the cover!"

She sat on the sofa, and I took my usual seat across from her. I, too, was excited about co-authoring a novel with her, but there was something weighing on my mind about the book I had ghostwritten. I decided to share with her what was troubling me.

"Connie, if it had not been for you, I probably would have given up my writing career by now due to financial reasons." Pointing to the pile of books on the coffee table, I said, "The money you paid me to ghostwrite that book kept me afloat financially. What bothers me is that the money *you* make on the book may be far less than what you paid me to write it. I know that per the ghostwriter agreement, you are the sole owner of the copyright and that all royalties will be paid to you. Nevertheless, you may well get the short end of the stick when it comes to receiving the financial rewards that the book generates."

Connie looked at me compassionately and asked, "Linzie, have you forgotten how the author in the novel struggled and struggled to get ahead before she met the editor that became her husband?"

"No, I could never forget that. Her struggle will forever be etched on my memory."

"Did you forget that the author's life in the story is based on my life?"

"No, I could never forget that either."

"Then, dear, you should not be surprised to hear that I empathized with your situation. I sensed that you were getting close to quitting your writing career when you came here the second time and mentioned that you were struggling to stay afloat financially. What a pity it would have been if you had quit writing! An exceptional talent would have gone to waste. It made me happy to offer you the ghostwriting job. It served as a life preserver that kept your writing career from going under."

"But, Connie, if you don't make out at least as well as I did monetarily on the book, I'll feel selfish."

"Linzie, I wanted the book written for a couple of reasons. Believe it or not, making money on it was not one of those reasons. Therefore, if I do not fare as well as you moneywise, you should not feel selfish."

"I'm afraid I will feel selfish, Connie."

"Come now, Linzie," she said laughing. "Use your head and think this through. It is I who has been a bit selfish. I knew you had talent as a writer, and I tapped into that talent. Where would I be now if I had not tapped into it? I certainly would not be sitting here with you at this moment, admiring that novel on the table and looking forward to the one we'll write together. Working with you gives my life purpose."

"I am excited about writing with you, Connie. Who

knows? Maybe after we finish this book, we'll co-author others."

Connie smiled and said, "That would please me to no end."

She then grabbed the two pads of paper and the two pens that were next to her on the sofa and handed me one of each.

"Are you ready to begin a new adventure?" she asked.

Nodding, I replied, "I sure am."

"Good. Let's get started."

As we sat in the living room, we giggled quite a bit as we bounced ideas off each other and made a preliminary outline of the plot. The book was to be a summer romance with a comical twist in it.

Shortly before 1:00 p.m., Connie looked at her watch and said, "I guess it's time to call it quits for today. You don't want to be late for your luncheon date with Mr. Rockfeld."

I looked at my own watch and gasped. The time was 12:54 p.m. I had been so involved in the storyline we were developing that the time had escaped me. I quickly rose to my feet and started to fill my briefcase with papers.

"Linzie, take three copies of the book you ghostwrote. Naturally, you'll want to keep one copy for yourself, but maybe you have some friends who would like to read the book. I'm going to order more copies soon, and you can have some of those too."

"Thanks. Would it be all right if I offer a copy to Mr. Rockfeld? When I met him last December, he told me that he knows you. He also told me that he is an avid reader, so he may want to read the book. I think he will be quite surprised that I ghostwrote it even though I had mentioned to him that I am a writer. That day I met him, I was coming here to offer my services to you as a volunteer companion. Little does he know that you were really interested in engaging my services as a writer."

"Sure, I see no harm in offering him a copy," Connie said.

"Let me know how that works out."

Connie and I exited the living room and followed the hallway to the closet. She removed my jacket and handed it to me.

"Well, Linzie, we have been on quite a journey together. It is nice to know that the journey will continue."

"I believe we have many more miles to travel together. See you Friday, Connie."

She opened the door leading to the hallway outside her apartment and said, "Enjoy your lunch, Linzie."

As I approached the elevator, I glanced at my watch. The time was 12:58 p.m. Fortunately, the elevator was free, so in no time, I was on the third floor. As I drew near the dining hall, I saw Norbert Rockfeld standing at the entrance. Sporting a red blazer, a white turtleneck, and gray slacks, he looked dapper.

"Hello, Mr. Rockfeld," I called out.

"Hello, Miss Cole. It is so nice to see you again," he said as he walked over to me.

He gave me a hearty handshake with his right hand while keeping his left hand atop his cane.

"I apologize for taking so long to dine with you," I said.

"No apologies are necessary, dear. I'm sure you have been quite busy."

"Yes. So much has gone on in my life since I met you. In fact, I spent three months in Rockport. I came back to Boston at the end of August."

"I am anxious to learn what has been happening in your life. Let's get seated first. I reserved a table in my favorite section of the dining hall."

Mr. Rockfeld gave me a gentle nudge on the back as a gesture for me to precede him into the dining hall. A male maître d' greeted us and led us to a table situated in front of a large picture window. That window provided an excellent view of the rolling hills, which I had often admired while peering through the window in Connie's living room. Once we were seated, the maître d' placed two menus on the table and wished us a good dining experience.

Before opening the menu, I gazed at the hills. Many of the trees had lost all their leaves.

"The view of the hills seen through this picture window must have been spectacular when the foliage was at its peak," I commented.

"Ah, it truly was," Mr. Rockfeld said. "You'll have to dine with me next October when the hills will be sparkling with brilliant colors. I'll reserve this table for us."

"I would love to dine with you in October. The fall is my favorite time of the year, largely because of the leaves changing color."

"Nature truly is remarkable when you think about it, Miss Cole. A tree that loses all its leaves in the fall looks dead, but when spring comes along and the buds burst open, the tree seems to come alive again."

"It's like a rebirth," I commented.

"How true, my dear! Nature gives the tree another chance to flourish."

As Mr. Rockfeld began to study the menu, he said, "Please order anything that your heart desires. You are my guest, my very special guest."

"Thank you."

I looked over the choices and quickly decided on the scrod dinner. Mr. Rockfeld chose the same. He beckoned to the waiter, who immediately came to our table, took our order, and then headed for the kitchen.

"So, what is new and exciting in your life?" Mr. Rockfeld asked.

I raised my right hand off my lap and placed it on the table. Then I wiggled the finger on that hand that bore an engagement ring.

"You're getting married?" he asked with excitement in his voice.

"I am," I replied.

"Who is the lucky man?"

"His name is Jack Grumey."

"And how long have you known Mr. Jack Grumey?"

"It will be one year in January. We're getting married next May. The ceremony and the reception will take place at Jack's brother's house, which is in Gloucester. I was wondering if you would like to come."

"I certainly would like to come. The union between two people is an extraordinary thing. The biggest disappointment in my life is that the institution of marriage managed to escape me."

"I guess the right one does not come along for some people," I said consolingly.

"Oh, the right one did come along and quite early in my life. She and I were high school sweethearts. Before I would tie the knot with her, I wanted to better myself so that I could feel worthy of being her husband. It was important to me that I could support her financially, so while I held down a job in the daytime, I attended college at night. I eventually obtained a degree. It was quite a blow to me when the love of my life dropped me and married someone else."

Mr. Rockfeld's voice cracked when he said that last sentence. It was obvious that the pain of his disappointment had not been wiped away by all the years that had passed.

"The loss of her to another man must have been terribly hard on you," I commented.

"It sure was. When my former girlfriend got married, I was beside myself. In need of some companionship, I started to date another woman. Dating that other woman was a mistake on my part because I was on the rebound. One thing led to another, and in time, I proposed to her. She accepted. I am ashamed to say that I left her at the altar because I could not go through with the wedding ceremony. I was still in love with that special person I met in high school."

"Was the woman you left at the altar bitter towards you?" I asked.

"She was as bitter as bitter can be, and not only towards me but also towards the woman I truly loved and still love. The fiancée I jilted claimed that I wrecked her life. She accused me of robbing her of my love and the financial security I had promised her. I felt so bad that I was instrumental in getting her an administrative job here."

"So, you've had some sort of tie to this place other than just being a resident?"

"Yes. I was an architect who performed quite a bit of work here at Elsbury Place."

The wheels in my head began to spin. On that cold December morning when I first stepped foot into Elsbury Place, with the intention of performing volunteer work, the strange behavior of certain people had created a puzzle in my mind. The more Mr. Rockfeld talked, the more the puzzle was getting filled in with pieces of information that I never imagined would come my way.

"As for the woman I truly love," Mr. Rockfeld continued, "I believe she felt she was doing the right thing when she married that other guy. You see, she was a gifted author who was unable to make a success of her writing until she met an editor who opened the door to opportunity for her. She married the editor. He eventually became a publisher. Unfortunately, he also became a louse. The marriage collapsed."

All the pieces of the puzzle were now in place. I was able to ask a question without feeling bold.

"So, have there been any new developments between you and the woman you love?"

"Yes. She hired a ghostwriter to write a book based on most of what I just told you."

"Did you read the book?" I asked.

"I sure did. I started to read it on Monday, right after the love of my life knocked on my door and delivered the book to me. I finished reading it last night."

"May I ask what you thought of the book?"

"The book was an eye-opener for me," he replied. "I

learned that when the marriage of the woman I love collapsed, she truly regretted that she had not married me. She always wanted to renew our relationship but felt she was unworthy of me. It was through the book that she let me know that she has been grieving all these years over the loss of what we once had."

While the novel served as an eye-opener for Mr. Rockfeld, his words served as an eye-opener for me. The novel had far more purpose than I had realized. Just a few hours earlier, Connie mentioned to me that she had wanted the book written for a couple of reasons, neither one of which was to make money. One reason had been clear to me all along—to fight bigotry aimed at homosexuals. Mr. Rockfeld had now opened my eyes to the other reason—a reason that was very personal to Connie. Through the book, Connie poured her heart out to Norbert Rockfeld, making him aware of all the feelings she had bottled up inside herself for years. How I admired her courage to knock on Mr. Rockfeld's door and present the book to him!

"So, do you think there is any hope left for the two of you?" I asked.

"Absolutely. Think of what we said about a tree a few minutes ago. When a tree loses all its leaves in the fall, it is not dead, but it appears to be dead. Then, when the spring comes along and the buds burst open, the tree seems to come alive again. It's like a rebirth—another chance to flourish. My feelings for Connie never died, but when she came to my door on Monday, new life was breathed into them."

I smiled and said, "I would say that when Connie came to your door, spring came to your heart."

"That is a good way to put it," he said nodding his head. "Connie feels the same as I do. We both want to start anew. We are much older now than we were when we first fell in love, but we would rather have each other now than never."

"I cannot tell you how happy I am for both of you."

With a sparkle in his eyes, he said, "I must tell you, Miss Cole, that Connie and I have a dinner date Friday evening."

"Wonderful," I said.

"And there's one other thing I must tell you."

"What's that?"

"You're one heck of a writer!"

My eyes welled up with tears. Through those tears, I looked at him tenderly.

"Thank you, Mr. Rockfeld. Coming from you, that means a lot to me."

The waiter then appeared at our table with our meals. During lunch, we chatted about various things, one of which was life in Rockport. Mr. Rockfeld was very knowledgeable about the town. Thanks to a former acquaintance of mine—a history buff—I was able to make some intelligent comments about the town's past.

As we exited the dining hall, Mr. Rockfeld made me promise that I would dine with him soon. He suggested that Connie join us the next time, an idea I welcomed wholeheartedly. After saying goodbye to Mr. Rockfeld, I headed for the elevator to begin my journey to the reception area, where I would dutifully record my departure time in the guest book.

Once I arrived at my destination, I noticed that Bonnie Tulley was sitting at the small desk located behind the counter. The number of papers on the desk appeared to have multiplied since my check-in earlier. As usual, Ms. Tulley was engrossed in her work. I recorded the time in the guest book and, without saying goodbye to her, headed for the main door in order to exit the building. As I was about to pass through the archway that led to the foyer, I turned around and retraced my steps to the counter.

"Ms. Tulley," I said.

"What is it?" she asked while keeping her eyes focused on the paper she was holding.

"I just wanted to wish you a good day."

To my surprise, she looked at me and said, "Thank you."

As I walked out of Elsbury Place that November afternoon, my thoughts reverted to that December day when I paid my first visit to the facility as a volunteer. I shivered when I thought of the ice-cold weather that day and the even colder reception I received from Constance Cranshaw. How ironically things had turned out! Constance Cranshaw, who had originally been interested in me only as a writer, eventually embraced me as a friend, and I, who had originally intended to provide her with companionship, actually found a friend in her—the true kind of friend that is so rare.

The End

Made in the USA
Monee, IL
01 November 2020